Drapes drawn shut, door locked, materials assembled on the desk, Santry got to work. He crossed the room quickly and stood in front of an unremarkably small frame enclosing what few in the world would suspect was a priceless treasure. The contrast between its unremarkable, drab appearance on the wall and its radiance when gripped by giant olive-wood hands in the center of a vast hall was startling. Santry took it carefully in his hands, placed it on the desk, took a razor, and began his work of restoration . . .

RECKLESS PASSAGE

A NOVEL BY

GEORGE D. COLMAN

LYNX BOOKS

New York

RECKLESS PASSAGE

ISBN: 1-55802-222-8

First Printing/April 1989

This is a work of fiction. Names, characters, places, and incidents are either the product of the author's imagination or are used fictitiously. Any resemblance to actual events, locales, or persons, living or dead, is entirely coincidental.

Copyright © 1989 by George D. Colman
All rights reserved. No part of this book may be reproduced or transmitted in any form or by any means electronic or mechanical, including by photocopying, by recording, or by any information storage and retrieval system, without the express written permission of the Publisher, except where permitted by law. For information, contact Lynx Communications, Inc.

This book is published by Lynx Books, a division of Lynx Communications, Inc., 41 Madison Avenue, New York, New York, 10010. The name "Lynx" and the logo consisting of a stylized head of a lynx are trademarks of Lynx Communications, Inc.

Printed in the United States of America

0 9 8 7 6 5 4 3 2 1

RECKLESS PASSAGE

Chapter One

The bones were found three days after digging began and excited no one. That is not to say they went unnoticed. Even in this corpse-strewn century, the chalky remains of a man continue to intrigue. We will pass a parade of living heads on the pier during an evening's walk and one or two may get a second glance, but the solitary, entirely anonymous skull, unearthed unexpectedly, still brings a moment's pause.

Little more than that, however, from those who dig for a living and unearth bones every day. For them, the line between dead sheep, burros, and men has lost most of its significance. Especially in a land where invaders have fallen and been buried below the rocky-soil surfaces for three thousand years. Romans, Slavs, Germans, Turks: They have all come to Greece. These and more. And they have all remained: quietly, peacefully, inconspicuously, underground.

Alexander Ross leaned against the idle Komatsu bulldozer and watched men in the pit below toss the bones aside. He had worried about this moment for years, sure that when the grave was opened, it would lead police directly to him. What happened was more prosaic. The bones led nowhere. No one gave a damn.

His eyes slipped from the workers and rose to distant mountains, eased across sheep-grazing land down through wind-silvered olive groves to the Aegean Sea. The low hills of Turkey lay brown and somber beyond the gull-flecked water. A freighter moved slowly toward

Mitilini. Nineteen sixty-seven seemed a very long time ago, but the voice of white, skeletal shards was clear and insistent. Ross was twenty-one that year and on the road. After Vietnam, he hit Detroit just long enough to see his folks, fight with his old man, and take off again. It was, intentionally, a short road. He was no wanderer. Certainly no drifter. He was a driver, an intelligent, high-energy charger who knew that for him to go with the flow meant getting stuck in the backwaters of southwest Detroit. Educational credentials, success, and money were on his mind. He gave the road six months and headed for Greece. The trail led to the island of Lesbos, the port city of Mitilini, and a backstreet bar where he sat in a dark corner, drank ouzo, and watched suspiciously as a paunchy Greek baited a silent man across the room. He couldn't figure out what was going on, but the drama absorbed him. He caught the words "Fool!" and "Thief!" and wondered why the fellow in the business suit sat there and took it. If anybody laid that kind of shit on him, chairs would be flying. But the man didn't move, didn't speak, didn't even look at the brawler. He drank his wine and gave him nothing. Infuriated, the screamer hit the table, jeered, stabbed the air between them with an angry hand, and shouted, "Coward!"

Ross tensed as the steel-haired man got up, leaned on his cane, dropped a few coins on the table, and crossed slowly toward the noisemaker. The face behind the dark glasses was stronger than he had expected: thin and chiseled deep with a nose as sharp as a predator's beak. The thickset man pushed out of his chair, clenched his fists, rolled his shoulders forward, and got ready. The man with the cane stood close, stared briefly, and walked out. Two men, who had kept their faces averted, now turned and watched the standing man. Something passed between them, something that made the heavyweight nod curtly as if saluting superiors and then leave the tavern quickly. Ross followed. A few hours later, a Greek was buried deep in the hillside pasture, but Alexander didn't know whether he or the man with the cane had killed him.

He fled to Athens and on to JFK. He got none of the attention feared. Nothing happened. Nothing at all. No police came. No one called. Even the letter didn't arrive for months. It carried Greek stamps and a return address in Mitilini.

My dear Alexander Ross,

My apologies for not writing sooner, but it has taken me this long to find you.

Please accept the enclosed pearl as a token of my profound gratitude for your action—and for your silence.

I suspect we'll meet again. Careless men remember life's accidental dramas. Willful men build on them.

My sincere regards,

Andreas Korachis

Ross kept the pearl and kept silent. There were boozy times, of course, when he was tempted to open up to a friend or two, but he never did, and that night in Greece, like the pearl he had received, took on a luster of its own. He sometimes wondered, long after the anxious edge was off, if Korachis might reveal him. Not to the police—that was inconceivable—but to his wife, or, more likely, to an old friend over brandy who in turn might raise an undesirable ghost. It never happened. Over long years, the only word from Greece was a friendly one: the occasional note from a silent man with a cane, dark glasses, and a gaunt face that had once turned fierce and deadly.

In 1984, seventeen years and a lifetime later, Ross was a transformed thirty-eight years old, a prominent and successful Detroit executive, long gone from the working-class neighborhood of old Delray, green-pastured in Bloomfield Hills, and itching for more: more power, more wealth, more excitement. When the unexpected letter came from Korachis inviting him to Greece "to discuss a business proposal," he was intrigued, and in early May flew to Lesbos, in the eastern Aegean. A limousine met him at the airport and took him directly to the excavation site of the new hotel. The chauffeur explained, "Mr. Korachis thought you should begin your visit here."

Ross took a final look at the grave below and at the startling red poppies scattered wildly across the fields. He told the waiting driver he wanted to see Korachis.

The chauffeur pointed to an old, stone farmhouse a hundred yards up the slope. "He's waiting for you there."

It was the fieldstone house to which they had gone after burying the corpse. Korachis was taking him step by step over vividly remembered ground. Ross liked the measured style. There was to be no hurry, no rushing at each other. After seventeen years, two impatient men should take their time.

A figure appeared in the whitewashed doorway, stiffly erect, and cast in the image remembered: vested business suit, cane, dark glasses. Flesh and change appeared at closer range. The wiry hair remained full of gray, and his features were leaner still, as if the sculptor had decided to take him down to bone. He was of average height and shorter than Ross. There was neither small talk about the trip nor any affirmation of pleasure at the sight of each other. There was only a hand placed warmly on his shoulder, the faintest of smiles, and the smell of coffee inside. Black, cast-iron pots hung from ceiling hooks over a bare concrete floor. A sheepskin was stretched on the wall, parched and dry. Ross drank his coffee, then placed the small cup on the sturdy kitchen table and looked through the small window at a horse hobbled outside. He was a long way from Detroit.

Korachis stood quietly by, watching the powerful animal and giving Ross all the time his different temperament required. "I think I know where we'll end," he said. "Why don't you decide where we start?"

Alexander didn't hesitate. "Who was he, Andreas? Who did we kill? And why was he after you?"

Korachis sat down, rested his cane against the table, and noted Ross's well-tailored suit. "Your uniform then was frayed jeans and a sweat shirt. Do you miss the carefree days?"

"There's nothing to miss. My life now is better in every way." He pressed: "Who was he?"

A slight rasp in Korachis's voice gave his words a whispered edge. "I am inclined to say 'no one,' because on any scale, he was worthless. We killed a fool, a dolt who thought his time had come. He worked for me. I fired him. My enemies tried to use his anger."

"There was no investigation? No inquiry?"

"Not really. There were questions and a few rumors, but nothing worrisome. Remember, you were here in April 1967. The colonels had taken power and a great many people disappeared. Boatloads were shipped out of Mitilini to other islands. I had relatives among them. The state decreed them dangerous. I decreed the state illegitimate. It was a troubled, tumultuous time and people behaved as they always do in a crisis. They looked the other way, they kept their mouths shut, and they watched to see who'd win. That historical period provided excellent cover for assorted personal treacheries. Only in such a time would the fool we buried dare to insult, let alone assault, me. His fascist credentials fed the fantasy that he'd prosper under the colonels and made him reckless. In fact, few missed him. No one cared." His voice grew quieter as his eyes searched Ross's long Scottish face. "Strange that you should be there. Stranger still that you followed. It wasn't your fight. Why did you jump in? I assume you don't know."

"I know," Ross replied with a self-assurance as casual as it was characteristic. "No big mystery. I was half in the bag, still furious about getting ripped off in Athens, and kind of looking for a fight. One thing led to another. When I found him clubbing you, I couldn't just walk away."

Korachis lit a cigarette and wondered, "Well, maybe. Maybe that's all there is to action: anger plus alcohol plus spark. Maybe one thing does just lead to another. I don't think so, but I'm not as sure as I used to be. In any case, after that I had to follow you. You were a young, unknown stranger who appeared out of nowhere, saved my life, and disappeared, but with information that could destroy me. I've paid far more attention to you over the years than you realize. At first, it was because you were a possible threat. I was a successful businessman, a little older than you are now, and I was not going to let either that fool or an unknown American boy jeopardize my life."

"You followed me to Detroit?"

"Yes, it was the simplest thing to do, especially since all I wanted was the assurance that you honored the pledge made at this table." Korachis ran his fingers along its edges. "We've changed the oilcloth, much as you and I have changed our surfaces, but the structure, the grain of the wood, is exactly as it was, only more mature." He lingered on Ross's face. "Except for the photographs, I'd never know you. Something familiar about the eyes, but otherwise all changed. The executive patina gives you a smooth, untroubled air." He sipped his coffee and added, in the manner of a frank confession, "Your success surprised me. It forced me to recast my impressions. All I had seen was a somewhat drunk and rangy American who was curiously good in a fight. I had no idea what else was there. You've done exceptionally well. And that's made it easier to keep track of you. Not because I've been worried about a revelation exposing the secrets of this hillside, but because I had grown interested in you. Associates kept me informed of your rise through corporate ranks—until the merger stopped you. Were it not for that, you'd be the company's president now. I'm sure that was a discouraging period, but it may be for the best. As a chief executive, you'd be less willing to consider the proposal I intend to make."

The coffee gave way to retsina and the men's guards drifted down and away. They acknowledged the curious impact of that death on their lives, the way it had bound their safety to a stranger's silence, and their growing trust as the pledge was kept. That brief but savage fight, the sudden corpse, the hurried, exhausting burial in rocky ground, the vows urged, repeated, sworn, the flight, and the years of secrecy had made them close as brothers. Their talk wandered leisurely through the years since '67 until Korachis, encouraged by what he heard, revealed more of his hand.

"Alexander," he said earnestly, as if dropping the last of his hesitations, "there are rivers of gold flowing in this world of which you know little or nothing. Holy waters in which men can be baptized and saved if they are naturally graced and prepared to repent of their sins: the sheep sins of dependence, habit, and servile obedience to the laws of others."

He leaned closer, as if narrowing the world to the two of them.

"In addition to the satisfactions of an entirely legal and prosperous import-export business, I've discovered the charms of enterprise in the less-fettered realms of freedom beyond the law, which is to say, beyond the rules made by other men. I'm inviting you to join me there. To start, take the lead in a single project. It will give us time to confirm our opinion of each other. If we don't work well together, you leave an enormously wealthy man. But if, as I anticipate, the match is right, then you join me in the expansion of an international organization that will satisfy all your taste for power."

Ross said the unfettered realms of freedom didn't interest him that much; he was free enough in Detroit. But power, money, and change of pace *did* appeal to him. He knew that the gems, drugs, and mercenaries of which Korachis spoke were growth industries, but he wanted the man to get more specific. What valuables had he recently delivered?

His curiosity ripened as the elegant Greek replied, "Excellent. The examples will lead us easily into the project I have in mind for you."

Smoke from Korachis's cigarette curled upward toward the ceiling of the still room as his eyes focused on the white-stone wall behind Ross, as if watching the events described. "We receive numerous requests for the release of zealots, enthusiasts separated from their cause. We recently arranged the liberation, as they would say, of an excitable young man who had spent the last two years in a dismal African prison—ever since the afternoon of his failed revolution. An exile community based in Paris wanted him and raised extravagant sums of money for his release. This month we were also involved in the return of certain photographs to Belgium that were being used to blackmail a rich client's overweight daughter, a voluptuary whose exotic appetites were unfortunately coupled with an impulse for exhibitionism. A different service, distinct in complexity and cost, was the secret purchase order received from the Treasury Department of a small nation for the printing presses and, of course, the printers who were flooding that country with exquisite counterfeit currency."

He gave the slightest of shrugs and said, "Those are a few of our present accounts, but don't misunderstand me, I am not a closet activist of either the right or the left, nor am I a humanitarian. I am committed only to my freedom and my few friends. I try not to betray either. Apart from that standard, I select my accounts case by case. And money is only one consideration. In fact, money's often unimportant. The uniqueness and the delicacy of the task, the opportunity to scorn established power, the possibility of a stylish, elegant resolution, my excitement, my intuition—these are the weights that tip the scales. And, of course, I have to consider the availability of people capable of such creative work."

He paused. No need to look at Ross to underline the point. His first card was on the table. Ross covered it and surprised himself. "I might be available, Andreas. What's involved?" It sounded like more of a commitment than he wanted to make. He had intended to circle the proposition with hard questions, but his "I might be" told the blunt truth. His life was at a turning point: late thirties, divorced, excellent but predictable career. Sure, he'd talk about opportunities with anybody. And if the money was good and the work interesting, he'd think about it. Why not? Key advances in the company had come because he welcomed offers and took risks. So what surprised him? It was, he realized, the unanticipated glint of excitement below the honest words. It was the strange hope set glowing that the intense, softspoken Greek would make an offer he couldn't refuse.

"The first thing involved, Alexander, is what you and I have honored for seventeen years: uncompromised secrecy. We've earned from each other what can never be purchased: trust. That and that alone makes this conversation possible, and it will be shared with only one other person." He got up, walked to the window of the small kitchen, and stared into the settling darkness. "It is now May. If you accept my offer, your work could be completed in August." He turned and faced him. "The risks? You could be jailed or hunted for life. The rewards? Six million dollars and the first step toward an empire."

Ross was not swept away by the amount. A single Turner painting had just been auctioned at Sotheby's for ten million, and Korachis had to know he was earning hundreds of thousands every year between investments and a safe, reputable job. To exchange that for a life at large and endangered by still-undescribed forces was going to cost. The money was enough. He was more interested in the "valuable." "What's the project, Andreas? What is it you want?"

"Permit me, Alexander, to tell you about the 'project,' as you call it, my own way—somewhat obliquely, circuitously. It is a way I enjoy, and these projects should be as pleasurable in their development as in their completion. It should go without saying that I would not invite you to Greece to discuss a simple assault on life or the usual forms of wealth. There are executioners waiting in line for work, and robbing banks can be exciting only to the desperate. But I've found for you a project of rare symmetry, a valuable that represents in itself treasure, art, antiquity, Christendom, and the Greek nation. A wealthy collector has decided he must have it. I've agreed to secure it. Its value will, of course, soar to the heavens once stolen because the inevitable publicity will make it even more famous and desirable. Even so, the collector will probably keep it or give it to one whose favor he seeks."

Korachis spoke slowly, pausing occasionally, as if to consider another thought.

"My interest? It will bring me millions, of course, and will also enable me to flaunt the parasitic power of those worst of shepherds: the Church and the State. I will increase my wealth by feeding on the unearned fatness of our rulers and will enjoy the spectacle of their frantic and frustrated search. I will take a priceless, some would say 'sacred,' document from their soiled hands and place it in the small circle of those who can appreciate the tortured beauty of its history and the ironies of its acquisition. And if no one else sees it the way I do, so much the better. I am responsible only for my own satisfactions. Which means, Alexander, it is unnecessary for you to challenge or to endorse my motivations. It is enough if you find something in the project for yourself."

Korachis, who spoke in the mildest of tones, took a sheaf of papers from a nearby drawer and placed one on the table in front of Alexander. It was a newspaper article dated June 24, 1928, reporting speculation that a millionaire named Constantine Theodopoulos, a Greek shipbuilder, had initiated negotiations with the government of Turkey to secure the return of the "Ephesian Fragments" to Greek soil. The papyrus manuscript, known to scholars as "P-04" or "Codex Lauticus," contained passages of the New Testament book Ephesians, the letter St. Paul wrote to the church at Ephesus. Discovered by an archaeological unit from the University of London working outside Alexandria, Egypt, in 1893, the Fragments set off a dust storm in academic and ecclesiastical circles because they varied at significant points from the received canon. Controversy surrounding the Fragments heightened when they were removed from Egypt in 1895 and presented to the Turkish nation. The Greek government protested immediately, arguing that Ephesus, admittedly part of modern Turkey, was a Greek city in Paul's day and that the early documents therefore belonged to the treasury of the Greek Orthodox Church.

Ross read the report twice. It was the first time he had heard anything about Ephesians since he left the Immanuel Presbyterian Church in southwest Detroit at age sixteen. When finished, Korachis handed him another sheet, but Ross raised his palm to stop him. "Please, Andreas, no more bits and pieces. At this point, I need an overview, a summary of all the relevant facts. Then I can make good use of the detailed file."

Korachis agreed. "It's important that we proceed your way, not mine, because if you accept, the project is entirely yours: research, planning, choice of accomplices, acquisition, delivery—all. I will interfere in no way. We are back to trust. I must trust you to deliver the Fragments and ensure my anonymity. You must rely on me to protect yours—and to deliver six million dollars.

"As briefly as I can put it, then, Theodopoulos succeeded. He paid the Turks a fortune and secured the Fragments in 1930. In the process, and as intended, he became a hero of the Greek nation. And in 1931, before an international gathering of kings and queens, prime ministers, archbishops, and business leaders, the Ephesian Fragments were officially and forever placed in the ancient monastery of St. David the King on the island of Kallos in the eastern Aegean. That particular monastery was chosen because it lies thirty miles off the coast of Turkey and just fifty miles from ancient Ephesus itself. You'll find it on a map just one hundred miles south of Lesbos between Ikaria and Patmos.

"Since that day, the fame and wealth of the island has grown enormously. It is not cynical to note that tourism is second only to shipping in its importance to the Greek economy and that antiquities of one kind or another are among the country's foremost attractions. New Testament scholars are not the only ones with a keen interest in the Fragments, nor are classicists alone dependent on the glory that was Greece. Lay an ax to any branch of the delicate tourist tree and you threaten enormous profits. Hundreds of thousands of Greeks and foreigners, most of them Christian, stream through Kallos annually because of the Fragments, for no sooner had they been deposited on that lovely island than the stories of miraculous healings multiplied like mosquitoes in the marsh. If I ever come upon proof that Theodopoulos owns every restaurant and hotel on that island and personally planted the stories of the first miracles, I won't be surprised. All you need, of course, are the first ones. The shepherds and the sheep take it from there. Speaking of the shepherds, I should tell you that the Greek Parliament declared the monastery and the Fragments 'sacred' in 1980. At the time, I thought my religious friends might object to the determination of holiness by roll call, but few if any Greeks seemed either amused, annoyed, or outraged by Caesar's latest pretensions.

"One additional feature should be mentioned. In 1970, the World Council of Churches and the Roman Catholics accepted the invitation of the Greek Orthodox Church to establish an International Center for Pauline Studies on the island. It operates in conjunction with the monastery but has an independent board and attracts the world's finest scholars to conferences and its famous library.

"The important thing for me to stress, Alexander, is that the priceless and historic value of the Fragments themselves, the drama of acquiring them from the Turks, the nationalism stirred as memories rose of a once proud Greek civilization in Asia Minor, the miracles and the pilgrims, the streams of tourists, the assemblies of scholars, the attentions of royalty, and, of course, the enormous profits—all these have worked a miracle. The Ephesian Fragments are no longer simply the important, priceless, even beautiful manuscript discovered by archaeologists in 1893. No, by the mysterious alchemy common to all herds, they have been transformed into that which is esteemed far more than gold. They have become representations of the flock itself. They have taken on spiritual significance and grown holy. They have become Greece. They have become Christendom.

"Count on it, to take them means to be a hunted man, perhaps for the rest of your life. And the Greek nation and the Greek Church will get the eager cooperation of every state and all churches in their pursuit of the barbarians who dared to steal that which has been officially declared sacred. I don't think I'm overstating the risk. On the other hand, if I didn't believe there was a safe, even elegant way of securing the Fragments, I never would have mentioned them to you. I am, however, sure it can be done and have imagined ways for you to consider if you're available for the work."

Outside, somewhere in the hills above them, a night-bird called. Ross listened to the high, clear tones and said, "I want your ideas before I decide."

Korachis grasped him briefly by the shoulder, pulled his chair closer to the table, and spread a series of photographs in front of them. They talked for another hour, locked the farmhouse, and drove to Andreas's nineteenth-century mansion by the sea. Ross said he'd make his decision within twenty-four hours.

The next day Ross was overheard calling the United States, seen swimming in the bay, and observed drinking ouzo outside a port café. And that evening, as Korachis opened the second bottle of wine in his wood-paneled dining room, Ross placed a long-treasured pearl on the table.

"You sent me this seventeen years ago and wrote that willful men don't remember accidental dramas, they build on them." He raised his glass and flashed the easy smile featured in his corporation's annual reports. "I liked the sound of that in '67. I like it even more tonight."

Chapter Two

Mike Santry felt the hard muzzle of the gun pressed against his head. He couldn't see it because he was face-down on a grimy linoleum floor staring at jugs of Gallo wine and wondering if this was it. Party-store holdups were not, of course, unexpected in Detroit. On the contrary, they were as common as funerals, but like that last, long ride in a black Cadillac hearse, they usually happened to somebody else. Santry was, in his own way, an authority on east-side crime. He knew far more about it than most and therefore had no illusions about his own safety in a neighborhood terrorized by guns and junkies. At fifty-three, he was old enough to remember unlocked houses and drugstores without two-inch-thick bullet-proof plastic shields, so he knew which way the storm was blowing. That early night in May he walked into Farouk's corner store for cigarettes and caught its blast: man in a crouch whirling toward him, security guard stretched out on the floor, the snarled command hurling him "Down!," and the immediate promise of essence condensation in the *Free Press* obit columns. *Don't move*, he told himself, *don't look, don't talk, don't provoke*. The gun went away. Quick footsteps crossed the floor. A man begged softly, "Please don't. Please don't shoot. Please."

A shout, "Leave it! Let's go!"

The door slammed. Absolute silence.

The soft voice: "I think it's safe."

Santry looked up cautiously. All clear.

The black security guard dusted himself off and called the police. Farouk, a small, balding man with a crisp moustache, checked the till. Farouk wasn't his name, but he was from the Middle East, and neighborhood kids made the appellation stick—usually with a "King" in front. Santry got his cigarettes and walked out. He was running late for the meeting, but when he got to his car he rolled the window down, leaned back, and smoked quietly for a long time.

An hour later, he was on his feet telling thirty people from as many funding organizations, "We're running out of time on the east side, but the story's twice-told and too familiar. The crisis has become a bore. Everybody knows what's happening and everybody's a little sick of hearing about it. Unemployment, crime, desperation, anger—how many times have you heard that litany? The question is, 'Can anything be done?' The mayor says we've got to attract industry. We say the evidence is in and that's a dream. We say we can't count on the private sector. That's a hard and clear conclusion—business decisions have gone against Detroit for thirty years. The East Side Community Organization's heard all the talk, read all the signs, and knows that if we want jobs, we've got to create them because nobody's going to give 'em to us. And that's what this project's about: jobs, food, and community self-development. It's a good, solid program. It may be our last chance. We need your help to get started."

He spoke quickly, passionately, and quietly, his black, deep-set eyes brightening the rugged Mediterranean face, his manner direct and serious. "Six months ago, the largest bread producer on the east side moved out. Five hundred out of work. Add families and we're talking about two thousand people. A disaster. Hundreds of leaders from all over the east side came together and worked out a plan: We propose to buy that factory, remodel it so it needs more workers, hire eighty percent of the needed labor right from the community, and begin making healthy bread available for little more than cost. People can pay for it in cash or labor and there'll always be a way to earn a loaf at one of the coop's outlets. Our community networks blanket the area and ensure the sale of everything produced. The business will be an expertly managed, well-run success. Profits will go for wages, plant improvements, and community development. We've got a pile of studies that say it's feasible. As experience, skill, and morale increase, we can produce other goods. We've got leadership, vigorous organizations, community support, workers, and a guaranteed market. We need capital to get it going. That's why I'm here."

He answered their questions and left discouraged. He was getting to be an expert on predicting negative responses. In one-half year, they had raised less than fifty thousand dollars. They needed at least a million, but it was nowhere in sight. Much later that night, he turned the key in the door of the old house where he lived alone and climbed worn, wooden stairs to a small room furnished simply with a narrow, hard bed, a table, and a straight-backed chair. Only a crucifix, stark above the bed, relieved the unadorned, light blue walls. He stood for a long time by the window in the darkness, looking toward the river, where a police helicopter churned. He had always believed that people struggling together could win an increased measure of justice for themselves and their children. And he was certain that without struggle, the poor could expect only wrung necks. He was no longer the innocent priest he had been at thirty, recently returned from the slums of Recife, Brazil, and full of words like "renewal" and "transformation." The helicopter moved toward the church, its searchlights uncovering the darkness in alleys and side streets as scout cars prowled the edges of the fierce moon brightness. He had been born down there and, except for seminary and Brazil, had never lived outside the neighborhood. He followed the helicopter's scouring lights and took a hard, dark look at the "transformation" coming to the city below: neither community renewal nor merciful death was on the way. Only slow, terrible decay lay ahead for this wilderness of the poor, the old, and the black. All able to flee the danger and rot would do so.

He turned on a small desk lamp, unlocked the drawer in which he kept his journal, and wrote:

> O Lord, my refuge and my strength, you know the anger and frustration in my heart. If there is a way, open it. If there is light, show me, for I cannot see. If there is hope, help me find it, for I am weary but cannot rest.

* * *

There are women a man never forgets. And men. The men are more privately remembered. Any of Alexander Ross's corporate peers or squash partners could name a few of the tall, photogenic women he preferred, but they'd be hard-pressed to identify male friends beyond club and business circles. Even those who shared keys to his love nest along the river and kept close watch on the ladies in his life—observing the vagrant vial of perfume, the telltale scarf, and the earring left behind—had little interest in the men important to him. It was a rare month that passed without sly references to the latest beauty in his bed, but of the men in his life beyond corporate walls, he was rarely asked and never spoke.

And just as well, Ross thought as he went to the phone in JFK and made two calls. The first went to full-bodied, red-haired Laura, who agreed to meet his plane in Detroit and save Saturday for romping. The second went to Father Michael Santry, whose answering machine took the message: "Hi, Mike. Alexander here. Just landed in JFK after a week in Greece. It's urgent that we talk. Please save Sunday night for me."

Ross had a window seat on the flight to Detroit and

remembered looking through the larger window of an army bus on a somber, slate-gray Detroit dawn in 1964. It was the first time he saw Santry. He and the other army recruits waiting to leave were watching thirty or forty demonstrators parading up and down the sidewalk on West Jefferson who were getting their pictures taken by the Detroit police. On the bus there was some "what the fuck!" resentment and "piece at any price" taunts at the women in the line, but most of the guys were quiet and curious. Only eighteen then, Ross hadn't cared much one way or the other and was reading the *Free Press* when he heard a sudden explosion of shouts outside and looked up in time to see a couple of cops tumbling out of their parked cars and running across the street toward the protesters. Everybody in the bus crowded against the windows, so Ross couldn't make out what was going on, but he glimpsed the police forcing a heavyset, middle-aged man to spread his hands on the roof of the police car while they searched him. In the next wild minute, Ross jumped out of the bus, raced past a startled M.P. at the gate, and was screaming at the cops to take their fucking hands off his old man. Twenty years later, he could still feel the club that jammed into his gut and hear the big sergeant's voice booming "Calm down, sonny! Calm down!" There wasn't much more to it than that. When the police learned that Ross was leaving for war that morning and that the man who attacked the demonstrators was his father, they gave everybody warnings, told Ross to take care of himself, and said he had better get back on the bus.

At just that point, one of the demonstrators, a priest, started across the street toward them. Everybody stopped and watched him coming. The sergeant signaled his men to hold still. The priest, a stocky man in his early thirties, walked straight toward Ross's father, whose flushed face was fixed in a frightened smile, then handed him the cap that had been knocked off in the brief scuffle, and said, "I'm Mike Santry. Maybe we could talk sometime. We don't have to be enemies just because we disagree." His father had looked at the cops, then told the priest they had nothing to talk about and to get back across the street with the other monkeys. The priest turned his dark good looks and easy manner on Alexander. "You his son?" Ross nodded. Santry said, "Good luck. When you get back, I'd like to see you. You can tell us how it looks on the inside."

In his first letter home, Ross asked his folks to send him any articles that showed up in the paper about Santry and the antiwar movement. His father responded with the zeal of an enraged librarian, so Ross got a two-year running account of Santry's activities along with his father's editorials. In the beginning, Santry was "confused" and "misled," but with the public announcement of a new Draft Counseling Center in the church, he had moved "dangerously close to treason." And when the newspapers carried a photograph of Santry on the platform of an antiwar rally in the company of "known radicals," his father was triumphant and wrote in the margin beside the priest's black-and-white figure, "If it walks like a duck and talks like a duck, it's a duck. Whatever Santry thinks he's doing, objectively he's joined the enemy."

The correspondence convinced Ross he had inherited none of his father's spleen. It was impossible for him to get so excited about anything. He had not been demoralized by the home-front marching, and if Santry helped a couple of draft dodgers get to Canada, so what? He read everything about the war that came along, concluded it was a mixed bag, did his job, and took every promotion he could get. At eighteen, he had been passionately committed to only a few things: getting ahead, getting out of southwest Detroit, and getting away from the stalking shadow of his father.

The man had been good to him, but he hated his

style. As a kid, on the way home from hunting trips up north, he had watched his father drop game off at some politician's house and asked him why. His father had answered with a knowing wink and the wisdom that good friends looked after each other. But Ross never saw anybody drop game off at his house, and by the time he was fourteen, he had reached two painful conclusions. The first was that his father had been blinded by his own bullshit. He had no friends and no one looked after him except Alexander's mother. The second and more profoundly disturbing conclusion was that his father's basic approach was to kiss ass. The neighbors regarded him as something of a buffoon and tolerated him with a smile. Alexander saw it all and cringed from the insults his father barely comprehended. He was, finally, a weak and uncertain man. The bravado on the morning of Ross's induction made the parting only more painful because it was all grandstanding for the cops. If Santry had come to their house alone and had handed out antiwar pamphlets, his father would have invited him in for coffee and promised to come to the next meeting.

Ross didn't see Santry again until the fall of 1967. Vietnam, Greece, and Andreas Korachis were memorably behind him, and high marks at Wayne State University were a priority and hard to get because he was working full-time to help pay for his mother's hospital bills. The escalating war protests intruded in his life as little as they had when he was overseas, but the campus announcement of a speech by Father Michael Santry was irresistible. The priest remembered him immediately and invited him for coffee after the meeting. Before saying good-bye, Santry surprised him by asking if he played handball. The following week they met at the YMCA and went to Greektown afterward for dinner.

The evening was repeated, a once-monthly pattern established itself, and the two became friends. The fourteen-year difference in age and the world of difference between their religions and politics made each one more, not less, interested in the other. They watched squash players on nearby courts, tried and loved the game, knocked themselves out, and then soaked luxuriantly in steam baths. They ate flaming saganaki, mussels, and curried shrimp at the best of the least-expensive restaurants, and they talked endlessly over Stroh's beer and red wine.

Less than a year later, after dinner at the Himalaya, an Indian restaurant across the river in Windsor, Santry handed Ross an envelope and said, "It's a loan you didn't ask for and won't want to take, but you need it anyway. You've got to hit the books harder. You need better grades if you're going to get an M.B.A. from a top school and dazzle the business world. You've got to quit that job and be a full-time student. Like it or not, there's no other way. I'm not giving you anything. I expect the money back. In ten years, I'm going to need a rich executive in my life, and, surprisingly, you're my best prospect."

Ross hadn't argued at all. He knew Santry was right in offering him the break he needed. The future he wanted felt suddenly within his grasp. More than wine had made him lighthearted that night.

Santry faded as the stewardess announced their descent into Metro Airport and Laura came into full-color focus. Ross had checked Detroit's temperature before leaving JFK to anticipate her clothes. It was a warm May night in the Motor City so he guessed a pastel floral print, heels, and a wide-brimmed, soft hat haloing that glorious sunset hair. She was, perhaps, the loveliest woman he knew. When he told her that, she almost smiled and said he should leave his rating sheets at the office. There was no need to rank her. And that made her exceptional, too. That and a face always on the edge of a smile that never came, freckled skin stretched smooth over marvelous terrain, and hands that loved to touch.

They talked little that night, their ritual silence after a week apart, and a pattern as predictable as her pastel print unfolded: the affectionate airport kiss, more than business, less than passion, the joint shared as soon as they reached her car, the glow rising from another in the darkness of his apartment above the river and freighter lights, where there was wine and WJZZ and they lay naked and moved slowly and took hours to take each other higher than either could remember into that unimaginably thin, near-screaming zone of pure, pure pleasure.

On Saturday, they sailed his ensign into Lake St. Clair, watched a flurry of terns above the Belle Isle breeding grounds, ate black olives and feta cheese while he told her nothing important about his days in Greece, and by Sunday morning she was sure.

"You're leaving, aren't you?"

"For a couple of hours. I'll be back by noon."

"No, I mean you're leaving Detroit."

He turned in the shower to face her, his fingers drifting along her shoulder and over her breasts. "Why do you say that?"

She arched slightly, lifting toward him. "Because in two nights and one long, extraordinary day you haven't mentioned the corporation. Something's going on."

Ross watched the hot water streaming down her body. She was on the mark: Detroit was receding fast, but in the age of jets, its pleasures were movable. "It's possible," he told her. "I'll tell you when I'm sure, but even if that happens, it doesn't need to end anything between us. You've always liked to travel."

She closed her eyes and almost smiled. "You probably believe that, don't you?"

"That you like to travel?"

"No, that it doesn't end anything."

"You see it differently?"

She shook her head and looked away.

"What's wrong?" he asked.

"Nothing, nothing, it's been a beautiful weekend." She held his face in her hands and held his eyes with her own. "You know I mean that. And if you leave, yes, of course I'd love to travel. Leaving doesn't end what we have. It's just that, well, leaving doesn't begin very much either."

Within the hour, Ross pulled his Peugeot into the Big Boy opposite Belle Isle on Detroit's east side, fed the street machine quarters for a Sunday paper, and went inside for coffee. It was early, bright, and cool. He took his coffee hot and black and looked out the front windows. Joggers, cyclers, kite fliers, even West Indian cricketeers were crossing the bridge to Belle Isle for a long, laid-back day in the sun and shade.

He glanced at the cops hunched over their cups at the counter beside him, then at the black waitress whose magnificent, young body pushed against all the right seams in her starched, tight, yellow uniform. It was hard to look away. She saw his eyes and asked if he wanted more coffee. He nodded, thanked her, and wondered about the long scar ridging her neck just above the collar. One of the cops was watching him. Ross looked over and watched back, then looked at himself in the wall mirror behind the waitress and knew how they saw him. Peugeot, cashmere sweater, and designer jeans over Italian loafers: pure suburban and rich, a blue-eyed white trolling for black women. He lingered over his coffee, left a good tip, and walked out, turning back at the door to catch the cop staring after him.

He headed east along the river, passed U.A.W. International's headquarters, turned near Chrysler's sprawling Jefferson Avenue plant, and saw that everything had gotten worse. He hadn't been in the neighborhood for a year. A third of the homes looked bombed out, FOR SALE signs were rampant, windows were broken, and glass was all over the goddamned, filthy streets. It was grim, but it improved his chances with Santry. Knots of black kids crowded on corners outside party stores, hanging out, watching his Peugeot, watching him, waiting for him to park, just waiting.

He drove slowly down silver maple-shaded streets, counting abandoned houses, nodding at old-timers sitting on porches, and smelling the first barbecue fires. By late afternoon, Detroit would be simmering in a cloud of rib smoke. People were beginning to move around. A gray-haired man, naked to the waist, watered a backyard garden and nursed a beer in the early sun. Two women laughed somewhere above him. Easy, good-time laughing that floated down like leaves. And in an empty parking lot, roller skaters wearing shorts and knee-high socks flashed arms and thighs, improvised, moved tight to the music, spun webs of black and gold, got hot, looked cool.

The streets got worse. Ugly. Peeled paint, cardboard in windowpanes, rain spouts down, dog shit, throwaway fliers hawking cheap chicken, and gutted houses. A woman was in the street. He stopped. They talked. She was maybe fifty, sleepy in a housecoat, bent over a dustpan and sweeping up glass from bottles smashed against her house when she was inside and alone in the dark and shaking every time one hit the wall and worrying that the angry fists and the howling voices were going to tear the front door off and find her hiding there and . . . Yes, she *had* called the police, but the police didn't come. And yes, she had a gun. Everybody had a gun. The wild ones outside had guns. It wasn't an advantage anymore. The only hope was to sit in the dark and hope to surprise them if they came. No, that was wrong. It used to be "if," but not anymore because they're coming. Count on it. Everybody gets their turn. Read the papers, look at the TV, open your eyes: nothing but beatings, knives, and worse. For Christ's sake, they're even starting school late to cut down on the rape of children. "Animals," she said, almost whispering, "animals!"

She quieted, smoothed her hand on the front fender of the white car, and asked Ross where he lived. When he told her Bloomfield Hills, she said he was lucky. If she wasn't trapped, she'd be getting out, too. She asked for a cigarette. They smoked and talked. Then Ross said he had to go. He watched her in the rearview mirror as he drove away and thought about his folks. They had been able to get out. The twin spires of St. Jude's rose just ahead. What the hell did Santry think he was doing here? Why did he stay? The question was rhetorical. He knew exactly why Santry stayed and half admired him for it. But only half. He didn't admire and didn't trust the other half, the Christian, romantic half. Santry was as hard-nosed and knowledgeable about the real world as any man he knew, but he gave himself away too freely and wasted enormous energy in reckless battles over lost causes. A failing of the best, not the worst, of men. His problem was he didn't take losing seriously. When Ross saw red ink, he knew he was in trouble and had to make changes. Santry had the luxury of living in a saint's world—moral victories counted. St. Jude's made his point: here stood an old building constructed when the neighborhood was full of Catholics and energy was cheap. Now the Catholics were gone and the place was always cold. A losing operation. If Ross were the cardinal, he'd have shut it down years ago.

He pulled the Peugeot off the narrow street and into the church parking lot. He double-checked the lock before going inside. The nineteenth-century Gothic building was enormous, the vaulted ceiling rose high over a cavernous chancel that stretched, long and narrow, toward a distant altar. All but the front pews had been roped off, as if in memory of the thousands who once sat there when the neighborhood was young and the Italian community strong. The small congregation, huddled in the front of the practically empty church, called more attention to ghostly absences than to their own presence. Ross sat in the back among the departed. He had come early, but not to worship. By ten o'clock, a few hundred people had walked down the long aisle to the front, as if attracted by the light high above the altar, a strong, golden light that swept the holy place and took the eye to the flickering reds of votive candles on the sanctuary floor.

A strong hand suddenly gripped Ross's shoulder from behind and an easy voice whispered, "What are you doing here?"

He imagined Santry's smiling face behind him, covered the hand on his shoulder with his own, turned his head slightly, and said in a low voice, "I come bearing good news for a struggling priest. Repent and believe. The Kingdom may be at hand. You okay for tonight?"

"How about the Pegasus at seven?"

Ross nodded, the hand slipped from his shoulder, and the priest was gone. He hadn't seen him in six months. The long evenings of sport, food, and drink that revived him in student days had given way to the demands of a young family and an executive position that took him frequently out of town. By the early eighties, their visits were down to two or three a year, but their pleasure in them never diminished.

A full-throated organ, altar boys swinging smoky censers, men carrying bright, multicolored banners high above their heads, and a choir of fifty strong voices announced a stately procession that moved slowly and solemnly down the center aisle. Santry would have it no other way. The poor would not be slighted. Worship should look and sound the way it was supposed to: divine. And that meant, above all, beautiful music. Later in the service, the priest climbed the hand-carved wooden stairs, began to speak, and Ross leaned forward to hear. Loudspeakers mounted on marble columns set off flights of echoes in the vast interior until some unseen hand on the sound system brought one voice out of many. Santry looked tired. Same dark hair and shy smile, but his face had thinned and caught more shadows. He began by reading from the Gospel of Luke. "It were better for a man that a millstone were hanged about his neck and he be cast in the sea than that he should offend one of these little ones."

His manner in the pulpit was identical to his way on the street: direct, quiet, and self-assured. He had been a priest for twenty-five years and harbored no illusions about the power of talk to change any firmly held conviction. Oratorical flights sometimes pleased, but they never persuaded, and he refused to be an entertainer. He therefore offered neither entreaties nor threats when he connected the passage from Luke with the plight of peasants suffering in the Guatemalan highlands and to the misery of the unemployed in Detroit. Besides, he and the listening men, women, and children knew one another well. They knew what he thought and were sympathetic, or they would have left with all the others.

"Our Lord," he said, "was upset and clear on this point, wasn't He? Something terrible happens to a man who offends 'these little ones,' something far worse than being thrown overboard with an anchor around the neck." He described the miracles of feeding and healing as the "good news," frequently asking the congregation in an offhanded manner, "Isn't that right?" Or he reminded them, "Well, you know the stories as well as I do." His tempo increased slightly as he concluded, "So I don't think He's issuing warnings here or anything like that. I think He's simply saying that if we want to see what He sees when He looks at the world, then look at suffering children. And if we want to be where He is in the world, then we will do something about that suffering."

Ross left his pew before the service ended, but lingered at the rear doors to watch men and women file to the front of the church, get down on their knees near a simple railing, and receive the host from Santry's fingers. He imagined Korachis's reaction to the scene, Korachis with his sheep and shepherds. The parishioners didn't bother Ross. They were there voluntarily. Most of them were poor and had been brought up Catholic. Some kind of needs were being met.

"You see the lamb on that spit? That's the east side, Alexander: slaughtered, skewered, and turning slowly in the fires. It's a wild country. Two or three generations is all a city gets." Santry turned from the roasting carcass, glanced across the crowded, noisy restaurant, and drank more wine. "My father left Italy for Detroit. He was lucky—he caught it on the rise; he did all right."

The two men had been talking, eating, and drinking in the Pegasus, a popular Greektown restaurant, and had caught up on the odds and ends of the past six months. It was an enjoyable night, and, for Ross, exciting. He knew that sooner or later the conversation would reach that luminous intersection of human suffering and priestly devotion appropriate for the revelation of his project. "Mike," he argued, "there's as much opportunity in Detroit today as when your father got here. It's just in different places. The economy's shifted and people have to shift with it."

Santry leaned forward on the table, no longer tired, his olive-black eyes shining as he studied the good face and expensive clothes of his younger friend. Little remained externally of the young hothead in sweat shirt and work shoes who had swung at a police sergeant while screaming "Get your goddamned hands off my old man!" But years of listening to confessions had taught Santry something about appearances, and years with Ross taught him that he kept only one of his selves steadily in view: that of the cool, achieving executive. If he had not personally experienced the squash-court rages and seen the rackets smashed after poorly played games, he never would have suspected the heat below that charming, suburban surface. And if they had not been friends, he never would have known the sobbing, drunken Ross who was desolate, childishly innocent, and uncomprehending when his wife finally left him. So Santry had been sure the moment he read about the merger and the corporate shake-up and saw another's name where his friend's should have been, that Ross had to be in a spiritual crisis. He had just lost the major, longest-running battle in his life. He had been publicly defeated. No way he could shrug that off calmly. The emotional investment had been too extreme. Ross was a volcano with a well-crafted seal and a serene, snow-covered crown, but between fire at the core and a sprinkling of snow on the summit, there was no contest. It was a law of nature. The snow had to give way. So in this, their first conversation since that loss, Santry listened for signs of the shock waves that were still reverberating below that self-possessed and affable surface.

A slight smile on his dark Italian face softened the bite of his words as he bore down on Ross. It was a new round in an old and serious disagreement. "C'mon, Alexander! A man's shot in the street and you say he didn't move in time. 'The economy's shifted and people have to shift with it.' That's sanitized business talk designed to hide the crime. The economy doesn't 'shift.' It's not part of the natural order. Winds shift, economies are manipulated. The east side's not dying a natural death, it's been knifed by corporations moving out. You know it and I know it." His voice grew quiet and earnest. "And it's not going to change. That's the harder truth. Disinvestment's been going on since the fifties at an ever-accelerating rate. There's no 'renaissance' coming and no friendly business cycle's going to bail us out. We're in a free-fall zone. Anything's possible. The only certainty is that we're going down."

The more he talked, the more restless Santry got with the conversation. Twice-plowed ground. He and Ross had argued about corporate decisions too many times to come up with something new.

He finished his wine and said easily, "Look, why don't we go to a movie or walk by the river or talk about the Tigers. This is going nowhere."

The waiter came with their bill and Santry started to get up, but Ross interrupted the move. "No, don't go, I have to talk to you about something."

It was a good place to begin: privacy assured by hundreds of people coming and going, movement and noise all around, and Santry's mood was right: hard-nosed and pessimistic. The priest gave him a curious look and settled back in his booth.

"I told you this morning I had good news. I do. If I helped you find three million dollars, how much good could you do with it?"

Santry shrugged. "Who knows? It's a new question for me, but three million must buy a lot of good."

"A while ago you were all afire for that bread factory. You told me it was the east side's last chance. You still believe that?"

The priest brushed the crumbs from the tablecloth with an impatient sweep of his hand. "Sure I believe it, but it's hard going. Six months of begging and we're not even close. I've got meetings coming up with a couple of foundations that seem interested, but we'll have to see."

Ross leveled with him. "No, Mike, you don't have to see. You have to give it up. You don't have a chance. I've made a few calls, talked to the Community Affairs man in the corporation and the Torch Drive executive who switchboards the big contributions. They're not going to give you a dime. On the record, they'll smile, say it's a fascinating project, and hand you a list of five other places to go for funding. Off the record, the U.A.W. and the Democratic Party are pissed off because your organization keeps running independent candidates and the corporations can't get excited about a parallel, cooperative economy that dreams of controlling markets. You're not going to like this, but your leadership's no asset. They can't insult you publicly because you're a popular priest with a following, but, my friend, you've been out there on the wrong side of the barricades for twenty years. You can't expect them to love you, and you don't have enough power to make them give you money. The bottom line is, they don't owe you a thing."

Santry poured more wine and fumed about cynical cronyism and mindless back-scratching. The truth stuck in his craw like a fish bone, cutting deeper each time he moved angrily against it. The merits of the project and the needs of a desperate community were incidental to the fact that he was in the wrong camp. Talk about inflated rhetoric! Barricades! Bureaucrats didn't fight on barricades, they sat on safe committees, voted as instructed, and played games with workers' money. He knew he was no threat to them, no offense. He simply wasn't on their team. He supported other candidates. Whether those candidates were bad, good, or better made no difference at all. The point was simple and stark: He was not one of them, he was wearing the wrong colors. He wouldn't get a dime.

"Hold it, Mike," Ross urged. "The east side can have the food-manufacturing plant if you want it badly enough. There's a price tag, but you can pay it. That's the good news; it's within your reach. Now listen carefully. This is going to sound wild-assed to you, so be your patient best and don't slam the door till I've told you the whole story."

Alexander kept his voice low, urgent, and unhurried, glancing occasionally at busboys carrying heavy trays and the loud party of six at the table nearest them. It was impossible for anyone to hear. "I've agreed to remove certain ancient Christian documents, popularly known as the Ephesian Fragments, from the monastery of St. David the King on the Greek island of Kallos and sell them to a trusted friend. If you're prepared to help me, then I'm prepared to contribute three million dollars to your East Side Development Corporation.

"The risks? Practically none if you and I do it together." Santry gave him a "can't believe what I'm hearing" look. His frown said disapproval, but a smile said his friend had to be kidding. Ross raised his hand quickly to block comment. "Give me a chance to explain why I'm bold enough to ask you. First, the theft will be only technically illegal. No real crime will be committed because neither objects nor persons will be deprived of value. No one will experience either hurt, loss, or injury. The Fragments themselves have been photographed thousands of times, printed in innumerable books, and scholars work entirely from copies. Those seriously interested in ancient documents never even glance at the originals, whose remaining value is entirely that of tourist attraction. Years of publicity have made them famous. Were it not for that, they'd be decomposing in a basement and no one would give a damn, but because of their notoriety, thousands of tourists, not ten of whom would read Paul's letter to the Ephesians in their family Bible, travel long miles to Kallos and stand for thirty seconds in front of a glass-enclosed, locked, and guarded icon because they want to feel the ancient vibrations, pray for healing, or just tell the kids they've been there.

"Even that value will be neither decreased nor threatened, because at the same time we remove the original, an exact copy will be substituted, an imitation so good that only experts could distinguish it from the second-century manuscript. And there's no chance of that because the experts don't go near it. You could probably put *The Wall Street Journal* under the dark glass and no one would notice the difference.

"The amazing truth is that the Fragments will never be missed. Life on Kallos will go on exactly as before.

Neither Greece nor Christendom will be offended. The miracle is that all present value will be preserved and, at the same time, simply by transferring the Fragments' resting place, millions of dollars will be released to feed the poor. I think even St. Paul would be pleased." He paused, tried to guess Santry's reaction, and asked, "Shall I go on?"

Santry retained all the external signs of priestly composure, but admitted freely, "Alexander, I'm glad you're a good friend and certifiably sane, because otherwise I'd be laughing in your face or just walking out of the room. What you propose has the ring of genuine madness about it, and you must feel the same way as I do. You must know it's crazy! How could you even dream of doing such a thing?" He looked around to be sure no one had heard and said, "Let's go for a drive. We need to talk about this in private."

Once outside on the busy sidewalk in front of the Pegasus, Santry took Ross by the arm and called his attention to the restaurant's large front window across which flew a magnificent, winged horse mounted by a youthful rider.

"You know the story?" Ross shook his head and the priest told him, "The horse is Pegasus. The rider is the beautiful and gifted Bellerophon, a favorite of the gods. He and the horse were victorious in all sorts of battles, apparently unconquerable, but Bellerophon's ambitions got out of hand and he tried to ride Pegasus to Olympus, the home of the gods. The wise horse refused, threw the rider, and Bellerophon had to wander alone and despised till death—his punishment for excess."

Somewhere behind them a man shouted, "Roses! Dollar apiece! Roses!"

Santry went on quietly. "Alexander, you're extremely talented and ambitious. Don't throw it away. Don't want too much."

The two men stood together near the curb, their backs

to the slowly moving cars. Santry, in black suit and white collar, leaned relaxed against a parking meter, his dark face and alert eyes moving between the large window with horse and rider and the face of his taller friend. People crowded on the sidewalk near them. Ross's eyes were also on the window but lower, below the horse, where the glass was clear and the spit-seized lamb inside the restaurant turned slowly through the fire, roasting in its own juices.

"I know what you're saying, Mike, but flying free of the corporate canary cage doesn't sound like storming Olympus to me. Anyway, I could end up wandering and despised by staying right where I am. This way at least I'm going to have a glorious ride." He stopped, looked from the lamb to the priest, and asked, "Okay if I push you hard?"

Santry nodded and waited.

"Mike, you started out tonight by claiming the east side was like that seared flesh, but as soon as I gave you a chance to do something practical about that suffering, your eyes shifted to the horse and the rider and the lesson swung from the necessary works of love to the evils of excess. There may be something in that window for both of us. I may be too ambitious, but you may be too timid. That's rough but right. You may not want anything badly enough to really go after it. I know that sounds strange as hell because everybody thinks you're bold. You're always speaking out, writing articles, slashing the rich with the sword of the Lord, leading demonstrations against the evil utilities for cutting off service to the poor, and getting arrested at military installations. A lot of people don't like what you do, but nobody thinks you're conservative. I do. I don't think you've ever gone beyond preaching and street theater. You're a master of dramatic gestures. It's not posturing because you're sincere about it, but deep in your heart and in spite of all your experience, you still believe that 'witnessing' or 'testifying' makes some kind of dent in the real world, and I say it doesn't even scratch it. You preach about 'contending with the principalities and powers' for the sake of the blessed poor and it all sounds good and pure and high tone, and it all makes not one goddamned bit of difference.

"Forgive me if I'm out of bounds, but we owe each other at least our best judgment. You've always been willing to take a public stand and openly violate unjust laws for the sake of a cause. But there was no real risk involved. You weren't going to lose your job or go hungry or even stay in jail very long. So the moral question for you is: Will you take an unpublicized real risk and secretly violate an irrelevant law in order to accomplish the good you've absolutely failed to do any other way? That food factory's within your grasp. You say it's important. Well, if you want it, you can have it. Inside there, you threw up your hands and called my idea crazy. And I'm telling you it's a lot worse than that because it's not going to let you go. A crazy idea's easy to get rid of, but this one's real and should torment you because, whatever you decide, you're going to be involved in criminal behavior. Join me and commit a technically illegal act that injures no one and gives you resources for the creation of jobs and food for thousands of people, or turn your back on the poor and walk away on high moral ground. I ask you seriously, which is the more criminal act? One way you accomplish something enormously positive for the poor; the other way you keep your skirts clean. I see nothing at all crazy or mad about what I propose. It only sounds wild because it threatens to dig you out of that protected moral cloister and confronts you with a decision about the real cost of discipleship."

Ross stopped, anxious, aware he may have offended. His words had come like a torrent, a rushing stream that overflowed the banks of careful speech. His mind

raced back and forth over that current, aware of the
half-formed observations, the sharp criticism, and the
undertow of resentment. He admired no man more than
Santry, but he had none of the priest's impulse toward
saintliness and more than a few questions about all the
Christ-on-the-Cross talk. He liked Santry best as a
sweating, east-side grown Italian pummeling the squash-
court walls with an incredible mix of aggressive drives
and drop shots. He loved the man's loyalty to people.
No if's, and's, or but's, a person could count on him.
And he admired the independent, gutzy advocate of decent causes. But Ross suspected that a hell of a nice
guy had gotten trapped by the goodness dream. Why
should Santry beat himself up because he hadn't saved
the east side? Who did he think he was? Talk about
excess! Talk about wanting too much!

But even as his mind whirled over what he had said
and worried that he had said too much, even as he
waited for Santry's first response, Ross knew—he did
not feel certain or think or guess—he knew that he had
spontaneously played his cards exactly right. Exactly!
He had offered Santry the crown Santry could not refuse: the lonesome valley, self-sacrifice for the blessed
poor, the way of the Cross. It would be a complicated
process, but Ross was sure the good man would find a
way.

Two Months Later: July 15, 1984

He polished his reading glasses with a clean, white
handkerchief, touched the seat belt once again, and saw
Manhattan toward the west as the Iberia 747 arched
gracefully over JFK, then curved slowly toward the east,
the Atlantic, and Spain. The evening sun was behind
him, but its light went far ahead, rimming the sky with
flecks of gold. The earth had slipped away. He flew over
fields of purest fleece, remembered how much he

missed such beauty, and thought that this alone was worth the trip.

He would have breakfast in Madrid, dinner in Athens, coffee under the Acropolis. All that was imaginable. The rest of it was not. All the rest was strange and frightening and necessary. Yes, it was necessary. Of that he was now certain. And he knew, because he had been in strange and frightening places many times before, that his emotions would soon parallel his will. The strangeness and the fear would gradually subside, thaw like ice in the sun, and disappear. The imagination and the will—those swift horses were always in the lead. The emotions, powerful contenders for the mind's throne, resisted change, sounded alarms, dug in their heels. He turned to the voice speaking from the aisle of the plane, saw the cart nearby, and said, "Yes, I would. Scotch, please."

He did not, as others imagined, go calmly through the world. Every fight took something from him, every battle wounded. Sometimes it was so bad he ached for quiet and rest, but early in life he had chosen to go another way. Had chosen or had been chosen? He often wondered. He hoped it was at least that complicated. He would never claim to be simply an instrument of Holy Will. That arrogance was not in him. But he had to believe that God gave him leadings, had answered prayers and opened doors. Yes, he had to believe that much.

And hours later, while others stretched out on seats and slept, the solitary man took a hardbound journal from his traveling bag and began to write:

> Thou who hast heard my supplications and answered my prayers, help me now to obey Thy will. The familiar is swept away and all about the land is strange. I am alone and have only Thee. Do not turn Thy face from me, but make me a faithful

instrument of Thy Holy Love. O Thou, whose voice comes in the whirlwind and fire, cleanse my heart of fear and my mind of troubles. Grant me the strength to act boldly and not to count the cost. And if the powers of this world revile and persecute me, then grant me safe lodging and peace at the last.

Chapter Three

She held the barbed spear in tense hands and whispered sharply, "Soon, Ross, soon! I know when they're close." Her thin, near-naked body, famous to thousands of Greeks who would never know her face, leaned over the edge of the small boat. The wind died at sunset. The sea was as quiet as a dark, untroubled pool. The deadly spear moved gently in the night waters. "Keep it just ahead of me," she commanded.

The intense white light poured from the torch in his hands, tunneled effortlessly through five feet of dark, shallow water, and caught stones, sand, needle-backed urchins, and green sea grasses in its blaze. Gabriella kept the hovering spear on the edge of darkness, behind the moving light, a few feet off the bottom. Small fish circled lazily, unalarmed by the white beam or the trailing, knife-sharp lance.

The boat drifted, the light moved, she warned again that one was near. A match flared in the rear of the boat. Ross saw the quick flame die in a cigarette's glow. The other woman never spoke. He felt Gabriella's bare leg against his own as she shifted beside him in the bow. "Look! Don't move the light!" His eyes went back to the bottom and saw it glowing there. He heard Gabriella's quick breath and saw her tighten on the lance as he held the torch over the feeding octopus. She brought the spear quietly above the animal, held it motionless, then raised up and plunged her golden arms downward in a smooth, powerful thrust that carried the barbs deep into the white and writhing flesh.

She brought the octopus up slowly. Ross moved the torch and glimpsed the face staring at the struggling mass. Nothing triumphant there. Deep-shadowed sadness in the eyes and strain on the full, unsettled lips. He had seen the same intense face among the photographs. The night before over drinks he learned she had been a model. He asked to see some photos and she showed him a few in the yacht's lounge. She did not show him the album discovered among the books. The fashion magazines loved her body and what her movements did for clothes, but they kept that somber countenance obscured or hidden. The spear's point, buried in flailing tentacles and dripping seawater, came over the side. She told him to hold the animal against the floorboards of the boat, took a knife, bent quickly over the pinioned octopus, and, with a few sure strokes, settled and rocked the blade from eye to eye until the creature quieted. Then, holding it limp and bloody in her hand, she heaved it out to sea.

Ross snapped off the light. It was her party, but if she wanted more octopus, she'd get it without his help. Taking them with a light was like shooting sheep behind the barn, but if one wanted them for food, okay, call it harvesting. She was satisfying stranger appetites. A cigarette flipped from the rear of the boat, scattering red sparks across the water.

A soft voice asked, "Now?"

Gabriella slid the point of the spear into the notch of the bow, rested the shaft across the seats, and answered, "Yes, love, now." The powerful engine caught on the first turn of the key, rumbled quickly to life, and turned the boat seaward under a star-ridden sky. No one spoke during the ride to the yacht, neither Alexander Ross, nor Gabriella Antissa, his contact in Athens, nor her beautiful eighteen-year-old daughter, Ladrea.

Ross had arrived in Athens the day before and called

Antissa from his hotel. She canceled an engagement and met him within the hour. The meeting was brief. She was sailing to the island of Mykonos that night on Korachis's ninety-foot yacht and invited him to come. A business trip. She was entertaining buyers from Latin America. There'd be time to conclude all arrangements related to his project on the sail. One of her jobs was to ensure that neither Ross nor the Fragments could be linked to Korachis. He would therefore be Ian Marshall on the yacht, a personal friend and English teacher from the States.

"The Latinos will assume you're my lover and keep their distance. You'll have your own cabin and won't need to see any more of them than you want. My daughter, Ladrea, will be along. She'll know your real name and that you work for us, but nothing about the project."

From the small boat, he saw Mars, Saturn, and Jupiter shining out among the stars of late July, the dark mass of the island moving slowly away on portside, the open sea to starboard, and, after half an hour, the low silhouette of the anchored yacht stretched across the sheltered, private harbor. The motor slowed, idled, and stopped as the small boat moved gently to its side. Gabriella threw a line to waiting hands, shouted at the crew in Greek, and climbed aboard. Ross watched the silent daughter on the ladder. When he reached the deck, Ladrea was gone, but Gabriella waited.

"We'll eat in an hour," she told him. "The others are going to the island, so we'll be alone."

He shrugged off the imperious tone and focused on what he wanted: a swim, a hot shower, fresh clothes, a comfortable chair on deck, and a very dry martini. In minutes, he stood alone on the diving platform mounted on the stern of the yacht. Lights from the ship threw shimmering lances across the gently rippling waters. The air was cool, sea-fresh, and came on a light breeze. He dove, swam fifty easy yards, rolled on his back, and watched the stars.

He heard their voices before he saw them and looked across the water toward the ship. The two women stood on the rear deck. There was enough light to distinguish between them, though little was needed. The mother was reed thin and angular, a coiled spring, wiry and lean. The daughter's body was a swirl of crescent moons. She stood like a young animal: quiet, full-fleshed, attentive. Ross had watched her for an hour that afternoon, caught by her natural moves and beauty. Brown as the hills that swept up behind her, she had walked the stony beaches collecting shells, swam in the cool Mediterranean under the hot summer sun, spoke pleasantly, and went her own way. And where she went, eyes followed.

One of the men from Venezuela had walked with her on the sand and came back to knowing winks and smiles from his buddies. Ross knew a little Spanish and a lot of bullshit, so he could keep up with the ravings of the half-plowed Latino who went on and on about the *chica* who was going swimming with him naked that night. Yes, he assured them, the purple bathing suit that molded those young, high breasts and ran the edges of those glorious, surely aching thighs would be peeled and he would teach her the ways of South American love. Like the Venezuelan, Ross had felt the genital surge. The eighteen-year-old's body was a magnet of intense power and heat. But over the years he had learned to proceed with caution. Too often, the woman he had to have today was the same woman he couldn't stand tomorrow, and walking away was more complicated than the boys made it sound. He judged the Venezuelan to be all mouth and glands, a clown clamoring for a circus that would never come his way, a rum-swept waste trying to impress traveling companions, succeeding only in kidding himself. He'd never touch her. He wasn't in her league.

It was then that he heard the warning that collapsed the Latino's rooster crowing. One of the businessmen, anger and worry creasing his face, reached over, gripped his friend's arm, and hissed, "Quiet, fool! She's Korachis's daughter." The Venezuelan was as surprised as Ross by the revelation and instantly quieted. That night, when Alexander heard the women's voices and watched from the water, he thought he could see the rich blend of the mother's beauty and the father's quiet power. Gabriella was stretching her lithe-as-a-cat body through a series of exercises, preparing for a swim, while Ladrea lingered above the water, running her fingers through thick, black hair. He knew they had done this many times because when they dove, they dove together, swam side by side, stroke for stroke, and traced an easy circle around the yacht. At the ladder, they rose like sea goddesses, streaming water from brown shoulders and glistening flanks, wrapped all in darkness. Then, a brief murmuring on the deck and Gabriella left. Ladrea stayed behind, alone, half hidden in shadows, motionless, listening to tremulous Greek music coming from deep within the ship. Almost imperceptibly, she began to move. Her feet barely shifted and her body held to a stately, sinuous, slightly undulating line, but her arms moved as easily as tall willows in a breeze while her fingers circled intricately, snapped, and wove a seductive spell high above that long, arched back and regal head. The dance was brief. A few minutes, a little more. But as Ross came out of his own darkness and swam slowly toward the yacht, he was sure that violets rode the water. And once on the empty deck, he went and stood where she had danced, reached out, and touched her there.

It was midnight before Gabriella asked about his accomplice for the work on Kallos. Conversation during the lobster dinner, served with a flourish of Greek wines to the two of them alone, avoided the business that brought them together. But now on the deck with Metaxa brandies in hand, the time had come. Ladrea and most of the crew had taken the South Americans to the island and would leave them at a party designed to honor and exhaust. The drinking and dancing would continue till dawn or until the three Athenian voluptuaries flown in for the occasion took the Latinos to bed. Ladrea was spending the night with a school friend vacationing on Mykonos. Ross surprised himself by wondering about the friend's gender. In any case, no one would return before noon the next day. Except for the Greek cook and security crew, Antissa and Ross were alone.

"The identity of my accomplice is my business," he told her. "Andreas and I have a firm agreement. There's no reason you should know it, just as there's no reason for him to know yours."

"I'll accept that," she said, as if she had a choice in the matter. "Tell me about your plan. That *is* my business." Her face had softened somewhat during dinner, the alternating fierceness and sorrow relieved by wine and quiet talk.

"My partner's on Kallos now," Ross told her. "We'll meet in two weeks to shape the final scene. You'll have the Fragments by mid-August."

"How will you travel between Athens and the island?"

"By night boat."

"Why?"

"Because boats don't check passports and don't leave computer trails. There'll be no evidence anywhere that I've been on Kallos."

"How are you going to get away? There'll be an explosion of publicity, rewards for information broadcast on radio and TV, headlines, an international search."

"You're wrong. There'll be none of that. Only five people in the world will even know it's happened: the buyer, Andreas, you, my accomplice, and I. Andreas has pledged the silence of three. I guarantee the remaining two." He reviewed the plan in detail.

"Where will you have the substitute prepared?"

"It's finished. Friends in Mexico City led me to artists who specialize in illegal documents. I flew there with thirty color photographs to guide their work. They did a beautiful job."

"And if an expert should look closely at the one you'll leave behind?"

"No expert ever will. But if one should, he'd spot the fraud instantly, so I had them use and fade the most common European vellum. The trail would lead, if anywhere, to the larger cities of Germany, France, and England—not to Greece or to the United States."

"You know that hotels and banks will ask for passports."

"I'll rent rooms in private homes on the island, and I brought all the drachmas I'll need with me."

"And afterward? Where will you be?"

"Unreachable. I'll call once a year in case there's news."

"How do you want the money?"

"Five hundred thousand dollars in cash to be picked up in New York, the balance divided equally between two accounts: one in Switzerland, one in the Cayman Islands." He gave her the numbers.

She filled his glass and, as if announcing the completion of their work but not their night, lit a joint, inhaled deeply, and passed it to him. They smoked in silence until she stood, surveyed the star-choked sky, and pointed. "There, just to the left of the mast—the bright one's Mars, God of war. In Greek, Ares. The Romans loved him more than we. Either way, he is the only God. None of the rest survives. He endures and grows."

Ross looked at the planet riding close to Mars. "I have a friend who believes in the other one. He doesn't call him Saturn but he works for the same Golden Age: peace, equality, those things."

Gabriella drank more and remarked, "He must be a discouraged, pitiful man."

"Discouraged? Yeah, I guess so," Ross told her. "But not pitiful, not pitiful at all. I don't agree with him, or with you, for that matter, but he's a helluva man."

Michael Santry was appalled. He stared out the window, followed the erratic flight of swallows feeding over the sea, and wondered about two things: whether those swallows migrated in winter, and whether he should say anything. If he were in Detroit, there'd be no hesitation, but on the island of Kallos, should he do anything that called attention to his presence, anything that would make him stand out among those who had come to attend the annual summer conference on New Testament studies? His life was suddenly full of new questions. He turned away from the swirling birds, having decided they must migrate, looked back over the heads of several hundred conferees toward the distant podium, and focused on a buttoned-down, self-important, young historian named Temple from an East Coast university in the United States who was arguing for "the irrelevance of the New Testament."

The priest leaned forward in his seat, leaned back, crossed his heavy legs, lit another cigarette, and returned to the window. He knew the argument by heart and had been fighting it for thirty years. Now here it came again, more popular than ever and packaged for sale in Dr. Steven Temple, an articulate, charming, good scholar. Santry listened to him take off from Paul's letter to the Romans. "You can almost open the New Testament arbitrarily, let the wind choose the page, and prove my point. These verses from Romans are well known and frequently cited not because they're unusual, but because they represent the wisdom of the whole. 'Let every soul be subject to the higher powers for there is no power but of God: the powers that be are ordained of God. Whoever resists them, therefore, resists God and will receive damnation.' "

The young professor continued with an amused smile on his face. "That is, admittedly, not popular teaching in some quarters today. It is, in fact, anathema to those who oppose the existing order and propose to storm the ramparts in the name of 'liberation theology.' Their eyes are fixed, however, on an entirely imaginary Jesus. The hard—and I think the indisputable—truth is that neither Jesus nor Paul was a political activist and those engagé priests who would transform them into big-city councilmen or Central American revolutionaries are simply wrong. They have a perfect right to do whatever they want, but they should be honest about it and not try to wrap their political causes in Christian garb."

His manner became more serious, quiet, even pious. Santry knew an accomplished performer when he saw one, and Temple certainly was rehearsed.

"Any informed reading of the New Testament must conclude that from its point of view the world will be transformed not by the works of men, and not transformed at all in the way liberals desire, but transformed only by and in the way and at the time of God's own graceful choosing."

Santry had been irritated by the speaker but was shocked by the enthusiastic and prolonged applause that followed—a scattering of people were even on their feet. He had studied the roster of participants: most came from congregations in the United States and Europe. It was designed as a popular rather than a scholarly conference, attracting serious parishioners and lay leaders in numbers nearly equal to the priests and ministers present. He and Ross agreed that it provided exactly the right cover and access they needed. It explained his trip to Greece, and conveniently occurred when the island was packed with tourists. It sheltered him in the camouflage of other Christians, and legitimatized any special interest he exhibited in the Ephesian Fragments.

He would be on the inside, attending a conference officially sponsored by the monastery: he was welcomed to all its functions, and was encouraged to use its impressive facilities, which included, of course, the museum whose main attraction was the Fragments themselves. There could be no better vantage point from which to observe all security arrangements and to plan the unobserved removal of the island's treasure.

The applause ended, the chairman invited "questions and comments from the floor," and Santry decided.

He got to his feet, hunched his shoulders forward even more than usual, and took the long walk down the center aisle to a floor mike in the front where he nodded toward the featured speaker, turned, and addressed the conference. "I'm Father Michael Santry, a parish priest in the United States. I'll be brief. I agree there's a basis for the position argued by Dr. Temple, but the wind blows my New Testament open to different pages: to stories about Jesus healing and feeding and telling those interested to 'love one another as I've loved you.' The disciples of John came to him and asked if he was the Messiah. He told them to report what they had seen and heard: The blind see, the lame walk, lepers are cleansed, and the poor hear good news. I don't know if Dr. Temple's 'liberals' want those things or not, but Jesus did and the weak and the poor believed him, not because of what he preached or promised but because of what he did. He did good works and he said 'Follow me.' I believe Christianity is just that simple and that profound. The speaker says the world will be transformed only by and in the way of God's own choosing. The difference between us may be that I think Jesus has shown us what that 'way' is and that where his spirit moves in power—as I believe it does even in these dark days—there you'll see the same signs of his presence: health for the brokenhearted, deliverance for the captives, sight for the blind, and liberty for the oppressed."

Santry spoke, as always, quietly and unpretentiously, raising neither his voice nor his arms, but his rough-cut Italian face and compelling eyes moved steadily as he talked, reaching out to any in the audience whose eyes would hold on to his. He had learned long years ago that the purpose of a speech, at least any speech he could make, was not to persuade anyone of anything but to identify those few people in any group whose spirit was already prompting them along similar lines so that he could talk with them later. He had already found one: a bearded priest near the back of the room whose expression said *I'm with you*.

"One or two more comments and I'll sit down," Santry promised. "I've always found the question of obedience or disobedience to the state, or what Paul calls the 'higher powers,' to be far more complicated than Steven Temple suggests. He argues that we should be obedient. Period. But Jesus was, to put it starkly, a law-breaker. He didn't break all laws, of course, because he came to fulfill them, not to throw them out. But where the law blocked the works of love, he chose love every time. We should be clear on that. Dr. Temple quotes Paul promising damnation for those disobedient to earthly powers, but that's not who Jesus went after. You know the stories: He had a millstone for the necks of those who injured children, an ax for the root of the unfruitful fig tree, a whip for the money-changers, and wrath for those who frustrated the Kingdom of God, which he certainly never confused with the Roman Empire. I believe the way of discipleship is the way of obedience to Him and not to anybody else, especially not to the principalities and powers of this earth who are responsible for so much of the suffering that I see every day of the year in my parish where people can't get jobs and can't get food because the so-called 'higher powers' are pulling their plants out of Detroit in order to make more money in Arizona or Mexico or Taiwan."

As he walked away from the microphone and down

the aisle toward his seat, he was surprised by the applause. No one stood and cheered, but there were no boos, and people were being either polite or appreciative. He knew that didn't mean they agreed with him. Folks respected mavericks as long as they were on the same team, and his black suit and collar certified him as a member in good standing.

Temple's voice was coming over the loudspeakers even before Santry got seated. "The imitation of Jesus is a risky approach to discipleship," he was arguing, "especially when it comes to breaking the law because, as I'm sure Father Santry would agree, we don't have the wisdom and the grace that marked His life. Once a man steps beyond the law, once he goes beyond the social constraints so necessary to maintain the order without which justice is impossible, he is dangerously on his own and, in my opinion, is almost certain to go too far. We are a willful lot, much more committed to self-advancement than to the works of love. The law is therefore a necessary boundary, a human defense system, a moral wall that we should not cross lightly. Somewhat regretfully, I must side with Paul: better the Roman Empire which ushered in the Pax Romana, a period of extended peace, than the barbarians and the dark ages." And then Temple asked the question that caught Santry. "Where does the law-breaking end, Father Santry? Where does it stop and say 'enough'? And when it gets there, how does it know?"

Santry had a theoretical, public answer to that which would advance the conference debate and satisfy those who agreed with him, but he had no interest in it. It had been a mistake to respond in the first place. The frames of reference were too dissimilar. Most of the people in the room had never gone through a stop light. How could they possibly understand a priest who had been arrested on and off for twenty years, who talked about discipleship in the morning at a conference on New Testament studies, and then surveyed museum security in the afternoon so that he and a renegade executive from one of the "higher powers" could rob the island's treasure?

And the question worried him, seriously and persistently. Not because Temple raised it, but because those were the words he kept hearing through too many fretful nights. *Where does the law-breaking end, Michael? Where does it stop and say "enough"?* He wasn't sure of the answer to that one. He knew what it should be: It stopped as soon as he got the money for the food factory. It ended as soon as he was back in Detroit. This was a one-time exception to a necessary law against theft, not the advocacy of a new norm. But what happened when the money would run out and the three million was gone, as it surely would be in a few years? What happened when there was more suffering, more cries for help, and friend Ross sidled up in another Greektown restaurant and whispered about another treasure? If once, why not again? He worried about that and he worried about Ross. Would he be satisfied with a one-time strike for wealth? Not a chance. He was going to throw all those get-to-the-top energies into the new game. And what if this one went as smoothly as it should, but the next one, the one without Santry, failed? Could the trail lead back to the first one, back to Kallos, and back to a priest who talked too much about breaking the law?

He got up and walked out of the conference center. He was feeling a long way from home and on a road that might never end. The narrow cobblestone street wound downhill from the monastery through a labyrinth of gleaming white houses, pastel doors and shutters, geraniums, marigolds, and zinnias bursting from crowded clay pots and olive-oil cans. Cats watched from tiled roofs, stretched out and sleepy in the sun. The road ended at a pleasant harbor tavern. Santry ordered a cold beer and drank to his own health. It was time to visit the museum and see the Fragments, time to figure the whole thing out, time to do what he came to do, then get out of there and not look back.

At four o'clock that afternoon, he sat on a wooden bench in the monastery's luxuriant gardens reading the *International Herald Tribune*. He searched for news from Nicaragua, glanced at articles on the Olympics and the Democratic Convention, and watched the policemen near the museum door offering help to travelers. Neither carried a gun or club, and they were the only uniformed guards in the garden: a large rectangular park with flower beds, trees, and benches placed along its pathways. He had chosen a shady spot under a fig tree so he could see all the buildings surrounding it: the conference center, the library, and the ancient museum, all stone-and-castle dark. A line of people, many trailing cameras and children, had gathered outside the museum doors for the late-afternoon opening. A few priests, most of them Greek Orthodox and bearded, moved quietly from place to place. In the distance, motorcycles whined and growled and threw themselves up steep streets, gnashing at cobblestones with hard rubber teeth.

When the doors opened, Santry joined the slowly moving line, paid less than a dollar for admittance, and soon stood in the dimly lit, stone-walled, cavernous interior lined with display cabinets and filled with ornate vestments, jeweled mitres, gold and silver chalices, hundreds of manuscripts, gems, and icons. He saw that everyone who entered the hall immediately grew silent. On three walls, colorful tapestries and paintings of the Apostles, the Fathers, and the Saints of the Church hung above the exhibits, and, on the fourth, a powerful, full-wall mural collapsed the centuries and depicted the legendary arrival of St. Paul on Kallos, striding boldly through the shallow surf from an ancient boat with his letter to the church at Ephesus extended forward toward the abbot of the monastery. Onshore, kings and fishermen, farmers on tractors, businessmen and factory workers, women in olive groves, and members of the Greek Parliament dropped their work and stared in fixed amazement at the visitation. Ceiling spotlights threw sharp narrow beams downward through the gloomy medieval room, played on the stern, immense face of Paul and the fervent, openmouthed abbot, then took the eye along a path of light toward the precise center of the hall where dramatically sculpted arms rose together, then flared apart into immense hands of olive wood which held the holy, illuminated Fragments high above a dais raised and draped in velvet.

A priest stood at the base, permitting visitors to climb the four steps to the brilliantly lit platform one at a time. Once there, the great majority of pilgrims centered themselves carefully before the treasure, made the sign of the cross, and prayed. Santry counted two policemen inside and four priests, each moving unobtrusively among the visitors, answering questions, and watching—always watching. He opened the illustrated brochure purchased at the door, though he already had the contents memorized. Ross had given him the pamphlet and thirty photographs of the exhibition hall the day he agreed to join the project. While waiting his turn in line, he reread the brief description of the manuscript he was about to see:

> The Ephesian Fragments are a sacred treasure of the Church. Our Lord left nothing in writing. The letters of St. Paul are the earliest Christian documents, dating from the middle of the first century. The four Gospels—Matthew, Mark, Luke, and John—were composed later, between 70 and 100 A.D. None of the originals of these works survives, but as many as 5,000 handwritten Greek manuscripts have been preserved and provide the basis for the various translations of the New Testament.

The most ancient manuscripts of the New Testament were written in Greek on papyrus and have been discovered, without exception, in Egypt within the last one hundred years. Less-ancient manuscripts, uncials on parchment and minuscules, have been known for centuries.

The Ephesian Fragments were discovered outside Alexandria, Egypt, in 1893 and date from the early third century. They contain portions of Chapter Two of Paul's letter, measure 6½" by 11", and have 27 lines to the page. They have been sealed archivally between sheets of clear lucite to preserve them from air, fire, and moisture.

The line moved, a priest nodded, and Santry crossed the thick carpet, went up a few stairs, walked to the center of the platform, and saw immediately that the unknown draftsman in Mexico City had served them well. The sealed copies his friend had with him in Athens matched the ones before him exactly—right down to the slender, silver pins in the four corners of the lucite sheets and the barely visible scuff mark left where a tool had slipped. The Fragments, bathed in light without glare, lay on a bed of velvet within a glass-topped wooden case that rested in the open olivewood hands. The lock on the case was, however, out of sight, underneath. Or was it possible that the case had been sealed? He had to find out, but how? He had quietly counted the seconds taken in front of the Fragments by those who preceded him in line and knew his time was nearly up. Better to return later when a different priest was on duty than call attention to himself by lingering. He glanced quickly at the waiting line. They were all looking at him. Meaning? Meaning nothing, he told himself, sure that his suddenly worried thoughts had not rippled across his placid face, sure that the people stared only because they were waiting. He walked off the far side of the platform, down the stairs, and out into the late-day sun, irritated and angry with Ross. He had been so sure and made it sound so easy: Simply substitute one document for the other and live happily ever after. Ross would bring an array of picks to deal with any lock, but what if the case was sealed? He returned to the shaded bench under the fig tree, aware of habit's quick comfort, and tried to figure out how to get back in there after dark, after the museum was closed. He grunted, exactly the way he did when playing squash and lunging after a distant drop shot. He glared through garden greenery at the thick museum walls. He wasn't going to tunnel in there, and the windows looked as if they hadn't been opened since the Turks took over five hundred years ago. He took the conference schedule from his pocket and decided to attend the evening session. The abbot was speaking on the history of the Fragments. Santry's innocent questions would be welcomed.

Late that night after the abbot's speech, Santry sat with six or seven others in the comfortable, upholstered chairs at one end of the conference center's carpeted lounge. The abbot, Father John Simonedes, was, to his surprise, the bearded priest who sat in the rear of the lecture hall that morning signaling his silent appreciation of Santry's remarks. He now stroked and smoothed his wiry beard, while listening to a question about how seriously he took the stories in the village that members of a Turkish sect had committed themselves to the return of the Fragments to that nation's soil.

The Greek priest, whose swollen eyes behind thick, severely magnified glasses gave his face a perpetually astonished stare, tilted his head thoughtfully to one side and said that someone or other was always whispering that the Turks were coming. "But who's to say?" he asked, the deep lines of his forehead pulling up against the downward tug of his mouth. "We hear the rumors and we are responsible to the nation for the Fragments' safety so, yes, we have to increase security, but at the same time we tell the people not to worry because it's very unlikely that any Turks are on their way here."

And with that, a great and gradual peacefulness settled over Santry. Settled, that was, after the initial shock of the words "we have increased security" had passed. Waves of unexpected contentment calmed his mind as he realized, *Dear God, it's all over, it can't be done!* The theft had become impossible because increased security in a small village meant only one thing. It did not mean more uniforms, guns, road inspections, plastic shields, helicopters, attack dogs, or alarm systems. It meant something far more effective than all those big-city systems combined: It meant more eyes, more of the same quiet, watchful, prowling eyes that had always been the first line of village defense against internal deviance and external assault. Grizzled old men glancing slowly up from cards as a stranger passed; women in black looking over porch geraniums or sitting silently in windows over cobblestone streets; shopkeepers on duty along the harbor, where all ships must come and all travelers must walk; the garbagemen who picked the village clean and swept through it every day; the postal clerk who worked in Germany, picked up English on the freighters, and read all the cards; the out-of-uniform policeman drinking with the Swedish girls; the restaurant waiter who was related to the grocer who was married to the daughter of the farmer who drove his sheep past a deserted strip of beach and saw . . . And Santry knew instantly that tomorrow, when he returned to the garden, he would find not only two policemen outside the museum doors, he would also see two men playing chess and another behind a newspaper and, now that he thought about it, he knew they had been there every day since he arrived. And inside the museum, there would be the two guards, the five priests, and, he was sure of it, how many familiar faces among the tourists!

It couldn't be done. The village had been alerted and

there was no way to escape its prying eyes. He and Ross had assumed a relatively tranquil, unguarded scene through which they could filter one night, anonymous and unnoticed, assisted by little more than Santry's intimate knowledge of the guards, the grounds, the buildings, and the drawers or rooms in which the keys were kept, plus Ross's skill with picks and locks. He leaned back in his comfortable chair, appeared still interested in the conversation, and attended to the pleasantly rising river of peace within him. He was glad to be out of it. Grateful. His spirit had been tense as a deer hunter's bow: flexed, drawn, and held by sheer muscled will on the still too distant, steadily approaching tawny target. He let go gladly and silently watched an arrow hurtle straight upward toward the stars where it would do no harm. He could enjoy the conference now, read long-awaited books, walk by the sea, and return to Detroit as empty-handed as he had come. All that terrible apprehension could be laid down. The whole idea had been wild from the start—insane. How had he ever talked himself into it?

The abbot continued talking and answering questions, now about the annual Festival of St. Paul held on August 1, a celebration that was, apart from Easter, the island's most important event. A candlelight procession would climax at the harbor, where, according to local legend, Paul first came ashore. No, there was no "evidence" for the visit, but the Apostle had clearly been to many of the adjacent islands, including, as Acts 20:14 testified, to Lesbos or Mitilini. "So why not Kallos?" he asked with a smile and a shrug that said it didn't make much difference one way or the other, that the misty line between legend and fact should not be chiseled too fine, and that the important thing was the festival's meaning for the people. "There will be a brief service in the center of town," he said, "and then the procession will wind its way up the dark hill to the monastery, where the Fragments will be returned once more to the museum."

Santry glanced quickly around the small circle to see if any had noticed the intense curiosity, even confusion, in his face. The Fragments were going to be out of the museum, out in the open, for at least a few hours! The abbot expressed his hope that all members of the conference would participate in the celebration and ensure its international character. The circle nodded, of course they'd be there, and the conversation moved on. Santry had a quick vision of his mind as dark, rich soil into which an alien seed had just been thrust. His will worked against it, struggled to dislodge it—fast before it took hold, sure of its impossibility, and alarmed by this unexpected threat to his newfound peace. But his imagination, going its own, more colorful way, danced a little, hovered over the seed, nurtured it against his will and wondered. That was all. Just wondered. He told himself it wouldn't hurt to think about it, and so he thought and wondered and gave it time and walked through lonely streets for most of the night. And by morning, he knew the seed had taken root. He could feel it. And his will began to bend. It may be possible, after all. Barely possible, but he had come this far; he should at least be sure. He may not have to go home empty-handed after all.

Late July 1984
Athens, Greece

If there had been sufficient light, their similarities, not their differences, would be observed, for the bodies coupled and sleeping on the bed were, in general form, musculature, and leanness, about the same. But his preoccupation was with a difference and so there was no light. Remarkably enough, she had never seen him naked, though her fingers knew his body's every line and pleasure. She could have seen, of course. Over twenty years, even those who loved but never lived together could observe anything they chose. But she chose not to see, chose not to see as he left the bed, back toward her, and reached for his cane, the cane with the pearl grip, the cane he brought from the war in 1945 but couldn't use until 1948, when the next war, the civil war, left him with a paralyzed and withered limb. She loved him even then, but as an adoring child.

The wars had given Gabriella Antissa two dead parents, a home on the neighboring Korachises' farm, and a new brother, Andreas, who spent the 1940s, the decade of his twenties, fighting. He ended it by getting shot. She grew from girl to woman in the fifties, the same years in which a relentless Andreas grew rich, married into a powerful family, and moved from his parents' farm to a fashionably old, large, and wealthy home in Mitilini. He and his wife, Maria, welcomed her there. She moved in and Andreas became not only brother, but father and guardian. Maria helped her with school and traditional lessons; Andreas pressed her beyond them with endless demands for independence and excellence.

By the age of sixteen, no one on the island of Lesbos doubted her independence, but few considered her excellent. The complaints were unconventional and, though only partially true, made it hard for her to stay. There was evidence for the charge of crime, but torture was never proved. Andreas's stylish car had been seen throughout the island too close to the places and times of repeated night robberies to be coincidence. And a girl, thin and taller than most, had been seen running. It didn't help that everything stolen was always found the next day, piled along some beach or country road. That only made it worse, convicting her of three offenses: theft, strangeness, and ridicule. She was Korachis's adopted daughter, she didn't need to steal, so why was she doing it? Sick and self-destructive were the usual explanations, with the suspicion "laughing at us" coming hard behind. The accusation of torture was untrue, though woven from the half-accurately reported experiences of school friends who had gotten involved with her "experiments in pain." No one had been coerced, but many had been encouraged to see how far they could go with pins, ice, and flames. One child had burned herself, the parents had called, and an alarmed Andreas confronted her. Gabriella met the claims directly: She was entirely responsible for the rash of robberies, called them "a phase in my development that's now over," and acknowledged a "special interest in the dynamics of pain and suffering."

They agreed she'd be better off in Athens, and over the next years she excelled in private school, read eagerly, and began her career as a successful fashion model. By 1963, at the age of nineteen, a fast circle of Athenians considered her the finest of them all, a judgment from which Andreas, then in his late thirties, had never deviated. And that year, the brother and sister who had become father and daughter transformed themselves once more and became lovers. Uninhibited by genetic, legal, or communal restraints, fiercely committed to personal freedom, and supremely self-confident, they honored their longtime obsession.

He expressed concerns. Their love could not interfere with his marriage to Maria or Gabriella's life with other men, they could never live together, and there would be no children. She had no concerns but told him he sounded fatherly and had to shed the role. Nothing happened as planned or promised. Their love interfered with all other relationships. It became primary to both, and neither Maria nor Gabriella's various husbands adjusted well to the fact. They lived together far more than either had thought possible because Andreas kept an apartment and office in Athens. And Ladrea was born within two years. Gabriella was married at the time, but physically and emotionally divorced, so no doubts surrounded the child's parentage.

But over the next twenty years, one pledge was kept: She never looked long at the withered leg and never offered help. "It's my trailing weakness," he told her, "the one foot already in the grave. I don't want to talk about it and I don't want you to see it. Your interest is already excessive." She tried to assure him in familiar ways, but he stopped her. "One right is inviolable: to reveal or to hide what we choose. I've got to deal with this wound my own way."

She respected the right, for she had wounds of her own to heal. And so his crippled leg became an emblem of sorts, a reminder of the terms of love, of wars and graves, of dark, numb shadows dragged behind, and of their choice: absolute silence where others whined, fingered, and enjoyed old wounds.

In 1984 he was sixty-three and she turned forty. His severe face, always behind steel-rimmed, dark glasses, looked his age, but his body, except the leg, was younger. Her face was any age, depending on her mood, which was usually tense and angry, so most of the time she looked older. In body, however, she could be Ladrea's sister, but where the daughter was voluptuous, Gabriella's skin stretched smooth too close to bone.

Uncoupled, they lay on their backs and watched the curtains move in the late breeze. "His partner's on Kallos, but he wouldn't give me his name."

"I have his name," Korachis replied evenly, knowing from her voice that she had relaxed. "I assume you're completing the file."

"Tapes, photos, and daily logs of activities will be on your desk Monday."

"When's he going to Kallos?"

"In ten days. His friend will be in Athens next week to make final plans."

"What else should I know?"

"Your American warrior is charming your daughter."

His silence was prolonged.

Gabriella asked, "What's your reaction?"

His untroubled voice came slowly. "What you might expect—that's her business, not mine. I thought they might enjoy each other." He grew quiet and reflected, "Interesting, he's in his late thirties and she's eighteen—about the same age when we became lovers."

"They live in entirely different time zones. There's light-years between us."

"He's about your age."

"Only in years. He knows nothing about war."

"He didn't mention Vietnam?"

She was silent and surprised. Korachis asked what she thought of him. "I think he'll get the Fragments and be valuable in the years ahead. The plan's good; he's imaginative, forceful, and careful about the work, sufficiently distant and untalkative. About what I expected."

"What else?"

"He's a moralist, vain, somewhat humorless, and didn't like my octopus hunt."

"He may simply lack your appetite for death scenes."

"I have no appetite for death scenes, Andreas. Only a modest interest in violence."

"He may also lack your capacity for self-deception. Your modest interest in violence is the mainspring of your life, the coiled, steel serpent at the very center."

She smiled, rare for her, and rolled on top of him. "No, dear friend, you are the mainspring of my life." She moved her pelvis slowly against him. "And this is the only coiled, steel serpent at the center."

"Sorry, but the call came as I was leaving the hotel. There was no way to reach you."

She shook her head and gave him a smile he couldn't figure out. "Don't worry about it. Warriors shouldn't apologize." She had told him that her father called him a "warrior," a compliment, unlike the words "soldier" or "mercenary." Ross had trouble taking that kind of talk seriously.

It was a bright, hot, Athenian day, the last Saturday in July, a sweltering time when the pale blue dome of an overheated sky enclosed and sealed the concrete city like the vault of a steaming Turkish bath. Tempers sizzled in traffic jams. Tourists crowded restaurants and paths to the Acropolis, and breathed hard in filthy, stagnant air. Patience was in short supply. Greeks moved as little as possible or hurried off to the islands. The Balthazar was their oasis, their place in the shade, where thick hedges, leafy trees, flower beds, and thick old mansion walls surrounded the cool, cornered hubbub of men and women whose drinks and smokes and eyes were always on the move. It was their second time together since the sail to Mykonos. Santry had called unexpectedly at noon to say he had just gotten a seat on an afternoon flight from Kallos and would arrive at four. Ross had to clear the evening.

"Well, warrior or no, I'm sorry about tonight. I had looked forward to it."

Her necklace was of island shells and her full-sleeved shirt was silk and violet—for him, she said, because he liked the color. Her long black hair swirled easily about her face. Leaning forward, intent on the peel of lemon in her water or one of her curious thoughts, it flowed across her cheeks and left little more than nose, lips, and black, green-flecked eyes visible. "How long can you stay?" she asked.

"Today a few hours. Altogether, a few weeks. Unless my meeting tonight changes everything."

"I don't want to know what you're doing," she said without looking up from her drink, "but you should be more careful."

He passed the warning off lightly. "Have you seen something I should see?" He had learned during a long walk on a remote pebble beach that her name, Ladrea, was a blend of "Andreas" for her father and of "lathreos," meaning "clandestine" or "secret." It was Andreas's decision to name his firstborn girl after himself, thereby declaring his parentage and pride openly after a two-year lapse from freedom into a secret love affair. He had grown sick of the lies and deception involved with Maria and Gabriella's husband, despised the deceit, and felt like a hawk with clipped wings. Her birth forced a decision. He chose to tell Maria about his life with Gabriella and to celebrate the newborn child openly. As the girl grew, Andreas learned he had named her better than he had known, for if her mother's special interest was in pain and suffering, the daughter's was in the secret images that came to her.

By secret images she meant exactly what others meant when they said, "I had a dream last night," except for two differences—she dreamed night and day, and she took all of her dreams seriously. While others learned to ignore or discard dreams for the sake of the "real world," she did almost the reverse. She did not exactly ignore the real world for the sake of more interesting dreams, but she did, far more than most, experience daily life through the ever-shifting filters of her fantasies. As a child, she had startled and worried her parents until they got the hang of it and realized she was not mad. But in the beginning, her conversations seemed four parts wild and one part normal. The most pedestrian question, such as "What did you learn in school today?" elicited dreamy, unsettling responses full of shrunken elephants with trunks that produced waterfalls, teachers whose three-fingered hands floated in the air over crescent-shaped rainbow boards, and a girl in the balloon beside her who never wanted to go away. The principal called and said she needed help. Gabriella said she needed a better school. A psychologist tested, listened, and announced, in more technical terms, that her unconscious was simply streaming over all the circuits and that they shouldn't worry; the content was relatively benign, the kid was happy and exceptionally responsive, and she'd learn soon enough to keep the stuff to herself. Society had its ways. And, indeed, adjustments were made. Gabriella and Andreas did nothing to block or dam the round-the-clock flood of images. On the contrary, they prized and encouraged them. But at the same time they helped the child to learn the more prosaic sights and sounds she needed to use when buying oranges, passing multiple-choice exams, or talking to people who, as they told her, wouldn't understand.

She learned her lessons well, exactly as one learned a foreign language that was necessary, challenging to master, and even fun to use when with people who lived in the fixed, measured, and predictable world of photographable images. When she was with them she continued to see the world her own way, but talked as if she lived in theirs. The ever-flowing images went unrevealed. They remained her secret. But when meeting someone new, especially someone attractive like Alexander Ross, who had in ways never described saved her father's life, she would share a few images from the stream in hopes that he or she might be bilingual, too.

Alexander's time came when she returned to the yacht unexpectedly one night and found him sitting on the rear deck, alone, absorbed in darkness. He told her that Gabriella had gone to bed, invited Ladrea to join him, and asked about her evening on Mykonos. She told him a little of what she had seen: glistening black dragons flying above the harbor road, a heaven-high curtain of light opening to a north wind, and a succulent peach dropped carefully into her extended hand from the gentle mouth of a brown-and-white whippet.

And Ross had said, "That sounds like a pretty good light show. Too bad you missed the one here—there was a shower of violets on the sea."

Everything was easy after that. She had told him to

close his eyes, then reached over, and touched them with her fingers. "Now what do you see?"

"Your fingerprints," he told her.

"No, no." She laughed, correcting him. "You see millions of white doves fluttering round and round the mountain's throne and . . ."

He picked it up in midsentence. ". . . and settling like mayflies, luminous on the river piers."

"What's a mayfly?" she asked, her hand still warm on his face.

"Every spring millions of them hatch in the Detroit river and blanket the shoreline for a day or two. It's all the time they get to breed, lay eggs, and die. They have very beautiful, very delicate wings."

"And there are millions of them?"

"Yes, all at once and all over—on the water, across piers, along the river road, on storefront windows, under streetlamps. They come like a snowfall."

"They're all dying and they're all beautiful?" she asked.

"Looked at in a certain way, that's true."

Her fingers left his face, but one returned to touch his forehead, where she slowly drew a circle, then cut through its center with a long vertical line. "What's that?" she asked, her voice still light and playful.

"The world split in two."

"No, it's just the opposite, so you were closer than you knew." She traced it again and told him, "It's the first letter in the Greek word *philos*. It means 'friend.' "

"You're branding me?"

"No, I'm making a wish."

The suddenly serious voice surprised him. He opened his eyes and saw her face, near and searching his for something. Without turning from her eyes, he reached behind his neck, unfastened the clasp of a silver chain, and held it toward her. "The pendant's black coral from the West Indies. I found it at eighty feet, near the hull of an old ship. I think you'd like it down there. It's another world."

"Won't you miss it?"

"The coral? No, not if a friend wears it, and someday I'm going back to dive for more. Hopefully very soon."

And it was in that brief exchange that another sort of dream edged into the twilight corners of his mind and played on his private screen. Perhaps he'd like to have her there, perhaps she'd like to come, perhaps . . . And that was as far as he allowed the dream to go, because there was work to do before the play began. It was on the work that he focused when, over drinks in the Balthazar, she told him to be careful and he asked if she had seen something.

"No, I don't see the future or tell fortunes or have second-sight or any of that. My fantasies aren't practical that way. They're more like your coral reef: a different world to visit and enjoy. Sometimes you bring something back, but more often you just leave it there." She glanced about the busy room and said, "No, I mean something different. I mean you should be more careful because you're being watched. You're always being watched."

"Always?" he asked. She said nothing. He looked at the waiters, the distant bartender, the crowded tables. "Now? Here?" She nodded. "But who? Who is it? And why?" Her eyes searched his face, and something in them, something troubled and knowing and insistent, passed through the silence and he caught it, caught on, and said, half wondering and half bitterly, "It's you. Seeing me is part of your job."

She laughed as she reached across the table and touched his hand. "Me! Alexander, they wouldn't ask me to watch a parade at the zoo! Can you imagine the reports? I've been sitting here watching fields of wild flowers growing from your hair. They'd never be able to sort it all out. Anyway, Andreas won't permit it and that ends that. From the heart, new friend, there have been no traps, tricks, or lies from me. The truth? I know that someone in this room will file a report tomorrow, but I don't know who it is. And I know that Andreas asked me to give you this package, but I don't know what's in it." She reached into the shoulder bag hanging from the back of her chair and handed him a sealed manila envelope. "I'll be back in fifteen minutes," she told him. "My fantasies are wild enough without getting mixed up in yours."

He watched her cross the room and disappear beyond a door, then took a knife, inserted it beneath the seal, and slit it cleanly open. The envelope contained prints and negatives, cassettes, a sheaf of typed pages, and a letter from Andreas.

My dear Alexander,

Please forgive this unusual intrusion in your life, but do trust me. It is all for the best. I have watched you closely since your arrival in Greece, not out of any mistrust or lack of confidence, but entirely because of my unusual affection and respect. As in any new endeavor, there are things to be learned. It is in that spirit that I send you the enclosed materials.

Ladrea has seen none of them. Gabriella has seen the photographs taken on the yacht. Only I have reviewed all the documents. You now have them. All of them. No trace of these exists anywhere else. I am sure you will draw the necessary conclusions from this packet and take their clear lessons to heart.

You tend to think of life as a race in which the laurels go to the swift and the strong. That wisdom must now be joined with Gabriella's truth that life is a Balkan war and not the Olympic Games.

The revelations enclosed are utterly trivial and insignificant, but they suggest how easily an enemy could learn far too much.

                        My fondest regards,

                              A.

Ross sorted quickly and anxiously through the material, glancing up frequently to catch the eye or suddenly averted head of the someone watching him even then. There were dozens of photos taken on the yacht trip to Mykonos. He had seen the cameras. No surprise there, except that they'd be used this way. Then it got deeper and worse: a list of everything in his luggage on the ship and in the hotel, transcribed tapes, including the one with the love sounds of a high-class hooker who kept repeating his name, something he had noticed but disregarded at the time, and twelve sheets of single-spaced type detailing his activity right down to the paper read over his morning cappuccino. The worst was the last: an enlarged photograph of a man sitting on a park bench beneath a tree. On the back of the glossy sheet was the following:

Kallos Project: July 24, 1984
Inquiry: Alexander Ross's accomplice.
Tentative finding: Father Michael Santry (see photo).
Level of Assurance: Probable.
Rationale:
1. Detroit base and known friend of Ross.
2. History of illegal activity and advocacy of selective disobedience to "principalities and powers."
3. Visited museum and Ephesian Fragments on three different occasions in one week.
4. Luggage and personal effects include a funding solicitation brochure for "East Side De-

velopment Corporation" and a personal letter referring to the hope for "new financing."

Ladrea returned and sat beside him. "Your face says it's not good news. I hope it's not all bad."

He slid the photos and cassettes into the envelope and wondered if he could trust her. "You're right about the watching. Your father's had a spyglass up my ass for a week." He wanted to keep it easy and light between them and didn't trust his growing anger. "Maybe it's okay, and maybe it's not. I've got a lot to think about." He watched her face and realized how little he knew about her. "But it makes me suspicious of everybody, which I suppose is the point of all this." His fingers drummed slowly on the thick envelope. "Best to think of it as in-service training for the new boy. Well, it doesn't thrill me, but it's a useful lesson." He was sure she'd report every gesture, every word, and he was steaming. He had allowed himself to be suckered by the extraordinary grace and beauty of an eighteen-year-old whose mind was either blitzed or, quite literally, fantastic. *Don't blame her for being a good daughter,* he told himself, but her eyes were on him and he knew there was an edge in his voice when he asked, "You still see the wild flowers growing?"

Her smile was halfhearted and strained and she looked down at her empty glass. It was the first time he had seen her uncertain and awkward. She was suddenly very young and on the edge of something painful. *Remember, Ross,* he told himself, *it's a Balkan war and she's on active duty. A puppet. Beautiful, but still Andreas's puppet. Testing, checking, probing for weaknesses. Every expression, every word, has probably been rehearsed. Keep it cool and keep it distant.*

"No," she said, her eyes still on the glass, "the flowers stopped growing and the violet spell's gone." She looked up. "And the reason's clear: You think I'm an informer. We're caught in an evil trap, Alexander. Your suspicions are false but understandable. They may even make you a better warrior. But I'm not very good in war zones and I refuse to play the proving game.''

The cab pulled away and Ross handed Santry the manila folder. "You'll be interested in the enclosures. Don't react till we're alone." The packet included everything received from Korachis except his night with the call girl. Fifteen minutes later he saw a park coming up on the right and told the driver to stop. There were trees for shade, kids on swings, an ice-cream man, and white geese floating on a pond. The two men sat on a bench and watched the road. Ross was sure no one had followed. "I think the letter means exactly what it says, so there's no real problem. They were able to identify you only because they knew me and could link up Detroiters. If anything goes wrong on Kallos, there's still no trail that anyone else could follow, but we'll be safer if we assume that someone's after us."

"Let me remind you, friend, that everything has already gone wrong on Kallos." Santry had worn a sport shirt and slacks for the quick trip to Athens, in part for comfort, but primarily to prevent any "priest plus Ross" combinations from being observed. He had already decided that his younger friend was headed for a life of trouble, and the letter from "A" only confirmed his fears. "Nothing on Kallos is what we expected. The security is intense and village-wide and the case containing the Fragments is sealed, for all we know." He reviewed the problems in detail, then said, "There's only one way I can imagine getting them, and I'm honestly not sure we should try."

They talked for two hours and agreed it could be done. Ross wanted to go ahead. Santry was hesitant but willing.

"Michael, the people I'm working for obviously know who you are. I'm not worried about that, but I'll give you their names if you want just to keep it even all around."

"Forget it, Alexander. I'm going ahead with this for the same reasons I got into it, but it's not my game. I just want to get it over with and get back to the east side. The less I know about your friends, the better. This is Saturday. I'll be back on Kallos tomorrow. You arrive Tuesday. And on Wednesday, August 1, we will celebrate the Feast of St. Paul together for the first and the last time. I can't wait to get this all behind me." He touched the arm of his taller companion. "Two things before we go. I want you to promise me that no matter what happens next Wednesday, there'll be no violence. That's important to me."

"You mean no more than we've already agreed is necessary?"

"Yes, that's right. No more than that."

"Agreed. What else?"

"It may be a long time before we talk again. Take care of yourself."

"Thanks, Mike. You, too."

There was a quick, affectionate embrace. Then the two men went separate ways.

On Kallos

Santry watched the thin, middle-aged waiter swivel-hipping his stylish way through the crowded outdoor café, balancing a tray high on one hand and waving people aside with the other. Like a ringmaster in baggy pants and soiled apron, he kept the sidewalk circus moving: sliding coffees—hot Greek, iced, or Nescafés— onto shining tabletops without a spill, collecting dirty dishes, drachmas, giving change, pointing people to empty chairs, and collecting shouted orders with the bored look of a juggler who hadn't begun to show his stuff. The wide sidewalk, sheltered from the morning sun by a faded blue-and-white awning, was jammed with hundreds of Greeks and visitors. The summer crush of tourists peaked with the Feast of St. Paul and the crowds were streaming in. Postcards of these sidewalk scenes always looked inviting, failing to show the snarl of traffic that lay to the right of the picture. The camera also failed to record the clouds of road dust, lung-collapsing noxious fumes, and head-splitting jackhammer noises distributed impartially over the coffee by racing cars, diesel-smoke-spewing buses, and fool-powered motorcycles.

Santry thought his mood was a perfect match for the environment. The only pleasant thing on his mind was the date: July 31, the day before the *day*. Kallos would soon be far behind him. He glared at a young cycle fiend revving his motor and tried to read a book, a copy of Aeschylus taken from the conference library. It was no help. Everything made him doubtful, uncertain, and restless. He closed the book when he came to the line "Ancient arrogance loves to bring forth a young arrogance . . . irresistible, unconquerable, unholy recklessness." He didn't want any more warnings about recklessness. He was tight and tense with them already and the die was cast. Whether his recklessness was unholy, as he sometimes feared, or holy and necessary, as he hoped, the question had been decided in favor of action and boldness. The road had been chosen. He told himself to lay down his doubts and to focus on what had to be done.

His eyes followed the enormous cruise ship entering the harbor and scanned the faces of travelers crowded along its railings, some already waving happily to people on the shore. The boat brushed gently against the pilings, heavy ropes dropped from the deck, the bow opened wide like a yawning mouth, and trucks lumbered out of the cavernous hold with food, beer, construction supplies, and machinery from the mainland. The tourists were close behind and fanning out in all directions. Santry saw him as soon as he cleared the ship and moved toward town: taller than most, alone, leather bag in hand, one of the few in a lightweight suit and tie. He had the bearing of a man who had been on the island many times, though Santry knew this to be his first visit. There was something very purposeful and proud about him: no looking around, no questions asked, no hesitation, and right on time. And Santry guessed that was about the way Ross was feeling. He watched him go by on the other side of the street without a glance in his direction. He checked his watch. An hour to go. He ordered another coffee and was feeling much better. Yes, he was happy to admit it. His friend's presence on the island increased his confidence. Ross had that gift. Right or wrong, he was sure about what he was doing, and Santry was suddenly glad for Ross's touch of arrogance. If one was going to deal in recklessness, one had better have some of it to back himself up.

At exactly noon, Santry left a hundred-drachma note on the table to pay for his coffees, picked up his recently acquired leather attaché case with its specially designed combination lock, and walked two blocks to a busy kiosk, where he set the case on the ground beside him while examining the magazines. He was vaguely aware of the people coming and going around him as he glanced at *Newsweek*'s report on the Democratic Convention in San Francisco. He decided to buy the issue, and walked the few steps to the front of the newsstand, where he paid the shopkeeper. Recovering the case, he left the harbor road, turned up the steep cobblestone street that led to the monastery on the hill, and trudged slowly back to the conference center. The twenty-minute climb in the midday sun made him hot and sweaty. When he reached his small, clean room, he locked the door, placed the case on the white-sheeted bed, and went to the corner sink to wash and to drink. He watched the case suspiciously while drying his hands and listened for sounds in the corridor. There were a few members of the conference who had been impressed by his speech and liked to drop in on him, but they would all be at lunch. He sat on the bed, rested the case on his lap, and examined the hand-tooled-leather initials near the lock. The case he had taken to the kiosk had been initialed "A.R." This one, identical in all other respects, carried the initials "M.S." Each man now had the case with which he would leave the island. He moved the numbers of the memorized combination, raised the lid, unwrapped the package inside, and held in his hands the exact replica of the Ephesian Fragments fashioned by Mexican craftsmen and sealed between two sheets of the finest lucite.

On the other side of the village, Alexander Ross opened his matching case and read the enclosed brief note:

Proceed as planned and *pax vobiscum*.

He felt relieved. No new problems had emerged requiring a meeting. He had nothing to do for twenty-four hours. The plan was firm. They were in position. Santry was ready. All right! After the first jolt of Korachis's letter had worn off and his attention had shifted from the embarrassing foolishness with the hooker to his promising future, his imagination had taken off. This was the beginning, the new start he needed after the setback in Detroit. If he played it right, by the time he was forty-five he could be running and expanding Korachis's empire. He went through his luggage in case the man was still tagging him, shifted passports and airline tickets for the West Indies into the inside pocket of his coat, and walked out of the house. The woman who rented the room to him was in the front garden watering the zinnias. They nodded at each other. He didn't wander long before finding a cool tavern with cold beer. Tucked into a quiet corner, he recalled Santry's note and thought, *Peace to you, too, Mike, and get a good night's sleep. You're going to need it.*

August 1, 1984

Santry was awake long before the church bells pealed at dawn. He had watched for hours and had seen the last bright stars fade over the sea and disappear in the rising light: gray, then silvery, before the first hints of rose. The bells announced the fateful day and evoked familiar stirrings within the building: water taps on and off, showers running, footsteps up and down the hall, the occasional voice. All background. All in the distance. His mind was focused entirely on the evening, when a procession with an unknown ending would begin.

The hours in between went slowly. Afterward, he'd remember every step, sound, and sight of the long, strange night, but little about the day. The conference was not in session because of the festival, so he drank coffee with a few friends, gave half an ear to their stories, and took little part in the rambling conversation. The scare about a Turkish plot to seize the Fragments had washed up onshore like a jellyfish: dead, harmless, no sting left in it. Was he going to walk in the procession? He glanced at the attaché case that never left his side that day. Yes, he thought he would. It seemed important to the abbot, and the man had extended himself for them. What else was happening in the village?

A teacher from England grimaced and replied, "Oh, the usual. Some magnificent bull's been reduced to the bloody-bloodies, the crowd down there's thickening fast into immobility, and every peddler on the island is hawking his wares from a row of stalls on the waterfront. Everyone's gone mad. The children are running around with plastic machine guns, the disco's warming up the masses with hard rock, and the traffic's so snarled that the police have run up the white flag, admitted defeat, and are quietly drinking ouzo at the station.''

After hearing that a delegation from the World Council of Churches had arrived that morning and that a correspondent from *Time* magazine was asking questions about the interrogation of the island Turks, Santry decided he needed a long walk and spent hours roaming a deserted stretch of bluff and pastureland miles outside the village.

By eight o'clock that night, Santry was ready and walked across the monastery garden with all the self-possession and self-consciousness of an actor about to play a well-rehearsed part. The procession would form in front of the museum, and Santry was there early enough to establish his place. The abbot had honored the several hundred conferees by inviting them to walk with him and welcomed Santry by name when he arrived. Their friendship had been the one positive outcome of his early contention with the keynote speaker. They exchanged pleasantries and Santry remained at the priest's side, admiring the embroidered jeweled vestments he wore for the festival's concluding pageant. Conference participants arrived steadily and took their places behind him. Monastery priests, many with religious banners or swinging glittering incense pots, assembled in front of the abbot to lead the way. And all the while, anonymous robed figures scuttled back and forth, showing people where to stand, distributing candles, carrying messages from the abbot, making sure that all was well.

A little after nine o'clock, the monastery bells tolled slowly and, on signal, the thick wooden doors of the museum swung dramatically open to reveal a tall bearded priest accompanied by an honor guard of three villagers on each side. They stepped out together, waited until all fell silent, then walked to the abbot and ceremoniously placed the Fragments, still encased in their protective lucite, in his hands. He offered a short prayer, and instantly priests moved through the assembled people, bending long tapers to light the marchers' candles. The flame spread quickly, as if touched to a fast fuse, and the stationary procession that circled the entire garden was transformed into glowing gold. Santry was moved by their beauty in the failing light: He saw the abbot give a sign, felt the line begin to move, and adjusted his pace to fall a half step behind the monastery's leader. In his right hand, he held a burning candle. And in his left, secure within a large black folder, easily opened, he gripped the Fragments the abbot would carry home. The parade, led by three hundred priests in disciplined ranks, soon left level monastery ground and edged down the steep hill toward the waiting village and the distant sea.

It took them half an hour to get there. People cheered along the way and children ran ahead to spread the news, but no one joined them. Village tradition insisted that the monks and their foreign guests come first to the shore where the Fragments were received, and then the village as a whole would escort them safely to their place of honor in the oldest local church. The last five hundred yards were carefully staged for dramatic impact. The road down swung sharply to the left and came out on a level place directly above the pavilion in which thousands of villagers stood, staring uphill, waiting, expectant. As soon as the hundreds of priests, recognized in the dark by the blazing light of their massed tapers, rounded the corner and came into view like the triumphant phalanxes of an ancient and invincible army, thunder rolled across the water as cannons fired from the beach. Fireworks laced the sky with streaking reds, greens, and sizzling whites, and the people's roared approval threatened to wake the peaceful dead and unsettle distant hills. The procession streamed quickly then to the beach, where the reception of the Fragments from

St. Paul was reenacted and the abbot held them high above his head, the crowd cheered again on cue, and the priests moved toward the church for the rededication of the Fragments and the village that protected them.

It was a short half-mile walk, but dark and impossibly crowded. Most of the candles had been burned down or blown out by the wind coming off the sea. Faces were indistinguishable. Santry pressed close to the abbot, looked ahead, and knew there was no way to funnel that crowd into the narrow street toward which they all were moving. But everyone knew that. It was part of the excitement and everyone was supposed to try. Thousands surged toward the narrow gap, some running ahead of the leading priests, most pressing in from the sides, no one content to trail behind. The abbot turned before reaching the first buildings and shouted, "Don't worry, Michael! We've done it this way all my life!"

Santry struggled forward, switched the folder to his right hand, held it close to his body, and was glad for the crowd, the intense darkness, and the weight of anonymous bodies pressing relentlessly from all sides. He was glad for the noise and the shouting, glad even for the insane firecrackers that started going off in the crowd, glad for the way it all got worse when they finally jammed into the narrow street and he could move his feet only a few inches in any direction. Everyone was pushing, shoving, and pressing them up the hill. Santry counted the streetlights overhead, and when he got exactly between the second and the third, he was relieved and exhilarated to feel a sudden hard push from behind and strangely thrilled to hear his own voice yelling, "Stop pushing! Please stop pushing!" And he was excited to shout the cry of fear that he was going to be crushed if he went down. "Please, I'm falling! Don't! Please don't push!"

But no one paid any attention and the crowd surged

and caught him as it was catching others, knocking him and everyone else forward and off balance.

He shouted louder and louder. "Stop it! Stop . . . !

But people were careening into one another and he was falling and afraid and reached out desperately for anything to keep him from going down and caught the abbot by the shoulder and heard him suddenly gasp and moan terribly as somebody hit him from the other side and they were all going down, sprawling, lost in the darkness of the crowd's heavy, treacherous herding feet and the abbot's anguished scream cut through it all like a knife.

"*Apokoma! Apokoma!* The Fragments! The Fragments!"

And Santry, his knees cut on cobblestone and fighting to get back on his feet, yelled and yelled, "*Eco! Eco!* I have them! I have them!"

But the pushing, the trampling, the screaming only got worse, because the crowd in front pushed back to see what was happening and the people behind surged forward so they wouldn't miss the excitement. Santry crashed forward like a charging tackle, forced his way to the fallen abbot, set his legs on both sides of the body, swung his thick elbows wildly to clear a space, and struggled for air while shouting angrily, "Get back! Get back!"

The shocked villagers nearest saw the abbot between his legs, caught the crisis, locked arms uphill and down against the crowd, and a woman shouted, "In here! Bring him in here!"

A man ran to Santry's side. The two of them lifted the abbot from the ground, carried him into the streetside home, slammed the door against peering eyes, laid the abbot on a couch, stared at him, and told the woman to call the police. An ambulance was needed immediately.

* * *

Three hours later, a chartered plane took off from the tiny island and flew to Athens, where the still-unconscious abbot was rushed to a hospital's emergency room. He was accompanied by the island doctor, a monastery priest, and Father Michael Santry. There was little small talk while they waited. They were used to silence, and each of the men had his private thoughts. Santry sat grimly in a corner of the antiseptic room, staring out the window at nothing, smoking, grateful only that no one spoke to him, quiet and immovable as cold stone, focused hard on the fact that Simonedes might die. None of this was planned, he told himself. None of it was desired or dreamed, or even considered possible. Of course. The worst never was. How could a man in his fifties be so innocent? So self-righteously full of good that he'd turn so quickly to this? He told himself not to leap too far ahead, not to reach too fast for guilt and the sickly comforts of remorse. He had known that anything might happen. He had judged the balances and he had gone ahead. He had gotten himself to Greece. *Nothing more to do about it now, so lay it down. Maybe it'll work out. Wait. Don't rag it like a terrier. Wait till there's some word, something definite.*

The island doctor returned with a hospital specialist at three in the afternoon. Santry turned to face them. "He's regained consciousness and he'll be all right, though a long time recovering. His wrist was broken in the fall and half his face is badly bruised. He wanted to see you, but for no more than a few minutes, please. He's under sedation and will want to sleep."

At bedside, Santry looked down on a heavily bandaged, swollen face and, as he had at hundreds of other bedsides, reached out to touch the patient's hand. The abbot smiled weakly through dry lips. "Michael, oh, Michael." His eyes closed and his head drifted slightly to one side, but he continued to speak. Santry leaned closer. His voice was little more than a whisper. "The doctor says you saved my life. Thank you, thank you,

Michael. Whatever would have happened if you hadn't been there?"

August 10, 1984

The Pan Am jet traced a low silver curve above the island's coral shore, came in from the south, leveled out, eased down, and rode the white ribbon to a stop in front of the concrete terminal. It was hot and humid, and storm clouds were building mountains in the sky. Inside, they cleared customs and told the English-speaking driver they were staying at the Blue Dolphin. The ride took forty-five minutes. Their room had a balcony, a great mahogany bed, and opened on a white-sand beach that ran for miles along a blue-green sea. The storm held off until they had their swim. Later they watched the torrents of blowing rain bending palms and banana trees from the sheltered veranda where the house drink, a piña colada with coconut milk, was served by black women with glistening skin. He had been there before, in the same hotel, but not for many years. "What do you think?" he asked.

She laughed excitedly. "It's a green and wild garden and you should never leave. The waterfall pouring over your skin is full of orchids."

He excused himself before dinner. "One more wire and I'll finish all my warrior responsibilities."

Many on the veranda watched him leave and cross the lobby toward the front desk. Many more couldn't take their eyes off her.

"Send this wire and charge it to my account," he told the clerk. "I'll need a copy." The cable was addressed to Father Michael Santry, Monastery of St. David the King, Kallos, Greece:

Congratulations. All is well.

Ian Marshall

August 15

Excerpts from an article found on an inside page of the *Athens News*:

> The International Conference on New Testament Studies, an annual event on the island of Kallos, ended its month-long deliberations yesterday with an address by the abbot of the host monastery. Father John Simonedes spoke of the importance of such conferences for the ecumenical movement and for international understanding. A highlight of the final proceedings was a special award presented to Father Michael Santry of Detroit, Michigan, who had, in the abbot's words, "saved me from more serious injury, if not death, and preserved the Ephesian Fragments, one of Greece's greatest treasures, from unimaginable harm." Father Santry expressed his gratitude for the abbot's recovery, but beyond that would say only that the month in Greece had been one of the most important times in his life.

Chapter Four

"The editor, please."

"I'm sorry, he's in a meeting. Can I help you?"

"Yes, tell him Varga's calling."

He read the newspaper on the table in front of him until he heard the familiar voice. "Dimitrios, what a pleasant surprise. What can you do for me?"

"A series on frontier relations with Turkey: seizure of fishing boats, war rumors, arms buildup, treatment of visitors, fantasies and facts. About six articles. A major piece."

"Good of you to call. When can I have them?"

"Research for two months, another to write. You can run the first article in your Christmas issue."

"Good. Thanks very much for the call."

Varga's phone rang five minutes later. "Hello, Ted Vatis here. See if you can work Kallos in. There's some strangeness going on: A lot of talk about Turkish plots and a priest who got trampled in a recent festival. There may be something there."

Dimitrios Varga was one of Greece's most respected investigative journalists. At the age of forty-nine, he commanded the highest fees and could choose the publication for his work. Every serious editor wanted him; he was a gifted storyteller who combined the passion of a hungry ferret on the prowl with the even-handed judgments of the village wise man. No publisher ever got burned on the facts, though in the early years lawsuits were as common as the endless awards. He had begun his career as assistant professor of history at the University of Athens, but after completing the research for his first book on the Greek resistance in World War II, an editor friend suggested he do a series of popular articles on the subject. The money, the type of writing, and the nationwide audience appealed to him. So did getting out of the university. The articles were controversial, sold well, led to more, and in a few years he resigned from the History Department to become a full-time writer.

He dialed *Ta Nea*, a prominent Athens newspaper, and asked for the library. "Hello, Maria, this is Dimitrios Varga. Do you have a file on recent events on Kallos? Anything about an injured priest?"

She checked.

"Yes? Good. I'll come down in a few hours."

By seven that night, he had read through the afternoon's gatherings from several libraries and newsstands, including the brief articles on "disturbances" that marred the annual festival of St. Paul on Kallos, and was back on the phone. One call went to Father John Simonedes, abbot of the monastery of St. David the King. He explained his interests, said he'd be on the island in a few days, and requested an interview. The abbot was cordial and invited him to stay at the monastery. A date was set. Before hanging up, Varga asked how many people had been in the streets the night of August 1. Simonedes estimated four or five thousand.

"And how many others were injured that night?"

"To the best of my knowledge, none. I've heard of no other injuries."

Varga stopped writing on the legal-sized pad beside the phone and looked at the opposite wall, where an owl stared back from an enlarged photograph given to him by friends. They thought the resemblance was striking. Varga thought it was slight, but suggestive. "How do you account for that? Out of four thousand people, isn't it strange that you alone were hurt?"

"I've wondered about that, too," replied Simonedes, "but at my age you go down faster and get hurt quicker. When you see me, it won't seem so strange. I'm wearing a pair of grotesque binoculars without which I'm blind. But with them I'm goggle-eyed and lift my feet six inches too soon for steps. No, I'm afraid it was nothing but an accident."

"Why do you say 'afraid'?"

"Well, I assume you're looking for a story to sell, and I'm 'afraid' there's none here. It's just an expression. Perhaps I'm also a little afraid of reporters who will invent a sensation for the sake of a few dollars. We've had some unfortunate experiences along that line, but I know your reputation and I do welcome you, Mr. Varga."

"Some people on the island hold the Turks responsible."

"Some people on the island," Simonedes countered, "hold the Turks responsible for drought, jellyfish, and unfaithful wives. I've seen no evidence for any of it."

"A priest from the United States rescued you that night?"

"Yes. Father Michael Santry from Detroit."

"I'd like to talk to him."

"Sorry, he returned to the States a few weeks ago."

They said good-night and Varga called Dr. Apollo Petrides. The response was enthusiastic. "Dimitrios, where are you? Why haven't you called? Are you in trouble?"

Varga offered to buy lunch if Petrides had friends on the staff of the Health Hospital.

"Of course. I have friends in every hospital. I knew you were in trouble. How can I help you?"

Varga listed his questions and Petrides promised to

deliver the answers the next day over an expensive bottle of wine.

When he realized he was waking people up, Varga laid the phone to rest, heated milk for his nightly cup of cocoa, and threw darts at a well-punctured board mounted on the opposite wall. He lofted them high, sending the feathered steel across the room in long, drifting arches that sliced into the board from above. Occasionally, he'd mix it up, bear down, and throw fast and hard. "Four thousand people on a narrow street," he mused while throwing. "It's dark. One man goes down. Only one man goes down. One man gets hurt. Only one man gets hurt. He's holding a national treasure. He calls it an accident. And maybe it was. And maybe it wasn't." He reviewed the little he knew about Kallos, wondering about the "accident" and the many actors that could hide behind that curtain. Several of his most important stories had developed because he thought "actor" when others settled for "accident." His last dart buried itself in cork, he stirred the cocoa, carried it into the dark living room of his eighth-floor apartment, and looked down on Athens, a city far more beautiful by night than by day. He had expected more resistance from Simonedes. How many other abbots would welcome a journalist's prying into a near-miss on a Greek treasure just when government officials were calling for more control over monastery holdings? But if the abbot had not been hurt in an accident, then who did it? Personal enemy? Anticlerical fanatic? Religious or nationalist sect? Turks? A plain old thief? Probably not. Why would anyone increase the risk to himself by assaulting a religious leader in a crowd of four thousand, when safer ways to hit, hurt, steal, and run were easily accomplished. Then again, why not? Or was it done precisely for the publicity? Were those who wanted ecclesiastical properties broken up and used for public purposes threatening the Fragments to demonstrate clerical incompetence and church negligence in the care of Greek treasures? Had Simonedes received threats? If so, why had he chosen not to disclose them?

Varga let the stream of restless questions roll and drank his hot milk. He played with them all but refused to jump to conclusions. At the beginning of a story, all doors should be open and none closed. They'd be slamming in his face soon enough. Years of carefully criticized practice taught that if one gave even the most improbable explanations a hearing, the wheat and the chaff separated themselves soon enough. He knew he'd eventually see a pattern, but that would take time and could not be hurried.

There was a second reason for withholding judgment. One of recent origin. He didn't care. In the past year or two, he had grown increasingly indifferent to the dramas that had for almost two decades excited and absorbed him. And why not? Most of his successful investigations simply documented another case of corruption in high or low places. The details varied, but the greed, the grubbing, and the tawdriness were depressingly constant. He had long ago surrendered the hope that his exposés made much difference. They did not. People loved to read them only because his stories endorsed their cynicism about others and ratified their own corruption. *See, everyone's doing it, says the building inspector to his partner as he pockets the bribe and signs off on the faulty construction.* So he had little hope of finding anything very new on Kallos. He'd go after it just as hard. That was his job and he had his own standards, but his interest was tempered by the knowledge that once he clawed his way to the heart of the story, he'd probably find just one more greedy, mean-souled little man with his sweaty hand in the till and a frozen smile on his face. He still enjoyed the chase, but he had grown more interested in the occasional virtues he found along the way than in the larger vice he wrote about at the end of the hunt.

Within a week, he walked slowly across a deserted

football field listening to an older, taller, black-robed man tell his story. September's first rain, little more than a heavy mist, settled softly around them. The abbot nodded toward the village. "There, just to the left of the restaurant, that's the street."

Varga turned his collar up, pulled his jacket shut, and said, "Please show me where it happened."

The flat, bare clay field gave way to a narrow cobblestone street. It was glistening wet, slippery, and steep. They quickened their pace up the hill against a sudden wind and heavier rain, and Varga was glad when the abbot stopped and said, "Here, we were right here."

Varga absorbed the empty, quiet scene. There were no people in sight. No voices. No music. All doors and most shutters bordering the road were closed. Simonedes, bearded and peering from behind thick lenses, suggested they get inside.

The small restaurant was warm, its tables Greek-taverna rickety and covered with oilcloth. A few old men looked up when they entered, greeted the abbot, then went back to their card game. A parrot squawked from a dark corner. They drank coffee and watched the rain streaming down the windows as Simonedes told Varga about thousands of people jammed into that narrow corridor, the growing pressure of the crowd, the screams, people falling, his own shouts when he dropped the Fragments, and then—nothing, nothing at all until he opened his eyes in a hospital bed.

Varga watched a young policeman enter the taverna, then hunched over the table, tilted his head slightly toward a knot of men across the room, and said, "I wonder if they think it was an accident."

Simonedes gave Varga a curious look and shrugged. "I doubt it. Imagined intrigue wins over dull fact every time. In a village this small there are very few mysteries, so they must be invented. People need drama the way they need coffee—something to get the heart going on dreary mornings."

"Let's ask them."

Simonedes was amused. "You want to go around the circle and conduct little interviews?"

"No," Varga replied, interested in the quick tension his proposal generated. "Let's all talk together. They're listening anyway, so why not include them? We might both learn something. Just introduce me and I'll get it started."

The abbot hesitated, then called out, "Nikos, Anastassios, Vasilis!" He quickly named every man in the room and each turned toward him. "I want you to meet Dimitrios Varga. He's a well-known reporter. Remember how shocked we were four or five years ago to learn that powerful businessmen like Kosmas and Segas in Salonica were part of an international heroin ring? Well, Mr. Varga's the man who discovered all that and wrote the articles. Now he's on Kallos to see what he can see."

A few chairs turned and men shifted in their seats to get a better look at the thickset man beside the abbot. They saw a middle-aged Greek with good clothes on his back, thick brows over friendly eyes, and a heavy moustache on a broad face. Worry beads clicked softly in his right hand as he explained his interest in Kallos and assured them that he knew nothing at all about their Festival of St. Paul. "Nothing!" he repeated with an indifferent flourish of his hand, except what he read in the papers, and he was as skeptical as everybody else about what he found there. He had come to Kallos ignorant but interested. He wanted to learn. And if they could help his understanding, he'd be grateful. "Now," he said, as if the time had come to get down to work, "Father Simonedes got a broken wrist and a battered face on the night of August 1. I suppose most of you were there. What do you think happened?"

The policeman, a slight man with a thin, sharp face,

began talking immediately, and Varga wondered if his presence was accidental. He saw quick glances pass among the other men as the officer began his recitation. A few kept their eyes down on small white coffee cups while he talked. The policeman had been on duty that night, he had talked to everyone, he had reviewed the investigation that followed, and there was not a hair of evidence for a plot, an attack, a theft, or a Turkish raid. There had been a most unfortunate accident and people should now forget about it unless they had some new evidence to offer. He concluded a rambling, agitated summary of police findings with an appeal to authority. "The abbot tells us it was accidental. Who should know better? Who was closer?" Looking at Varga, he added, "We've got to be sensitive to the international implications of all this. A lot of Greeks are looking for demons and terrorists under their beds and they're inflaming a dangerous situation." He stared pointedly at two men on the far side of the room. "This is a frontier island and we've got our share of armchair desperadoes with nothing better to do than sit around in coffee shops, curse the Turks, and hope for the worst."

Varga saw the abbot's hand come off the table just as the policeman finished, signaling his intention to speak. He pleaded for an end to idle speculation, attributed his fall to his failing sight, and scotched a few rumors circulating about his plans to leave the island. By the time he finished, it was clear to Varga that no one else was going to say a word. Why should anyone go public against the weight of the police and the Church for the sake of a stranger? If they had something for him, it would come later and it would come privately.

The policeman was on his feet, standing in polished shoes and a sharp, tailored uniform, saying to the abbot, "I've got to get back to the station. If you want a ride, I'll be glad to take you."

The abbot looked outside at the pouring rain and touched Varga's arm. "Perhaps we'd better. It could go on like this for a long time." Varga nodded and told the men he'd be on the island for another day and would be back to talk with them. The abbot walked halfway to the door, then turned unexpectedly and fixed his large, sorrowful eyes on the men watching him. "Only two of us had a chance to say anything." He spoke quietly, awkwardly, as if caught in an embarrassing situation. "I'm sorry about that, but I do think we need to be more careful. There are so many rumors—but I didn't mean to silence anyone. No, I didn't mean to do that. If we can help Mr. Varga, we should. I should and you should."

The abbot apologized again when the three were in the car. "Demos and I were a little heavy-handed in there and I regret it. But try to understand—my fall during the festival has excited endless questions and speculations. It's hard to get anything else done."

The lieutenant kept his eyes on the wet road and spoke against the heavy drumming of rain on the roof. "You're the fourteenth reporter since the Festival. We even had a television crew fly in from Athens. We cooperated with them, but there's just not much to say after you look at the facts we've got."

Varga thought about the men in the restaurant, wondered if they'd be there when he returned, and explained to the lieutenant that what happened in August wasn't important to him unless it tied in to his story on Turkey. If there was no connection, he was moving on. In the center of town, he leaned forward from the backseat, tapped the policeman on the shoulder, and said, "Let me out here, please. I want to walk on my own for a while." Turning to the abbot, on the seat beside him, he added, "I'd like to take you to dinner tonight— someplace quiet where there's good fish and wine. I brought some pictures I want to show you."

They agreed on a time and place, the police car pulled

away, and the abbot asked, "What do you think, Demos?"

"You handled him very well, Father."

"I didn't mean that!" Simonedes snapped, immediately regretting his impatience. He was getting irritable with everyone. "I meant, what do you think of him?"

"I'll be glad when he's off the island, but I don't think he's going to print any garbage. He's after a bigger story than he can find here. He'll drink a couple of ouzos with the old-timers, hear it all, and leave in the morning. Where are you putting him up?"

"In the conference center. Why?"

"Just wondered. There are plenty of rooms in town if he's in your way."

"Is there anything new?"

"Not a thing. Nothing at all, Father. I'm beginning to think it was some drunk after all."

"That would be a relief, wouldn't it?"

The policeman pulled up a long, curved driveway and stopped under a sheltered entrance to the monastery. "I'll call you in the morning to see if you've found out what he really has on his mind."

Simonedes looked at the driver, thinking that was an odd expectation. "Yes, if you want to, though I'm sure it'll be just like the last journalist who wanted to eat with me: nothing but a series of questions about the rumors he'd heard. If there's anything new, I'll call you."

They waved good-bye and Lieutenant Demos Forticos turned his car toward town, rode the brakes down the steep hillside, and parked on the harbor road opposite a restaurant. An octopus hung from a line, dripping in the unusually heavy rain. He turned off the motor and blew his horn twice. In a few minutes, a stiff-legged, grizzled old man walked slowly to the open window on the driver's side, leaned over, and talked briefly with the officer. Forticos then watched him return to the restaurant, and he drove to the police station, closed the door to his office, and sat quietly for a few minutes, as if to compose himself. He then dialed an Athens number, listened to the familiar message from the answering machine, waited for the tone, and said, "Dimitrios Varga on Kallos. Advise."

The fingers of the abbot's left hand, tender from a lifetime of work with prayers and books, curled on the wineglass, displaying a ruby ring to the candle's fire. Varga watched the red flares erupt in the stone and blaze like a miniature sun. "It's a better evening than I had anticipated," Simonedes told him. "We're on the second bottle of Kallos's finest and you still haven't plagued me with the terrible rumors you heard today."

Varga shrugged. "There are more important things. At least one or two. And to tell the truth, Father, I didn't hear any rumors today." Varga's thick arms rested on a cleared table in a large, noisy room. Only wineglasses, a bottle, and the flickering candle remained. He spoke easily, comfortably as an old friend might, adding a running commentary with assorted gestures and shrugs. "I wandered in that marvelous rain after I left you and your little friend and I thought about what I'd already heard and what I probably would hear if I went back to the café and I decided this is not my story." His eyes went up from his wine and watched the abbot through heavy brows. "Although there's a story here. I'm sure of that now. Not because I've heard anything new, but because of what I've thought and . . ."—here he paused, waited until the abbot wondered what was coming, and concluded—". . . because of what I see in you."

Simonedes, who had enjoyed the previous hour's conversation as much as any he'd had since Santry left, tapped his wineglass impatiently and urged Varga to go on. "Yes, yes, what do you see?"

"A good man who is puzzled and irritated." Varga laughed a little at his words. "You understand I'm not sure of any of this. I don't know if you're good or not, but I liked the way you apologized this morning. Those men deserved an apology and you did it well. I'm sure that was good because I liked it. The little lieutenant with the cat's eyes would never do that. The rest, the impatience and the confusion, well, that's obvious."

"Please, please, Mr. Varga, if I'm as impatient as you claim, you know your obliqueness has got to infuriate me. So please get to the point. I hate being brusque but . . . I'm sorry. Yes, it's been a trying month. Nothing like this has ever happened before—but go on, I'm interested in what you think, especially in why you think there's a story here."

Varga pulled his chair a few inches closer to the abbot. "I want to tell you exactly what I think and then maybe you and I can stop the fencing. Maybe we can even dance around the truth together and get one or two good looks at her. That would be something new, wouldn't it? A priest and a reporter looking for the truth. Ha! No one will believe us. So we begin where you ended: 'Nothing like this has ever happened before.' Never! In fifty years, the Festival was never disrupted. In fifty years, the abbot was never injured, but this year it's reported that the abbot broke his right wrist in a fall and suffered severe bruises to the left side of his face when he hit the street. Why did that happen? Four thousand people on the march! An unruly crowd! Pushing and shoving! How many others got injured in that night storm? None! Not one. And, of course, that makes people wonder, but the world's getting stranger, and the abbot, who is a truthful man, says it was an accident.

"That, I think, is a fair summary of the public record at this point, and most people go along with you. Believe it, don't believe it, they don't care. They go along. It's a matter of indifference to them. Oh, there's some talk of Turks and terrorists, but it means nothing, absolutely nothing, although it involves you in a lot of tedious conversations like ours this morning in the café.

But that will end in a month or two. For practical purposes, it's over. There is no important, public challenge to your version of those events by any representative of a powerful institution, and, finally, they're the only ones that matter. The sparrows of the world will chatter endlessly and peck at any available horseshit, but no one pays any attention to them.

"And I feel like most of those who just go along, Father. I'm glad you're healing, but it's no real concern of mine. You say it was an accident. That's all right with me. Why should I care? I don't! That's the truth. But, Father Simonedes, I confess that I begin to care a little when I realize that you're hiding something, maybe even hiding someone." He stopped abruptly, leaned back in his chair, and challenged the abbot directly. "Hiding, covering up, telling less than the full truth. You know it and, of more importance to our little dance with the truth, I know it." He reached into the briefcase by his chair, withdrew a large packet, and passed it across the table. "These are the pictures I promised you."

The magnified size of the abbot's eyes behind the thick lenses accentuated his startled appearance as he looked quickly back and forth between Varga and the package on the table. He started to protest, "I can't imagine what—" But he broke it off, stopped himself in midflight, quickly opened the package, and took out six X rays. He sorted through them, shaking his head, and laid them back on the table in front of Varga. "I don't understand. I honestly do not understand what these are or what you're trying to tell me."

Varga's voice was conciliatory. "These are the X rays of your wrist and head taken at the hospital in Athens when you were unconscious. I've had them evaluated by specialists. Not one of them believes that that break occurred in a fall from a relatively motionless, standing position. Hand-to-hand combat seems more likely to them. Their best guess? You were clubbed or, more probably, chopped by an expert, someone skilled in karate, someone who damned near tore your hand off with the flat edge of his palm and then went for your throat but missed in the darkness because you were falling and he caught the side of your face instead. You were lucky. A hand that could do that to your wrist could have killed you—and that may be exactly what he wanted to do."

"But Mr. Varga," the abbot pleaded, "there was no 'he.' No deadly attacker exists except in your imagination." He waved his hand over the X rays, as if dismissing them from consideration. "These prove nothing. The doctors of your choice see a karate expert in them; my doctor sees an old man with brittle bones falling on stone. Why should I believe yours? The police tore this village apart investigating. They closed the harbor and the airport, interviewed hundreds of travelers, talked to everyone within a hundred yards of me that night. And they found exactly what Demos told the men this morning: nothing. I realize that everyone would be far happier if they found a masked bandit in the hills, but on the evidence gathered thus far, the incident must be called an accident."

Varga nodded and poured more wine. His next question would tell him how much of a taste the abbot had for the truth. "Do you remember what you told the nurse shortly after regaining consciousness in the hospital?"

"I'm not sure. I suppose I said something about feeling a terrible blow and falling. And I'm sure I asked about the Fragments. Why?"

"Because I talked to the nurse and wanted to see how much of the memory had faded. Not much. You have a good mind. And when the police questioned you later, you probably said the same thing, didn't you?"

"Of course, but where's all this going?"

"It's going to the coffee shop this morning where the lieutenant quoted you as calling it an accident."

"Well, it *was* an accident. That's the only possible

conclusion you can come to after looking at the results of the investigation."

"No, that's not true. It's only the conclusion that you came to, Father. Let's go slowly here, very slowly. And remember I suspect you of nothing. I believe what you tell me, and I never say that unless I mean it. Now, listen to me and see if we can understand this thing together. Originally, you said there was a 'terrible blow.' But in little more than a month of repeating the story, the 'blow' has disappeared from all descriptions of that night and has been replaced by another word: 'accident.' But if the police had actually found the masked bandit of the people's dreams or, better yet, the Turks, or a drunk monk who hated you the way sons are supposed to hate their fathers, then today in the coffee shop you would have said something very different, wouldn't you? Yes, you would have said, 'This monk or this Turk came crashing through the crowd and gave me a terrible blow and so forth.' Yes?"

For a moment the abbot shook his head as if bewildered, then spoke impatiently. "Are you crazy? Of course I would have said something different, but that's not what we found, is it?"

Varga pressed the abbot's arm reassuringly. "Let's be careful here. The words are very slippery. You say 'That's not what they found' as if they found something, but they didn't find anything, one way or the other. The masked bandit, the Turks, the drunk monk could still be the best explanation, but the police prefer their usual card tricks: they come up with an empty hand, but they've got to show results, so they announce triumphantly, 'We found nothing,' as if that was some kind of success story, as if 'nothing' was really 'something,' the result of another incredible painstaking investigation. And then they deepen the mystification by transforming 'We found nothing' into what Demos said this morning, 'We found an accident.' But that, Father, is not a logical conclusion—that is a leap of faith. You see what I mean? No? Then look at it this way. If you had been shot or killed, then the situation would be starkly unambiguous and there would be no card tricks. A killer is out there. Have you found him? Yes or no? Answer: No! But in your case, there was so much going on: the darkness, drunks, kids throwing firecrackers, thousands of people packed and frantic on a narrow street. All that makes it easy for a 'terrible blow' to fade into 'accident,' and gradually be forgotten as long as that's the official interpretation. I am simply saying that 'terrible blows' come from attackers and not from stumbling drunks, and it would be more honest for the police to label it 'case unsolved' instead of 'accident.' I understand why they do that, but I don't understand why you go along with this fooling the people."

"I haven't gone along with anything! The police are continuing their investigation and, at the same time, we're working together to reduce the hysteria created by endless rumors of Turks and terrorists."

"Aha!" Varga smiled. "No one said anything about a continuing investigation this morning. You and the lieutenant saluted each other, dismissed the citizens, and marched out the door as if the file had already been deposited in the archives. So what are you continuing to investigate?"

"Mr. Varga, we're islanders but not children. Forticos and I know an attacker is a possibility, however remote, and he's continuing to question some people and watch others, but we've agreed it's best to say nothing about that unless something definite's found."

Varga hit the table with the flat of his hand. "Wonderful! We're making progress. A minute ago, no attacker existed except in my imagination. Now you and the police acknowledge a possibility. The investigation continues. I suppose that's why you searched my room this afternoon."

"What!!" The abbot all but shouted the word and quickly looked around to see how much attention he had attracted. A few people turned toward the outburst, saw nothing, and returned to their own food and problems.

Varga spoke quietly. "Someone walked into my room this afternoon and went through my papers and unlocked luggage."

Simonedes's reply was abrupt and angry. "I begin to understand how you get your stories. You go around bullying and bluffing until you stumble into something. I can't take what you just said seriously."

"He was about sixty-five, three or four days without a shave, slight limp, black wool cap on his head, about my size. I was reading in the lounge and heard his footsteps. As you know, and as he seemed to, I'm the only one on that floor, maybe in the building. I thought I heard the footsteps stop in the center of the hall, near my room, so I got up and watched. Fortunately, nothing was disturbed. An excellent camera remained untouched, or at least unremoved. He was no thief. What, then? My guess is Forticos sent him. Your friend had every reason to believe I'd be downtown all afternoon and he wanted to see what kind of pictures I was going to show you tonight."

Simonedes's anger gave way to alarm and apology. "That's terrible! I can't believe it. I mean, I believe you, I just can't believe Demos would do that. The man you describe is certainly Stelios. He's the maintenance man for the monastery and has free run of the place. No one would think twice about seeing him around. He must have been checking the plumbing or the wiring or something. Though I don't understand because I thought he had finished that unit for the winter. We should go to his home right now and ask him. There must be an innocent explanation. As you say, he didn't take anything."

Varga watched the abbot running the maze, hitting dead ends, blind corners, reversing himself, scrambling down corridors, looking for a way out, trying desperately to make sense out of an event that he couldn't but had to believe. "I wouldn't even mention it to Stelios. If he's given you good work for years, why worry if he's picking up a few drachmas from Forticos for odd jobs. But if the lieutenant's behind that room check and didn't tell you about it, then you may have a problem, because it suggests he doesn't trust you to tell him about the pictures I promised to show you tonight. Or, on the other hand, it may mean he's nervous about what I've got. That would be even more interesting, wouldn't it? Why should he be nervous? You know the man. What do you think?"

"Please! You're leaping way ahead again. You jump from a probably innocent inspection of your room to a conspiracy with Demos and then ask why he's nervous! If he's not now, all he needs is an evening with you! You're too full of suspicions, Mr. Varga."

Dimitrios watched the abbot's swollen eyes grow worried and told him, "I wouldn't show Forticos those X rays."

"Why not?"

"They'll make him nervous. He'll assume I'm going to expose his mediocre work. All I have to do is run these pictures in a prominent newspaper, quote medical specialists that you were attacked by a sober, disciplined, and powerful man, place that beside a photo of you and the lieutenant, mouths wide open pleading 'accident' or, better yet, pointing to some dismal drunk, and people all over Greece will roar with laughter. That may not bother you, but it will sure as hell torpedo the officer's long march to power. And a story about illegal room searches wouldn't do much for your conference center either."

"Now you're threatening me!"

Varga smiled and spoke slowly, deliberately. "Not really. It doesn't interest me that much. Ten years ago, maybe, but not now. There's not enough there: unknown assailant, inept police, good-willed but innocent abbot. The world's full of better mysteries. For your sake, though, I hope he doesn't come back."

"Who?" asked the abbot.

"Who!" snapped Varga, reaching for the bottle and filling the priest's glass. "You need more wine. Somebody damned near killed you! Why? What did he want? Where is he now? Is he coming back? The truth is that nobody knows. A little more suspicion in your brittle bones would help you keep your skeleton together."

"I'm not worried about anyone coming back, Mr. Varga, but any publicity at this point would hurt us—especially any report about these." He fingered the X rays and added, "Or about the incident this afternoon. No, that wouldn't help us at all. I have your word that you're not going to do that?"

"You will have it."

"Will?"

Varga hunched over the table as if to speak more confidentially. "Yes, you will if you satisfy my curiosity on one point. Only one. Do that and I promise there'll be no story from me unless you ask me to write it."

The two men's heads drew together and their voices grew quieter as they talked. At one point, the abbot shook his head in vigorous dissent, pushed his chair back, and threatened to leave. Varga told him to go ahead, assured him it didn't matter to him one way or the other. He'd send him an advance copy of the story so he could prepare for the storm. "You think there's too much talk now? Wait till next week!" Simonedes stared at Varga the way a trapped rabbit watched the approaching fox, then stood up, walked to the telephone, and made a call. When he returned, he remained standing and said stiffly, "Demos will meet us at the station in an hour."

The taxi stopped at the monastery's great wrought-iron gate. The abbot told the driver to wait, and the two men climbed out. Varga looked down at the village and dark sea below them and pointed to the lights of an approaching ship. The abbot refused to speak, continuing the angry vow of silence he had taken in the restaurant after Varga beat him down. The spacious grounds, well known to monks, were without lights. By day, the large garden made it a pleasant place to linger, but at night it reminded Varga of a prison: massive stone walls, shadowy turrets, severe rectangular construction, and, within those walls, the innumerable cells.

The abbot's keys chinked together in the blackness as his fingers sorted through them, selected one, and slid it unerringly into the large, antique lock of the museum door. In moments, a few ceiling spots scattered the darkness into corners and played brightly on the raised glass case held by enormous olive-wood hands in the very center of the room. In early September, even after months of bright dryness outside, the room remained damp and cold. Simonedes suggested Varga wait by the door, but the reporter refused and stayed close to the abbot as he crossed to the collection's prize, climbed the few stairs, knelt briefly in front of the display, inserted a key beneath the case, then rose and lifted the exhibit's top. The ancient and priceless Fragments lay before them. Varga, who had seen them that afternoon during regular museum hours, reached in quickly, closed the folder on which they rested, and withdrew them. Simonedes looked at him sharply, closed the case, and took the folder from him. "The last night I took these out turned into one of the worst in my life. This one already ranks among the most unpleasant, thank you."

"If you took things less personally, they'd be less unpleasant," Varga told him. "If you'd give old John Simonedes, the son of peasants, a little more room, a little distance from the abbot of the great monastery, you wouldn't complain so much. This isn't unpleasantness between you and me. It's between institutions: two big businesses, the media and the Church. You took your job voluntarily. Well, this goes with it. You wanted a national treasure, so don't object when the public wants to know what you're doing with it. Above all, Father, don't whine. It's a bad example for the young."

The abbot glared, turned abruptly away, and descended the stairs, looking back only once and long enough to say, "Come! I want to get this over with."

The police offices, laboratory, jail, and garage nestled close to the harbor. Forticos waited for them outside and brushed away the abbot's immediate apologies for taking him from his home. Simonedes asked if the lab technician had arrived. Demos assured him he had, and suggested they go inside so "you can tell me what this is all about."

His office furnishings, Varga thought, were much like his car: on the luxurious side for a cop. His eyes went from the rich drapes and fine watercolors to the weasel-faced man behind the desk waiting patiently for an explanation. The door was closed and no lights came from adjacent offices.

"Demos," the abbot began to explain, "this afternoon Mr. Varga met—" He broke off, turned to Dimitrios, and said, "You might as well tell him, it's your idea."

Varga offered cigarettes. Neither Simonedes nor Forticos smoked. He lit one for himself. "Today in a café a man insisted that it was he, not Santry, who found the Fragments after they dropped from the abbot's hands. He claims he heard the abbot crying out and, at the same moment, felt something hit his foot. He seized it and rushed toward Father Simonedes, but Father Santry blocked his way. He surrendered them to the American priest, but afterward, after all the publicity and the awards and the attention, he grew annoyed and bitter that the glory was not shared with local Greeks. Now, this is a small thing, Lieutenant, even insignificant, but I can't leave Kallos tomorrow without a story, because my editor asked specifically about the dynamics here. The good abbot and I had a long talk today and he told me many things. He made me sensitive to your needs for an investigation that continues—but quietly, even secretly. I understand that and I don't want to interfere in any way by publishing my idle questions and speculations. They wouldn't help your work, as the abbot knows, because I see things here differently than he does. I'm prepared to move on, but I must submit something. You can understand that. Well, this stranger's story would make a nice center for an interesting but slight and altogether complimentary piece. If he did find the Fragments first, then I'll take his picture and give him a little national attention. He's happy then. He puts it on his wall and shows his friends. But if he didn't find it, I can still use it as evidence of local interest in the Fragments, the groundless rumors, and so forth.''

Forticos noted briskly that it was the first time he had heard that story, a remark that caused the abbot to scurry into the conversation and argue, ''I think we should just cooperate, Demos. Speaking frankly, we are better served by Mr. Varga's absence than by his presence. I have his word that his interest in Kallos ends tonight, and his departure will be helpful to us simply by convincing other reporters that there's no story here.''

Forticos shrugged. ''It's all right with me, but how are you going to check his story one way or the other?''

Varga dropped a sealed white envelope on the desk. ''These are his fingerprints. We'd like your technician to check them against the Fragments. If they're present, I'll take his story seriously. If not, I'll develop another angle.''

''Simple enough,'' Forticos said. ''You want to wait for the results?''

''Yes, certainly,'' replied Simonedes. ''The Fragments have to go back tonight.''

* * *

They made no attempt to small-talk their way through the expected hour of waiting. Varga told them he was going for a walk along the harbor and left Forticos and Simonedes talking together in front of the station. He was sitting on the concrete jetty, feet dangling toward the shimmering water, his eyes idling over innumerable boats and ships, when he heard the abbot calling. He got up slowly, refusing to rush. In the next few minutes he could be taking on the most interesting and important story he'd had in twenty years. The abbot met him outside. "Nothing there, Mr. Varga. No trace of your friend's prints, though there were plenty of others."

Forticos came out through the doors of the station behind the abbot and ratified the results. "Sorry, Varga, no story there, but I like your idea of using it to show the flood of baseless rumors."

Varga shrugged his heavy shoulders, thanked the lieutenant for his help, and concealed his sudden excitement. The results proved all his suspicions. He declined the offer of a ride to the monastery, explaining that he wanted night air and a long walk. They shook hands, wished each other well, and Varga assured the abbot he'd see him again before leaving in the morning.

It took Varga unexpected hours to reach the monastery grounds and sanctuary. Breathless, frightened, and exhausted, he staggered across the well-kept lawn until he reached the dark garden with its trees, hedges, and thick, clotted shrubs and flowers. He forced his way through the low bushes and sank to his knees against the black trunk of a tree, staring anxiously back at the gate. He took long, deep breaths to quiet his frantic gasping for air. The feel of the wet earth reached his knees as he pressed his body close to the tree and felt the leaves of lower limbs against his face. He was sure he couldn't be seen and struggled to control his wild breathing.

He had first noticed the stranger sitting on a stone

wall when he came out of a store carrying the brandy he intended to share with Simonedes. At first there was nothing either furtive or ominous about the man. He sat in a well-lit place staring amiably at those passing by. Varga barely noticed him, even when he looked back after a few blocks and saw the man walking behind him. It was a small village. The same faces reappeared endlessly. But he could not deny the special way the stranger watched. He had stopped again on the edge of the commercial district and sat on a sidewalk bench. One café remained open across the street. A couple wandered in the park behind him. Otherwise, the eyes of the village were closed. The stranger came and sat beside him. He wore loose clothing and moved gracefully. Varga offered him a cigarette. The man accepted one without thanks, inhaled deeply, and blew smoke rings toward a streetlamp. When not smoking, he held the cigarette upward between his thumb and index finger and stared intently at the small, white cylinder. He did not look at Varga and he did not speak.

Varga dropped his cigarette on the pavement, ground it out with his heel, and looked at the man beside him: late thirties, delicate, fine features, long blond hair, good arms and chest, flat stomach, an athlete of some kind, perhaps a dancer. He saw the relaxed, sinuous body and the quick, catlike intensity in the pale eyes. "What do you want?"

The stranger looked surprised, stared back coldly, and said quietly, "Nothing, of course. I have everything."

Varga turned his back on the cool stranger and walked up the steep, cobblestone street toward the monastery. The stranger followed. Varga waited. The stranger approached and stood quietly by. Varga started the long uphill pull. The footsteps stayed behind him. He had been followed before, but always from a distance and always in a way meant to be hidden. This was very different. More intimidating, more frightening. *Want?*

Nothing, of course. I have everything. What the hell kind of talk was that, thought Varga. Highly stylized and purposeful? Or simply demented? The calculated mannerisms of an actor? Or was the man gone, out to lunch, a crank? A harmless pain in the ass or an ominous threat? He didn't come from the village. The clothes, gestures, and airs were all big-city. Varga turned left and drifted downhill toward the harbor and the police station. If the guy wanted company, he'd introduce him to an officer and arrange a room for the night. He certainly wasn't going to lead him, sane or crazy, directly to his room in an empty dormitory.

He stopped suddenly and turned: no one there. Gone. He considered going to the police anyway, but the dancer hadn't done anything except make a pest of himself, and not even much of that. He told himself to lose him and forget it. No reason to get jumpy. He took a sharp turn, stepped into an empty doorway, and waited. No noise came from behind. The stranger had gone, or was he somewhere back there waiting and listening? Varga knew that in the silent-as-a-grave village his footsteps could be heard for blocks. He slipped off his shoes and started up the hill, angling away from the light, shifting suddenly to different streets but always heading upward toward the monastery that crowned the summit, stopping frequently but hearing and seeing nothing. He became convinced that the demon stranger had been born of his own fatigue and overheated imagination.

He stopped near the top to catch his breath, sat down on a low curb, and put on his shoes. He was close enough to the monastery gate to see it. His chest was heaving, prompting a quiet commitment to lose some weight, quit smoking, and get back in shape. The roofs of the village were below him, and, in the distance, lay the always alluring sea. He never heard him coming, not a sound. There was only the sudden scarf, the throat spasm, the quick jerk backward, the violent twist. He tried to scream, but there was no voice. He struggled to breathe, but there was no air. He threw himself backward, felt a quick, sharp pain, and knew he was going. His last sight was of a violent sky rushing away and his last feeling was complete astonishment at the nature of his death. Then there was only the peaceful, fading flow of the purest blue. . . .

He awoke where he fell, stretched out on the sidewalk. His hands rose slowly to his throat and touched the terrible ache. His head throbbed as he leaned on one elbow and looked around, bewildered and frightened. His watch said two o'clock. He had been there an hour. He had not been robbed. The stranger could still be around. *Get up! You've got to get up! You've got to hide!* He forced himself to climb the hill. The monastery gate was just ahead. He reached the grounds. His eyes searched the shadows frantically for the stranger. He could be there or coming back or close behind, and he began to run with painful, shuffling, staggering strides toward the garden, where at least he'd be safe and could rest and breathe and try to think. Nothing moved. The leaves were still. The black paint on the monastery's iron gate glistened under the streetlamp. The dark mass of the buildings lining the garden lifted broad shoulders against the night sky and promised to shelter and to protect. His gasping mouth and lungs gradually quieted, his back felt the tree's strength, his eyes took on weight and closed. He was still alive. Still alive.

The abbot's voice came from a great distance and through thick filters of wool. "Dimitrios! Dimitrios!" Over and over again, insistent, urgently chanting his name. Varga stirred, listened, and opened his eyes, squinting against the light. The black-robed, bearded abbot rose above him like an ancient statue. Flowers grew high about his knees. Varga tried to speak, but the words couldn't get out. His eyes closed. "Dimitrios!" A hand was on him, pushing, refusing to let him go. Someone shouted, "Yorgos! Stefan! Help!"

* * *

Later, after sleep, a hot shower, and strong tea had restored much of his shattered poise, Varga sat in the abbot's comfortable study describing the stranger, his presumed assailant, to the abbot and Forticos. They agreed that he was an outsider, certainly already off the island and, to judge from the calling card left behind, either crazy or a highly skilled professional. The card, discovered neatly tucked among the credit cards in Varga's wallet, enriched the mystery swirling around the two words "Who?" and "Why?" On one side of the card, the single, capital letter "G" was elegantly engraved. And on the other side were three words: FUTURES AND FORTUNES. Varga refused to believe it was a personal enemy, as proposed by Forticos, someone hurt by an earlier exposé, meting out delayed punishment. There was no need to follow Vargas to Kallos for that, and, besides, the attack seemed much more of a warning than an act of vengeance. No, if it was not the random work of a violent crank, and Varga dismissed that possibility, then the attacker was somehow related to Kallos, the abbot, and the attack of August 1. But if so, they had only unsatisfying guesses about the possible connections. When Forticos left, he said he'd file a report and call the mainland to ask if the mysterious "G" had presented his credentials to others.

The lieutenant, who had remained impressively calm about this latest outbreak in his usually peaceful jurisdiction, also asked, "Will I see you again?"

Varga told him probably not, that he'd be leaving the next morning. "But I'll call you from time to time to ask about the investigation."

Forticos expressed the hope that with all the tourists gone, there'd be no way a stranger could remain unobserved. "So if there's going to be any trouble, I won't expect it until next summer. By that time, we'll be ready for anything." The lieutenant gave each man a brief salute, told the abbot he'd see him soon, and walked out.

Varga massaged his stiffening neck muscles and watched the abbot pace the floor until he heard Forticos's car roar to life outside. The abbot was unusually upset. "Dimitrios"—he had begun calling Varga by his Christian name since finding him that morning—"you can't imagine how quiet this island has been for the last thirty years, so you can't imagine how strange and disturbing all this is."

"Father, your troubles are just beginning," Varga told him. "Yes, today they've begun."

The priest turned and stared, his face drained of color. "What do you mean?" he asked, adding almost immediately, "It's got something to do with last night, doesn't it? You've learned something and you didn't tell us. That's right, isn't it? I thought there was something suspicious about the whole performance."

Varga nodded. "Yes, you're right. But the time's come, and that worries me because I have to trust you not to talk to anyone: not to Forticos, not to state officials, not to family, no one—at least not till we agree on it."

"Why should that worry you?"

"Because it's a matter of life and death for you and me. It's that serious. I don't know 'who' or 'how' or 'when' or even 'why' yet, but out there in the big world some game's being played for enormous stakes, and the players aren't going to allow a small-country journalist and an island priest to get in their way. Your broken wrist and my sore neck are the merest nudges along life's way, little pushes toward the true path of silence, tiny reminders of our terrible weakness. They know they could kill us anytime, anytime they decide to. They want to make sure that we know it."

"Dimitrios, please!" The abbot, who had been pacing the floor, raised his arm in a sign of desperation. "You're so dramatic."

Varga shot straight back. "And that kind of reaction is exactly why I worry about you. You're locked in a see-no-evil straitjacket that's going to get us both killed. You find me damned near buried in your rose garden and then you have the nerve to tell me I'm getting dramatic. That, Father, strikes me as peculiarly void of any redeeming imagination."

Simonedes stiffened, took two steps toward him, and said in measured, hostile tones, "I am sincerely sorry you were hurt. Beyond that, your brief visit leaves me with little but bitterness toward you. Since you arrived yesterday, you've been furiously spinning evil webs, secret plots, and now conspiracies to murder. And what have you used for material? Bits and pieces of memory, hearsay, and fantasy. And when you run out of those solid foundations, you invent whole schemes like Stelios's visit to your bedroom. And then to make sure that I understand your exalted rank in the world, you threaten to publish your infantilisms. So, Mr. Varga, if you have something to say, now is the time, because it's the last chance you're going to get. And you don't have to worry about my word. Abbots of monasteries have long training in keeping secrets, which is far more than can be said for the journalists of the world."

Varga looked at the floor, letting his huge head rock slowly from side to side like a great caged animal. This was the abbot he liked. This was a man he could deal with. "You have anything to drink in here? Anything besides tea? This is going to take a while, and I'd like something cool and strong in my hands." The abbot prepared two ouzos. Varga lifted his glass and said quietly, "Now we begin." He set his drink carefully on the table in front of him and waited for the abbot to sit. "Yesterday afternoon, I visited your museum. The story of the Fragments had excited me as a boy, so I wanted to see them. But when I stood there looking down at them, something bothered me, something didn't seem right, though I didn't know what it was. I know you don't like my suspicions, but I love them and let them pull me around by the nose because they're always the key to a story. Most of the time they take me to a blank wall, but they're all I've got so I follow them. I'm sorry to say that yesterday they led to something. I had gone back to the dormitory and was reading in the lounge when it hit me, and I almost ran back to the museum to see if I was right. Father Simonedes, there's not a scratch anywhere on that sealed lucite cover, and there should be. Where you were attacked, cinders are all over the street, and they were almost certainly there on August 1. So unless the Fragments flew directly from your hands into those of Father Santry or rested peacefully on someone's shoe in that mob, they had to hit the surface of the street and there should be at least a mark or two on them. But that lucite looks like it's just been polished: not a scratch or scrape on it.

"Which proves what? Nothing. I understand that. It only raises more questions, although now fascinating ones. And that's why last night I invented a pathetic story about the antagonized Greek who felt left out of the publicity. I'm sorry I had to do it that way because I don't enjoy deceiving you, especially when I wonder out loud if you are trustworthy, but you understand these things. I did it and you and Forticos reported that there were no prints on the Fragments that matched the ones I brought in. You were sure that nothing like them had been found, and I felt my stomach roll over when I heard those words because they worried me as much as any two words since in the war when my mother yelled, 'They're coming!' Listen to me, dear abbot, you carried the Fragments on August 1 right up to the time you lost them. You read from them in the square and you raised them high over your head so the people could see and cheer. Your hands were all over them. But Father, it was *your* fingerprints I gave to the lieutenant last night and your fingerprints are not on the Fragments. Not one! And they should be!" Varga leaned closer and began to whisper, "At least they should be if the Fragments we took to the station last night are the Fragments you carried August 1. You see what question is driving me, Father? You see why I'm worried? The real Fragments, the ones with your prints on them, where are they, Father? Where are they!"

"Please join me for a drink."

Phillips slipped the small card into his shirt pocket and looked around. He had caught his smile on the first glance: straight across the smoky lounge. Alone. Phillips returned a discreet nod, looked about the noisy room once more, eased off his bar stool, and walked over. The black piano player hunched over his keys and watched them both. A waitress brought gimlets, straight-up. They drank silently.

Phillips wore work clothes: a dark, permanent-press business suit. The trousers sagged permanently at the knees. The stranger with the long blond hair wore turquoise beads, and long strings of them looped over one another. He had rings on the fingers of his left hand, and wore none on his right. He also wore an embroidered light cotton shirt, white as a cloud and open at the neck. But one noticed the jewelry first—after, of course, the beautiful face. His skin was golden brown and smooth as a boy's.

"My name's John Phillips."

"Yes, I know who you are, Mr. Phillips." The stranger spoke softly, reassuringly.

Phillips sipped his tart drink, already imagining the delicious peace that would slide down the mountains and envelop him after two more. "We've met somewhere?"

The stranger shook his head. "No, we know each other through friends."

Phillips hesitated. The conversation had taken a peculiar turn. The stranger's long, ringed fingers played slowly over his turquoise beads. His right hand rested quietly on the table. Phillips guessed he was thirty-five.

"We need your help."

His words sounded strangely sincere, without the irony Phillips had to believe was in them. How could he help anyone? He was barely keeping himself afloat. "I'm afraid you've got the wrong man." His smile was apologetic, the deferential grimace of one who'd been confused with, if not a superior, at least a more capable equal.

The stranger ignored the disclaimer. His unusually pale blue eyes lingered on Phillips's solid brown tie and dull white shirt. Phillips knew he was being judged harshly, though nothing in the stranger's manner suggested this. He had been thinking about a new suit for some time.

"We've prepared two offers. If you'll agree to be a regular consultant, we'll pay you one thousand U.S. dollars each month for a year."

Phillips laughed, a little too heartily. "Sorry, definitely the wrong man." He finished his drink and signaled for two more. He had been at the bar for an hour and was feeling pretty much in sync with what he called fate's "starts and farts." This wasn't the start of anything. "No, my friend, I'm no high-priced consultant."

"We know exactly who you are and what you do, Mr. Phillips. You're a clerk in the shipping department at L. P. Gerson. You've worked there seven years and enjoy a reputation for reliability. You're also deeply in debt. Our offer would relieve you of that and would require very little of your time." The stranger's voice was as smooth as his skin. His fingers continued to caress the beads.

Phillips was dazzled. Except for his occasional sexual adventures, he led a boring life, and this conversation with a total stranger was the stuff of romantic dreams. But he was, at heart, an orderly man who could sniff the skirts of chaos on any wind. "Why don't you tell me exactly what your offer *would* require of me."

The stranger brushed the golden hair back from his forehead. "It would require exactly one sheet of paper each month of the year, on which would be detailed the dates, destinations, and contents of all of Gerson's shipments from Pireaus."

"But that's illegal. It's impossible. We can't give out information on munitions shipments. The last one who did is still in jail."

The stranger nodded, indicating sympathy with the problem, and placed a photograph beside Phillips's gimlet. "If our first offer is unsatisfactory, this is our second."

Phillips suddenly wished he had less alcohol in him and, at the same time, craved a fast double. He recognized himself immediately, even at the peculiar angle. And he remembered the man. It was the one in the felt hat who approached him in a public park where he sometimes ate lunch. He had wondered why he never saw the man again. "This is blackmail!"

"That's just a word, Mr. Phillips," the stranger said calmly. "Call it as easily 'payment for services rendered.'"

"No, I can't do that. It's not in me to do that."

"Fine," replied the stranger as he got up and dropped a few bills on the table for the drinks. "You need time to think about it. Decisions like this should never be rushed. I'll visit you tomorrow."

Phillips left his home before dawn the next morning, hung over, bleary-eyed, and desperate. He'd call in sick when he reached the shore. He had to get where nobody could find him. He needed a day by the water to think. That fucking pig! A thousand dollars would do him a lot of good in a cell. What the hell was he going to do? This may be the time to just totally disappear. But if there was no way to trace the information, how would they ever catch him? And who were they, for Christ's sake? Those miserable photographs—his supervisor would love one of them below the calendar. How long would he last after that got flashed around? Not very goddamned long!

He drove for two hours. The long pebble beach was empty and the water was quiet when he got there. Just what he needed. A slender, well-built young man in swimming trunks came over and sat near him. Phillips looked around. *What the hell! An empty beach and he crowds me.* He walked on the firm, wet sand by the waterline, where a few sandpipers scurried back and forth. He glanced around. The young man was behind him. *Not today, Junior!* He decided to get back in his car and drive on. He didn't need this nonsense. Not today. The path from the beach to the parking lot led through a stand of pines. A breeze was coming off the sea and whistled through them. It was a sound he hadn't heard in years. Someone was standing in the path up ahead. Not moving. Phillips thought of cutting through the trees to get to his car and then he looked behind him. The kid was still there, keeping a steady twenty yards away. A tree branch snapped above him and Phillips almost jumped off the path. Jesus Christ! He was wired tight, but a few more minutes and he'd be out of there. He heard the motor behind him and recognized the stranger ahead at the same time. He was wearing a T-shirt and tight jeans and he was waiting.

"Have you come to a decision, Mr. Phillips?"

"Hey! What is this? I can't decide anything that important overnight. You said yourself I needed time."

The stranger wore no turquoise or rings but carried worry beads and flipped them quietly. "Is there information you need, or is it simply worry that's postponing your decision?"

"Yes. Who are you? Who do you work for? How can I trust that you'll do what you say?"

"If it would help, we'll pay you a year in advance."

"I've got to think about it. I'll tell you something tomorrow."

"I'm afraid we need the first month's information today."

Phillips looked and sounded bewildered. "Today! I obviously can't get it today. I already called in sick."

The stranger smiled. "I suppose an inventive man might find a way. Let's walk on the beach."

Phillips considered bolting for the car but gave up the idea. His hope for survival lay, as it did in the office, in some form of limited cooperation. As they cleared the pines, he saw a motorboat churning up and down the coast at incredible speeds, as much out of the water as in it. When they appeared, it dropped speed and idled toward them.

"You're going water skiing."

"I don't know how."

The stranger shrugged. "You'll pick it up." He pointed to the young man walking toward the boat. "Go with him."

Phillips followed. He actually skied well, but didn't understand the game they were playing. At the waterline, the young man held a rope and began to tie his hands. "No!" he yelled, broke away, and ran down the beach. When he stopped, out of breath, and looked around, he saw the young man kneeling, watching him, as were the two men in the boat, which was rocking twenty-five yards offshore. The stranger was coming toward him. He heard the rocks scratching under his boots as he walked slowly across the pebble beach. He looked frantically for other people, other boats—anything. Bent by fear, he crouched slightly as if preparing to wrestle.

"Please relax, Mr. Phillips. All these reactions are primitive. There's no reason for self-torture. Think of yourself as a trapped animal. We're offering you freedom, goodwill, and a great deal of money. If you turn us down, we will have to kill you. Be clear on that. You can even choose the method: water skiing with hands tied, a beach burial, a quick knife—it makes no difference to us if that's your choice. It offends only because it's a stupid way to die. The important thing is to know that you're trapped and that you've been offered freedom. A healthy animal wouldn't hesitate."

Phillips hesitated and barely saw the stranger's quick, slashing move, felt his head slam into stones, and his arms pulling from their sockets. His vision blurred but he knew the stranger was walking away, someone else was tying his hands, and the motorboat was roaring angrily. The pressure was building up in his head but he couldn't swallow, couldn't relieve it. The beach began to move beneath him, slowly at first, then faster and faster, tearing at his head and body with a thousand blunt, terrible blows. He was being dragged across the rocks toward the water and he was screaming, "No! Don't! Please!" A wave caught him across the shoulders, cold and hard, and rolled him facedown. The boat surged forward. He screamed, wild with fear, but he couldn't get his face out, couldn't get his mouth up, couldn't get the words out, and inside his head he heard someone shouting, "I can't breathe! I can't breathe!" Then he was coughing, gasping, wanting to throw up. His arms still pulled over his head, but his body lay on sand.

The stranger's voice reached him from above: "Mr. Phillips, have you decided?"

His head scraped back and forth on the sand in a sick frenzy. "Yes, yes!" he cried. "Yes, God, yes!"

Later that night, the stranger talked quietly from a public phone. "Negotiations were successful and we have the first list. There's a shipment next week that will particularly interest you. A breakthrough, I'd say. Kallos? Last I heard Varga had departed for other islands and peace was restored. Why . . . ? Oh? When did he call you? How interesting he told you about that. Well, Forticos remains the two-bit flunky. When you talk to him again, tell him I said the card in the wallet wasn't self-indulgent—it was stylish. He won't understand that, but my challenge will give his brain a creaky turn or two before he goes back to polishing his badge. You can also tell him that when I get your job, he's the first to go.''

"No, I'm happy to say I've heard nothing. The reporter and I had our difficulties and I'm glad he's gone, so I'd expect him to call you, if anyone.'' When Simonedes hung up, he realized he had just lied to Forticos for the first time in all the years they had known each other. More forward motion on life's pilgrimage. He had, in fact, talked to Varga the previous night, immediately prior to the younger man's departure for Detroit. The abbot removed his heavy glasses, laid them carefully on the bedstand beside him, and massaged his smarting eyes. Was it better or worse that rough Dimitrios had come and smashed his ironclad ignorance? Perhaps worse, though he felt guilty to think so. No, it must be better to live in the real world. He shook his head wearily. That at least seemed to be the proper answer. Truth always was better than falsehood. Yes? Yes, he supposed so, but he was tired all the same. And when he wasn't tired, he was angry. The Fragments had been stolen. Yes, the truth was a wonderful thing. He stared vacantly out the window of his study, choosing to fix on the blurs and indistinctions there rather than on the vivid, sharp lines of the enormous problem that faced him. He had finally agreed with Varga not to report the Fragments' disappearance. The inevitable publicity would only alert the thieves, who had every reason to believe their crime had gone exactly as planned—undetected. Varga wanted two months to move on his own. If he found nothing in that time, then national officials would have to be notified. And what a glorious day that would be! Politicians would launch special investigations, reporters would swarm over monastery grounds, editors would denounce church security, and the abbot would have to answer to all of them. He put on his glasses and peered curiously at the desk calendar. September 20. At least the next two months would be quiet ones. But then . . . ! He realized it was the prospect of having a little time to prepare himself for the onslaught that finally led him to agree to his silent pact with Varga, not any hope that the man could recover the Fragments or identify the thieves in two or twenty months. How could he hope to find them? What could be gained by a long flight to Detroit and a conversation with Santry, pleasant as that might be? The abbot shrugged and got up from his chair. He wanted to walk. His spirit was as stiff as his bones and needed limbering.

It was unusual for him—or anyone on Kallos, for that matter—to be out so late at night. The streets of the ancient village ran to the fields and its rhythms were set by the sun. Simonedes ordinarily got up at dawn and so most nights by nine or ten he lay quietly in bed. But on the rare nights that worry or anger kept him awake, he'd take a short walk and end it, always, in the monastery garden, where he would sit and let his mind drift among the shadows. The garden, of course, was choked not with weeds or even flowers but with memories. His daughter, born before he entered the priesthood, had wandered there. He saw her tottering down the walk, arms reaching toward him, just past the trees where he found Varga, near the bench where Santry sat, by the roses that Peter used to tend. The roses were still there, but Peter, a young monk of exceptional tenderness, died the year Simonedes turned fifty—over twenty years ago.

A sudden spot of light intruded in his reveries and distracted him from garden shadows. It had come from the administration offices of the monastery. Only once, but it *had* come. Quickly. On and off. As if someone jerked a switch rapidly up and down. The building was now settled in darkness as deep as the garden's. He looked around, trying to imagine a distant light reflecting briefly on the administration building's windows or even shining through from the other side where the village road wandered. Impossible. The light had come from within. But of those who had any reason to be there, he was the only one who ever went at night. He wondered if he should go back to his room and call someone. Or awaken another priest. No, no need to excite others. He'd remain where he was and watch. But there were lower-level doors out of sight on the other side of the building. If he stayed where he was, he could watch for a long time and see nothing at all.

Why, he asked himself, was he being so fearfully timid, knowing, even as he irritated himself with the question, exactly why. The physical beating on August 1, brief as it was, had smashed him unconscious and given him a broken wrist, a swollen face, and an old body that ached in every nerve. He had used up all his capacity for pain. He didn't wail or even talk about it in front of others, but the pain had filled his mind's eye, threatening him, telling him in no uncertain terms about a boundary over which he didn't want to go again. He was being overly dramatic, he told himself. Even so, he knew he didn't want to get beaten again. The warning corollary followed: Don't go looking for trouble.

Yet a light had flashed. He couldn't erase the memory, cover his eyes, and slink back to bed, but he could watch from some safe, unobserved distance. He got up and walked from the garden, down the slight incline past the museum and toward the modern administration building. He dismissed the idea of entering the building quietly and surprising the intruder, fearing that *he* would end up getting the surprise. If great age had not brought wisdom, it had at least freed him from the courageous pretensions of the young. And the wise place for him was not on the path of dangerous encounters, but under the sheltering boughs of an enormous plane tree, where his black robe and the tree's massive trunk would merge into one and hide his fragile body. From that dark, secluded spot, he could observe anyone leaving the monastery grounds from any building. He stayed in shadow while moving slowly toward that vantage point, looking frequently behind and stopping often to listen for strange noises. He had almost reached the tree when he heard a sudden scraping noise. He whirled and, at the same time, stooped low, almost kneeling. The lower rear door of the administration building, less than seventy-five yards away, had swung open. There were two of them. Thank God he hadn't gone in there by himself. And they were coming his way. He pressed himself against the tree, stared out, and watched incredulously as they passed less then one hundred feet from his impromptu blind, ignorant of his presence, whispering hushed words, and soon disappearing down the steep road that led to the village.

They were gone, but a great disturbance threatened him, and, suddenly, as from a great distance above him, he saw himself cowering in the shadows of the tree and heard himself cry, "Enough! Enough! Enough!" Lower limbs scratched against his face as he ran stiffly toward open ground, out of hiding, furious at himself for playing the innocent, peace-keeping, innocuous, good-willed abbot. "What's going on!" he demanded of himself and the night. "I'm in hiding and they're walking in and out as if they own the place!" His raised arms trembled beside his face and his fists clenched as he vowed, "Enough! Nothing's worth this!"

Within the hour, the abbot stood in front of Stelios, his finger jabbing the air between them, his voice sharp and rasping. "Listen to me, Judas! Forty years now I've counted you as a friend. We met when your children were baptized, we drank at their weddings, we cried together when your wife died, I gave you a job and the keys to the monastery because I trusted you. '*Adelphos mou*, my brother,' you called me, and so I never suspected, never once, not even when Dimitrios Varga saw you leaving his room. 'Impossible!' I told him. Never Stelios, never *adelphos mou*. Brothers do not deceive brothers. Oh, maybe in the cities, but not here, not on the islands where we still have the old ways, the family ways, the way of a man's hand and a man's word. Forty years I've known Stelios! Impossible! Yes, that's what I told him. And one hour ago, this man's weak eyes saw you sneaking away from the monastery with Demos Forticos and this poor man's mouth finally opened and said, 'Enough!'

"So listen to me, Stelios, and don't go scrabbling among the cinders of your mind looking for excuses or explanations, because there is no way to make this right. There is only one thing to be done, and that is to end it all. No! I'm sick to death of the lying, the deceit, the intrigue, the . . . yes, I will name it for you, Stelios, I'm sick of demons reversing everything natural. The rivers are running uphill in Kallos. Thieves wander freely. Good men inflict speechlessness on themselves, and for the sake of a few drachmas, a brother makes a brother bleed!"

Suddenly tired, Simonedes slumped into a chair and turned his face away from his old friend.

"You're finished at the monastery and I'm filing a complaint against you and Demos in the morning. You can tell your lies to the police and the courts."

"No! It would be dangerous to do that to Forticos."

Simonedes hadn't expected that tone from Stelios. Apologies, maybe; pleadings, probably; but not warnings.

"I mean it, John. He could hurt you."

"You should have thought of that before you began robbing me."

"I never took a thing. Not a fig. Not a rose. Just information and a few pictures with Demos's camera. I didn't see how any of that hurt anybody, and I needed the money. I'd never do anything against you, Father, never. In your heart you know that's the truth. Demos said it was routine police work—like being his deputy."

"Pictures? What pictures?"

"Of a priest this summer. I don't know why."

"Which priest?"

"I don't know his name. American—he was at the conference."

"What else?"

"Very little."

"What else!" Simonedes demanded.

"Between us? Your word?"

Simonedes heard a trapdoor swinging open on an unseen, unsuspected room. He looked critically at the grizzled, bent man beside him and remembered a proud, handsome father, head swathed in a bright scarf, riding a mule. The mule was dead now. Stelios wasn't far behind. "Yes, between us."

"Varga's luggage and things on your desk."

Simonedes flared, "How long has this been going on?"

"Since you got hurt."

"What were you looking for on my desk?"

"Anything about the Fragments and what happened August 1. He told me you were working with him on the investigation, but you were busy and sometimes missed things."

"And did you find anything?"

"Nothing. That's why it didn't bother me enough to tell you or to stop. I never had anything to tell him except that I hadn't found anything, and he kept giving me money, very good money, so I thought, why not keep looking?"

"Why did he go with you tonight?"

"I don't know. He either doesn't trust me or he's looking for something he doesn't think I'd see. We weren't in there twenty minutes. He sorted through your mail and took some telephone numbers you had written on your calendar. It all amounted to nothing. You should do the same with it: nothing."

Simonedes's confusion doubled with every revelation. Photos of Santry? Varga's luggage? His mail? What were they looking for? He had cooperated fully with the police. It didn't make any sense. Then, with something of a start, he realized that the one man in the world he most wanted to talk to at that moment was Dimitrios Varga. He'd know what to do. He'd at least know what to suspect. Varga was blessed with great suspicions. "Stelios, when a man breaks into your house, do you ignore him and hope he stops? Of course not. You stop him. And if you can't do it yourself, you go to the police. You understand me?"

Stelios moved uncomfortably in his chair. "Oh, I understand what you're saying. The problem is that Demos Forticos is . . . well, I don't think he's alone." Stelios leaned forward in his chair, as if worried about being overheard. "What I mean is—tonight when we were walking away from the monastery, I said in a kidding kind of way that I hoped the mysterious 'G' wasn't hiding out there in the bushes waiting to jump us the way he did Varga. Well, Forticos just laughed at that and told me I didn't need to worry about 'G.' And that's all he said, but underneath the laugh and the words, it sounded like he knew all about that man."

Simonedes shook his head from side to side, as if to clear it, fighting off his confusion. His racing heart and a strange tightening of the lips worried him. "Stelios, let us think about this together. Varga thinks he was assaulted to warn him away from Kallos. If he's right and if you're right about the lieutenant and 'G,' it means they may be working together to block, not to complete, any investigation of August 1. Why? We don't know except that they must have something to lose if what happened then is fully understood."

And as he said the words, perhaps because he said the words, Simonedes began to suspect that Forticos was somehow involved in the theft of the Fragments and that "G" had been the man who bolted from the shadows, broke his wrist, and beat him to the ground.

"Stelios, I'm beginning to agree with you. I should do nothing. And you should continue to do what Demos asks, but now every day you and I will have to talk about what we see and what we find and after a while we may even give Lieutenant Forticos and 'G' something to worry about."

Anyone watching might assume that he was showing her a ship in which he had recently purchased majority interest or a warehouse packed to its lofty ventilators with goods being shipped to Thailand or Venezuela, because the striking couple standing on the deck of the *Sea Plow*, a freighter docked in Piraeus, the great port of Athens, had the look of active wealth and easy command. She had turned away from the long yellow arm of the loading crane that absorbed him, moved to the ship's railing, and looked down on the swirling lines of heavy trucks spewing road dust and diesel smoke over tangled cars, people, and cargo waiting jammed on the piers, wharves, and access roads below. Shouting stevedores and peddlers competed for attention with horns, music blaring from a nearby kiosk, and angry motors.

His eyes, however, rarely wandered from the crane or the enormous wooden boxes it lifted from the adjacent pier, swung high over the freighter's side, and lowered gently into the dark hold. But when the last boxes had settled into place, he walked to her side at the ship's railing, touched a wisp of hair that fell attractively across her forehead, and said, "We have two hours, Gabriella."

The late-afternoon sun streamed through a sudden rift in the clouds, showered on the people gathering to board a nearby cruiser to the Aegean islands, and swept across their faces. His was the more tranquil. Hers was darker in color and in mood. His edged toward insolence and pride, hers toward tension and bitterness. Few things made her truly happy, but some brought intense pleasure. She smiled, raised a slender golden arm toward his face, and placed a finger on his slightly parted lips. "Let's go below," she told him.

The two had been lovers for a few years, and despite the usual difficulties, their relationship had succeeded where most failed or floundered. Their coupling had become more, not less, intense, an unusual circumstance due, in large part, to their insistence on mixing business with pleasure. The combination wouldn't work for all, but their business was unusually exciting, so they gained from the spillover effect. Even more, their business was exciting because it was dangerous, so dangerous that any reference to it served as a powerful reminder of how often they were threatened by death, separation, and ultimate loss, a combination that rarely failed to intensify breath, light, and sex.

Larus had worked for Andreas Korachis since 1980 but saw him rarely. That was not unusual. Only two people in the organization saw Korachis with any regularity: Gabriella Antissa and Savonon, his director of field operations. Burly, no-nonsense Savonon first heard about Larus in the Golden Horn Hotel in Nairobi where he was meeting prospective clients from Zanzibar. After only three nights of heavy duty at the hotel's ornate, trophy-rimmed bar, he had heard fourteen different versions of how a man known only as "G" for "Ghost" had decimated the entire security system of a large isolated prison and led four well-known political detainees to safety. It took three months but Savonon had tracked him down and flown him to Athens for extended talks with Korachis. Gabriella watched from a distance for a year or two, knowing that eventually their time would come. Even the first year, they were together twice a week for lessons. She taught him Greek, then changed clothes and roles to follow his lead in the martial arts. She liked his coolness, his quiet, controlled arrogance and physical grace. She moved as beautifully, but with the consciousness of a model on the runway. He moved as if alone, unseen in the dark, the way a leopard stalks. And she liked the stalking, the uncertainties and quick reversals. Each of them was a hunter, each sought prey, and each knew there was some of that tricky excitement between them.

One morning Korachis called her from Mitilini. "You may not know that he's leaving today." Their attraction had never been concealed, so there could be no confusion about who was leaving. "He will be involved in very dangerous work for an extended period. I thought it important that you know."

She called Larus immediately and arranged to meet at a hotel near Athens's airport. The room would be in her name. She would be waiting. In her own time and way, she had decided to move on him. He was gone for six weeks but returned safely and full of praise for long afternoons in airport hotels as the only necessary preparation for journeys. They were together frequently after that, but always, ritualistically, before a trip—and as close to the place and time of departure as possible.

The porthole of his cabin on the *Sea Plow* opened to the east, away from the setting sun, so she lay in muted light, her dark body looking even darker against the uncompromising white of sheets and pillows. She wore only his turquoise beads in a single strand that traced a serpent's way from the black hair falling about her face, across small, well-formed breasts, and the smooth plane above the pelvic rise. His body, longer, fuller, stretched beside hers, one hand under the beads, smooth against her skin. Her thin fingers threaded casually through his hair.

"The *Sea Plow* sails west at seven, and straight for Gibraltar," he told her. "When it clears the Mediterranean, it's scheduled to turn south, run the coast of Africa to Nigeria, then unload and return." He stopped and asked, "You saw the boxes being loaded?"

"Yes," she said, stretching her leg across his stomach and straddling him. "All stamped L. P. Gerson. The *Sea Plow* has taken on munitions." She moved against him, lowered herself, and watched his eyes. Her hair fell toward his face and her eyes closed as he wrapped his legs around her and kneaded the muscles in her back—tight, always tight, always better for his touch. She took long slow breaths, felt the tension easing, let her head drift down along his shoulder, drowsy, her mouth open against his neck. "And what happens now?"

"I'm one of twelve scheduled passengers, but the only one on board when the ship sails. The others are technically no-shows. In fact, they don't exist. We bought every space." Her arm reached down his leg. The nails of one hand scratched lightly on his skin. "Late tonight between one and two, I'll enter the cargo hold, dismiss anyone on duty there, wait quietly for a minute or two, and tap gently on four of the L. P. Gerson boxes. Those inside, sixteen in all, four to a box, will be happy to see me, no doubt having wondered what would happen to them if I hadn't paid attention to the loading and made sure that four boxes of munitions hadn't been lowered on top of the ship's new crew."

He eased off her, watched her stretch, eyes still closed, back slightly arched, breasts raised, inviting. His hands moved along her edges as she reached and held him. He took a long, slow breath.

"Every man knows his assignment, each has intimate knowledge of the ship, and each is armed." He stopped, leaned over, and kissed her breasts, felt the ache deeper. "We'll be in command within an hour and follow the same route to Nigeria. Observing planes or boats will see nothing unusual. But the night before reaching there, we'll drop off course, anchor, display lights, and wait for a pilot boat to lead us into port. I should be right where I am now within twenty-four hours after delivery."

She took the turquoise beads, looped one end about his neck, and raised herself to meet him. "Right where?" she asked.

"Right here," he whispered, driving deeply, steadily deeper against the ache. "Right here! Right here!"

They took their parting drink in the ship's small lounge. A steward brought the Scotch and then left. Gabriella asked about Kallos. He told her briefly about Varga and his pledge to Savonon that Forticos would be the first to go when he took over field operations.

"You shouldn't count on that," she told him.

He frowned and waited. Their two-year assumption had been that when Savonon retired, Larus was the obvious choice.

"Andreas may want someone else. I can't say more."

"Do you know more?"

"A little."

"Then I want to hear it."

She looked at him curiously, as one might look at an intemperate child, sipped her Scotch, and stared out the window at the metal sides of the ship in the next berth. "If I could tell you, I would."

"I thought you were free to do and say what you want."

"I am," she said, her head rising slightly and her eyes darkening. "And when I say I will keep something in confidence, I do." She turned back toward the window. "No one ever said that job was yours. You and I thought it was a good idea, but it may not work out that way."

His hand slipped quietly through the turquoise beads around his neck as he said evenly, "I've met most of them, Gabriella, and not one can keep up with me." He reached over suddenly and shook her arm. "Look at me! Don't say a word, don't break any promises to His Holiness, but look at me!"

She turned angrily, her eyes on the hand that shook her.

He withdrew it slowly, leaned back, and said, "He's bringing in an outsider, isn't he? Yes, that's exactly what he plans to do. And the outsider's name is Alexander Ross. Am I right?"

Gabriella said nothing, but her lips parted in a light, triumphant smile as she got up and walked from the room.

Chapter Five

The stranger sat in the back, off to one side, alone. He had been in church Sunday but left before the service ended. He was heavyset with a broad face, thick hair, a great bushy moustache, and bristling brows. Michael Santry, who stood in the front of the room going over the agenda with the meeting's chairman, turned to the black woman standing nearby and said quietly, "Betty, check out the stranger in the back, will you, please?"

She, too, had seen him the minute she walked into the room. In fact, if Santry had turned to any of the sixty or seventy people in the community center and asked, "Who's the stranger?," no one could have told him, but everyone could say exactly where he sat. Betty Forbes eased away and moved down the aisle, reaching out, touching, and talking to people the whole time. "Hey, girl, how you doin'. . . ? Fine, fine! Glad you came! How's your mama . . . ? Good. Tell her I asked. Yeah, the project's good, eh? Looking very good! You want some hot coffee? C'mon with me. Doughnuts, too. Fat? You blind? Lean as a bean, woman. I could use some fat!" She rolled her eyes, tossed her hips, laughed, and moved on. Eyes, smiles, and chuckles trailed her like gulls after a fishing boat. She checked the sign-in sheet. Sixty-three names and not a stranger on it. She stood beside smooth Percy at the coffee table and looked over the backs of people's heads toward the front. "Good turnout, eh, Percy?"

"They smell the money," he said sourly, offended by the sudden increase in attendance.

"You bet your ass," she told him, smoothing her red dress down one long thigh. "And it's one helluva smell after all these years of nuthin' 'round here." She sipped sugared black coffee from a white Styrofoam cup. "You ever seen the dude before?"

Percy stared straight ahead, arms folded across his chest. "No. Nobody's seen him before. See you later?"

"If you wait. Mike'll want to go over the meeting."

She said good-bye by leaning into him, shoulder and hip grazing his, bright red against blue jeans, very lightly, just a touch. *Nice,* he thought, *yeah, very, very nice.* His eyes went up and down the length of her as she moved across the back of the room and stood beside the stranger. Checking them was routine as coffee, a sign-in sheet, and the agenda printed in big block letters on the blackboard up front.

"Hi, I'm Betty Forbes. Like some coffee?"

The stranger got to his feet, took the extended hand, returned the smile, and thanked her. "Yes, coffee. Good." He followed her to the table and took his with milk. "No, no doughnut, thank you." He laid a large hand on an ample paunch and shrugged, as if to say that a life with no sweets was sad but that the time had come to show restraint.

"What's your name?" She asked the question directly, looking him over, and keeping it light and easy.

"I'm sorry, I should have said. My name's Dimitrios Varga. I was in church on Sunday and read the announcement about this meeting. Is it all right for me to be here?"

"Open meetings, Mr. Varga. You're welcome. You don't live around here, do you?"

"No, no, I live in Greece. Athens. Just a tourist— I'm here only for a short time."

"How in the world did you ever get from Greece to St. Jude's on Sunday?"

"Yes, I see the puzzle." His manner was easy and his English fluent. He sounded to Betty Forbes a little like the old Italian men who used to work at Chrysler. "Well, I read about your priest in the Athens newspapers when he was in Greece this summer and I thought, well, while I'm here I'll go and meet him."

She was surprised. "He made the Greek papers?"

"Yes. You didn't know?"

She shook her head and watched his olive-black, shining eyes while waiting for more. He told her, "Yes, the Father rescued a Greek treasure and saved the head of an important monastery from harm. They said many fine things about him."

Forbes laughed, clapped her brown hands, and looked toward Santry, in the front of the room. "That's him, all right, that's just like him. He never mentioned it and never would. We got to talk more, Mr. Varga—just you and me. Stay after the meeting. I want to hear about Greece, and I know Father'll want to meet you."

A heavy woman three rows in front of Forbes was waving a handkerchief and calling, "Pssst! Betty! Betty! Hey, child, c'mere!"

Up front the tall chairman, a teacher at Martin Luther King High School, was trying to get the meeting started. "If everyone will please take their seats . . ."

Forbes motioned to the woman and mouthed, "After the meeting, okay?" She saw the chairman waiting for her, flashed a quick smile at Percy, in the back, hurried down the aisle, and slid into the seat Santry had saved for her. And as the room quieted and the chairman reviewed the agenda for the meeting of the East Side Community Organization, she leaned close to the priest and whispered what she had learned.

Santry listened, then turned slowly in his seat and looked back, finding the stranger's eyes, as expected, on him. He nodded quietly and offered a welcoming smile. The stranger returned the nod and the slightest of smiles. Too slight, Santry thought. Too slight a smile, too bold a look, too improbable a story. Much too improbable. He wasn't even trying. A wandering Greek just looking up the priest who had been honored in his country? Not likely. Santry heard the voice vote approving the secretary's minutes and the chairman's call for the treasurer's report.

It was early October. In the six weeks since Greece, Santry had moved through remorse and fear to acceptance. The remorse hadn't lasted long, but the fear surprised him. It came as he considered a likely future: excommunicated, cut off from the Church and the people he loved, imprisoned without a noble cause, exposed as naïve, impatient, and untrustworthy—a failed priest, lumped in people's minds with alcoholics and pederasts. He had never wanted or worked to be honored by all men, but, if found out, he would lose the favor of even those few whose esteem he did need. Of course, some of them would remain loyal. They'd visit and write, but when together they'd shake their heads, remember the man he used to be, and wonder where he had lost his way. That would be very hard to handle because the object of pitying, misty-eyed loyalty could only be the pitiful. Something like acceptance followed the remorse and fear. If he had been wrong, it had been for decent reasons. And if those motives were misunderstood, it wouldn't be the first or last time. The food factory would get its chance. A great many people would be helped. *Lay down the worries,* he told himself. *One day's evil at a time.*

He heard the chairman call his name and glanced at the agenda. Betty Forbes swung her legs to one side so he could pass. At the podium, Santry saw Varga leaning forward in his chair, elbows on his knees, head up. He saw no accusation or anger in his broad, inquiring face. Only a searching intelligence and unusual interest. The priest smiled at the slight, illusory relief he experienced and proceeded with his report. Yes, as the documents in their hands made clear, the organization had at least enough money to get the food factory started, and the executive committee had hired a business consultant to guide the project through its early phases. Everyone should be pleased and everyone should be prepared to work even harder. He detailed specific tasks that had to be accomplished in the next four months and said that Betty Forbes would be contacting people with suggested assignments. He assumed everyone would cooperate because, he noted, "This is the chance we've all wanted, and it is almost certainly the last chance we'll get."

When he asked for questions, Varga surprised him by getting to his feet, and everyone's head turned to see the unknown man in the back of the room. "Father Santry, am I allowed to ask a question?" He had a good voice, deep and pleasant.

Santry said immediately, in his quiet, comfortable way, "Forgive me for not introducing you earlier." His eyes moved across the room. "Friends, this is Mr. Dimitrios Varga—I hope I've got that right—who is a traveler from Greece, a country you know I visited this summer. He and I have not talked yet, but Betty assured him that all of us welcome him. Of course, Mr. Varga, you may ask anything you want."

Varga, whose coat was draped over his heavy shoulders, smiled back at the people looking at him, gave a quick tilt of his head to one side, and thanked them for allowing him to come to their meeting. His manner was modest and engaging as he apologized, unnecessarily, for his poor English. "I'm very happy to read this report that you gave me because I like the food factory very much. It is a big idea. I wish we had such a factory in Greece. My question is, how do you pay for it? And where do you find the money?"

A light wave of favorable fluttering ran through the group because the stranger had been complimentary, polite, and asked a reasonable question. Santry, externally as polished and low-key as ever, explained that after six months of fund-raising, they had almost given up because less than fifty thousand dollars had been pledged, but last summer a prominent Detroit businessman took up their cause and secured a commitment for several million dollars. One of the terms of the gift, however, was that the donors remain anonymous. He added the reassurance that, "It's the only string he attached."

Varga, unexpectedly, remained on his feet. "Yes, thank you for the answer, Father. May I ask just one more. The way an organization like this works and the way secrets are kept, how many people know the giver of the money?"

Santry replied evenly, "At this point, I am the only one who knows the name of the donor." He looked into the faces watching him and added, "I am not entirely comfortable with that fact, but it was a necessary condition and the members of the organization urged me to go ahead."

Scattered affirmations were heard across the room. "Yes!" "That's right!"

Heads nodded vigorously, and one or two swung in their seats to stare at the outsider and make sure he didn't think they weren't informed or that they had any questions about the way Father Santry was handling the deal.

"Anything else, Mr. Varga?" Santry asked amiably.

Varga squinted against the smoke unfurling from the cigarette he held close to his face. "Maybe one thing, please. I am wondering why you said nothing to your friends about the Ephesian Fragments."

It was, Santry thought, either an exceptionally insensitive and blunt, even rude, question, or exceptionally bold. The man, whoever he was, was either attempting to ingratiate himself, trying to win the priest's favor by calling attention to his honored role in saving the Fragments, or he was issuing a public, though veiled, accusation. He studied the standing figure in the last row and felt an unanticipated, strange pleasure in the thought that Varga might be the man of his worst dreams. "I'm afraid I don't understand your question, Mr. Varga."

There was a sudden flash of red to Santry's left as Betty Forbes got up and told everybody, "I understand it and I can answer it." She turned to Varga. "But to tell you the truth, it's a funny kind of question to ask. Anyway, the answer's simple: Father doesn't flash his medals." She shifted her attention from Varga to the group. "Father saved some kind of Greek treasure this summer and got written up in the papers over there. That's how our visitor heard about him and that's why he came to St. Jude's on Sunday and to the meeting tonight. That's all there is to it." She stared back at Varga as if she wanted to say more, but just shook her head as if it was hard to understand such a dumb question.

Santry had watched Varga closely while Betty Forbes was on her feet explaining everything and saw in his manner no trace of apology, embarrassment, or awkwardness. He seemed, in fact, to be barely listening, sat sideways in his chair, one leg crossed over the other, smoking, his face actually turned away toward the wall, absorbed, it seemed, in his own thoughts.

Sometime later in the meeting, Betty leaned over and said, "Mike, your Greek man just slipped out the door. You want Percy on him?"

Santry nodded and Betty turned in her chair to give the signal.

Two days later, Santry got a call from a reporter at the *Detroit News*. He was a Catholic and a friend. "Hey, Mike, Charlie here. I wanted you to know that a guy carrying press cards from a couple of Athens papers and calling himself Dimitrios Varga has been in here reading your file and asking questions. . . ." They talked for a few minutes. Then the reporter said, "Yeah, I could do that. No problem."

The reporter called again the next day and told Santry, "If the Varga we're talking about in Detroit is the Varga they know about in Athens—and the descriptions do fit—then your man's an investigative journalist. My contact says he's one of the best and knows what he's doing. He was surprised to learn that he was over here. Why's he so interested in you?"

Santry told him about Kallos and the near-riot at the Festival of St. Paul, adding, "It hardly seems enough to bring a journalist the whole way to Detroit."

The reporter agreed. "It's not. He's got to have some other angle on you. Could be a liberation theology hit. The Pope's putting the heat on your Sandinista friends in Nicaragua. If he's working on that, the views of North American priests would be useful."

Santry told his friend he was probably right, thanked him again, and slowly returned the phone to its cradle. He reached immediately for his cigarettes, glanced out the window of his church office, and told himself that Charlie was certainly wrong. A reporter who wanted his views on engagé priests did not get them through a series of mysterious, back-pew appearances and offensive questions about the Ephesian Fragments. What did he know about Varga? Little. He was a Greek journalist staying at the Pontchartrain Hotel. That was about it. Percy had followed him there, followed him right into the Salamander Lounge off the lobby, and watched him through two beers. Beyond that, he knew nothing. Santry crushed his cigarette in the glass tray near the phone. It was only one o'clock in the afternoon and he had already gone through a pack. *At least Varga's not the police. Or is he? Any collusion is imaginable these days.* But certainly Ross would have called immediately if the theft were even suspected. True, if Ross knew about it. But where was Ross? He had no idea. Couldn't reach him if he wanted to. He watched two boys at the far end of the outdoor basketball court going one on one. Fake to the left, drive to the right. The old tried-and-true. Fake, drive, and never lay back. Santry thought about that for a while, reached for the phone, and dialed the operator. "Yes, I want to place an overseas call."

His phone rang again in thirty minutes. "Hold on, please. We're ready with your party."

"Hello! Hello!"

"Father Simonedes! This is Michael Santry in Detroit." Santry realized with some relief that Simonedes was genuinely excited and pleased to hear his voice. "Yes, I'm fine," Santry told him, "but I've had no news from Greece since I returned and was thinking about you." He heard his voice booming in the high-ceilinged room. The connection was good, but all that distance made it seem necessary to shout. "So how are you? Has your wrist healed?"

"Oh, yes, I'm fine, Michael, but, no, it's been a terrible month. We've been besieged by reporters and there have been a few troubling incidents that I can't talk about over the phone. But we're doing our best. Someday I'll write you a long letter and tell you all about it. I'd love to get your thoughts on a number of things, Michael. I do miss our talks."

"I hope you will write. I'd be very interested. Father Simonedes, does the name Dimitrios Varga mean anything to you?"

"Well, yes, Michael, it means a great deal. I was wondering if he had contacted you. I take it he has?"

"Yes and no. He's in Detroit and has come to one of our community meetings, but he hasn't stayed to talk to me. He appears and disappears. Who is he?"

"He's a journalist. And he's a good one, though he can drive you crazy. At least, he almost drove me crazy. But Michael, he's forceful and extremely perceptive. A very clever man. He discovered things here that I'm still having trouble believing, but there's no real doubt left.

When he arrived, he struck me as the most disagreeable person I had ever met, but he won me over. In the strangest of ways, he's almost a friend. Yes, you can trust him, Michael."

"But I don't know if I'll see him again."

"Oh, you'll see him! He won't leave Detroit without talking to you. You can count on that."

"Can you give me an idea of what he discovered that you had trouble believing?"

"I wish I could, believe me, but I'll have to write you about it. Better yet, when you see Varga, tell him we talked and that I think you should be told everything. He'll know what I mean. But when you hear it, you won't believe it either. Yet it's true, Michael. What he'll tell you is fantastic but absolutely true."

Santry stared at the phone for a long time after hanging up. His day may have come. Over the past twenty years, he had been with hundreds of people on the day they got the news, the paralyzing word, the shattering report from friends, doctors, newscasts, telephones: "I'm sorry, but the tumor . . ."; "The man is armed and dangerous . . ."; "The boy said when he woke up and saw the flames . . ."; "Hello, this is the police department, there's been an accident . . ."; "We'll do all we can to relieve the pain, but . . ." He had seen many others on bent, disfigured days when their orbit suddenly shifted and life's hopes collapsed like a huge tent when the ax was laid to the ropes. *The theft may have been discovered, but they're saying nothing, telling no one. That's why Ross doesn't know and hasn't called. But they don't know much either—or at least Simonedes doesn't. The good abbot actually wants Varga to tell me everything. And Varga? He's sure of nothing, but he knows who was nearest Simonedes when the Fragments were seized, and he knows who yelled, "I have them!" So he must be probing, chipping here and there on a mountain of conjecture, hoping to strike a few loose rocks, dislodge them, and start a slide. Fake, drive, and never lay back.*

He called the Pontchartrain Hotel and asked for Dimitrios Varga. There was no answer from his room. "I'd like to leave a message. Tell him to call Father Michael Santry at St. Jude's."

But Varga did not return the call and Santry did not try again, certain that the journalist would show his face, if not his hand, within a few days. It happened on Friday night in St. Jude's parish house. Santry came down from his room on the second floor and there he was, exhibiting his curious predilection for the left edge of the back row. It was a meeting of the Latin American Peace Committee, a citywide group of Catholics with a sprinkling of liberal Protestants who gathered monthly for study. The speaker that night, as announced in the church bulletin on Sunday, was Sister Mary Margaret Quinn, recently returned from El Salvador, where the government accused her of illegal activity in support of the guerrillas.

Santry walked directly to Varga, extended his hand, and told him, "You disappeared the other night before we could talk. If this meeting doesn't go too late, let's have a drink afterward."

Varga said he'd like that very much. Neither man said anything about the unreturned call, and Santry said nothing about his conversation with Simonedes. Standing together, the two men looked the same height, but Varga's weight and thick, unruly hair gave him a slightly disheveled appearance. Santry, in contrast, had an old-fashioned, short haircut, clean-shaven face, heavy shoulders, and a body that looked trim and strong. There was something of the old athlete about him, something easy and self-confident, the suggestion of unexcitable strength. Varga was restless by comparison. The priest stood casually, hands in his pockets, eyes either steadily on Varga or down, quietly watching the floor in an attitude of careful attention to what the journalist was saying. When speaking, Varga was rarely still. His great head moved from side to side, his brows arched expressively, and his right hand made small, slow circles in the air.

At the beginning of her remarks to the fifteen people present, Sister Mary Margaret, who had flown in from Milwaukee for the meeting, encouraged interruptions. "Please don't hesitate," she said brightly. "We all know the issues and need to hear from one another. Most of you have traveled in Latin America." She nodded toward a lanky priest on her right and then at Santry. "Jim and Mike both worked in Recife for years." Her quick eyes went next to an older woman in slacks and sandals. "And Helen, you were in Chile during the coup, weren't you?" Right through the small group, she found something to say about each one, even if little more than "You remember the conference in Philadelphia where we met for the first time?" Then she'd laugh a little and recall some after-hours incident. During her report on El Salvador she repeatedly stressed the importance of the work carried on by the people in the room. Santry was delighted to see her again. Her desperate times in Central America—the surveillance, the jails, the interrogations—had not stifled or turned her. There was no hint of grandstanding, not the faintest whiff of sweet saintliness, and a blessed absence of war whoops.

While listening, Santry glanced occasionally at Varga, sure the journalist would try to pry some rocks loose, and saw the reporter's interest quicken as the speaker traced the influences most important to those Christians close to the sister in Central America. He leaned forward as she spoke of Camillo Torres, the Colombian priest who had joined the guerrillas in the mountains of that country and had been killed.

In a pause, Varga broke in. "Sister Mary, do you

think it is morally correct to kill? Do you think justice can be reached through violence?"

"In some situations, unfortunately, I believe it is morally necessary, yes." Her light blue eyes and fair Irish face hovered sadly over the words. "Our work must always be to reduce violence and to build peace, but, yes, there are situations of such terrible oppression, situations in which whole families—really whole generations of the poor—are being killed, that only armed struggle has any chance of saving them. You're from Greece, aren't you? I suppose most Greeks would celebrate those who killed to drive out the Turks, the Italians, and the Germans, wouldn't they?"

Santry saw the clear trajectory of the question, saw it coming straight at him.

Varga pressed on. "So if killing can be morally necessary, as you say, then other things that people think of as bad, like cheating, lying, and stealing, these can also be sometimes necessary, even good?"

"That seems to be the case, doesn't it?" she replied steadily. "I'd even say that's the A, B, C of it, so clear that it's little more than common sense. Certainly there's no rule to guide us in every situation. What mother wouldn't lie to save her child from death? What father wouldn't steal for a hungry family? Such exceptions are commonly recognized, even honored. But you'd never be tempted to make a rule of that either. Action must always be weighted toward building, not tearing down, and prohibitions against killing, lying, and stealing help to preserve life. Generally, they must be observed. But there are exceptions, special circumstances, crises in which love requires good rules to be broken."

Varga studied the smoking end of his cigarette for a moment and looked up, but not at the speaker—at Santry. "And do you believe the same way?"

The question's tone rode the edge between interrogation and accusation, but only Santry guessed its real meaning. He was in the habit of giving direct answers to direct questions, so almost told Varga exactly how and why he agreed, but went a different way. Not to evade the man, but to meet him more directly, he asked, "Why is that important to you, Mr. Varga?"

People who had been making a few notes on Sister Mary's statement stopped writing and looked at Santry. His blunt rejoinder had the sound of a whip crack about it and the meeting's mood of easy amiability shifted toward uncertainty.

Varga didn't hesitate. "Because you were honored by my country, Father. The papers called you a good man, a friend from America." He shrugged and stuffed his cigarette out. "So I'm surprised to hear good people promoting theft and murder. I'm sorry if that offends, but it's important to me. If a friend is able to kill and steal from me, how is he different from my enemy?"

Mary Margaret offered the trace of a conciliatory smile and argued, "But you surely misunderstood what I said. No one here is promoting murder or theft. Year in and year out in anything like normal circumstances, it would be impossible for a Christian to do either. But there are extraordinary times, crises, such as those faced by the Sandinistas, when that which is normally unimaginable becomes the morally responsible action."

Varga settled back in his chair, folded his hands across his broad stomach, and gestured his appreciation to the nun for her words. It was clear that he intended to say nothing more, but she wouldn't let him go. "Is that a useful clarification, Mr. Varga? Don't hesitate to press us."

Most eyes and all attention were now on the journalist, who was rubbing his forehead as if suffering from a headache. "I don't know," he told them. "Looked at one way, I understand what you say, but most of the time, I'm thinking it's exactly like everybody else, only fancier and bolder. For twenty years I've written about corruption, and I know it when I see it. Not many murders, but lots of thievery. I've found many strange hands in the public's pockets, but most of them only worried about getting caught. They didn't even think about the bad and the good of it. Tonight I hear you thinking about it, but you come to the same conclusion. They just say, 'I want it.' You say, 'The poor want it and we'll help them get it.' That's because you're full of love and have the weight of the cross on your shoulders. So I can't decide if your argument's better than what I hear from the ordinary corrupt people I know, or whether it's just got more holy cleverness in it. To me it all sounds a little slippery."

The group rallied predictably to Varga's challenge and several others tried out their own formulations, but he refused to argue. He thanked each in turn but remained silent, and Sister Mary Margaret went on with her presentation. Everyone noticed, of course, when he got up and walked quietly from the room.

Santry thought he might find him waiting outside after the meeting, but the dark, high-ceilinged corridor was as empty as the street and sidewalk beyond the steel-reinforced door. He was pleased and irritated. Pleased because now he was free to have a drink with Mary Margaret, but he and Varga had at least one more round coming before the journalist was out of his life. Even assuming the theft had been discovered and that the journalist suspected him, there was nothing at all linking him directly to the loss beyond his recovery of the fake manuscripts, an act that in itself proved nothing. He had found them at the abbot's side when he fell, thrown there, no doubt, by the unknown man who had seized the original. But Varga had to ask his questions before those explanations could be offered, and Santry was in the mood to get it over with.

A horn sounded. He pressed the old button switches on the wall over the exit, walked out, and pushed back on the door to make sure the lock had snapped. A new Plymouth, light green under the streetlamp, waited for him. "Where to?" asked the man at the wheel. "Sinbad's, okay?" General murmurs of assent circled inside the car and they moved down the block toward Jefferson Avenue. "What's with the guy from Greece, Mike?"

Santry did not reply immediately. He was staring out the side window, looking back toward the dark shape of the parish house. Buildings and trees blocked a clear view, but he was sure he had seen a light on the second floor. "Jim, I'm sorry, but would you mind driving me back? I'm suddenly not feeling well at all and think I've got to lie down."

Expressions of concern and offers to help surrounded him.

"No, no thanks, I'll be fine—a good night's sleep is all I need. Mary, how about lunch tomorrow . . . ? Good. I'll call you in the morning."

He watched the car drive off, then looked up and down the deserted street and at the drab, three-story building in front of him. Only the light over the entryway offered illumination. The light he had seen from the car was on the other side. A cat dropped quietly to the street from a nearby wall, crouched for a moment when it saw him, and shied away. He opened the large front door quietly, closed it softly behind him, and stood motionless in the interior darkness. There were always sounds in the old house, but he heard no strange ones. He worked the nearby switches, flooded the corridor with light, and walked up the wide stairs directly ahead. As he reached the second floor and stared down the long, dark hallway, he felt a strong impulse to turn, go quickly to the first floor, and call the police because a line of golden light shone beneath the closed door to his room, and from within came faint, unmistakable sounds of occupancy. But an ordinary thief would have heard him climbing the stairs and taken off, so he thought he knew who was in there. He made no attempt to approach the room quietly. His fingers reached, turned the knob, and pushed the door wide open.

Varga was sitting at his desk, back toward him, head bent, apparently reading. The realization of what he probably had in front of him chilled Santry. Varga neither turned from his studies nor acknowledged the priest's sudden appearance. Santry closed the door, leaned against it, and stared at the intruder's broad back. "John Simonedes said I could trust you. He was obviously talking about someone else."

Varga's head lifted slowly but did not turn. He seemed intent on something outside the single window ahead of him, something out there in the night. His voice, when it came, rumbled softly. "It's good priests don't breed. Your innocence would cripple the species." He turned in his chair, studied Santry with open disdain, and looked back through the window. "The abbot's also an innocent man, but humble and therefore harmless. He even does some good. You are equally naïve, but arrogant—full of messianic illusions and posturing."

"Thank you," Santry replied calmly. "When I need a judge, I'll call you. At the moment, your views don't interest me, so please leave."

Varga closed the book he had been reading, pushed his chair back, stood, and faced Santry. His voice was threatening. "If this is the end of the story, I'll leave, but if I do, you should offer emergency entreaties to Jehovah, because Zeus will soon be raging all over you with thunder and lightning." He thrust the book toward the priest like a sword.

Santry stared at the journal, furious that anyone would read it, and frightened at how it could be used. He had been careful when writing, scrupulously avoiding any names of people or places, so any casual reader would learn nothing except that Santry had a far more complex emotional life than suspected. It contained only prayers and meditations, but it was dated, and a suspicious, inquiring mind might unravel its meanings.

"When I discovered the Fragments had been stolen," Varga told him quietly, "I wondered about you right away. It was you who presented Greece with a fraud, it was you who managed to stay closer than anyone to the abbot for three hours in a wild crowd, and it was you who said nothing to the police about seeing anybody attack Simonedes. In Detroit, I learn that an anonymous donor has given you millions of dollars and that you are willing to turn thief for a price, the price being whatever you consider to be a good cause." He opened the book, turned a few pages, and said, "This one is dated August 1, the day Simonedes got broken up and the Fragments got taken. 'The end is near and all this will soon be behind me.' And the next day, August 2, the abbot was in the hospital and you wrote, 'It is over. I begin to breathe again. And vow: never again.' " Varga closed the book, looked up at the priest, and said, "Like deathbed contrition, your repentance is somewhat touching, but too late to be of consequence."

The small room had one chair, one desk, one bed. Even in normal circumstances two men would fill it. Santry felt hemmed in, pressed, cornered. "Let's go downstairs, where we can sit and talk. I've got some Scotch if you're still interested in a drink." As they walked down the stairs, he asked, "How did you find out about the Fragments?" Santry refused to play the pretender's game. The worst had just exploded in his face. Crises should be taken head-on.

"We learned that Simonedes's fingerprints were not on the object you left behind. An expert confirmed the theft. You realize your accomplice tried to kill Simonedes that night?"

Santry stopped abruptly and cautioned him, "You're getting way ahead of yourself."

Neither man spoke again until they reached the small lounge off the kitchen and had drinks in hand. Varga examined the books on a display table in the corner. Most were about Central America. He wasn't looking at the priest when he asked, "When did you lose your interest in religion?"

Santry ignored the taunt. "It's time to say what you mean, Mr. Varga."

The heavyset man turned from the books and offered Santry a look of mild surprise. "There's no mystery about it. I'm a journalist and I've got a good story. Not all of it, but more than I need for the first articles. The rest I can get, or the police can get, or you can get." The ice chinked softly against the sides of his glass as Varga swirled the Cutty Sark. His mood shifted away from accusations and became, if not amiable, at least more neutral. "All I want from you is a decision about who's going to get the rest of the story. The police will want more than that from you, but not me."

"I don't understand what you're saying."

Varga leaned forward in his chair, nursing his Scotch between two large hands. "Well, the story's over or it's not. That's right, isn't it? If you decide it's over, then I have to decide who gets the rest of it. Do I track down your friends, or do I let the police do it? Do I find the missing Fragments or let the police search for them? Right now I could go either way, but that's my decision. You just have to tell me if the story's over."

"And what if I tell you nothing at all?"

Varga shrugged, as if it made no difference to him. "Then the story's over, isn't it? Then there's a little more investigating, we publish the facts we have, the public and the police go crazy, there's an international scandal, Greece and the United States throw their arms around each other, you're arrested, your friends hide, the Fragments are buried. Something like that, I suppose. But if the story ends where it is now, you're finished. Your life as the humble saint of the east side is over." Varga looked into Santry's eyes and said with a sincerity approaching personal concern, "And you know that's true. If the story ends here, you'll be extradited and you'll stand trial in Greece for theft of a sacred treasure and for conspiracy to commit murder."

"What!"

"Your friend, whatever else he is, is a professional killer, skilled in hand-to-hand combat. The broken wrist and the head injuries suggest he tried to kill the abbot. I have medical testimony to that effect and I'll certainly print it."

Santry's face clouded. It was worse than he had imagined. For something to do, he took the empty glasses to the kitchen, opened a new ice tray, and poured doubles. Extradited! Theft of sacred treasure and murder! Could that be true? Could Alexander have tried to kill Simonedes? He found himself wanting Varga to know and to believe that he would never have gone to Greece if he had known the abbot would be injured. The impulse passed. He had known and accepted the risks he could see, but he hadn't seen them all. What else was there to say? The thought of just disappearing occurred: slipping away, vanishing before the story broke. There were places in Latin America—a plane to the Indies, local freighters to Venezuela, overland to Brazil and friends. He'd never be found. He handed Varga his drink. "You keep saying 'if the story's over.' I don't understand that."

"That's because you're thinking of me as the police. You've done something wrong, I've caught you, the story's over. But I'm not the police, I'm a journalist, and I don't want to write it up until it's really over, finished, completed. And that's your decision, not mine. I'm only asking if you're going to do anything else."

Santry asked impatiently, "Like what?"

"I can't tell you what," Varga snapped. "It's your story. It't not my job to write your lines." His fingers stroked his bushy moustache, vainly trying to smooth it into place, as he added, "But there are many things someone in your place might do."

Santry stared out the window, watching shadows running wild on the sidewalk as a rising wind swayed the old lamp suspended over the parish hall entryway. Varga wasn't behaving at all as expected. It was as if the man wanted him to do something else, as if he was leading him to someplace he couldn't see.

"You could tell me who's behind the thieving, who planned it, who attacked Simonedes. You could tell me where the Fragments are. You could run away." There was a long pause and then the astonishing suggestion that suited Varga's purposes and changed Santry's life. "And, of course, a creative, desperate man could also decide to recover the Fragments and return them before the public and the police hear anything about it."

Santry responded suspiciously, "But then you wouldn't have a story."

Varga shook his head. "No, I'd have a better story. A priest looting the public treasury is good, but a repentant priest stealing from fellow thieves to replace the loot is better."

Santry moved toward the bait. "The police would come anyway. I might as well deal with them now."

"Maybe they would and maybe they wouldn't. I might work it out with Simonedes. Make it his story. Claim this unnamed priest confessed to him. They wouldn't press him."

Santry leaned back in his chair and closed his eyes. "It's a frightening but powerful idea. However, Mr. Varga, the truth is that I don't even know where the Fragments are."

Varga scratched the side of his face. "Don't waste time telling me about the problems. You have enormous problems if you just sit in that chair with your eyes shut. You're trapped, finished, so just tell me if your story's over so I can write it up or if you want me to hold off for a while."

"What about the money?"

"What about it?"

"You don't care if it's not returned?"

"I don't care what you do. I've got a story either way, but if the police get into this, your East Side Development Corporation's dead, factory and all. If you keep the police out of it, who cares how thieves cheat thieves? Your principles apparently allow you to do anything, so why not keep quiet and save your neck with the same crime—find the Fragments, steal them back, return them to Kallos, and leave the fraud with your unsuspecting friends. That way you get your money and Greece gets its treasure. A nice twist: retribution with restitution. Then you persuade me not to publish your story for a year. That gives your organization time to collect the rest of the payments and build the factory. It also gives you time to establish a new identity in an obscure part of the world so your friends can't find you when my story comes out."

"There's something very strange about the way you're talking, Mr. Varga. There's something for you in all this that you're not talking about."

"That's true, Father Santry, but irrelevant. You're the man in trouble, not me." He stood and told the priest to call him the next day. If he didn't hear from him, he'd run the story he had, concluding it with an account of the trial.

Santry's first impulse after Varga left was to find Ross somehow, tell him a bomb had exploded in their lives, and that their only hope was to return the Fragments. By morning, he had second thoughts. In the first place, he had no idea how to find Ross and no expectation of hearing from him. But even if he knew, he'd hesitate, because Alexander would as likely decide to silence Varga as get involved in a complicated attempt to restore the Fragments. The priest wanted nothing to do with more violence, and Ross had committed himself to working for an organization that thrived on it. But what could he do on his own? He had no idea—none at all. Yet if he did nothing, things would be even worse—

hopeless. Inaction guaranteed exposure, disgrace, imprisonment. He called Varga and asked to meet him.

It was a bright October day, warm in the sun, cool in the shadow, Detroit's best season. They walked from the Pontchartrain to the nearby river park, leaned against the railing at the water's edge, and looked across to Canada. Santry watched the river, a short strong-current chute surging south toward Lake Erie. He did not look up when he told Varga, "I've decided to make a public statement describing my involvement in the theft of the Fragments, explain my reasons, and take what comes. I'll give no information about anyone else. It's almost impossible for me to get them back, and even if I did, I'd still have to go into hiding. If you publish now, the police are after me. If you publish a year from now, the thieves are after me. Dead end either way. It's over."

Varga turned his back to the river and pulled his collar up against a sudden breeze. "You say 'almost impossible.' You mean a recovery's possible?"

Santry had spent a good part of the night wondering about that. "I know very little. The names of a few people on the edges, that's about all. I can imagine ways to reach them and try to learn more, but . . ." His voice drifted off without completing the thought. He had little interest in talking more to Varga. His mind was already drafting the public statement.

Varga huddled over a match and a cigarette. "How old are you?"

"Fifty-two. Why?"

"I was trying to figure out which one of us will die first." He leaned closer. "Unless you're passionately committed to jail, I have an idea that might help us. Think about it. If you recover the Fragments, I won't publish the story until your death. That way you won't have to hide from anybody but God, so you can keep your parish and even build your food factory."

"Why would you do that?" Santry asked cautiously.

"I told you yesterday. It makes a better story. One that gets better the longer you live. I'm in no rush. Corruption's not going to dry up and leave me out of work. There's only one condition: You have to keep me informed, because there are side stories that will tumble out of this in which I do have an immediate, even urgent, interest."

"I couldn't give you names."

Varga shrugged as if it didn't matter. "They're unimportant. The story I'm after is about what you do—and about certain things going on I want to understand. I'll get the names myself."

"What if I try and fail? Would the agreement hold?"

Varga hesitated only briefly. He wanted the priest in motion and wasn't overly concerned about how he got him moving. "Agreed. If you do all you can to get the Fragments and keep me informed, then no story about you till you die, whether you get them or not."

Santry looked at the river for a long time. The way out had suddenly appeared. His life might go on, but . . . He shook his head. "I don't know you well enough. How do I know you'd keep your word?"

Varga countered, "How do I know you'd try hard?" His voice grew sharp and angry. "Do what you like, Santry. Trust the police, honor thieves, go to jail, bleed all over the public with a self-serving statement, play the devil's martyr, but don't climb up on the cross and look down on me with questions about trust. In my eyes, you have no moral edge. None at all." He took paper and pen from his coat pocket and wrote down a few numbers. "I'm leaving tonight. You can reach me in Athens at these. If I don't hear from you by the end of the week, your story's going to the papers. If you decide to recover the Fragments, I expect weekly calls on your progress. In return, not a word from me about the saint of the east side until he goes to his eternal reward."

Athens, November 1984

He had gone to bed early the night the call came, weary in spirit and body. The phone startled him. "Father Michael Santry?" The voice was a man's.

"Yes?"

"You inquired about Ian Marshall."

"Yes."

"Leave the hotel in thirty minutes. Bring your passport. A black car will be parked in front of the entrance. Get in the backseat."

Santry hung up, flicked on the overhead light, and dressed hurriedly. It was two A.M. He had been in Athens for a week. The call had finally come. He had actually made some kind of contact. He was excited, frightened, and vaguely disappointed. In Detroit he had sifted through every summer memory but found little, and had arrived in Greece with only one name to begin his search: the name on the wire sent by Ross from the West Indies. He did recall the photographs of two attractive women in swimming suits standing with Ross on the deck of a large yacht, and an "A" had signed the letter Ross had received at the Balthazar and shown him in the taxi. So he had placed a bold ad in every Athenian daily after arriving in the city: "Father Michael Santry seeks information on Ian Marshall from 'A.' Call Hotel Porfyris." After four days without response, Santry had begun to lose hope and to take heart. He was committed to the Fragments' return, but knew that if he exhausted all his physical and imaginative resources in seeking them and still came up empty-handed, he could go home without penalty. At the same time, he would never take advantage of his agreement, because he had given his word. He buttoned his white collar in place, slipped his passport into a coat pocket, and rechecked his suitcase. If they had searched his room on Kallos, they'd certainly do it in Athens. Any link between him and Varga had to be destroyed, including the telephone numbers he had taken so much time to memorize on the flight.

He dropped his key on the counter in front of the night clerk, walked to the door, stopped abruptly, and leaned against the wall. Why had they called him in the middle of the night? He should have refused, should have insisted on a day meeting in some public place. Anyone might have answered that ad. He watched the street through the glass doors and saw the car pull up. He looked at his watch: exactly two-thirty A.M. As he crossed the deserted sidewalk, the back door opened and he was motioned inside. There were three of them. Two in front, one on the backseat beside him. The car pulled away slowly.

"May I see your passport?" The directive came from the man in front. He had not turned to look at Santry when he spoke.

"Please tell me who you are and where we're going," Santry said.

"Yes, we may do that, but only after we know who you are and what you're doing. Please understand, our instructions are to treat Father Santry well, so if you are the priest, all your interests are served by immediate and civilized cooperation—which I define as having that passport in my hand within the count of five." He paused briefly and began to count: "One, two, three . . ."

Santry extended his passport toward the front seat. The man beside him intercepted it and passed it forward. "Please close your eyes." A light instantly blazed in his face, blinding him. The light stayed on while the man asked, "Now tell us what you want to know about Ian Marshall."

"I want to know how to reach him. He is a close friend."

"Why must you talk to him?"

Santry shook his head and turned away from the blinding light. "I can't tell you if I don't know who you are. You can understand that. Anyone might answer that ad."

"Who is 'A'?"

"I don't know. I only remember Ian referring to his friend 'A.' "

"Who are Marshall's other friends in Athens?"

"I have no idea. He never mentioned them to me."

"When were you last here?"

"This summer."

"Why were you here this summer?"

Santry was shocked by the question and the sudden realization that he might be talking to the police. He remained silent.

The light went out but the voice continued. "Here are ten photographs. Ian Marshall is among them. Show us your friend."

The man beside him held the flashlight while Santry went through the pictures. "He's not here. The Ian Marshall I know is not among these." He handed them back, sure that if they were the police, they were fishing, but if they were not the police, they suspected that he was.

The flashlight stayed on and another photo was handed to him. "Where was this taken?"

Santry was looking at himself in a group picture. "In the garden of the Monastery of St. David the King on Kallos."

"Identify the people."

"The abbot of the monastery is on the bench beside me. The man in uniform is a local policeman named Forticos. The rest were at the conference with me." He named them all.

The man in front gave a signal to the driver and in minutes the car pulled to a stop in front of his hotel. They had completed a carefully timed circle. The man handed Santry a card and told him, "Come to this address at eight o'clock tonight."

* * *

Hours later, Santry stood in a phone booth talking to Varga. "Yes, they searched the room. Didn't take or disturb anything, but they found the airplane tickets, so they'll assume I'll be gone day after tomorrow. The bag with my other clothes is downstairs in the check room."

Varga was insistent. "You should tell me where you'll be tonight. It could be dangerous."

"No. A friend of mine is right in the middle of all this. We'll have to talk about it later."

"We shouldn't talk much longer," Varga agreed. "They're certainly watching you right now and wondering who you're calling, but you should know that I talked to Simonedes."

"You didn't . . . ?"

"No, nothing's revealed. Look, Santry, don't keep insulting me. You've got your own load to carry; you don't have to worry about mine. I told the abbot we had a good visit, got repeatedly drunk, and love each other very much."

"How is he?"

"A tough old goat getting tougher. He caught the police lieutenant going though his mail but is saying nothing till he learns more. My guess is that Forticos is working for your people. Look, I'm sorry to stop this, but you really should get out of that booth. And remember, you're being followed. I'm sure of it."

Santry hung up feeling relieved that Varga had been there. He felt less afraid of his isolation. Outside the booth in the early sun he imagined another blazing light blinding him and a hostile voice demanding, *Who were you talking to!?*

He was ready: *The airport to confirm my flight home.*

He looked across the small plaza toward a domed church on the other side of the traffic-snarled street. Thousands of people in cars and on motorcycles churned impatiently on all sides, shouting, blowing horns, and racing engines. Only one was watching him. His eyes drifted over a few men lingering in the park and coffee drinkers at nearby tables. Which of them would he see again? He had broken through. He had, unimaginably, flown to Athens and reached through the darkness of his ignorance. He had touched a strange and ominous shore and was prepared to do what he had to do. At a local kiosk, he picked up a copy of the *International Herald Tribune,* walked to a restaurant for breakfast, and over terrible coffee looked vainly for any news about Detroit.

At seven-forty-five that night, the cab stopped in front of a large, old house that sprawled half hidden behind a six-foot iron-spear fence and an enormous, sidewalk-buckling tree. Except for one room on the first floor, the house appeared to be in total darkness. At the door, a uniformed guard picked up a phone mounted by the dimly lit entrance, repeated Santry's name, and ushered him inside. A wide flight of stairs, illumined by two peach-colored lamps, rose directly ahead. He looked up. At the top, a man with shoulder-length blond hair leaned against the banister, watching. His legs were crossed. One hand rested lightly on his hip. The other held a cigarette.

"Good evening, Father Santry." The chilling insolence of the voice that had questioned him from the front seat of the car was unmistakable. Santry nodded, offered no greeting, and followed him down a wide hallway lined with somber nineteenth-century landscapes, brooding marble busts, and a huge painting of a stag at bay. The red Oriental carpet was badly worn and frayed. Altogether, the place had the look of a seedy private club simmering in the must of memory. He watched the man ahead and thought of Ross. They must be about the same age, each well built and tall, but much different in manner. Ross met one straight on and hard. One never doubted one's status as friend or enemy. This one affected an easy, supercilious air rimmed with haughtiness and "count to five" arrogance. *An-*

other of the world's cold ones, Santry thought. The stranger opened an ornately decorated door at the far end of the hall, offered a slight bow, and encouraged the priest to enter. As he went by, Santry smelled the perfume, saw the jewelry gleaming on fingers and wrists, and the piled loops of turquoise twined loosely about his neck.

The door closed, a voice shouted, "Hold it!," and Santry stared across the room at a dark, regal woman in a full-length silver gown, motionless in a flood of light, arm extended toward him. A magnificent cheetah pressed against her legs. Another lay on the floor beside her. The photographer, circling, called again, "Beautiful! Beautiful! Now work the cats."

Santry glanced away from the low stage in the center of the high-ceilinged room, saw a woman sitting alone along the wall, heard the door being locked behind him, and felt the stranger's hand on his arm pushing him toward the model. He pulled his arm away and walked slowly toward the stage, where the glamorous woman with jet-black hair now reclined imperiously among dozens of enormous, brightly colored cushions. The rest of the room was drab and bare, but she was a sultry focus of light and magnetism. Her hands stroked the awesome animals stretched beside her, but her eyes were on Santry.

The photographer, a short, wiry man wearing tight designer jeans, sandals, and a loose-fitting painter's smock, moved restlessly about the stage, hovering over the model, suggesting moves. "Tighter, Gabriella, tighter! There! Good!"

A spotlight blazed suddenly from above and played on Santry's face. For a moment, he could see nothing beyond the bright center of the room, nothing beyond the elegant, shining woman, as poised and alert as the cats beside her on the vivid greens and reds of tropic-colored pillows. Their faces, less than fifteen feet away, were fixed on his, as if all three expected him to speak.

The large, tawny cats, with their heads raised and curious, blinked imperturbably in the floodlights and waited. The sleek beauty watching him was savage in contrast. The deft touches of a makeup artist extended the sweep of her eyes, heightened the arch of her brows, and exaggerated her facial planes into a feline mask set off by a single diamond brightness on one cheek. The photographer rested on a high stool and watched, camera ready. Santry felt like an ill-prepared actor: expected to say something but uncertain of his lines. Or was it a courtroom? A trial, not a play?

The photographer began to shoot as the dark woman straightened and glared at him. "You look like a priest!" She said the word as she might say "pariah" or "parasite." "You've announced to all of Athens that 'A,' Ian Marshall, and Michael Santry have something in common. Ross spoke of your virtues. He neglected to mention the vacant brain vault." She spoke slowly and precisely, as if to a wayward child. "Our agreement was strict: Ross was not to give you names."

Santry refused to be bullied. "Any agreement you had with Ross got shredded in July, when you had both of us followed, searched, and photographed. I had been promised absolute anonymity, but when Ross wouldn't give you my name, you tracked me down yourself. In any case, the ads reveal nothing."

The photographer slid off the stool and began to move, this time circling Santry. "Over here, Father! Good! That's good. Beautiful!"

Santry moved toward the camera as if to take it. He checked himself, asked the man to stop, looked at Gabriella, saw her mocking smile, and heard her say, "It's for the advertisement, Father. Ask in public, receive in public. You'll get my response in Detroit, but now we need exciting pictures. Father Santry on retreat in Athens. Your ads prove nothing? Neither will mine. Like yours, they will only suggest, tantalize, and shame. Oh, look alarmed again, Father, I'm not sure he caught it.

The caption might be: 'Santry sees police crashing through the harem door.' Perhaps we'll run a series: a new photograph to greet your parishioners every morning. They'll loathe you for a time, but they'll want you back. Wayward priests are rarely stoned; they're forgiven unto death. What better solace for the rotting soul than a rotten saint?"

She looked beyond the rim of light and called, "Larus! Come!" The cats grew restless and leaned on the pillows beside Antissa as the blonde approached.

Once settled, he watched Santry and moved the fingers of his hands suggestively along her thighs. "You've never done this, have you, Father? Never stroked a woman, never felt the fire." He smiled contemptuously. "No, of course not. How could you?" One hand slid idly along his turquoise beads as he wondered out loud, "I never understood why they call voluntary eunuchs 'Fathers.' Can you explain that to me? Perhaps it's a joke, meant humorously, like when I say, 'Father Santry, may I have your passport?' " He winked slyly and added, "Or, even, may I have this dance?"

Santry had heard enough and turned away, left the lighted center, and walked to the door. But it was locked. A ceiling spot flared and held him in its grip of light. No one spoke. He was immediately alarmed. There was another door at the far end of the room. He wanted to run but checked himself and walked quickly, reached, and turned the knob. Locked! He searched the room with his eyes. The windows were too high. The other woman had gone. Another spotlight flashed. He raised his arm to shield his face. What was going on? Who was working the spot? Who was the dismal adolescent taunting him? Why the high-gloss theatrics? The entire set reeked of emotional warp and torment. He should have told Varga more. He leaned against the heavy door and stared boldly into the light that pinned him. There had to be a control room and more people and more eyes and cameras, but he couldn't see them. He moved abruptly to one side, escaping the light. The couple onstage ignored him, but the photographer circled and snapped, recording every move.

Gabriella stretched and nuzzled the cats. Her voice was calmer. "These are the only gods, Father Santry: aloof, beautiful, and fierce beyond belief." Her fingers worked their sides. He saw her as if vividly magnified, larger than life, even as her voice became remote and distant. "Larus and I are only their novitiates," she said, "not their masters." Her eyes, black as obsidian, found and summoned him. "And now you, Father. Come here! Come!"

He stepped back, close to the wall, returned her stare, and slowly shook his head. No, it was over. He wasn't playing any of their childish games. And all the lights, as if waiting for that signal, began to fade, went dim, and out. An afterimage lingered: a receding silver crescent spiraling away. And then there was only a palpable, terrible darkness. He crouched instinctively and moved to a remembered open space on his left, as if to escape the blow expected where he stood. He felt out of breath and heard Varga telling him to be careful, and he saw Simonedes curled like a rag doll, unconscious, broken on stones. He suddenly knew why the shades in the windows were down and tight: he had been led step by step into this darkness. He didn't know what to do. He kept one hand on the wall behind him. The other groped slowly in the empty space ahead. His eyes strained to see shapes, but nothing emerged. Nothing came clear.

Then an ominous rustling in the center of the room and a scornful voice. "Come, now, Father, don't play the reluctant child. Walk toward my voice. Now!"

Santry turned his head toward the sounds, listened intently for more, but heard only his beating heart and breath. He was suddenly cold.

"Larus!" he heard her command. "Release the cats!"

My God! Santry thought, crouching lower, moving to his left along the wall, reaching blindly for the chair he was sure had been there. He heard the faint metallic snaps of leashes and imagined the cats dropping noiselessly from the stage on padded feet. Desperate, he ran to one side, stumbled into something hard, swore, grasped it in his hands, and threw himself backward against the wall, swinging the chair like a club in front of him. A flashbulb exploded in his face and someone laughed. He stopped swinging, the brilliant iridescent glow faded into blackness, and the chair began to pull away. Someone or something had fastened on to the legs and was dragging it and him slowly across the floor. He let go, heard a noise behind him, whirled, and, in that instant, felt an arm lock around his neck, a knee sharp in his back, his feet off the floor, and his body falling awkwardly out of control.

He landed facedown in a noisy thudding sprawl, crawled painfully onto his hands and knees, and tried to rest. He could hardly breathe. He felt numb and wanted to collapse, but he could feel someone close, someone coming from behind.

A voice shouted, "Now!"

And all the lights in the room blazed on. Dazed, he saw the photographer kneeling in front of him, swinging a motion-picture camera in his face as the man who had mounted him held his hips tightly against him and simulated copulation.

Santry bellowed, "No!" He got one foot on the floor and threw himself violently backward, swinging his elbows wildly and breaking free to see and face them all.

The woman and the cats remained motionless on the stage. The animals had never been released. The photographer stood nearby, smirking and ready, his camera held like a fist eager for the next round. Larus, naked to the waist, was within arm's reach.

Santry backed away, his arm outstretched to ward them off, his white collar torn loose and dangling from a button, his thinning hair across his forehead, breath coming in gasps, his rage struggling with his weakness. "Why? Why!" he demanded, glaring at them. "What kind of people are you?"

Larus moved toward him. Santry watched him anxiously. Though taller, the blonde probably weighed less but had tossed him like dry leaves. His face, delicate and sensuous, seemed all wrong for the lean, powerful body. "Take your clothes off, Santry," he said with undisguised malice. "And don't look so horrified. We know it won't be the first time."

Without warning, Larus's open hand struck the priest's face, once, twice, hard. Santry raised his arms head-high to protect himself; the stinging blows had come too fast to see. Larus studied him without smiling and snapped his fingers. The photographer ran to his side, draped a stretch of thin, translucent cord across his open hand, and backed away. Larus's eyes stayed on Santry as he wrapped the rope ends across his palms, held the garrote up for the priest's inspection, crouched slightly, and began to circle.

Santry took a half step backward, glimpsed movement on the stage, and heard the woman's voice. "Stop." No one moved. "Look down, Santry!" she commanded. He stared at the floor and saw he was standing on a large yellow X in a circle of white chalk. "For the next few minutes, no one should speak," she told them.

The lights went out and Santry straightened in the darkness. He had not surrendered but he had given up hope of escaping the punishment so clearly intended for him. No reason to believe he would be spared. The spirit could protect the inviolable center but not the shell. Even that would be miracle enough. He had few illusions about man's strength. The spirit was as tender as the flesh, as breakable as bone. He had watched too many souls crippled or broken entirely by pain to believe in invulnerability. Unconsciousness and death seemed more certain allies. If they failed to make all things new, they at least dependably ended torment.

A beam of powerful light streaming from a bright circle behind the stage flared against the nearest wall, a large door opened, and a man walked through. Santry looked about the room. Larus and the photographer had disappeared, but the woman and the animals remained behind him, reclining on their cushions. He stared at the wall in increasing disbelief. On it was a movie, showing him entering the building less than an hour ago. The camera must have been hidden approximately where Larus had stood on the top of the stairs, because the camera looked down on him as he came through the door, glanced up, and climbed with bent head toward the blond stranger. Then another shot from the opposite side. Two cameras had worked together. He was astounded that he had noticed nothing when he entered. A close-up of Larus: the same insolent smile on the petulant, well-formed lips. Then back to Santry approaching him and a zoom-in for the look on his face. But it wasn't Santry! Same general build, black suit, white collar, but definitely someone else. The images disappeared, and large block letters covered the wall:

> The Dynamics of Pain and Humiliation. Case #8: The Illusion of Choice. Object: Michael Santry. One in a series of studies on social conditioning and predictability. The film you are about to see, the eighth in a projected series of twenty, enacts the predicted responses of a Roman Catholic priest to a carefully orchestrated sequence of threatening interactions. These range from the mildest forms of gestural alienation to direct physical violence, and can be expected to evoke responses on the recessive-aggressive spectrum ranging from mere annoyance to panic and collapse.
>
> "A 'predicted scenario' using actors will be

followed by the unedited, filmed reactions of Father Michael Santry to identical stimuli. The audience can then compare and discuss the filmmaker's predictions with Santry's actual behavior. It should be stressed that almost nothing is known about Santry except that he has been a Roman Catholic priest for twenty-five years. The producers suggest that after analyzing that one fact, one can predict over ninety percent of the object's responses to the scheduled interactions. Know the role; know the man. Contrary to his self-consciousness, Santry is not a free subject but a social product whose genuflections have all the spontaneity of a lead soldier in fixed salute. This is an educational film and is deliberately provocative. Discussion will be spirited and the audience will come to its own equally predictable conclusions."

The text ended and a close-up of the actor-priest filled the wall. Small orange arrows on the film pointed to his white collar and black suit as the narrator on the soundtrack said,

"The knight's armor and the priest's garb are roughly equivalent in social function. Each is a public statement announcing and reinforcing prescribed roles. The white collar is the priest's armor and cage, an iron chain linked by invisible reins to the institutions and people who shape and control him. It is, at the same time, the halo sign, the perfect circle, and signals others to expect special behavior from him and to act deferentially in his presence. Whether they do that sincerely or insincerely is of no consequence, because either way the role and approved public responses to it are reinforced. Any who doubt the social utility of this ritualized deference are invited to read the collection of prayers for a nation at war to be found in the study guide. From the ruler's point of view, priests are a small price to pay for the passive compliance of the flock."

Santry, amazed, watched the film priest following Larus down the hallway exactly as he had done and listened to the narrator explain that his "distancing" behavior had been elicited by the stranger's "denial of deference," a response that set off the first "dissonance anxiety" in the priest. There was no mention of the previous night's ride or interrogation.

The actor's every step had been carefully planned and his every reaction filmed. Santry's fascination increased as the actor came through the door to the room in which he stood and actually shrugged off Larus's hand just as he had done.

The narrator commented:

"The role of shepherd has little room for guidance from the flock, especially from nondeferential rams who confuse sexual specifications by wearing perfume and jewels."

As the actor-priest stood in front of Gabriella Antissa, the commentator called the audience's attention to the yellow X on the floor where he stood and predicted that Santry would stand exactly there. His anticipated distance from Antissa was explained as the

"position a hierarchically conscious personality will take in relationship to superior power. The woman's elevation, regal bearing, great beauty, silver sheath, and exotic companions all together suggest an ancient Egyptian frieze. The priest will experience her as an earthly queen or Virgin Mother. He will be unable to approach any closer and remain comfortable. He may remain somewhat more distant, but 'the inner circle of royalty' has been carefully calibrated in other experiments, and a man with Santry's awareness of social rank will not cross into it.''

Santry saw the actor standing within a foot or two of the position he himself had taken in front of Antissa and wondered if there might be truth in it. In fact, he had not wanted to get closer, but, as he remembered it, that had more to do with the wild animals than with symbolic kings and queens. He watched his counterpart on film struggling with the two locked doors and trying to evade the light. The actor did not, however, pick up and swing a chair at his antagonists, a divergence that was satisfying to Santry. The film went momentarily blank and the wall went white. The next pictures, like all the rest in high-grade color, showed the actor flat on his stomach, not like Santry on hands and knees, but Larus mounted and riding him arrogantly all the same. In the film, the actor sobbed, shook his head, and moved his arms in pitiful protest. He failed, however, to struggle free.

Disgusted, Santry turned away, but he heard the soundtrack continue with the priest's whimpering sounds and Larus's cries of triumph. He looked up. The naked blonde had collapsed on the actor's back, forearm pressed down on the victim's neck. Santry knew the film was moving rapidly to the X on which he stood, the X marking the exact intersection of his vulnerable present and their predicted future. Two huge faces filled the wall. The actor-priest's face was twisted in embarrassed bewilderment and fear. Larus's face, contemptuous and vulgar, was saying, "Take your clothes off, Santry. And don't look so horrified. We all know it won't be the first time." The real Santry winced when he heard again the two sharp cracks as Larus slapped the actor's face. He reached up in the darkness to touch his still-burning cheeks while the man on the screen cowered and nursed his own.

They had now caught up with themselves. The film had reached the present moment. Santry looked around anxiously, but Larus was out of sight.

The woman's voice called, "Stop." Her thin, royal face looked down at him from the wall, speaking to an unseen audience—or, he wondered, was this entirely for him? Could all this be an elaborate, unnerving ruse, a corrupting, brutal game? Or did a series of films really exist? Were people actually going to watch an actor anticipate his moves?

Antissa's voice continued:

"At this point, Santry feels deeply threatened and confused. He dimly suspects the sexual assault that is to come, but can't face it directly. A feeling of numbness, close to paralysis, is beginning to spread. This has nothing to do with courage or will. It has only to do with the automatic response of the nervous system to a threat perceived as terrible and inescapable. Santry's fear is especially overpowering because of sexual inexperience, vows of celibacy, and the Church's abhorrence of homosexuality. His alarm systems have been thrown to full-flood alert and, consequently, his brain has downshifted from neocortical dominance to primitive flight-or-fight centers. But the physical exits are blocked so he can't flee and he is, by training, unequipped to fight. His behavior has become even more predictable.

"Alternative futures will now be presented to the anxious priest by our actors. The first offers short-term humiliation but complete freedom from physical pain. The second guarantees both extreme pain and worse humiliation. In such circumstances, the only sane 'choice' would be the first, but 'choice' has nothing to do with it. 'Choice' is an illusion. Watch!"

She vanished and, in her place, a full-length view of Larus, fully clothed, flashed on the wall. He spoke quietly to the actor-priest, who had combed his hair and refastened the dangling white collar. A worried, careful look was on his face, but the terrible fright and lurid color of the previous scene had gone. A portion of lost composure had been restored. Larus had also changed. His shirt was light brown, hand-embroidered, and open at the neck. The loops of turquoise accented the pale blue eyes. His earlier malevolence had moderated, and if he was not friendly, he at least wore the colors of sincerity.

"There is a way out of this," he told the actor calmly. "Do you want to hear it?" The actor-priest appeared uncertain but nodded.

Santry took a deep breath and sighed quietly. If not illusory, choices were definitely limited in a room with enemies and locked doors. The worst had been predicted by Antissa. She was now committed to making it happen. Their wills were on the line.

"We want you to know that we will do exactly what we say," Larus continued, speaking solicitously to the actor. "You now understand the scientific nature of the experiment in which, almost accidentally, you have become involved. We defeat our own purpose if we deceive you, so we'll tell you the truth." He ran one hand along the back of his blond hair as he said, "The way out requires no more than thirty or forty-five minutes of your time and involves no pain at all. You would, in fact, probably experience considerable pleasure. You understand? An hour from now, you could be walking out that door. Free. With no one following." Larus stopped and waited for a sign. None came from the troubled actor-priest, and so Larus asked, "You want me to go on?"

Santry watched impatiently, thinking that the film-priest accurately mirrored the apprehension that must be on his own face as Larus proceeded to describe the options: voluntary or involuntary participation in a seduction scene. The actor was told he could join Larus either consciously or unconsciously in his nest of pillows.

The film-priest began to back away, his hands open and raised defensively. "No, I can't! Please!" He looked as if he might, at any moment, kneel and beg.

Santry refused to watch the ending and stared, instead, into the dark corners of the room beyond the projector's beam of light. He would be next. He looked again at the film. He had to see what they had planned for him. The camera was on Larus walking toward the broken priest, counting. The light went out. There was absolute silence and then a strangled scream, which pierced him like a spear of fire.

The wall went black. He looked where the projector's bright eye had blazed. Gone. The room itself had disappeared in darkness. He took seven quiet, long steps to the right, the distance he had calculated to the wooden chair, pressed his leg against its side, and waited breathlessly. Across the room, a spotlight knifed a vivid line from the ceiling to the floor and cut a brilliant circle. Beyond the stage, a door swung open, and Larus, a thin rope in one hand, walked quickly to its center as an actor might. The jewels, turquoise, and open shirt were gone, replaced by beige T-shirt, well-laundered jeans, and unconcealed contempt. A second light flared, hit the floor where Santry had stood to watch the film, found him gone, and began to search. The spot moved slowly across the floor, this way and that, as if in doubt. All a game designed to make him run. A single switch would light the room. He knew there was no hiding and held his place. The spotlight, anchored in the center of the ceiling, caught him at an angle and etched his shadow on the floor.

Though he knew which words were coming, they stunned him just the same, for they summoned his final scene.

"There is a way out of this, Santry."

He stood in a shower of light, separated by some fifty feet of darkness from Larus. Two men, a large dark room, two beams of light breaking over them. He heard the soft whirring of a camera from somewhere high on the far wall. He was, strangely, breathing easier now, still tense but centered. Their eyes met. The other's were pale blue and cold, and Santry wondered what lay behind that frozen mask. It was possible for the soul to be drawn too thin. Unnourished, the image could only fade and finally disappear. Then what remained? Larus moved closer. The spotlight followed.

"Do you want to hear it?"

"I've heard it," Santry said.

"We want you to know we will do what we say. . . ."

"I know exactly what you're going to do."

"What is your choice, then?"

Santry stiffened as the count began. On five, the lights would go. Seconds later, Larus would be on him. His hands were cold but ready. ". . . Three," Larus said, "four, five!"

Darkness crashed around Santry and splinters of light drifted downward in his eyes as he seized the chair, swung it high above his head, charged straight for Larus, and brought it crashing down where he had stood. The chair pounded through empty space, hit the wooden floor, shattered in his hands, and tore free. An awful silence surrounded him.

Then a quiet voice taunted, "On your knees, Santry."

The priest whirled to face him in the dense, artificial night, legs bent, arms up, elbows out, listening. There was nothing. Not a breath. Then a faint scratching nearby. He turned slowly toward it, braced himself, and swung frantically when something brushed his cheek. Larus's ridiculing laughter stopped him.

"Only the faintest touch of what's to come, Father. What do you say? Shall we get this over with? Why not? But you should count this time. Count to ten. On ten it's over. Guaranteed. I'll start. Count silently if you prefer, but at ten we'll be together. One, two . . .''

Larus stopped and Santry picked up the silent count in the darkness. Three. If there was an exit, he'd run. If anyone could hear, he'd scream. Four. He was alone and he was trapped. Five. And he was no street fighter. Six. No illusions. But if he lived, seven, if he got through this, then, eight, one way or the other, nine, he tensed, fists clenched, legs ready to drive low and hard, the blonde had to be taken down, ten!

A quick tap, no more than a flick, caught him below the eye. He swung, blindly, and struggled against a scream as his wrist cracked into something hard as rock and a fist exploded in his center, doubled him over, and a bright explosion filled his falling head.

Somewhere beyond him the woman's voice came softly.

"Between humiliation with no pain, and worse humiliation with extreme pain, Santry has taken the path our script predicted. Men playing other roles would take different but equally predictable paths. His minor deviations from the actor-priest's performance were easily evoked by the writers. In the film, we showed him a priest whose carefully rehearsed simpering violated Santry's deep-rooted commitment to masculine Christian stoicism. Or, to put it more accurately, the film-priest contradicted Santry's own role-script and he therefore had to set the record straight. He had to play the courageous priest because that role is the only life he has. That its defense is impressive to no one but himself, as has been the case tonight, is entirely beside the point. And so Father Michael Santry marched, like the good lead soldier he was poured to be, into the arms of humiliation, pain, and even death, calling it all great faithfulness and true life."

Dark eyes glistened above him. He turned his head, saw an empty chair, a desk, a painting, and heard the voice.

"Hello, Michael."

He looked back. The eyes were still there. Enormous. And the moustache. He closed his eyes and said, with a sigh, "Dimitrios, Dimitrios, thank God! How?" He tried to move, but the pain stopped him.

"You're all right, Michael. A friend examined you. You're in my apartment and you're safe."

The words fell on Santry like a soft, warm blanket in the cold. It was the first time they had called each other by Christian names. "How did you find me?"

"I followed your taxi last night and waited outside. They drenched you with whisky and left you in the bushes. I brought you here."

"When? How long ago?"

"Not long. You've been asleep five or six hours."

"You saw them?"

"One of them: the one I had seen before—on Kallos."

"What was he doing there?"

"Strangling me is what I remember best."

Santry opened his eyes and looked up from the pillow. "You never mentioned that."

"We've been talking about *your* story, not mine."

"I need your help, Dimitrios."

The Greek looked down and smiled. "Yes, that's what I thought when I saw you in the bushes last night. The tickets in your pocket say you're going home tomorrow."

Santry shook his head. "I bought them only for the sake of appearance, only to throw them off. Do you know them? Do you know who they are?"

"No, but I've got questions—even a few suspicions.

We'll talk about that later, after food and rest, after you tell me what happened in there."

"You won't believe it. I was in a movie."

"A good part?"

Santry looked away and said quietly, "A familiar one, Dimitrios, and better than some I've played. But good? I don't know. I'm honestly not sure. I see certain limitations."

Chapter Six

Santry looked out the rear window of the cab but learned nothing by staring backward through the rain. The cars streaming behind all looked the same to him. He turned to the woman beside him and asked, "Are we being followed?" He expected her to tell him only what she wanted him to believe, but, impatient and suspicious, he asked anyway. She was an attractive woman. He had known that even before seeing her, from the moment he picked up the startling telephone and heard her say "Hello, this is Ladrea, Alexander's friend." That introduction alone told him she was endowed with physical beauty, because Alexander did not run with the lumpkins of the world. And she had a message for him, one that had to be delivered face to face. Fine. He'd be there. When he got in the cab at the appointed hour, he had been surprised by her age—early twenties, he'd guessed—but not at all by the remarkable face and the long, full body. The light raincoat she wore against the dampness of a late-November morning precluded much direct observation, but a photograph Ross had shown him that summer of two women in bikinis on a yacht snapped into hard focus when he saw her. He had not remembered names, but the images lingered without prompting.

Silver-dolphin earrings drifted in black hair along the margins of her face as she assured him, "No, no one's following." She saw his doubt and added, "They've decided there's no danger in you. They no longer take you seriously."

Santry said he welcomed the change. Midnight interrogations and films specializing in male rape, however simulated, were dreary affairs. "I saw the woman with the cheetahs in a photograph with you. Who is she?"

"Why didn't Alexander tell you?"

"Because at that time I didn't want to know."

"That's changed now?"

"Yes, it's changed. This summer she was a face to me. No, less than a face. She was one of the indolent rich at play. Now she's producer and director of my first film and sponsor of my first unconscious night on soaked muddy ground under a dripping, dark tree. Yes, I'd say things have changed. I'd even say that introductions and explanations are past due." He was saying more and saying it more angrily than he had intended, so he added quietly and with a touch of apology, "But that may have nothing to do with you. You said you have a message from Alexander?"

Yes, that was true, she told him, but he had to wait. Not long. A few hours at most. She was sorry to be evasive, but she had promised to deliver the message a certain way.

Dismayed, Santry shifted uncomfortably in the backseat. He worried about messages that had to be delivered "a certain way," reached forward suddenly, tapped the driver on his shoulder, told him to stop, then turned abruptly to Ladrea. "You may be Alexander's friend, but you're also related to that pair of psychopaths who caged me the other night." The cab pulled to the curb and Santry pushed his door open, but the barest parting of her lips and expansion of her eyes stopped him. He had seen that startled look before. "Now I remember," he told her. "You were there during the filming, weren't you? Sitting against the wall when I came in, looking just like that, just like you do now, but you left. I looked for you—but then the lights went out."

"Yes, I was there," she said with her hand on his arm, asking him to stay. "That's why I called Alexander. That's why there's a message. He's coming back. His plane lands in an hour. He wanted to surprise you."

Santry pulled the door shut, leaned back in his seat, and stared at the cars and trucks speeding past. "Why did you call him?"

Hurried explanations tumbled out. "Because you needed him, and because I can't stand that kind of thing. I thought the films had stopped a long time ago."

Santry told the driver to keep going and asked, gently now, for he thought he heard the twist of pain, "Who is she?"

"You really don't know?" Her tone suggested the information was such common knowledge in Athens that he could ask the cab driver and get it. He declared his total ignorance and pleaded for light, any light at all. The gates opened. She was eager to talk to "Alexander's closest friend," and wanted to tell him about "the other films." For the next two hours, most of which were spent at a nearby airport restaurant waiting for Ross's delayed flight, they huddled like conspirators over a bottle of wine.

Santry had watched long enough. He dropped his burning cigarette on the sidewalk, stepped from the building's deep shadows, and slipped into the phone booth. He counted five rings and kept his eyes on a solitary figure coming toward him on the vacant, windblown street. He heard the strong, familiar voice saying "Hello," and returned the greeting, while watching the stranger cross toward the park beyond. He hadn't talked to Varga for a week, hadn't seen him for three. Each week a different phone booth, each time a different part of town. If the tight link between them was even suspected, their enemies—and that was how Santry had come to think of them—would close in on them like wolves.

"How are you?" Varga's voice was warm and relaxed. But Santry was uneasy with the big man. He trusted him to keep agreements but knew he wanted more information than Santry was willing to give. "Some interesting developments, Dimitrios. Ian Marshall is back in Athens working with our sponsor. He's close to the center and has access to information that would never be available to me. For the first time, I can imagine ways to learn where the treasure's buried. Beyond that, it stills seems impossible, but I'm refusing to think about it. One step at a time."

"Is Marshall from Detroit?"

Santry ignored the question and went on with his report. "I had a long talk with a woman who was present during the filming the night you found me, Dimitrios. She's related to people in the organization, but not to the activity. It was an unexpected and strange meeting in many ways, but we've become friends."

"What did you learn?"

"Name, relationships, family problems, worries. Nothing with direct bearing on the project."

"You're a stranger. Why should she trust you?"

"My friendship with Ian and being a priest, I suppose."

"She and Marshall are close?"

"They're friends."

"What do they think you're doing here?"

"Seeing Ian, arranging earlier payment for the factory, considering a move to Latin America, taking time to think things over."

"No suspicions?"

"None. I'm sure of it. Ian shared a report received from Kallos that all's quiet there. He confided that the rulers in this kingdom were pleased with our work. No, they take me at my word. They've even invited me to Lesbos for a week. Ian has work there, so his friend and I can enjoy the island. Which reminds me—I learned that a series of films like the one they made with me actually exists. I'm trying to get Marshall to bring them to Lesbos. At the right time during that week, a casual question about the treasure's location may not be inappropriate. I assume Marshall could find out easily enough."

"How are you feeling about all this?"

"False but true. It seems to be the only way. Anything for me?"

"I talked to an art dealer this week, a true democrat who'll deal with anybody. He says he's heard nothing of a big sale, and when they get into the millions, it's hard to keep them quiet. It doesn't mean anything, but it doesn't mean nothing either. You should consider the possibility that the treasure has not been sold."

"But it has. The money's changed hands. We've seen it."

"No, you've seen money, not hands. Your sponsor could also be the purchaser. On a related matter, Michael—you might also ask a casual question about munitions. There's been some heavy-duty hijacking of Greek ships lately and some of the guns may now be fighting your friends, the Sandinistas. It's a possibility that may interest you."

When Varga hung up, he turned to the man sitting by the extension across the room. "Will you recognize his voice the next time?"

The man nodded without looking at Varga. "Easily. Is he always so low-key?"

"He only sounds low-key. The fact is that he's already my favorite wild man. A bomb waiting to go off—that's how low-key Santry is. You heard him: 'false but true,' he says. That's a priest talking, a serious man. In Detroit, they're sure he's a saint, but here he is lying to a friend in order to find the Fragments and save both their asses. All of this has got to be tearing him up." Varga, his tie pulled down and his collar open, leaned over the large desk in front of him and studied the dozens of photographs spread there. In one, Michael Santry, Alexander Ross, and Ladrea Antissa were walking directly toward the camera. Ross and Santry had luggage in their hands. Ladrea walked between them, her face turned toward the priest. "How'd you get the names?" Varga asked.

"The society editor knows all the high flyers, so the Antissas were no problem at all. The mother's file is an inch thick, but daughter has yet to attract much copy. Santry's friend is circulating with 'Ian Marshall' on his bags and a new Greek passport, but the correspondence in the attaché case is all 'Alexander Ross.' "

The photographer, who remained seated by the second phone, opened an onyx-handled pocketknife and sliced apples into thin wedges on two plates. Cutting completed, he placed one on the desk beside Varga and retired to the far corner of the room as if to suggest that his natural place in the world was on the edge. In the same way, he called himself "Nikos," which wasn't his real name, but he liked the common, familiar sound. He also liked it because it had been the name of his father, an unexceptional man who left no trace of himself in the world except in the memories of his only son, who considered him to be as fine as he was uncelebrated. And though he could afford better, Nikos chose to wear plain, decently fitting, inexpensive black suits, always clean and always pressed. In the beginning of his work with a camera, those clothes were all he could afford. Later, when cashmere jackets and tailored suits were within his reach, he wore the same plain clothes defiantly. They were him, Nikos, the father's son. He wasn't giving them up. It was only later, when he started to use his camera stealthily and for more money than he could ever make at weddings, that he realized how valuable they were. With them on, he never stood out in a crowd. Unless he spoke, no one saw him. Unless he moved, no one looked twice. The old clothes were the perfect, portable blind for shooting the world's wilder animals.

While Varga talked, Nikos took a white tissue from his coat pocket, cleaned the pocketknife, closed the blade, and slipped it into a velvet sheath. "Look at the one of Santry coming out of the library," he said. "If he let his hair grow and took off his collar, he'd make a decent Greek. He already has the face and the black suit." Then, wondering about the phone conversation, he asked, "Why won't he give you names?"

Varga answered without looking up from the latest batch of photographs. "He refuses to be an informer. That position is inconsistent and a little crazy, but in a principled sort of way. Santry is very fond of principles and guilt, which is fortunate for me, because that guilt-whip is driving him straight into the shark I'm after." He took a photo from the desk and held it toward Nikos. "Look at him! One of the wealthiest and most respected businessmen in Greece: intelligent, fierce, attractive, and entirely degenerate. A one-man corruption factory. I've been after him for years, but he buys everybody up. I could never get close enough to prove anything. But Santry can! Nikos, if I play that priest right, I may soon have this son-of-a-bitch by the gonchies." He looked carefully at the enlarged, full-face picture of Andreas Korachis and asked, "How'd you get it? It's a terrific shot. You've caught the bastard's incredible arrogance."

Nikos finished a wedge of apple, thanked Varga for the compliment, and passed it off as routine. "A well-known face and address, parked car, hours of waiting, telephoto lens—the usual combinations."

"No sign of the blonde?"

"Not yet, but he's got to turn up. How important is he?"

"I'm not sure he's important at all, but he's so dangerous we've got to keep track of him. He's one we don't want moving around behind our back."

* * *

He stood naked and motionless in front of the full-length mirror, admiring the lean, muscular body that filled the glass. He spoke without turning toward the bed, where she lay. "You've been very quiet. Anything wrong?" His tone was relaxed and effortlessly so. Larus had to work his body: stretch, press, and use it hard to keep it perfect, but to be casual, to be careless, required no discipline at all. His indifference was, or so he considered it, a gift that spared him the more prevalent forms of self-torture. He was not a worried man. He did not agonize. He needed and wanted no one intensely enough to make an issue of it. *Love* was a word he never used, reeking as it did of emotional confusion and instability. Yes, there were times when he needed and wanted a woman, but when the need passed, so did she. Gabriella? Good when together, unimportant when apart. Compelling, finally, only because she was Korachis's lover.

He knew she was watching and shifted to one side so he could see her in the mirror. She took his place in the glass: propped up on pillows, brown legs pulled close to her body, wearing the light purple robe Ladrea had brought from the Indies, all bundled up after sex as if the act had chilled her. Smoke from a cigarette drifted aimlessly from tense fingers and curled around her dark, imperious face—a face far more believable as a desert queen come alive from ancient sculpture than as a fashion model in Athens. Rich men watched and spent thousands to dress their women in her clothes, only to turn away in disappointment when that regal look had not been delivered with the gift-wrapped box.

"You haven't answered my question," he said, reaching into his bag and taking out a black turtleneck sweater. She gave him only more silence and, not for the first time, he wondered how close she and Ross were becoming. That possibility excited no commonplace jealousies because he didn't care where she slept.

He did care, however, if Ross was fucking his way through the family to edge him out. He pulled on his jeans and shirt, adjusted his watchband, and asked, "Okay, what it it? Why the chill?"

Her eyes and words accused him. "You went too far today."

He was surprised but kept it light. "I thought you liked the extras."

She got up and stood in front of him. "You're losing control," she said harshly.

"I thought that was the whole point."

"It's true. It was a mistake to leave Santry like that. It was a mistake to kill the sailor. And it's a mistake to leave that insulting card wherever you go."

He turned his back on her, faced the mirror, and nonchalantly combed his hair. "Well, I'm glad you told me, Gabriella. That's what friends are for, aren't they? Tell me, are there any other mistakes we should talk about? It'd be good to look at them all together." He caught her eyes in the mirror. "Make sense to you?"

"I haven't been making lists. If you want the details, talk to Savonon. I overheard some talk, that's all. Do with it what you want."

"Talk?" he repeated. "You heard some talk. How tidily unspecific. Well, what I'll do with it goes like this." He studied her insolently. "First, sincere apologies, lover, for overstepping the bounds of appropriate passion. You seemed to be enjoying yourself, but I obviously misread the grunts and groans. Next time let's try it without dope. In the clear light of everyday consciousness, I'll be less inclined to excess. Probably less inclined to any contact at all." He watched her face to see if the knife had cut, but he couldn't be sure. He had never met such an unyielding bitch. "As for the rest," he said, smiling with the memories, "Santry's disposition was a bit uncool, given his influence with Ross, the new crown prince and heir apparent, but if the priest is offended, dear one, it's more by the film than the outdoor sleeping arrangements, and for that you are as wickedly involved as I. The dead sailor? I honestly can't imagine whose tender sensibilities are offended by his passing. Certainly not Korachis's. His exorbitant love for the race is sufficient to eliminate all but a few disciples. Which leaves the cards. That bit of nonsense comes straight from Forticos, who is really complaining because I consider him worthless, which, in fact, he is. Why should anyone object if I sign my handiwork? An engraved 'G' goes nowhere." He dropped a few ice cubes in a glass, poured a drink, and sat down. "What interests me more is the peculiar conjunction of this rash of complaints with the arrival of Alexander Ross. I begin to wonder if a campaign is on to discredit me or even to ease me out."

"Stop it!" she commanded. "Your monologue is all wrong. Your edge *is* gone. A year ago you'd never justify yourself like that. You'd just walk out. Today I complain and you jump through the hoops like a wounded puppy." Her angry voice pummeled him. "Those cards are a disgrace! Vain, unnecessary advertisements revealing the childish need to have idiots in villages telling awesome stories about a mysterious 'Ghost.' Have you been sleeping through our films? Didn't any of it take?" She was talking fast now and clipping her words. "At the base of all predictability is the infantile itch for approval. You can't be free and scratch it at the same time. You know that! Or you knew it once. Either way, you've regressed to primitive addictions. I can't believe it. You're actually jealous of Ross, actually lusting after his job."

Larus interrupted and corrected her calmly, quelling the urge to tear the goddamned room apart. "It is not his job, Gabriella. It is my job! You certainly led me to believe that Korachis agreed to that some years ago, and for good reasons: My work in the field brought life and wealth to the old man. But now there's a change, the winds have shifted, and someone else is moving in.

Well, I consider that theft, and I'd argue that simple justice, not jealousy, requires me to object. When a man pulls a knife on me, I'm bound to defend myself. Right? Right! Now someone—I don't know who or in what combination—has just attacked me. Whether it's Korachis or Savonon pushing for Ross makes little difference. They're reasonably intelligent men, so they surely don't believe Larus is going to retire to a corner and suck his thumb while they strip him. And, finally, your little lectures on freedom and predictability have become a tedious, predictable pain in the ass, so have a heart and stuff that bullshit!''

She said nothing for a moment and then began to applaud softly. "Bravo, bravo, Larus! That had a very nice edge to it. I liked it very much." Her relaxed face confirmed the pleasure as she reached for his glass, drank, then kissed him. He knew she wasn't posturing and certainly not surrendering, because they had gone this way before: right through insult, bitterness, and acrimony to a sudden reversal. "And now what?" she asked, a smile on her lips. "How does the knight defend his honor? How does the 'Ghost' haunt the castle of the king?"

His arms went around her, one hand pressing gently in the small of her back. "Is Korachis's decision about Ross final?"

She pressed closer. "Yes. They have a longer history than you know. For Andreas, it's like bringing in a son, but, in this case, one with an impressive record. He'll work under Savonon for a few months and then take over."

"And you agree," he asked, moving his body against her, "that self-defense is appropriate?"

"I agree only that you and I should act unpredictably. The ruts rise on all sides. Before the gravestone caps the container, it is appropriate to use wings—even dark ones."

Mithymna, Lesbos

Santry stood by the west windows and watched the sun scatter its last light on the waters that carried Agamemnon's ships from Aulis to Troy and, he had read that afternoon, the head of Orpheus to Lesbos. Turkey's dark headlands rose in the north, a few miles across the sea, and Santry thought he'd like to visit Istanbul. He finished his drink, studied the empty glass, and went for another, glancing at the TV as he walked behind Ladrea and Alexander, who were talking on the cushioned wicker couch. Their idyllic month in the deep green foliage and mahogany beds of the West Indies was well behind them, but their pleasure in each other seemed undiminished. Santry didn't know how long that could last, given the enormous differences between them, but what did he know? From the outside looking in, who could know anything? His closest friends certainly didn't know what was going on with him. And if told, they wouldn't believe it. Too strange and unbelievable. Odd, he reflected, it was already becoming less strange to him. His conversations with Alexander no longer brought the quick cringe of regret experienced when he first lied to his friend by saying "I'm going to stay a few months to think things over. Then, who knows? Maybe home to Detroit, maybe Latin America."

Ross had even offered him work with Korachis's organization, and Santry had been impressed—not by the job, but by Ross's quick assumption of authority. His friend was ruggedly free of all new-boy-on-the-block awkwardness, and Santry was glad for that because he was running with a wild pack. A less-forceful man would be skinned and fed to the dogs by Larus alone. Ross would probably do all right. He hadn't lost many rounds in Detroit, and he had never been beaten down.

Santry looked up at the sound of the door, saw him coming, and felt his stomach tighten. He hadn't seen

Larus since the night of the filming. He watched suspiciously as the blonde kissed Ladrea on the cheek, ignored Ross, and came directly toward him, wearing at least the mask of amiability. The smile was easy and the manner seemed sincere as he said, "Father, I want to apologize for the rough treatment you got after the filming last month. The idiots responsible for leaving you outside in the rain are no longer working for us."

Santry, no believer in cheap grace and sure that no sadist changed his spots so fast, countered, "And what about the jackals responsible for the treatment inside?"

Larus gave a little laugh as he turned to fix a drink. "Yes, I can understand why you'd be upset about that, but, believe me, no harm was intended. You should think of it as an evening dedicated to science and religion." His smile veered toward a sneer as he concluded, "I thought the film would fit nicely in your parish education programs. Young Catholics would be inspired by such an accomplished, cosmopolitan priest."

Santry replied without effort at pleasantness. "I assume you brought the film. I want Alexander and Ladrea to appreciate the quality of your work."

Larus crossed the room and sat in the empty chair facing the couch, his fingers playing idly with the double-looped turquoise strands about his neck. "As a matter of fact, no. I got your request, but, unfortunately, the film's been lost." He lifted his hands in a gesture of helplessness. "It sometimes happens. I was very disappointed myself because I had looked forward to seeing it again." He gave Santry a suggestive smile and told him, "I had the impression that you and I worked well together, but I wanted to be sure. I think we can use you again."

Alexander interrupted to say the news was beginning, the brusque wave of his hand telling others to be quiet. Just as well, Santry thought. Nothing gained for him by sparring with Larus. *Don't get baited into an argument,* he told himself, *just keep away from him.* He retreated to the west window with his drink and stared at the dark sea. Ladrea, who refused to be diverted from the imagined world in which she lived by the monotonous brutalities called news, had gone to the kitchen to cook the mushrooms she and Santry had picked that afternoon in the olive groves. Larus moved to take her place on the couch beside Alexander. Perhaps five or ten minutes passed before Santry heard the newscaster mention Iraq and turned from his window in time to see Larus lean toward Ross, point at the screen, and say, "Watch this." Santry looked and saw smoking debris in the midst of charred, tangled steel and knew immediately that another Iraqi embassy car had been bombed in Athens. The fourth that month. "Credit" for the attack, in which two Greeks had been killed, was claimed by Al Dhama, a terrorist group unknown before this particular series of bombings.

The segment passed, and a meaningful look went between the men on the couch, although nothing more was said. Santry emptied his glass, and considered but refused another. He was sure he had stumbled accidentally onto cold, treacherous ground and had to tread carefully.

"Watch this!"

Had Larus seen the news clip earlier in the day? Not likely. He had just arrived from Athens. So how did he know what was coming? And why his special interest? And why should he assume that Ross would share the excitement?

The announcer said something about St. Jerome, as a famous painting of the saint filled the screen, and a voice explained that the painting had been stolen from the island of Malta. Then came a commentary linking the bombings and the stolen art as examples of rising barbarism. Santry wanted to object, wanted urgently to clarify the important difference between the terrorism that killed innocents and the theft that might bring food to thousands.

Ross and Larus had gotten up and walked to the door. Alexander turned and waved. "Back in a minute, Mike."

Larus left without a word or a look, and Santry recalled Ladrea's assertion—*they don't take you seriously.* He went to the television, snapped it off, and stared at the bare screen, remembering Larus's excited voice urging Ross to "watch this!" as two Greeks died in Athens.

Ross returned within the hour, fixed a drink, and told Ladrea and Michael that it was good to be alone with them. Santry waited until after dinner to press his question. "Did Larus have something to do with that bombing at the Iraqi embassy?"

"Why do you ask that, Mike?" inquired Ross, so casually the question might have been about the weather.

"Because before the story was announced on TV, he leaned over and told you to watch it. It was as if he knew what was coming."

Ross fingered his coffee cup and challenged him, "Why should that interest you one way or the other?"

The response appalled the priest. In the long years of their friendship, Alexander had rarely been evasive. On the contrary, he had worn "straight talk" as an emblem of his direct, no-nonsense style. In friendship as in corporate politics, he prided himself that people always knew "where he stood."

Santry didn't hedge. "It interests me for the same reason I assumed it would interest you. It suggests that Larus—and, therefore, your organization—was somehow involved. Otherwise, why his knowledge of what was coming? Why his excitement? And why his eagerness for you to look?" As he talked, Santry heard the anger rising in his voice and the harsh edge of accusation in the question. He glanced again at Ladrea. Was he imagining things, or had she silently urged him to press ahead? It was hard to be sure because he found her uncommonly interested in everything, but he had the impression that she waited until their eyes met and then gave the slightest of nods, as if to say that she had been wondering about many of the same things.

"You still haven't answered my question, Mike." Ross spoke quietly and Santry was annoyed by the reasonable tone of his friend, who was brandishing his cool, executive style. "Why should Larus concern you one way or the other? Why should you be even the least bit interested in what he or, for that matter, the organization does?"

The words came smoothly, and the honest Scottish face from which they flowed looked friendly and solicitous, but Santry knew he was being told that neither Larus nor the organization was any of his goddamned business. The faint, familiar smell of acrimony and rift sullied the air. Lines were being drawn and barbed. He was sure that threats, veiled or otherwise, could follow, because he had been there before hundreds of times. Never with Alexander, but more than often enough with landlords, cops, union bureaucrats, and civic leaders to learn the pattern and know the pace. Press too far and sooner or later came the flat palm in the face and the voice barking "Butt out!" Santry refused to be backed off.

"Then let me spell it out, Alexander. I'm interested because even among us thieves there must be some honor. Not much, perhaps, but some. At least enough remnant of a code to resist full moral collapse. As you know, I consider Larus vile, cruel, and capable of killing innocent people, so his excitement about the bombing doesn't surprise me. But I don't want to believe that you've joined him. I guess that's it. I guess it comes down to that: I don't want a close friend of mine killing people."

"Mike, Mike, what's going on!" Ross exclaimed. "Where's this craziness coming from? I honestly don't know what Larus meant, and I didn't care up to this moment, but if it's important to you, I'll find out and tell you. No problem. As for the rest if it, hey, Michael, have a heart, you know me better than that. No close friend of yours is killing anybody."

Ross reached over, pressed the priest's shoulder, and Santry felt the strong, warm hand and good affectionate smile easing suspicion's knot. Easing, but not untying. He had gotten no answers; he had gotten a massage. But surely that was predictable. Few men would admit to error, however trivial. When it came to murder, all were certifiably innocent. Had he really expected Ross to level with him? To tell him the truth? To say "Sure, Mike, we're selling dynamite to terrorists"? He was angry with himself. The questions had been naïve. Ross had taken vows. He had signed on with a new corporation. His job was to make it grow. Period. A company rep was a company rep and gave the company line whether that company was a union, church, city hall, or political sect.

Santry attempted a smile. "Sorry, Alexander. That was harsh, but Larus excites my worst suspicions. I really don't want to know anything about what you're doing. It's bound to be depressing, and there's nothing I can do about it. I just hope you'll be careful."

"Nothing to worry about, Mike. This operation's more like selling mufflers than you'd imagine."

Santry didn't bother to argue. Ross had given him classic public relations treatment: warm smile, hand on shoulder, meaningless banter. All the more reason to trust his own suspicions. Larus and the Iraqi embassy bombings were connected. Two women lay facedown on a cold sidewalk, guilty of being in the wrong place at the wrong time, trespassers in an unmarked war zone. Bags of groceries had broken open and scattered. A thin stream of blood trailed from one of the victims off the right side of the screen.

In all previous cases of well-publicized terrorism, that thin stream had led Santry nowhere. It had vanished in the thin air of remote places, unfamiliar names, and spotty reporting. He saw Larus stalking him again, his body hard, graceful, insinuating, his voice insolent and whispering "Watch this! Watch this!" The trail had not vanished this time and Santry wanted to look away, wanted not to see where the blood ran, but the contours of distant, abstract terrorism insisted on swirling into features and assembling into a face. The blood that disappeared off the right side of the screen ran to Lesbos and Larus and to where he stood. And a frightening thought flickered in the caverns of his mind. A brief, uncertain thought, quickly put away, but fearful all the same. Perhaps his presence in this place and at this time was no accident. He left it there. He didn't press, didn't scurry behind the screen of thought to search for providence or calling. He had always been uncomfortable with such claims. A man should do his job and resist self-righteousness. That was enough. But if no accident, then what? He couldn't answer, and, anyway, it didn't work like that. One just felt the harness brush one's skin and slip into place. One didn't know where one was going. One only knew one could no longer walk away. He folded his napkin, placed it carefully to the left of his empty glass, and pushed back his chair. "I don't know about you two, but I'm all talked out. How about some cards?"

Ross looked at his watch. "I'll take you on tomorrow, Mike. I've got to change clothes and get out of here. Larus and I have work to do. It may be morning before I get back." He saw Santry wondering and said, "Don't ask. I can't tell you what I'm doing."

Santry remarked dryly, "I assume you'll tell us when the streets are too dangerous to be outside."

Ross looked at him curiously. He was no longer smiling. "You're dead serious about this, aren't you? Let's get a good couple of hours together as soon as my schedule settles down. I want to fill you in on things."

In thirty minutes, Ross had changed into jeans, heavy sweater, and wet-weather gear. He kissed Ladrea goodbye, encouraged Santry not to worry, and walked out. They watched the door close and listened to his steps growing fainter on the cobblestone street running behind their house downhill. Santry noted that Ross turned toward the harbor, not toward town. An agreeable silence held between them until the table was cleared and the dishes washed. Then Santry asked her, "How much do you know about Larus?"

She seemed puzzled by the question, pushed her hair back from her eyes, and replied lightly, "Only the too much I overhear." Her thick black hair fell forward again in soft waves along the sides of her face.

"You hear 'too much'?" he asked.

"Yes. I don't want to know anything about Larus, but I can't avoid overhearing things. And," she added with a sly smile, "I was taught to share." She had been quiet and detached during dinner but now became playful, almost gay. "So I'll tell you things, but in my own way. Nothing's easy in this life. You told me so yourself. Are you ready?"

"Ready? I don't know what you're talking about."

"That's because you don't know how to listen."

Santry wasn't in the mood for games, but beneath the jaunty mood, he sensed a serious purpose, and told her he was ready.

"I'm glad," she said, urging him not to be impatient. "There's more than one way to tell the truth, and the game's sometimes better played in code. Tonight we'll do it all with questions. What prayer were you taught as a child?"

"Ladrea, please, I'm sorry, but I don't understand what you're doing."

"I'm answering your question with questions."

"What question?"

"You asked me what I knew about Larus and I'm going to tell you, but in a way that will tell me more about you. Fair?"

He gave a friendly sigh and answered, "I was taught the Lord's Prayer."

"Give me the first names of your friends and relatives. I'll tell you when to stop."

"Charlie, Sam, Alexander, Gino—"

"Stop! Do you spell Gino with a G or a J?"

"A G."

"Good. I like Gino. Remember him and give me the name of the fragments you stole from Kallos."

Something about that made Santry uneasy, but he told her, "The Ephesian Fragments."

"And why did you steal them?"

He began to tell her about hunger in Detroit, the food factory, and how the Fragments' existence as a museum piece was served just as well by a copy, but she stopped him.

"No, no, you're making it too hard. You stole them for a 'what'?" With work, she extracted "reward" from him. Then came his family life as a "son," an extended discussion of the "omnipotence" of God, and, finally, the significance of the nativity. She insisted she had made it too easy for him by asking religious questions. "Now give me each identified word."

He got one or two out of order, but eventually arranged them in proper sequence: Lord's Prayer, Gino, Ephesians, Reward, Son, Omnipotence, and Nativity. She thanked him for the discussion and told him to string the first letter of each word together. He got it right the second time: LPGERSON.

"Put a period after 'L' and after 'P.'"

"L.P. Gerson?" he asked.

"Yes," she said, suddenly sober and quiet. "That's one thing I know about Larus, but you'll have to get its meaning for yourself. There's more, but I want to see what you do with this."

The phone startled them. It had not rung all day and Santry had forgotten it was in the house. He listened to Ladrea's bright surprise when she learned it was Gabriella calling from Athens, but saw her quicksilver face shift from pleasure to worry about something being said. It was a brief conversation. Santry, who had looked away in order not to intrude, heard the phone returned to its cradle and Ladrea's anxious voice telling him, "She had a dream and wants Alexander to be careful around Larus. That's so strange."

"It doesn't sound strange to me," Santry countered, taking Gabriella's side. "I'm sure it's good advice."

"No, the advice isn't what I meant. Of course Alexander should be careful around Larus, but he's better at those things than any of us. I mean, it's the first dream she's remembered in years, and it's the first time she's ever warned me about Larus. That's what's strange. That's what worries me."

Larus pointed to the dark cove below them. "I'll come in with my lights off. If it's all clear, give a quick flash with the car's high beams. If I don't see that, I'll know there's trouble and go to the beach I showed you this afternoon."

The Toyota, parked on a farm road used only in the summer, purred smoothly and sent a stream of warm air curling about their legs. The glowing hands on the panel clock said ten before midnight. Outside, rocky headlands formed an ancient amphitheater, its sides rising high above them, darker even than the starless sky. Directly ahead the ground fell away and plunged downward toward the rough waters cascading against a narrow beach. A winding, deserted coast road, the one they'd use to run from Mithymna on Lesbos's north shore to Mitilini and the island's only airport, curved into the empty hills a few hundred yards behind them.

Two days before, five hundred miles to the east, a prisoner had been carried to a Turkish hospital for surgery. An armed guard accompanied him through a series of X rays, tests, and examinations. During the night, a fire in the laundry room blossomed savagely, licking walls and blowing hot, choking smoke into the wards. The panic was predictable, as planned. Those who could move at all fought for the doors. Those who could not screamed and pleaded. The incinerating flames took patients and hundreds of files. For four hours, chaos raged, which left more than enough time to drive far from Ankara toward the Turkish coast.

The trip to Lesbos would soon begin: a small, fast boat hugging the Turkish shore, running lights off, a high-speed dash across the strait into Greek waters, a sudden reduction of speed that would seem imperceptible to the jacketed passenger, who must jump the moment the green light flashed from the sheltered bay, the leap, the quick roar of accelerating motors, and the safety of the open sea. If the speedboat had been picked up on radar, doubtful on a bad weather night, there would be nothing in the Greek navy near enough or fast enough to catch it. And if there were, they'd find nothing: no trace of fish, drugs, munitions, contraband. Odds were they wouldn't be bothered. And as the boat powered away from Lesbos, a soaked and anxious Italian would be pulled over the sides of a rubber dinghy and flop awkwardly on the bottom, his mouth working like a distraught fish for the few minutes it would take to get to a small, isolated cove, warm clothes, and the car that would drive straight to the private plane waiting to carry him off to Rome.

The plan was well known to both of them, but Larus insisted on repeating each detail. Ross thought Larus was simply enjoying his moment as commander. In fact, the blonde was playing the baiting game. "I'll arrive at the cove between one and two. Under no circumstances can you leave the car during that hour. Your only job is to sit here and flash the lights when you see me."

Ross, who had suggested to Korachis that he spend his first few months observing their different operators in action, said he thought he could handle the assignment and stared out the window at the ghostly shapes of sheep sleeping on the hillside. "What other projects are you working on?"

Larus's fingers drummed lightly on the steering wheel. "Sorry, Ross, that's privileged. Only Savonon knows, and if he hasn't told you, neither will I."

Larus had been giving Ross the same childish hard time for days, and Alexander decided to nail him to the floor. "It's past time to drop that Little League bullshit, Larus. You can't play rough dude and whining loser in the same act."

"Listen, Ross, anytime you want to—"

Ross chopped the sentence off. He spoke as comfortably and directly as he would to any subordinate. "Forget it: We're out of grade school. No need for us to go into the alley and tear each other up. I've got an easier way: We figure out how we both win the game. You're pissed because I've got the job you wanted, and I'm unhappy because the best field man in my organization is somebody I can't trust behind my back. Better for both of us to figure out how to get along, because if we can't, then, my friend, you've got to go. There is no other way. But they tell me you're good, so I'd like to keep you. Therefore, a proposition: You accept the fact that you can't have my job, not now and not ever, and in return, I'll create a new position that gives you day-to-day supervision of field operations. It's not a free hand. You'll report directly and daily to me, but if we can get along, money and power'll move your way."

In the darkness, Larus smiled and felt the tide moving his way without Ross's help. Strong, solitary waves were carrying him high above them all. If these people weren't so pathetic, he'd despise them. Each one a loser, each a puffed-up clown's balloon, airy and vacant. Gabriella: a spent, anorexic bitch chattering mindlessly about unpredictability while panting after Korachis's furs and yachts. Santry: the failed moralist, exuding shame from every pore and trying to shift the jackal brand. Now this Ross: a second-string businessman from the American Midwest playing straight-shooter and trying to buy him. *Who do these sheltered assholes think they are? What does Ross think I'm going to do? Grab his smeared pen and sign on the line, slip on the cuffs, then go to the locker room and check in my balls?* His eyes peered intently over the steering wheel and focused on a distant light at sea. His voice, when it came, was cool and distant. "I don't think that'll work, Ross. No, I don't think that'll work at all."

"If you've got a better idea, it's time to tell me."

Larus laughed openly and asked sarcastically, "Is that how you do it in Detroit? Is there twenty-five dollars for the best submission? Well, why not? Maybe I'll drop a winner in the suggestion box one of these days." He checked his watch and moved the luminous hands on the car clock five minutes ahead. It was fifteen past midnight. "But right now I've got to meet a boat. Remember to stay with the car. We could arrive anytime in the next two hours and we'll have to move fast. Watch the dinghy pull out so you'll recognize its shape."

The door slammed and Larus moved quickly down the ravine toward the secluded beach. Winds blew flecks of rain against the car window and muffled the sound of the dinghy's motor, but Ross had no trouble seeing the boat ease into the rough water and head north along the coast. He took a Thermos from his bag and poured a cup of steaming coffee. Larus would probably come around. Ross had dealt with high-powered corporate competitors for years and took it as routine that after every battle for advancement, it was his job to deal with wounded egos and get them on his team. He'd give Larus a few more weeks to huff and puff, but then the golden boy had to make a decision: in or out, one or the other. And if he couldn't make up his mind, Ross was prepared to drive him out of Greece. He flicked on the car radio, found some music, and settled down to wait.

Out of sight beyond the rocky cliff, the rubber dinghy moved slowly through choppy waters toward Mithymna's small harbor. Larus squinted into the biting wind and spray whipping his face. Rain gear black as the raft itself kept him dry, but the temperature was dropping and his hands were cold. The scattered lights of the hillside village gleamed in the rain ahead, rising sharply upward toward the dark mass of the castle that crowned and brooded over all. Larus's eyes stayed on the water, the beach, and the nearby buildings. When he passed the pier of the old olive factory, he turned the boat straight for shore, jumped out in shallow water, and beached it in front of the winter-empty Molyvos Hotel.

His back braced against the driving wind, he took the green signal light from his shoulder case, lashed it to a post, and pointed it to sea. When he switched it on, his eyes fixed on a wave a hundred yards out and he imagined the boat speeding past, the sudden, unnoticed splash, and the quick shift in Italian eyes from anxious expectation to bright fear when no one appeared on the cold Aegean's treacherous surface to pick him up. *Fuck him! And may his thieving partners in Rome, soon to be in grief for their dear, departed comrade, fuck Korachis and tear him up for deserting one of their own.*

Larus was quietly exultant. By dawn, Korachis would be reeling: at war with an international drug ring, Ross dead, his daughter vanished. Larus's long, hard legs kept a fast pace on the deserted streets as he walked to his car, spurred on by visions of Gabriella reading the taunt he'd leave by Ladrea's empty bed, written, of course, on the card she considered childish, the one elegantly engraved with the single letter "G."

He made no attempt to approach the house quietly.

He wanted the sounds of car doors and metal gates to whet their anxiety. He wanted them to wonder who was coming at this late hour. Not Ross, they'd say. They knew he might be gone until dawn. His footsteps stopped at the door, where he refused to knock, refused to make a sound, knowing they would have to come. Reading would stop dead in its lettered tracks, eyes would meet and worry, fears would fester. They were in a strange house on a windy, dark night and the specter of a prowler had been raised. They'd have to check, have to get up and see. He watched the window by the door, anticipating the parted curtains and Santry's immobile face peering there.

And it was Santry who stared, but the door that opened. The priest looked immediately beyond Larus and asked, "Where's Ross?"

Larus pushed him contemptuously aside and walked into the house. "He's waiting for a fellow countryman of yours, another Italian sheep gone astray. Tell me," he said breezily, "why are you people so prone to sin?" He crossed to the bar, in the far corner of the living room, poured Scotch over ice, and looked around. One reading lamp was on and the stereo was off. Ladrea had clearly gone to bed. *Even better with her upstairs,* he thought. The hostile priest leaned against the kitchen door, staring. "You have a good indignant look, Santry. I imagine in your lifetime it's restored many to the paths of righteousness. A serious question for you. If you and Ross die tonight, will your souls fly heavenward or sink in hell? Or will they just simmer in their foul juices for a time? Come, come, Father, don't be coy. You must have learned a few things over the years. And if the answer's some kind of holy secret, then, cross my heart, it will go with me to the grave."

Santry turned abruptly, walked into the kitchen, and closed the door. Larus settled comfortably in a chair, sipped his Scotch, and listened to the water running in the sink, the footsteps, and the sounds of drawers being slowly opened and quietly closed. The water stopped. Silence. The priest apparently intended to remain in the kitchen. Larus was pleased and permitted himself a satisfied smile. He enjoyed these cat-and-mouse skirmishes.

"Santry!" he shouted gruffly, expecting but receiving no reply. He imagined the ridiculous priest standing motionless and bewildered near the kitchen sink and wondered if he was crossing himself. "I'm going to tell you something, Santry, and then you'll come to me as if Jesus himself was calling. I'm sure of it. You, the immovable object, will be subject to my irresistible force, and you will voluntarily leave your hiding place. It will be thrilling to see you, Father, as you open the door you've so impolitely placed between us. Where were you brought up? Did your mother teach you nothing of courtesy? Or was she as miserably mannered as the Great Mother Mary? Aha! You are now thinking I intend to drive you out with insults. No, my insults will not bring you through the door. Say 'mother whore' to some men and they tear the house apart, but you lack the balls for that, Santry. Your shriveled walnuts lead you nowhere. Now listen carefully—let this hook take you in the cheek! When I finish my Scotch, I am going to walk up the stairs to Ladrea's room, slip her in a sack, and take her off. You do what you please about that, Father. Try to stop me, or, when Ross asks where you were when his love was kidnapped, tell him you were cowering in the kitchen, no doubt on your knees."

Larus stood up, swallowed the last of his Scotch, and shattered the empty glass against the kitchen door. He checked his watch. Time to move. He took a three-foot piece of thin, nylon rope from his pocket and held it loosely in one hand as he walked toward the kitchen. But the door swung open before he got there and Santry confronted him. Larus saw the empty hands and the tired but steady eyes. He saw no excited, nervous reaction to the garrote. Then, unexpectedly and without a word, the priest turned, walked to the stairs, and climbed to the second floor. Larus let him go. He had always intended to leave him strapped to Ladrea's bed. His voluntary presence upstairs made things easier. Larus moved quickly to the phone and cut the cord. Then he proceeded to the kitchen, where he tripped all the circuits, and went swiftly on to the stairs. He took them one at a time and slowly, stopping to listen on every rise, letting his eyes adjust to the darkness, letting the careful, calculated pace intimidate his prey. The driving wind rattled the shutters and drove strange moans from the walls, but a different movement toward the rear of the house suggested Santry was at the windows, checking heights. The priest had panicked. He was much too high to jump and walk away. Larus reached the landing, waited, watched ahead for shadows, and listened. More noise at the far end of the long, second-floor corridor convinced him that Santry was trying to crawl out on him. *Time to take him down,* Larus decided.

He was ten steps from the top when he stopped abruptly, heard the running feet pounding down the hall, and, astonished seconds later, saw Santry hit the top step like a wild broad jumper and take straight off, feet churning the air, coming down the stairwell on top of him, knees and arms pounding into his head, smashing him backward off his feet, off balance, out of control, reeling downward. They hit the railing on the fly, broke through it, and crashed against the wall. Santry never stopped swinging his fists or driving his legs forward. Larus, momentarily breathless and pinned, took the blows on his arms, positioned himself carefully, waited until Santry raised a bit, then drove his knee violently upward into the unprotected crotch. Santry moaned and folded. Larus rolled, whipped his powerful right arm around Santry's neck, shook him like a child, squeezed him limp, tied him up, and threw the house switches back on. The fun and games were over.

No one had slept through that racket. Ladrea had to

be awake and frightened, waiting for him to come. He took the stairs three at a time and threw open her door. Empty! And the double bed was unused. He stared angrily at a small photo of her and Ross nearby, then raced through every room in the house, tore open closets, searched behind doors and furniture. And then he knew—she had never been upstairs. Santry had gone to the kitchen and closed the door because she had been there; Santry had then gone upstairs to lure him away. He bolted outside and circled the house: road on the front, open fields to the rear, harbor far below. A harsh wind was blowing. She couldn't have gotten far. And she was cold. Her coat had been left inside. She was going to be a lot colder before the night was over. But where? Where? He turned slowly where he stood, searching every shadow, near and far, tense, listening. Some movement uphill across the back field seized his eye. And then he heard the sheep bells and knew he had her. Up there in the dark below the castle walls, he glimpsed a figure and heard sheep running, hundreds of neck bells jangling and new lambs crying as they chased after frightened mothers. Ladrea had run straight for the deserted castle and was stumbling through the flock.

Of course! Where else would a girl with her fairyland imagination try to hide? Even without the wildly running sheep he should have guessed. He jumped into his car, drove to the road's end, ran the last hundred yards, and stood, breathing hard and excited, beneath the towering castle walls. He had wandered there a year ago and knew what lay inside. His light played briefly on an Arabic inscription chiseled in stone before he slipped quietly under a seven-hundred-year-old archway, up a narrow passage, and turned quickly through an iron-plated door to stand within the walls on castle grounds. Oleander trees brushed against him as he followed the slight incline upward toward the turrets. Massive blocks of stone rose like ancient sentries in the night or, fallen but unburied, served as giant steps across drenched soil where Greeks and Turks once fought. The wind had stopped howling, but a light rain, little more than mist, settled on him. He eyed the turrets all around. She could be in any one of them, huddled in a cold, stony corner. He climbed higher, crossed a walkway, flashed his light. Not there. He turned toward the other turrets, the obscure walls, the jumbled stones, and shouted, "Ladrea! Ladrea! Come out! The game's over!" It was almost two o'clock. It was almost time. "Ladrea! In sixty seconds you're going to see Alexander! Keep your eyes on the coastline beyond the Delphinia Hotel. You'll see him there!" He pulled his sleeve back to use his watch and began to yell, "Ten seconds, Ladrea! Eight, seven—keep watching—four, three, two!"

He stared and saw the fireball explode, tear open the southern sky, thunder back and forth across the bay, rip the air to shreds, and shake the earth for miles. Violent flames rose hundreds of feet above the ridge and clouds of black, oily smoke billowed high. The fire danced red across the sea and gleamed in Larus's eyes.

"See him!" he shouted exultantly at the surrounding turrets. "See him, Ladrea!"

And then he heard the sounds, all but imperceptible at first, like whisperings coming from within the wall or from the dark stones themselves. No more than uncertain murmurings when they first reached his ears, they were now a high-pitched wailing that rose beyond a scream. He had never heard her cry, and as he walked to tear her from her hiding place, he had never felt quite as serene and strong.

The long, dark silhouette of a speedboat shot by the cove, knifing a churning white swath through the water. No lights. Low and incredibly fast. A long arc of foam trailed as it made for open sea, white plume rising behind powerful, drumming motors. One-thirty on the panel clock. Drop completed, pickup in process. Ten minutes until the dinghy would arrive. Perfect. Time for that last coffee and cigarette. Cut the radio and open the windows to hear the motors. The nice, solid feel of the steel Thermos. The smell of coffee. Eyes on the water: boat already out of sight. No lights at sea in any direction. Again to the luminous dial: one-forty-five. He should have been here by now. Only the wind outside—and surf. No motors. Where the hell was he? One-fifty. Ross grabbed the flashlight and headed downhill to the beach, where he would climb over rocks to the end of the cove and could look straight up the coast toward the village. Had an informer called ahead? Or Greek radar picked them up? If there was trouble with other boats, he'd see the lights from the point ahead. And if they came while he was there, his voice and flash would be signal enough.

He moved quickly, almost jogging down the hard worn goat path, and had reached the beach when the volcano erupted behind and beat him down with scorching flames, flying rocks, dirt, fragments of shattered steel, and plain old terror. The debris settled fast, but the smoke and flames piled higher and higher above him and in their light he saw Larus's hands adjusting the panel clock and heard his insufferably arrogant voice telling him to stay with the car. Christ! And he heard Santry, too, putting his brand on the son-of-a-bitch: "a killer, vile and cruel." *Have to move, get back, find out—and by the shore. The blast'll bring everybody out—don't want to be seen on the road.* Flames rose high above him and lurid red reflected on the water as he scrambled along the rocky coast, carried along on an enormous surge of relief, shock, and pure, I-could-be-dead-now, thank-God-I'm-alive energy.

Two hours later, in a world hatefully worse, Ross hung up the phone in the house over the sea and told Santry grimly, "Korachis and Savonon are together. They don't want the police brought in. The airport and docks in Mitilini are covered. The company plane's still there—the pilot never heard from Larus. First Olympic flight to Athens is at seven-twenty A.M. No cruise ship till midmorning. I can't believe he's still on the island. He must have had a boat waiting for him at the harbor. Andreas is going to stay by the phone to take the ransom call. We'll connect later. Everything's piling up, Mike, and I need your help. There was a drop-off at the beach a couple of hours ago."

Santry remarked quietly, "I know. Larus was happy to mention it."

"I've got to comb that area. If we lose this one, it'll be a disaster. Will you give me a hand?"

Santry didn't like the sound of it, but it wasn't in him to turn down a rescue mission. "Sure, if you tell me who he is."

Ross wanted to tell him that, as well as many other things, but he knew how difficult the conversation would be when he did. "I will, Mike, but afterward. Okay?"

The people who had run to the streets or looked out their windows when the bomb exploded had once more closed their shutters and crouched in bed waiting for dawn and explanations. The north–south road had emptied. A quick drop down a steep path behind the Sunset Café brought Ross and Santry to a seaside park: small, a few trees and benches crowded between the Molyvos Hotel and the rock-rimmed water. Ross found the rubber boat on the beach and the light where it was supposed to be.

"Mike, he's close. The boat dropped him right out there and the light's his only connection to safety. He had to stay near it."

Ross flashed his light four quick times and waited, over and over again, but there was no response. The two men split up, went different ways to cover more ground, but stayed in voice range near the bushes, oil drums, and sheds along the shore. Ross walked the beach toward the south and the deserted olive oil factory. He peered through broken windows and cautiously followed recessed loading platforms into shadows. He heard the gasping when he reached the pier, swung his flashlight, and glimpsed the anguished face.

"Mike! Mike!" Steps running toward him. They stared together. "Hold the light. I'm going after him!" He eased off the seawall and dropped into waves that drove the shallow water over his head. Hand over hand down the length of the pier. What the hell was he doing there? In minutes, he looked into a purple, choking face, got a firm grip on a soaked woolen coat, and slowly dragged him out. Then he understood. The hospital in Ankara had not been entirely a ruse: one leg gone, the other slack and useless. He had been thrown overboard crippled and left to drift, carried to the pier by the waves that might as easily have drowned him.

Their lights drifted over the small, crumpled body and the contorted face. A doll's head, soaked and bone-cold, whose sullen eyes opened when it was raised, and closed when it was laid down. He was perhaps thirty years old, and as light as a jockey.

"He looks harmless enough," Santry mused, "but given the means of transport, I assume I'm wrong."

They went through his pockets. No identification and no money. He was being passed hand to hand, a kind of serial scalping. Everyone took his cut, wiped his knife, and shoved the body westward.

It was after five A.M. Ross took off to get a cab. "Call me day or night," the man had said. Warm clothes and food at the house, then a hurried ride to Mitilini, the island's southern port and only city, with Ross riding in front with the driver, Santry in back beside the Italian, who was wrapped in blankets sleeping. The worst for Alexander had been packing Ladrea's things: the full-sleeved, cotton blouse with floral patterns from the Indies, a vial of perfume, the small, framed snapshot by the bed, and black leotards, draped, lifeless, and empty on a chair. They had packed in silence; neither man was much given to expressions of distress, no matter how severe the pain.

By noon, the Italian was asleep in the Sappho Hotel. His new documents named him Anthony Tocaro of Naples. The examining doctor said he should be hospitalized and remain in Mitilini for a week. Ross said the man was staying at the Sappho and flying to Athens the next day. His call to Korachis came up empty. No contact from Larus. Not a good sign. There would be a meeting in the morning. With nothing to do but worry, Ross longed for strong drink, food, and sleep. He discovered that Santry was after the same things, so they found a tavern near the port and proceeded to tear up a bottle of ouzo along with generous servings of fried squid, fish, fava beans, french fries, and tomatoes.

It had been a long time since they had done any serious drinking together, and each was in the mood. "You look good in those clothes, Mike. Anytime you decide to leave the Church, you could make it as a dock worker."

Santry had hung his clerical garb in an Athens closet and replaced it with dark blue cords, a heavy turtleneck sweater, and a light windbreaker. He took the intended compliment with an easy smile and broke another piece of bread from the loaf on the table.

"I sometimes think of the last six months as an attempt by Alexander Ross to get me defrocked. And most days, I'm uncomfortably certain you're going to succeed." Then, more seriously, he added, "You know they're going to catch up with both of us, Alexander. You know this can't go on. Oh, for a while I hoped you were right and thought we might get away with it, but not anymore. Events are racing and have their own momentum. They make their own demands. We're being carried along now. A few months ago, Ladrea was an unknown name. Today you'd give your life to get her back. And so would I. She's a rare and—" He checked himself. Not the time for reminders. "But you see what I mean? At some point, it becomes impossible to walk away. Yet I had talked myself into believing that we could do exactly that: just take the Fragments and wave good-bye. Life as before, but, of course, better." He poured more ouzo, added a little water, and watched it cloud. He felt awkwardly poised on the edge of saying too much and backed off into silence.

Ross, who had grown puzzled and then impatient with Santry's self-inflicted dilemmas, asked bluntly, "Why can't you walk away, Mike? What's keeping you? Why don't you just fly out of Athens tomorrow and never come back?"

Santry thought for a moment before answering and took a cigarette from the pack Ross had laid on the table between them. He inhaled deeply and watched the smoke curl gently upward. "What's keeping me? Well, Anthony Tocaro, for one." He saw Alexander's frown and felt his own heat rising. "He's a drug dealer, isn't he? Larus practically said as much and you dodged the question. I didn't want to know anything about him. None of my business, I kept telling myself, but then you needed help. That's what I mean—the river keeps sweeping us downstream to some new place, places we hadn't even imagined before." He leaned across the table, speaking urgently now. "You know what heroin means in Detroit. You know what it does to people. It's a plague, Alexander, and those who spread it are filthy, money-mongering vermin."

Ross hadn't seen Santry so upset in years. This was exactly the kind of horseshit he knew was coming when Santry began asking questions. If he didn't like it, why didn't he shove off where he could pretend it wasn't going on? He was an incorrigible reformer who invented causes when real ones weren't handy. "Stop it! For Christ's sake, stop it! If you weren't able to deal with the Tocaros of the world in twenty long years in

Detroit, how the hell do you think you're going to clean up the world five thousand miles from home?"

Santry checked himself, certain he had gone too far, and resisted the strong impulse to tell Ross that while cleaning up the world was a dream long buried, there remained things a man could do. Small change, perhaps, but necessary all the same. However, why waste words and decent affections? Better to drink and reminisce; the waters were troubled enough. Just drift along on ouzo's golden glow. "You're right, Alexander, let's drop it. It goes nowhere." He felt suddenly very tired but couldn't let go. The bit was in his mouth and he had to work against it. "Doesn't any of this bother you? In a few months you'll be running the show. What happens then? Bigger and better, is that it? This year one Tocaro, next year twenty?"

Ross, preoccupied by fears for Ladrea and irritated by the ragging, snapped, "Sure, something like that. Look, get off my back, Mike. I've never pretended to be a reformer. I've never had a job that paid me to play angel. If we didn't save Tocaro, somebody else would have. That's how the money flows in the world today; that's not going to change, and if you don't like it, well, that's just tough shit, because there's nothing you can do about it."

The conversation bucked awkwardly and stalled. Ross poured one more, drank it too fast, said he was going to bed, and walked out. Santry lingered, glad to be alone, idling with a full glass and his own thoughts. He'd be happy to believe there was nothing he could do; he wasn't looking for more trouble, but there was always something if one didn't walk away early. He believed that if he believed anything. A spark flew from his ouzo glass to dry tinder and a flame leaped up. He watched it, a little frightened, and blew hard against it. It wavered but wouldn't go out. He tried to smother it with a napkin, but it kept on burning. A small flame, but rugged and bright. He fed it a few ideas. It blazed higher. *Impossible*, he told himself. *No,* he answered, *only necessary.* He pulled out his wallet and looked for Varga's number.

Savonon was on the phone when Ross walked into Korachis's opulent nineteenth-century mansion early the next morning. The man was huge. His barrel chest swelled magnificently at the belt, his quick, tiny eyes watched everything from within the folds of a deep-jowled, fat face. His head was bald, smooth, and, though it was a December morning, sweating. Repeatedly, he raised a blue tissue clutched in his left hand to wipe his broad brow dry. He was bullying someone, his voice low and ominous as a dog's growl when guarding food. He glanced up when Ross entered and nodded a curt greeting. Alexander took coffee from a side table and moved to high front windows, where he looked across a winter-green lawn to the sea. Korachis came shortly afterward and stood beside him. In dark, fashionably tailored suits, the two lean, distinguished-looking men, heads close together and voices low, might have been discussing stocks, bonds, or plans for the next board meeting.

"There have been developments," Korachis told him quietly. "Last night, Larus killed one of our men, a policeman named Forticos, on Kallos. Strangled him, then chained his body to the doors of the monastery museum."

Ross's eyes followed an intricate design in the Oriental rug. "You're sure it was Larus?"

"He left his card, a printed letter 'G' for 'Ghost,' his name when a mercenary in Africa, and a brief note saying only '. . . before the gravestone caps the container.' I have no idea what that means, but I suspect Gabriella will. She's dressing and will join us soon."

Savonon hung up and called to them, "Airline agents on Kallos report a tall, good-looking blonde on the first flight out this morning." The two men moved closer.

"I've got domestic and international terminals in Athens covered."

"How about his apartment?"

"Naturally," Savonon snapped. "That began yesterday, along with his bank, pharmacy, and liquor store."

Ross pressed, "Nothing else? No ransom note? No demands?"

"Yes, there's something else, but not demands. He's on the passenger list as A. Ross!"

The men looked at one another in silent astonishment before Korachis spoke. "It begins to appear that ransom is not the game. At least not yet." The older, carefully dressed man sat stiffly in a high-backed chair and spoke in the leisurely way common to men whose words commanded attention. The thin, chiseled face, hollow cheeks, and pearl-handled cane resting on the floor beside him carried Ross straight back to 1967 and the night they killed together. "Forticos's death and the use of Alexander's name," Korachis continued, "suggest a more serious intent. It's too soon to be sure, but Larus may have decided that if he can't succeed Savonon and lead the organization, no one else will, either. He may be out to tear it apart, destroy it, and do so in the name of his dead competitor. The next few days may bring bitter news." He fixed on Alexander as he concluded softly, "Forticos hoisted on museum doors suggests the basis for a pattern: pin dead agents to local projects. If I'm at all correct, he began on Kallos not simply because he dislikes Forticos, but because that's where the late Alexander Ross began his work with us. We must warn the others."

Savonon informed them, "I've already alerted every agent in the Athens area about the bombing and the kidnapping. If he's sighted, they'll call immediately. We should contact those outside Greece today. Beyond that, it's a waiting game."

"No! You can't wait till he murders someone else before going after him!" Gabriella's sharp voice snapped like a whip from the back of the room. She had been standing behind them, just inside the door, during most of the conversation. "You've got to take the initiative or he'll cut you to ribbons." Her gold dressing gown swirled about her legs as she moved to Korachis's side and rested one hand lightly on his shoulder. Ross watched Andreas's arm slip easily about her waist and wondered how they held it all together. Their daughter had been kidnapped by a man who shared the mother's bed. Larus, he thought, might be on a rampage against more than one competitor.

Savonon scowled and challenged her. "Your constructive ideas are *always* welcomed." His tone was abrasive and reflected years of argument between the two. Ross had seen them attack each other before and knew that Korachis would never intervene on her behalf. By his code, to do so would be patronizing, and those who worked for him were free to take her on. She didn't want or need his help to hold her own. "You might also shed some light on your boyfriend's calling card," he grumbled. "What do you think this means?"

She took the card and read out loud: " '. . . before the gravestone caps the container.' " Her eyes darkened and her voice was bitter. "He's telling me his behavior has become exemplary, which is to say—unpredictable."

"Does that help us seize the initiative?"

Her small regard for Savonon went undisguised. "Yes, of course, the way is crystal clear." She paused, as if waiting for Savonon to admit his dullness. "This note is obviously more than a taunt directed at me, though it is at least that. I agree with Andreas's judgment that he's out to decimate the organization, but he won't be content simply to bring it down. He must do it in a way that proves his superiority to all of us, so he'll leave these stupid notes wherever he strikes. And there's his fault. There's the chink through which we drive the spear. He's proving himself to others, always the fatal flaw. It's his driving weakness—he cares what we think about him. If we rub failure in his face, we'll force his hand, drag him out of shadows, and take him in a clearing." She stared at Savonon. "You still don't understand, do you?"

He glared and wiped his face. "This isn't quiz time, Gabriella. If you've got ideas, speak plainly."

She turned on Ross, testing him. "And you?"

"I think it's a good idea, but we could discuss it more easily if you'd drop the prosecutor's robe and take your place with the rest of us mortals. Your airs annoy me." He looked back at Savonon and saw in his eyes the satisfied glimmerings of one who had suddenly discovered an unsuspected ally. "As of yesterday, Larus assumed I was dead. The lesson for each of you was supposed to be that he could and would destroy anyone who violated his territory. But he failed. I'm alive and therefore a threat. When he learns I escaped, he'll assume we think he's incompetent and are smiling at his impotence. Beating up a priest and stealing a woman don't exactly prove a man's worth. So he'll have to come after me or I'm proved superior. As Gabriella suggests, we can drag him out of hiding by using me as the lure. I agree with her. It's the fastest way to make him come to us." Ross had their attention and increased respect. Gabriella especially searched his face with heightened interest, as if finding there something she had missed before. He saw the subtle change in all of them and held the floor. "Let me suggest a plan. If we can reach agreement this morning, I could get things moving in Athens this afternoon."

"Michael, hello, hello! I've been worried about you. I thought you had maybe left without saying good-bye, but here you are! My friend, I am not being polite when I tell you I'm glad to hear your voice. Crazy things are happening and we have to talk. Tell me, how are you? Are you all right?"

Santry listened to Varga's rich voice booming over the wires and felt like a man being given a great bear hug by a long-lost brother. He liked it. After the last couple of days, he was ready for some human warmth and companionship. "Yes, I'm all right, Dimitrios, but I need to have a very long talk with you about everything. It's been wild over here. Too wild to tell you on the phone. Can we meet somewhere tonight? Someplace in Athens? It's urgent."

They agreed quickly on a time and place.

"But one thing can't wait," Santry told him. "Are you alone? Can you talk freely?" As he listened to Varga's assurances, he felt suddenly exhausted. Two days without sleep had worn him down. The night before he had wandered too many streets and drunk far too much ouzo, but the waves of doubt had passed. The tension remained high but tolerable. And his mind was clear: He had made a decision, he was prepared to live with it. "Dimitrios, this afternoon I'm flying to Athens with my friend in a private plane. There'll be another man with us. Two nights ago a boat from Turkey dropped him off on the north coast of Lesbos and we brought him to Mitilini. He's crippled—one leg's gone— and he's traveling with forged documents using the name Anthony Tocaro. Sometime around six-thirty this evening, he'll get on a flight for Rome. I'm sure he's an important drug dealer—huge amounts of money were spent to get him out of Turkey. When we have more time, I can tell you why I'm doing this, but now there's only one question: Is there any way to use this information to make a dent in the heroin trade?"

They talked for a long time, longer than Santry ever imagined would be necessary, because Varga picked up his query on a dead run and took off with it. And only after reaching an agreement about Tocaro did Varga tell Santry about the call received from Simonedes in the middle of the night. There had been a murder on Kallos: the local policeman, who, Varga was sure, had been working for Santry's "friends." And the card found on the body was identical to the one left with Dimitrios himself when strangled in September. "What the hell are your people doing? It smells like civil war to me."

Santry told him he had heard nothing about it but might before they talked that night. "Is Simonedes all right?"

"Yes, yes, fine. He always asks for you, but he's getting nervous about the Fragments. He says he can't give me much more time. A few weeks at most, and then he's going to the police and the press."

Santry said he understood but still didn't know what, if anything, he could do about it. It was another matter for their meeting. "Dimitrios, does the name L. P. Gerson mean anything to you?"

"More than a little. Gerson's the biggest munitions manufacturer in Greece."

Santry's voice dropped in discouragement. "Just what I was afraid of."

"What did you say?"

"I said, 'Thanks, Dimitrios,' and we'll have to talk about it tonight—somebody's going to find me on this phone and ask the wrong questions." When he hung up, Santry knew the fat was in the fire.

At three that afternoon, their plane drifted low over the western Aegean and closed in on Athens. Santry straightened his seat in the small cabin of the company jet, pulled back his window curtains, and peered out at a distant, cold sun riding low behind bleak clouds. Ross sat across the aisle beside Tocaro, whose fingers had drummed nervously on his new crutches since the plane took off from Mitilini. Otherwise, the Italian's anxiety went unexpressed. His face was a mask, eyes half closed under thin, black eyebrows, and his mouth was a sealed slit, revealing nothing. With short black hair plastered flat and forward toward his sharp features, there was something of the ferret about him. Santry was glad he spoke no English. Even the worst of predators had their good moments, and he wanted no friendly words between them to complicate his feelings. Ross, relaxed and amiable again after the previous night's flare-up, had reassembled his cool executive self and exuded a contagious confidence. Santry admired the style. It fostered the pleasant illusion that someone had a firm grip on events rather than the other way around. Even Forticos's death, about which Ross knew little more than Santry had learned from Varga, failed to shatter his composure. On the contrary, it only made him more certain that his plan would work. With Forticos, Larus had shown his hands. With one, he swung a wrecking ball: killing agents and enemies, tearing the organization apart. But with the other, he was sculpting and displaying a proud image of himself as the unpredictable one, all-powerful, godlike. Ross alive frustrated both programs and mocked his conceit. Ross alive was the competitor acclaimed. And Ross alive was coming after him. It had become a matter of kill or be killed.

Hillsides of concrete-slab apartments, five stories high, slipped by the windows. Santry looked away and checked his belt. Ross leaned across the aisle. "I appreciate this, Mike. I know how you feel and—"

Santry waved the thanks aside. The plane touched ground in Greece, trembled slightly, and ran quickly toward a terminal. It had been easy to arrange and "the least I can do." Ross, focused on Ladrea, certainly had more-important things on his mind than Tocaro and gratefully accepted Santry's offer to sit with the Italian until his plane to Rome took off.

Two hours later, Santry's hands gripped the black rubber handles of the wheelchair and followed the bright red-on-yellow signs in the international terminal to the flight-departure area. In July the same building had looked like the staging area for an invasion of the Balkans, but in December, a calm month between package tours, it was only crowded. The last few hours stretched endlessly behind him: aimless wandering to pass the time, blackening fingers on English papers, nursing too many instant coffees and cigarettes in rooms already choked with smoke. Tocaro had taken cigarettes but refused food or drink. Now coming up ahead of them: ticket inspection, electronic surveillance, and signs warning PASSENGERS ONLY BEYOND THIS POINT.

Santry checked the time: five-ten P.M. exactly. A few minutes to go and no sign of Varga. Good. He was to show only if arrangements had been impossible. At five-fifteen he pushed the chair forward from the wall, waited briefly in a short line behind an older, bearded traveler, and placed Tocaro's passport and ticket on the counter. The agent examined each with no trace of special interest and told Santry to proceed to the waiting room. The priest looked down at his passenger. With head bent forward and hands holding crutches, Tocaro looked very much the helpless invalid. Santry found a seat in the boarding area and turned the chair so the cripple looked away from him. At six o'clock, a woman in an airline uniform approached them quietly, stared where a leg was missing, and said Mr. Tocaro would be seated before the other passengers. Santry thanked her and yielded the wheelchair. He did not say goodbye or wish him well. As she rolled the chair away, a tall, well-dressed man sitting a few seats away from Santry got up and followed. A door closed behind them. In Rome, other tall men waited to follow Tocaro and his driver wherever they might lead. Hopefully, Santry thought, to at least a dent in the trade. He knew there would be no crushing blow. The drug trade was by far too worldwide and powerful. He stared at the blank door. It was a grim and dingy business and he got no pleasure from it. He looked away abruptly, as if to erase a memory, and walked outside.

The Datsun waited in the dark behind the newsstand: motor idling, parking lights on, triple-six plates. He got in the front seat. The car raced down a four-lane highway toward the city, the streetlights flashing on the driver's face every other second: clean-shaven, thin, regular features. He leaned against the door and drove casually at a high speed, one hand on the wheel, eyes covering the dim night surfaces. He didn't look over when he said, "I'm Nikos."

"I'm Mike Santry."

"Yes, I know," he said, but Santry was too tired to ask what that meant.

How much Nikos knew became stunningly clear when they got to Varga's and saw the display: hundreds of photographs across an entire wall, each one dated and named, and arranged chronologically. When he walked into the room, an unusually stern Varga threw on the overheads and told him, "Time to turn the cards face-up, Michael."

Full of sudden suspicions, the priest moved slowly down the shocking wall, studying the photos. A high percentage of them featured him: coming out of the airport with Ross and Ladrea, standing on a corner with Alexander, leaving a restaurant with a puzzled look on his face. He was, however, even more surprised and disturbed by the shots of Gabriella and Korachis. Dozens of them. In one they appeared to be arguing. Korachis had turned toward her before entering a cab. His mouth was open, saying some last, angry word. Her face seemed drawn and frightened. Most of the pictures had been taken in public places: street corners, airport, restaurants, corridors of office buildings, a few even from moving cars. Ross, to Santry's dismay, was featured prominently coming and going with Korachis, Ladrea, and other striking women about whom Santry had never heard. It was clear that Varga had betrayed him from his first day in Athens, but when he faced him, full of sudden anger, he saw nothing of apology in those large, steady eyes. "I told you I refused to be an informer. You said my story and the Fragments were all you wanted, but you've been after more from the beginning. You followed me to Ross and from Ross to Korachis. You're after all of them, aren't you?"

The big man with the thick tousled hair and drooping moustache met him evenly. "Korachis, Savonon, Larus, yes. Aren't you? You were this morning. And if not, why not? You said you wanted to stop Tocaro because you wanted to stop heroin. Where do you draw the line? At the bottom rung of the ladder? Korachis has grown fat on heroin, arms, and terrorism. If Tocaro's worth an afternoon of your life, Korachis should command a year."

The lecture chilled Santry, but he recognized its truth. His own commitments, though not so clearly drawn, had moved close to Varga's. Dead women on Athenian sidewalks, murdered Sandinistas, and addicts on his own east side made the recovery of the Fragments a part, but not the whole, of what he had to do. The original agreement with Varga had steadily dissolved as Santry's knowledge of the scale and content of Korachis's operation pressed him toward action. He went back to the photos. It was hard to fault a man for working early in the morning on a project to which one gave oneself later in the day. "I see you were on Lesbos."

On the wall, he saw Larus and Ross leaving the hillside house in Mithymna, saw himself with Alexander and Ladrea in a restaurant, three bottles of wine conspicuously on the table, and then one photograph he said he'd like to have: open field along the northern coast, a sinuous line of oleanders curving gently downward toward dark cypress trees in a small cemetery, a stretch of blue, rolling water, and, beyond it, Turkey's shadow. What caught his eye was in the middle distance on the bluff near the sea: a man and a woman carrying baskets. The label was accurate enough—"M. Santry/L. Antissa"—but said nothing, could say nothing, about the easy beauty of that afternoon.

A sudden question turned him back. "Then you must

know what happened. You know she's gone—that Larus tried to kill Ross and has taken her away."

Varga sat beside his cluttered desk, hunched forward in a swivel chair, intent on Santry. "What does Ross think is going on?"

"They met this morning. Alexander doesn't tell me much, but he seems to believe that Larus is out to tear the organization apart because he can't lead it. Why else would he kill Forticos? There's been no ransom note—no demands of any kind."

"Who met this morning?"

"Ross, Korachis, Savonon, Gabriella."

"What's their plan?"

"Alexander wouldn't say. Just told me to watch the ten o'clock news tonight."

Varga began shuffling through the folders on his desk. "Nikos, where the hell are those blowups?" Nikos came off the couch, where he had been stretched out watching television, opened a drawer in Varga's desk, and handed him a large, manila envelope. "Come over here and look at these, Michael. There's something very strange going on."

He cleared the center of the desk, focused a bright desk lamp on the surface, and took out a glossy, black-and-white enlargement. The photograph had been taken at night, but Santry recognized instantly the harbor at Mithymna: crescent seawall, a few large fishing boats, a row of smaller boats tied to the concrete pier, and the café where he drank his morning's coffee.

Varga's pencil touched the dark stern of the ship nearest the café. "The next is a blowup of this section." He took another photo and placed it beside the first. "What do you see?"

Santry leaned closer to the indistinct, assorted shapes and markings. "It looks like a dolphin."

Varga glanced at Nikos and said, "Yes, that's what we think, too. And we *know*, we don't think, we *know* that this is the ship Larus used to take the Antissa woman away. Nikos had been following the blonde all night, lost him when he left Ross in the car, scrambled back to the house in time to hear a car screeching toward the harbor. He got these pictures just before the boat pulled out. Now look at this."

Santry saw a different, much larger port in the new photo: small signal lights in the distance, narrow channel between breakwaters, and a commercial fishing boat tied parallel to the pier. Nothing about it looked familiar.

"That one's taken from portside. This one's from the stern."

The picture dropped from Varga's hand and a large, painted dolphin broke Santry's silence.

"But where?" the priest exclaimed. "When?"

"Yesterday in Mitilini," Nikos told him, explaining that he had followed Santry and Ross south from Mithymna, watched them check into the Sappho Hotel, and then had gone off to a harbor restaurant. After eating, he wandered around looking at the boats, not with any thought of finding the one Larus had used to escape, but simply to learn how common the name was. He found the only *Dolphin* in port and decided to keep his eyes on it. There was no movement all day, though after dark he saw lights and late that night a man walked by the boat twice, watched from a distance, then went quickly aboard. He stayed less than fifteen minutes and the boat sailed as soon as he got off.

Varga placed the final photograph under the light: a full-face shot of a huge man on the deck of a ship. "Recognize him?"

"No, I've never seen him. I'm sure of it."

"Well, you've heard of him," Varga told him. "You're looking at Gans Savonon."

"Impossible."

Varga scratched his thick moustache. "If you're sure of that, then we've got two certainties—it's impossible and it's Savonon, which is probably not far from the complicated truth. Now listen to me, Michael, and don't think *impossible*. Think *maybe*. Maybe this is the same *Dolphin* that left Mithymna the night before. We can't prove that, but I've got no doubt about it. It means Larus and Savonon are in this together, and it means your friends are wrong. Larus isn't tearing up an organization—he's *building* one. He's a psychopath, but he's not crazy. And Savonon's definitely a profiteering warlord who deals only in hard cash, never in flights of symbols. He wouldn't play unless there was a fortune and a business future. But to build an organization, they need tremendous amounts of capital. Take my word for it, a ransom note will come. They wouldn't bother with Ladrea for any other reason. Forticos was probably killed as a diversion and a signal to other agents, not as a first strike. Korachis can keep Ladrea out of the papers, but a murdered policeman on Kallos makes the news. How many men does Korachis have out there? Fifty? A hundred? We don't have the numbers yet, but when Forticos went down they all suspected a palace revolt and will contact Savonon to get the word. And I don't think Larus killed him. He had him killed. He couldn't risk running Ladrea through the local airport because she's a well-known face on Lesbos, but he wanted Korachis to believe he had made it to Athens. Leaving his card and setting up a tall, fair-haired passenger to fly out of Kallos in the name of 'A. Ross' shifted the focus of the search and magnified his reputation.'' Varga stopped abruptly and pointed at the TV. "Time to find out what they're doing."

Nikos and Santry settled on the couch, while Dimitrios got beer from the refrigerator. Santry was glad for the break. Hard, rough decisions were coming down on him and he didn't want to get locked into them yet.

A few minutes into the local news, Varga muttered, "Here it comes," and began a running translation of the earnest reporter's words: "Police on Lesbos continue to investigate the explosion that destroyed one car and shook the village of Mithymna early yesterday morning. Tonight, a firsthand report. Alexander Ross, an American vacationing in Greece, saw it happen."

Alexander's handsome face and cool manner filled the screen. He explained that he had been out walking on the coast road when the fireball blasted the night apart. He was close enough to feel the heat but had not been injured in any way. He went on to describe the sudden lights in village windows, the people rushing into streets, distant voices shouting, even—and this surprised Santry—the alarm of animals. No, he told the reporter, the incident had no effect on his plans. He liked Greece and intended to remain indefinitely.

Ross vanished and the announcer leaped on to Salonica, where a political rally had been disrupted. Varga got up and snapped off the TV, grunted, and paced with hands in his pockets. "So that's it. Trying to draw him out." He shook his head. "Fools! They've got him all wrong. What do they think happens next? A duel? They can take Ross anytime they want him."

"You know that, but they don't," Santry argued. "Take Savonon out of the equation and there's nothing foolish about it. I've got to warn Ross before he gets killed."

"No, no, Michael, you don't warn Ross. Maybe soon, but not yet." Varga pulled a chair up to the couch and sat close to the priest. "Slowly now. Go slowly. Say I'm Ross. 'Why do you suspect Savonon, Michael? Oh, you have pictures? Let me see. Yes, it looks like Savonon, but he's just standing on a boat. What does that prove? Oh, Nikos saw him? Who's Nikos?' You see where it goes? It goes straight to you and me and secret deals with a journalist circling the wolf pack. What does Ross do then? Throw his arms around you and yell at the servants to kill the fatted calf? Invite me in for taped interviews? Like hell he does! He looks around for a lime pit big enough for the two of us. Well, maybe not for you; maybe you get banished to America, but Varga's writing days are over. Your charming friend knows what he's doing, and what he's doing is working for Korachis. The emperors of the world do not play around when the throne's at stake. Usurpers will be killed sooner than fed."

Santry shook his head. "So what do you propose?"

"First tell me if you agree with what I just said. I have a special interest in any opinion that so directly affects my future."

Santry nodded grimly. "Yes, I'm afraid so. At least I agree that the risk's too high to take. But I can't stand by and let them kill Ross. I can't do that either."

Varga reached out and gripped his shoulder. "No, you can't do that—and neither can Ladrea. That's why she'll warn him."

Santry was upset and puzzled. He remembered the photo on the wall and suspected he had looked slightly bewildered since coming to Greece. "What are you talking about, Dimitrios?"

"Look at it this way. Ladrea's locked in a cabin when Savonon comes aboard in Mitilini. I don't know any of this, but it's imaginable. She hears the talk. What do they care how much she knows? Savonon tells Larus that Ross is still alive! Naturally she thinks 'I've got to warn him!' So she writes an urgent note, which, now that I think about it, should include the boat's name."

"But how can she possibly get it off the boat?"

Varga shook his head, as if dealing with a backward student. "She doesn't have to, Michael. You do it for her! Bring me some samples of her handwriting and the rest is easy. It's a beautiful plan! And we don't have to account for anything. What do we care how many people wonder how she got it off the boat? The more confusion the better. The result is that we get what we want: Ross is warned of Savonon and a search begins for the *Dolphin*. But you have to be there when it arrives—you have to stay very close to Ross, because if Korachis is lucky and gets Savonon and Larus, it will be up to us to get Korachis."

Chapter Seven

Until the letter came, the Italians had merely annoyed Korachis with their threats. He had sat in his straight-backed chair and listened patiently to the hissings on the long-distance line, then replied quietly that while he regretted the news, he rejected their overly generous offer of responsibility for Tocaro's arrest. He had gotten the man from Ankara to Rome as pledged. If they wanted him to ensure safe passage for their own people in their own city, he was fully prepared to do so, but only under the terms of a new agreement. They accused him bitterly and issued warnings, but he had little use for screaming children. And when he hung up, it was without rancor, almost without feelings of any kind.

The thin fingers of one hand removed the dark, perfectly round, tortoiseshell glasses from his face and placed them carefully on the narrow wooden table at his side. The pain had gotten worse. His thumb and index finger rubbed the bridge of his sharp, hooked nose. A tumor, they said, and too late for cutting. He imagined a black, frenzied leech, swollen, gorging itself. No, no hospital, he told them, no radiation, no chemotherapy, no remissions, no illusions. He tapped three pale green capsules onto his open palm and thought about their obvious meaning. A month ago, he had looked at only one. Korachis heard a quick knock, the door opened behind him, and Apostolos, his aide and guard, announced, "A letter from Ladrea!"

Korachis knew the handwriting. "Call Alexander and

Gabriella. Tell them to come immediately. Contact the coast guard and major harbors; inquire about the *Dolphin*."

Gabriella sat by the window on deep blue cushions. Alexander stood, coffee cup in one hand, cigarette in the other. Korachis read it again: " 'Only seconds to write—Savonon on *Dolphin* with Larus!' " The note passed from hand to hand. They agreed it looked like her writing, but Gabriella called it a forgery. Larus was setting up Savonon, playing the spoiler's game, sowing suspicions and proving how unpredictable he could be. Savonon didn't have the nerve to come against Andreas. Too many years of obedience had weakened his will. Anyway, if Ladrea were on a boat, it would be impossible to get the letter off.

Not impossible at all, Ross countered. Not if the boat were in port. A letter could get to shore with a sympathetic crew member or even be skimmed onto the pier from the deck or an open window. If Larus had written it, he argued, there would be no mention of the boat's name, would there?

Of course there would, she snapped. The *Dolphin* probably didn't exist. It was a fiction designed to mislead. Korachis said they had to treat the note as genuine even if it should prove to be false, and he had no doubt about Savonon's capacity for treachery. Only loyalty surprised him anymore. They'd know soon enough because the letter announced a different game than they had imagined. Larus on his own might seek revenge and be satisfied with punishment, but Savonon and Larus together meant business. They were building a new organization. He told them about the call from Italy. It all fit, he said. Savonon tipped the police to Tocaro's Rome arrival in order to discredit the organization he intended to supplant.

"Which also means," Ross added, "that they took her for ransom and she's therefore probably safe."

Gabriella turned from the window through which she had been watching traffic flowing outside their Athens office. "Then why haven't they asked for it?"

"It's been only two days and he's moving by boat. He needs time to get her in place. If this note's real, we won't have to wait much longer."

Korachis agreed and expected contact within a day or two. "That is, if we don't find them first. In a few hours, Apostolos will at least know where the *Dolphin* is not. He might even find it, because if this came from Ladrea, Larus has no reason to suspect we know its name. And then there are the new possibilities presented by Savonon himself." His eyes lingered on the letter, resting in his lap. "We won't confront or challenge him in any way. Eventually, yes, because as soon as they collect the ransom, they'll move to kill the three of us and secure their future. So that danger will have to be removed—but at the right time. At this moment, we need Savonon. He may lead us to Larus. We must listen to his calls, read his mail, and follow his every step. If we're able to do that, we may surprise them. The question is: How many others have been recruited to their conspiracy? We must act instantly, but who can be trusted?"

Santry was summoned within the hour. Help? Yes, of course, in any way he could. No, he had never met Savonon. Had never seen the man. Good. They showed him a letter. Did he understand what this meant? He looked up from the letter he had drafted, wondered about a trap, and said, "Larus and Savonon?"

Yes, said Korachis.

Yes, said Ross.

Gabriella said nothing.

Santry had not realized how intensely he disliked Antissa and insisted, by waiting, that she also say yes and ask for his help. She refused. Korachis stared. Yes, she finally said, they needed him to follow Savonon. She still had doubts that Savonon was double-crossing them, but nothing would be lost and, just possibly, something would be gained. He'd need keys, he told them. Keys to enter after hours and search the mail, the waste, the desk, for clues. Gabriella frowned, Alexander agreed, and Korachis called Apostolos and had the keys brought. And if there was contact? If Savonon did lead to Larus? What then? Korachis told him to stay close to Larus and call him as soon as possible.

Alexander and Gabriella had to go. She without a word. He with a hand on his shoulder saying thanks. The door closed. Santry was, for the first time in his life, alone with Korachis. Korachis in his three-piece, pinstriped suit, dark glasses, pearl-handled cane. No, he agreed, they hadn't had much time to talk. The black lenses stared at him. Santry told him it was difficult to talk to a man who stood behind one-way glass. Thin fingers reached to the stems and removed them. The eyes blazed, self-possessed, angrier than the voice, less patient than the pose.

"I never thought a priest would work for me."

"This priest never did."

"Oh?"

"You must know why I agreed to get the Fragments. Alexander must have told you. It was not for you, and it was to be once—not to be repeated." He looked away from the baleful eyes and out the window. "You think you've taken a road, something to walk on awhile and then to turn back on, but the road turns into a river."

Santry drifted into silence and would have stayed quiet but heard the question, "What do you want for helping?"

He shook his head. "What do I want for helping to save a friend? Dear God, we've come a long way. Are you always so quick with insults, or just in the habit of buying everything?" Then, more gently, "She's a flower. One of the rarest."

"Yes." Silence in the room. Korachis stared at the

floor, holding the letter with two fingers. Pale light streamed through north windows. Early asphodels rested on the sill, white and green and gold.

"When will Savonon come?"

"Soon."

"I must go and get a car and wait. His calls?"

"Apostolos will record and give them to you. Tell him where you'll be. My numbers? Here. Any hour. Please."

Santry changed into jeans, a turtleneck, windbreaker, and a black woolen cap. He called Varga. It was hard not to speed. "It's all there, Dimitrios, all of it. Project files dating back five years, lists of agents, informers, cooperators, pay scales, telephone numbers, photographs. And a closet jammed with films—probably for blackmail. Certainly for more than Antissa's entertainment. I've got to get back. Tell Nikos he has to come now. I can only wait till Savonon leaves."

At three o'clock that Tuesday afternoon, Santry slouched behind the wheel of a light blue Citroën, ignoring the newspaper propped in front of him. His eyes were on the dry street, the bare trees, an empty tan VW, and the second-floor windows of the old mansion that sprawled behind a high, black iron fence and thick hedges. Children walked carrying books and never looked his way. A burly, heavy-shouldered dog muscled by without growling. He was more invisible than he thought he'd be. There was even another man slouched behind the wheel of an old Ford about five cars down, and Santry wondered who *he* was following. The doors of a neighborhood grocery store opened and closed, leaving a thin Greek of average height standing on the sidewalk. Santry watched through the rearview mirror. He was wearing a cap, clutched a shopping bag in his left hand, and appeared to be counting the change remaining in his right palm. When satisfied or reconciled to the sum, he ambled along, stopping only briefly at the rear of Santry's car to bend down and tie his laces. Like the schoolchildren and the dog, he paid no attention to the priest, and turned at a nearby corner. The keys that Santry had placed by the back wheel were in his pocket and he kept his eyes turned toward the house. When Savonon and Santry drove away, Nikos would make his move.

They waited a long time. They watched the dreary sky fade entirely from view and a single streetlamp begin its feeble burning in a rising wind. Santry's mood shifted in the interim. He had arrived apprehensive and cautious, but after four hours of waiting he drummed impatiently on the wheel and muttered toward the windows, "C'mon! C'mon!" When it finally happened, it happened fast. Second-floor lights went out. Santry sat straight up and started the motor. First floor went out. He shrunk slightly behind the wheel. The front door slammed, the iron gate swung open and banged shut, a huge figure hurried past on the sidewalk, the VW coughed, then sped off.

Santry gave him half a block, waited until he turned from the quiet residential street into heavy traffic, then powered in behind him. He was easy to find and follow. There were other VW's, but none with the long bumper stripe that glowed orange in the beams of other cars. Santry watched it weaving in and out of traffic ahead, moving fast, but he couldn't miss the gleaming orange line. "Thank you, Nikos, thank you." The VW took a sharp left and parked behind a restaurant.

What now? This could go on for days. Savonon could eat for hours, take in a movie, hang out in his favorite bar, then go home and talk to Larus by phone. And why not? *Because he's running a double game,* Santry told himself. *He fears discovery, worries about wiretaps and high-tech sound systems that pick up living room conversations at fifty yards. Korachis can afford all that.*

Savonon can't afford any mistakes because, as the Alpine mountain guide says, One fall, that's all.

Santry hated it, but he had to go inside. If this was the meeting place and Larus arrived first and left last, he'd never see him. It was a tense foray. He kept his jacket collar high on his neck and his wool cap low, lingered inside the restaurant doors, made for the john, leaned briefly against the bar, somewhat surprised not to feel the hard arm around his neck and that unctuous, sarcastic voice close to his ear whispering something like "Hello, Father, I'm glad you've come for more. Is this about right? No? A little tighter, maybe?" He almost sighed with relief when he turned slowly from the bar, surveyed the large room, and saw Savonon eating with a hefty woman in the far corner. More accurately, the bald man ate while his companion drank. They appeared to be enjoying themselves, so Santry turned back to the bar, ordered a plate of fried squid, and sipped his beer while he thought about his Italian mother, who would hoot at squid. He never had it as a kid in Detroit. "Bait!" she'd yell when he asked about it. "In America, I don't feed my children bait!"

An hour later, the orange stripe lured him up a winding road where traffic thinned to occasional and distant headlights, to a sign that announced Lycabettus Hill. The woman had left the restaurant with Savonon, but had driven off in a different car. Santry didn't know where the giant lived, but when all the buildings and houses disappeared, replaced suddenly by thick bushes and pine trees, he knew the man wasn't headed home. Nor, he thought, was he climbing this strange and steep hill, this forest in a city, in order to park, picnic, and enjoy the view. The car became uncomfortably warm as he worried, *Is Santry following Savonon, or is Savonon leading Santry into a trap?*

He reached across the front seat to make sure the other door was locked. At the same time, he slowed down and let Savonon drive on. Up ahead the lights stopped. He imagined a roadblock, a car pulling in behind him, a light blinding his eyes, and someone dragging him out, throwing him on the ground, and shouting "Who are you! What are you doing here!" Or, if Larus were waiting for him, his time was surely up, because the throat crushing wouldn't stop until breathing was gone for good.

Speed: twenty miles an hour. Closer and closer. Santry swallowed hard, took a deep breath, turned his face away, and drove past the parked car without a look. He stared in the rearview mirror, watched the VW's parking lights recede, and made a firm resolution: He wasn't getting close enough to get caught. He wasn't crawling through any underbrush to get back there. Dead men couldn't help friends. He drove straight up the steep hill and out of sight, pulled onto a service road, turned the car around, cut the lights, and started slowly down the macadam switchbacks. But at the first dim sight of distant parking lights, he eased onto the shoulder, turned off the motor, and got out. The VW was far below him on the twisting road, all but obscured by bushes and trees. Santry felt the sharp edge of car keys in his hand, the bite of a cold wind, and the anxious press of all-weather, general-purpose fear. He walked into a stand of pines to get protection from the wind and a better view of the hillside running down in darkness toward the mass of distant city lights. Afterward, Santry told Varga that he had waited about thirty minutes before he saw the second car enter the preserve, wind uphill, and pull in behind the VW, which immediately cut its parking lights.

One car door slammed. Then another. Quickly, wet soil sinking under his hurrying feet, brief struggle with the wrong key, motor jumped to life at the touch, dash lights out to obscure his face, high beams flashing, keep it slow as lovers winding down toward home, two cars coming up just ahead, almost on them, speed steady, now! Faces in the front seat turning toward him, staring out, momentarily, white faces frozen forever in his mind. He cruised by, checked quickly in the mirror for tailing lights, none, nothing! Drive to the bottom, wait outside the entrance in a row of parked cars, drop the VW, forget Savonon, let him go, but don't let Larus out of sight. Don't let that red Fiat get away.

Minutes later, Santry watched from his parked car as the Fiat moved slowly down the hill. A man unknown to the priest was driving, but Larus was in the passenger's seat, eyes straight ahead, intent. Santry followed from a distance. The Fiat stopped on a small street by a green sidewalk awning at the entrance to an apartment building sporting a storefront pharmacy. Larus got out, closed the door, turned back to say something, then walked directly inside, his blond hair brushing his shoulders as he moved. The car took off.

Santry had to see that driver's face. He hit the accelerator, shot forward, pulled up beside him two blocks later at a light, and stared. He was in his forties, thin hair, sideburns down to his earlobes, no glasses, pudgy, weak face, pinched and frightened mouth. Santry sped past as if simply in a hurry, turned off, and circled again, found the green awning, and parked in shadows, with a clear view of the entrance. If Larus intended to be brief, the Fiat would have stayed. Maybe. It promised to be a long, cold night. A couple hurried by, bundled against the wind. Who lived there? Larus wouldn't risk going to his own place. Santry got out, ran across, ducked into the entryway, and stood in front of the registry of names, each in alphabetical order, each with a small black button inviting touch. He started from the top, but his eyes soon fixed in disbelief at the name in front of his eyes: G. Antissa.

Her fingers moved slowly under the faces in the group photograph as she described the point of pride or position of power that earned each an invitation to the previous year's War Widows' Benefit. Two hundred men in all: Judges, editors, politicians, manufacturers, bankers, each with a well-adorned woman at his side, stared at the camera from the plush seats of a private theater. A few faces beamed. Most struck less-energetic poses, suggesting a quiet, alert intelligence. One or two scowled. As a group they appeared middle-aged and well-established. Not one was camera shy, poorly clothed, or ill-fed. Furs were abundant. She showed him a scrapbook. Clippings documented the enormous publicity received: long articles in news sections, headlines on society pages, feature articles in magazines, and clips from TV coverage. Ross wondered about all the attention.

"It's an exclusive gathering that raises a fortune for a popular cause," Gabriella explained. "Who can deny time or space for war widows? And every drachma goes to a pension. I cover administrative costs myself. It helps, of course, that I'm notorious around Athens: a famous model, Korachis's consort, a film producer, free woman—that sort of thing. I've become a fixture in the local fantasy trade: beautiful, rich, arrogant, and a bit degenerate. News about me sells. Five years ago, I began using that fact for my own purposes." Her hands passed over a pile of grateful letters from women receiving help. "This is one of them."

Ross was impressed and said so. It was a side of her he hadn't suspected.

"Don't be foolish," she told him. "It's the same side you've seen. I do exactly what pleases me. My parents were killed in the war, and half the older people I know live alone. Orphans reach for the missing women in their lives. If they have my talent and money, they do what's called 'good works.' In fact, it's neither better nor worse than stealing if you're hungry. In every case, people act from need, not abstract virtue."

She was, for the first time in his presence, smiling, and Ross was puzzled by the transformation. He liked it well enough. She looked immediately radiant, but the change was perplexing. Korachis had asked Ross to lend a hand with final arrangements for the benefit to be held the following Saturday. It was, he told Ross, the single most important night of the year for Gabriella, and he spared no resources to ensure its success. In this, its tenth year, she had arranged for live television coverage of her film describing the work, so he was committed to having things go well. Ladrea's disappearance prompted momentary thoughts of canceling, but the event proved a welcome diversion from that grim preoccupation and was no impediment to the search.

Ross said he'd help. Gabriella had said drinks at seven in her apartment. They'd be undisturbed and Ross should stay out of public places while Larus was at large.

"Looks like everything's arranged," he told her after reviewing the plans. "What do you want me to do?"

She watched from across the room while he studied the printed program. "I want you to get Santry for me. I want him to introduce the film, but if I ask he'll refuse."

Ross caught gold gleams from the bracelets, a white blouse open on a brown throat, the rise of small breasts. "That's understandable. You gave him a very hard time."

"Yes, but what do you think? It seems to me that Santry would add an intentional religious dimension that could help." One long leg forward, one hand on hip, her stance suggested a model at the end of the runway fixing a slightly superior eye on the audience.

"I don't know. We're using him pretty hard these days. I'll ask, but he goes his own way. What else?"

"Nothing else."

He got up and walked to the nearest wall, as if attracted by the paintings. His voice was easy and without complaint. "That's all? You invited me here to ask me to ask Santry to do a sixty-second introduction on Saturday night?"

"No, Alexander, that has little to do with your being here, and you know it as well as I do." Her face darkened like the sea when a quick wind dropped on a calm surface.

Ross's eyes were on the portrait, a somber face in swirling blues and harsh greens. "Gabriella, I don't know what you're talking about."

"Look at me!" she demanded.

He kept his back to her. "I don't like the painting. Not enough of you. The brooding and the bitchery are there, but it misses the rest." He faced her, keeping the tone amiable, and letting the words do the biting. "More exercises in unpredictability, is that it? Making another film and testing script ideas? What exactly do you want from me?"

"There are only two things worth wanting from anybody: truth and beauty. I want to know how much of either you can handle. If that makes you anxious, go now, because if you stay, I expect to speak and hear the truth. Beauty's less responsive to the will, but if we're honest, we may see her."

He took their glasses, poured more wine, and told her, "Ready when you are."

Her eyes glowed with satisfaction and she spoke, as always, rapidly and with great energy but with an eagerness he hadn't seen. "From the day I took you on the octopus hunt, there's been fierce antagonism between us, but there's also been a link, a hint of powerful attraction. In the boat, our thighs touched for a moment and I felt the spark. So did you. I won't believe denials."

"More antagonism than affinity," he countered. "You've got a bitter mouth and play too much the savage queen. I remember the touch and felt the draw, but there's already one too many in your bed."

She raised her head slowly and gave him a haughty

look. "Perhaps you're not so different after all. I had begun to imagine a sensitive man alive under that cool facade. But bravo, anyway, for that bit of ugliness, which actually sounded like a truthful opinion. Tell me, Ross, what's too many? What's the right number these days?"

"Korachis is one too many. I don't get cross-wired with the man who pays me."

She drank her wine and smiled. "So you loved Ladrea instead! And how do you know that dear Andreas is not between those sheets? No, strike that, it was a taunt, not truth. Believe me, he's not. Andreas is the last of a type. He won't violate his family and, as you've noticed, he counts me in that hallowed group. In things personal, he's an exemplary man."

"How do you keep him? How does he put up with lovers like Larus? He must know."

"Yes, he knows. He knows all of them—by name, face, and body type, but the only word he says is *freedom*. Over twenty years, the only word. But he never feels one among many. He knows he's the one. The others are the many. No one's confused on that point. What about Ladrea? What is she to you?"

Ross glanced at the severe, moody portrait of Gabriella on the wall behind her. "She's not the One, if that's what you're after, but she's a good friend and occasional companion. We're good together."

"You mean you're good in bed?"

Ross shrugged. "Beds, tables, beaches, sure, and more than that—seriously more. Wherever she is, she adds to life, she doesn't take it away. But there are others—for me and for her. We'll never live together." His uneasiness grew with the memories. "How the hell did you spend so much time with Larus and not know what he was going to do?"

"I knew some things. I knew he'd try to kill you. In a certain way, that didn't bother me. Strangers are killed every day, but you're important to her and to Andreas, so I called to warn you. From his point of view, you're a thief. You stole his job and a man has to defend himself."

"What's your point of view?"

"Changing. You're abler than I thought. At first there was a certain pulse followed by dislike. Recently, I've been attracted—and the crisis will bring us closer."

"Not so far it hasn't."

"You don't know the crisis yet. Andreas is dying. He's said nothing, but I found pills and bullied the doctor. A year at most. Control of the organization passes to me."

Ross let out a long, low whistle as he felt the world tumbling pole to pole.

She swept on. "I intend to disband it and sell the assets—unless you stay. I have no interest in the business and need time for my work, but if you remain to run it, I'd consider hiring you."

"On what terms?"

"Exactly those on which you agreed to work for Andreas, plus one: We explore the decent spark that passed between us once. Not as a matter of love, liking, or any of that superficial nonsense, but entirely as a matter of primal magnetism and life-force." She had gotten to her feet and had begun to pace. "Korachis has been husband, father, and brother to me. I am three times bereaved and desolate. The truth, Ross: There may be a man slumbering beneath those three-piece suits of yours worthy of the woman weeping under this high-fashion gloss and anger. Perhaps not, in which case we'll be the wiser, but the spark we felt is rare. When it comes, it should have its hearing because it doesn't wait, and death takes us all too soon."

Santry backed slowly out the entryway, his eyes fixed on the glass door through which Larus had disappeared, the well-lit, red-carpeted corridor down which he had walked, and the elevator he must have taken to the third floor. His scuffed black shoes reached a desolate street. He was cold, but the breeze that chilled him on Lycabettus had stayed in the pines. The night was still. Quiet as death, he thought, hearing only his excited breathing. Ruby lips, tanned, cocoa-buttered legs, long-lashed eyes, and flashing white teeth beamed brightly from cardboard women in the pharmacy window. He reached the center of the street, looked up, counted, stared, but the third-floor windows, a few glowing yellow behind drawn shades, told him nothing. In minutes, he was on the phone, listening to it ring, eyes anxiously scanning the racked magazines in front of the street-corner kiosk.

"Andreas . . . ? Yes, Mike Santry. I followed Savonon tonight. He left his office around seven. Three hours later, he met Larus on Lycabettus Hill. . . . Yes, I'm sure. I'm sure of everything I'm telling you or I wouldn't call. I followed Larus. He was in a red Fiat that dropped him off downtown. Andreas, ten or fifteen minutes ago he walked into an apartment building and disappeared. Forty-five Kalitsis Street. There's a G. Antissa on the register. Room three-one-six. That's all I know. I'm going back there now and will park outside. . . . What? A blue Citroën, but if he leaves before you get there, I'll be following him."

Korachis, alone in his apartment, called Apostolos first and felt the river flowing. The ice had begun to crack and move downstream. The waiting was over. The current quickened. "Santry has followed Larus to Gabriella's. Take four men and wait outside for me."

The second call went to Savonon.

"This is Andreas. Sorry to bother you at home, but I'm restless for news. Any word from your men? Any trace of him at all . . . ? No, I've heard nothing either. All right, then, we'll wait, but not much longer. The air is heavy with change. Good night, Gans."

He returned the phone slowly to its cradle, opened a lower desk drawer, and took out a small leather book.

The cover was acorn-brown and lustrous in the lamplight. Hand-tooled, Arabic lettering flowed across its front, and inside there were a few names and numbers, rarely used, and each in code. He selected a page, rearranged the digits in his head, and dialed, greeting the man who answered in the careful way prescribed. "Hello, the Dove, please. . . . Yes, we spoke at noon. Confirmation has been received. He's at home now. Please call."

Savonon was not alone. After leaving Larus, he returned to the restaurant where he had eaten earlier, picked up the waiting woman, and hustled her off to his place, where they were drinking when Korachis called. An hour later, the two were naked on the couch. She was watching TV. He was on top and asleep. Her eyes, bright from the TV's glow, fixed eagerly on the blond star. She didn't mind Savonon's weight. The couch was soft and supple in the right places. When Redford was off the screen, her eyes drifted over the room. It was strewn with clothing, fast-food boxes, and a few laughs. Savonon was good company and generous, grossly overweight and crude but rarely violent. Her hands moved along his backbone, rubbing gently. She felt his enormous haunches and giggled a little about solid citizens. She realized with something of a start that she was happy. She liked it after sex. Hunger satisfied, a pleasant buzz, his big, warm body, dark room, good show on TV, and hours until morning. Contentment. She closed her eyes and hummed along: ". . . the way we were . . ."

She never heard the door open, never saw the gloved hand coming. And she couldn't get the scream out, couldn't move, heaved against him, fought back, struggled until the quick explosion beside her ear brought peace and the gentle painless falling and a hundred TV's circling noiselessly, glowing out there in the distance, around and around beyond her. For a minute, long hours later, her head cracking and throat parched, she thought it was the booze. She had felt almost as bad on other mornings. Her eyes opened slowly, her body felt strangely numb, and memories began to flicker in and out, discontinuous, scary. No weight. No sound. Only the remembered press of a gloved hand harsh on her mouth. Her fingers explored the swollen side of her head and the bruised lips. She dragged her legs over the edge of the couch, felt the floor, and pushed herself up. She didn't want to know who, what, or why, but she was sure that Savonon wasn't ever coming back. She searched the apartment for money and small things to sell, cleaned up every trace of her presence, and walked out.

Three men: Korachis, Apostolos, Santry. A dark, one-car street. They were close enough to whisper but no one spoke. A shallow pool of light from the closed pharmacy lapped at their feet, but their faces hid in the shadow. Santry, who had been waiting the longest, leaned against the Citroën's fender. Their eyes were on the glass door of the apartment building, the third-floor windows, and the occasional cruising cab. Apostolos, the youngest and tallest, kept one hand deep in his pocket warming the short barrel of a .38. Korachis stood unarmed, straight as a rule, fingers on his cane. The four men inside carried enough firepower to take the building. One grizzled veteran crouched by the exit at the bottom of the rear stairs, where a door led to a parking lot. On the third floor, a twenty-year-old with nervous eyes pressed against the wall midway between room 316 and the elevator, his gun raised head-high, staring at two men in black jackets flanking the door to the apartment. Each was a trained killer. Each had fought as a mercenary in Africa, been with Korachis for years, and was eager for the bonus that would come for taking Larus down. That was how Korachis and Apostolos saw them.

In fact, Savonon had signed them on for the coup. They were to do whatever was assigned by Korachis, behave as usual, salute on schedule, make all the right noises and glottal stops, but when it came to Larus they were to use their heads, help if they could, and get out of the way if they couldn't. In a few days, after the ransom was received, the king toppled, pretenses ended, they'd be honored openly with rank and drachmas worthy of their loyalty. Low to one side, away from gunshots that might come through the door, a hand reached, inserted Korachis's key, turned the lock, pushed it open, and two men edged inside. The third held his assigned place but grew apprehensive at the short sounds of men laboring with heavy weights. He stiffened. A few seconds later when Larus filled the doorway, his pale eyes searching the corridor, the sentry waved his gun, urging him toward the back stairs. As he went by, Larus reached out, touched the faithful vassal on the cheek, and flashed a princely smile. The ranks were holding.

"There it is!" exclaimed Apostolos, alerted by the sudden flash of light in the window three stories high above them.

Korachis turned to Santry. "Come. Safer there than here alone. He could be anywhere."

In the third-floor corridor, a hurried report from a bearded, sweating face: "Gone when we got here! But inside . . . !"

"Is she there?" Korachis demanded.

The soldier looked away and Korachis rushed forward, aware that others were holding back their faster pace, allowing him to lead, deferring to the limp and the worries that Gabriella might be beaten, raped, or murdered. The betrayal imagined by Santry, that Gabriella was still involved with Larus, had never occurred to Korachis. In twenty years, she had gone with endless others, but never once had gone against him. She was not the woman others thought, but he refused to defend her because what others thought was invariably contemptible and worthless. Neither he nor she—and for this he prized her—needed or sought justification for their ways. They lived without apologies and without regard for the clicking lips of dried-up locusts from whom all vital juices had long been sucked.

His cane tracked his course, leaving deep round impressions on the red-carpeted corridor and the gold rug of her living room, and marked the abrupt, shocked stop in the doorway to her bedroom with a heavy imprint that remained for weeks. After a long hushed moment, he turned to the men staring over his shoulder, ordered the soldiers to wait in the hall, and said to Santry, whose eyes had already been averted, "I must do this alone. She would not want others near her now. Apostolos, get our doctor here." He closed the door behind him and stood inside the familiar bedroom looking down on the naked, bloody bodies of Gabriella and Alexander, tied together in a terrible embrace, face to face, chest to breasts, taped down the entire body line in a grotesque parody of the lovers' knot. The faint smell of Gabriella's perfume was in the air.

Close to bruised faces, he exhaled sharply in relief at the sound of breath, cut them apart, and searched for wounds. No cuts or bullet holes. An ugly blotch on Alexander's cheek and rope marks on both throats. He covered them with blankets and read the note found taped over Gabriella's mouth. Ross began to stir. She took air in gulps. Apostolos was pacing in the living room but stopped when the bedroom door swung open and Korachis entered.

"I think they're going to be all right," he told them. "Larus is extremely skilled when it comes to pressure. The blood appears to be from the mouth and face. He wanted them to live—but punished and humiliated. He could have easily killed them. I suspect they will—live, that is." He began to say something else, something about humiliation, but broke it off and held the letter in his hand toward Santry. "So strange to thank a priest for helping me. You're one of the few who doesn't make me laugh."

Santry kept his mouth shut and unfolded the letter. It was handwritten and signed with the letter "G." The bedroom scene had hit him like a fist in the gut. Had Larus found them like that? If not, how had he surprised them? Ross was armed and quick in a fight. Apostolos was asking him to read it out loud, but a glance at the first line stopped him. Apostolos could read it for himself. The acid note read:

> Korachis, the dottering cuckold who calls her fast-fucking freedom, can have Ladrea for the necklace of Hera. The exchange takes place tomorrow, Thursday, or not at all.
>
> Gabriella, Athens' most predictable whore, should consider a horse farm in Bulgaria where stud fees are within her means and a cure for insatiability guaranteed.
>
> Ross, Ladrea hardly knows how to thank you for the Polaroids. Your performance with her mother is a feast, a straight-up orgy for the eyes. She'll always remember your devotion to her in her time of need.

Santry passed the note to Apostolos without comment and got up to look again at the portrait of Gabriella on the wall.

Korachis, who stood at the front window, hands clasped behind his back, began to talk. "If there were gods, the necklace of Hera would be worthy of them. Larus knows the black markets as well as I do, and can sell the emeralds easily for millions. But without Savonon, he's crippled. A superb one-man show, he couldn't organize sheep into a flock."

Santry interrupted. "What do you mean 'without Savonon'?"

Korachis turned from the window and studied the

priest's weary face, as if to judge the seriousness of the question. "I mean it quite literally. At this moment, Larus is 'without Savonon,' just as Savonon is himself 'without Savonon.' Some would say he now dwells among the shades. You, perhaps, would say that his soul has departed that mountain of clay. I think of him as nowhere, as nothing. He has, in the strictest sense of the words, vanished into thin air." The disapproval clouding Santry's face prompted him to add, "Surely you knew I couldn't allow Larus to be 'with Savonon' after receiving your call? You must have anticipated his . . . departure."

Santry protested, "No, I—" But the clamoring phone cut him off and twisted all of them tighter. Apostolos answered on the second ring and passed the ivory receiver to Korachis. He was imperturbable, like a seasoned banker arranging a routine transfer of major funds.

"Yes, I found your letter, Larus, and the terms are satisfactory. The necklace will be yours, but only after I know that Ladrea is alive. No, the phone will not do. I am an old man and easily deceived. . . . No, it would not be wise for me to come myself. There remain a few who would pay a handsome ransom for my release, and I prefer not to tempt you. In any case, you might want me dead. Apostolos will come. . . . Who? I don't know. I can't speak for him. Just a minute."

Wanting Larus to hear it all, Korachis held the phone inches from his face and spoke to Santry.

"He won't agree to Apostolos or anyone who works for me. The danger of a hidden gun or trap is higher than he'll risk. But he says that you, an innocent in the dispute, may see her." Santry seemed to hesitate, and Korachis, remembering the dark glasses, removed them to increase sympathetic contact. "Please," he asked, "for her sake. My word: No one will follow. No one will interfere in any way, but we must know she's safe before we move another inch."

Santry nodded impatiently. "Yes, of course I'll go. How could I say no?"

Korachis held the phone toward him. "He wants to speak with you."

When Santry hung up, he sighed quietly, as if resigned to an unwelcome fate. Korachis and Apostolos watched and waited for his report.

The priest shrugged. "He wanted to reassure me that if there are any surprises, I'll be killed immediately. My guess is that when he learns you've murdered Savonon, he'll feel honor-bound to kill one of you or me or all of us together. Gangster morality, Andreas. It looks like a quick fix, but it's just another link on the death chain."

"And what did you expect to happen, Father? Contrition and forgiveness? Arms around and the fatted calf?"

Santry replied with that mixture of obstinance and weariness appropriate for a man who knew that he was right but that his opinions would influence no one at all. "I expected you to follow him, to keep track of him, and to see if he'd lead to Ladrea. You moved too violently and too fast." He looked toward the bedroom. "Count on it. Next time he won't leave them breathing."

Korachis countered, "There doesn't need to be a 'next time' if you do your job tonight."

Santry bristled. "My job tonight is to confirm she's alive. Nothing else."

Afraid he was pushing too hard and in danger of losing his help, Korachis pulled back. "I agree," he said reasonably. "I'm only saying that if you could learn where she's being kept, if you could see or hear anything at all to help us find her, the chances of keeping her alive would increase dramatically. His letter disturbs me and increases my suspicions. Will he really give her up for a necklace? I have my doubts."

Santry studied Korachis's reflection in the front window as he said, "You told us it was worth millions."

"It is, and he means to have it. The question is: What else does he want? Why, I ask myself, did he deliver the ransom note in this peculiar fashion—taped across his lover's mouth? Did he find Alexander and Gabriella on the bed, or did he arrange them that way? It makes a difference, I believe. Less to me than you'd imagine, but in terms of understanding what he'll do now. If, for example, he surprised them while talking quietly in this room and dragged them in there, it's a depraved taunt. If, on the other hand, he found her in there, in the arms of a competitor as virile, complex, and able as he, why did he let them live? Perhaps, I think, because Larus, now the emotional cuckold he despises in me, was so violently shaken and infuriated by the sight of her golden body surrendering to his enemy that he condemned her not to death but to the secular equivalent of eternal damnation: endless humiliation and pain. Notice that the message is intended almost entirely for Gabriella. And which words in it carry his fire? 'Fast-fucking,' 'predictable whore,' 'stud fees,' 'insatiability,' 'straight-up orgy.' All about her. And what does he do with those judgments? He tapes them tightly across her mouth, he seals her with them, shuts her up, insists on having the last word, then puts her on display, leaves announcements, calls immediately to make sure we've seen, and demands what for a ransom? Nothing less than the necklace of Hera, a goddess, the wife of Zeus! He's obsessed by her and will be moved as much by that addiction as by his need for wealth. He wants her punished, exposed, brought low. A dead daughter would satisfy his profound desire for the mother's endless grief."

Well, Santry thought to himself, he didn't know and didn't really care how much of all that was true, how much nonsense, and how much the older lover speaking for himself. He told Korachis that if it was possible to find out where Ladrea was, of course he'd do so, but he didn't have much hope. Larus would be anticipating every move.

Korachis spoke again of his gratitude. He didn't want to press the matter, but if "there is ever anything . . ."

Santry responded casually, as if mentioning something pleasant but unimportant. "There is something, Andreas. If it's possible when things settle down a little, I'd like to see the Fragments. They got me into all this, but I've never had a good look. I think I'd enjoy holding that piece of paper in my hands. It's not often you can look at something that changed your life forever."

Korachis made an expansive gesture, suggesting the request was nothing at all. "Easily arranged, Michael. They're framed and hanging in my library on Mitilini. Negotiations continue with several buyers, but I'm in no hurry. When Ladrea's back, please go there for a few days, stay with Maria—she's a religious person and would love talking with you—use my books, rest, get some sun. I'd be honored to have you in my home. We are all indebted to you."

There was a warning knock at the door, and a tall, well-dressed man of about thirty with black, shaggy hair falling across his ears and forehead walked into the room carrying a black bag in his right hand. Korachis ushered him quickly into the bedroom and closed the door behind them. Apostolos and Santry were alone.

"Did any of your men touch their bodies?" Santry asked.

"No. They found them exactly so. In a situation like this, they'd touch nothing till I arrived. Why?"

Santry passed it off with "Just wondering" and grew silent. He had nothing more to say to any of them and he wasn't conducting any investigation. He'd wait only long enough to get the doctor's assessment and get out of there before he collapsed. It was already two in the morning and he had been up half the previous night arranging the forgery of Ladrea's letter. Too much coffee, too many cigarettes, too much lost sleep, too much tension. Slumped back in his chair, eyes closed, he decided not to mention the dark, wet stain on the black jacket of the short, stocky man in the beret who had stood beside him in the bedroom doorway. Blood? Probably. It looked fresh. But if so, so what? So maybe the men in the hall found the bodies clothed and arranged them in bed. Or maybe they were working *with* Larus, not against him. And so? And so if he told Korachis, he'd kill them. Or he'd try, fail, and they'd kill him. Somewhere one had to draw the line. His reports had already gotten one man murdered that day. No more. It wasn't his war and it wasn't his responsibility to keep killers honest with one another. If he was still alive and ambulatory when and if Ladrea got freed, he'd take Korachis up on that invitation to visit Mitilini. The revelation that the Fragments hung on a wall in his home was the day's only bright spot, but too many "if's" were in the way and there was too much to do first. Santry's priorities had shifted. It would be good to get the Fragments. He imagined taking them to Simonedes himself and telling him the whole story, but that would have to wait. It was far more important to rescue Ladrea and to help Varga expose and decimate Korachis's organization.

Varga was exultant. Not only had Tocaro been arrested in Rome, but Tocaro was talking in Rome, and though the underground pillars of the Eternal City weren't trembling, they were sure as hell paying close attention to daily briefings from inside the police department. The big man couldn't sit still, stalked his prey restlessly through his cluttered apartment, pulled on his moustache, argued with himself, and stopped frequently to stare at Santry, shake his enormous head with pleasure and disbelief, and decorate the priest with another medal.

"Now you're reaching the sinners, Michael. Now your sermons are being heard!" Then more coffee, more almond cookies, more muttered, excited observations. "And you look better for it! You were getting pasty from all the talk, constipated on righteous exhortations. Holy zeal demands release in action. See? You're even smiling."

Santry told him he looked better because he got some sleep and he was smiling only because he wasn't dead, not because he was happy. Varga was confusing a nervous tick with religious radiance. And if they didn't hear soon from Nikos, who had gone to search Savonon's apartment, they should go after him.

"No, Michael, about Nikos you don't need to worry. Nikos will outlive all of us. He moves like a breeze, easy, quiet, and unseen. Even here, right here in this room, if I'm not looking at him, sometimes I have to stop and think: Is he still over there on the couch, or did he go? How soon do you have to leave . . . ? An hour! Then we've got to see your films right now."

The projector was on the coffee table, aimed at the wall where a large pale yellow rectangle marked the removed painting's place. They had saved the movies until last. Varga had listened to Santry's narrative like a starved man at the king's table. Every morsel a delicacy repeatedly savored: the entire route behind the tan VW and red Fiat, all visions in a bedroom door, the insinuations of the ransom note, Korachis's speculations, the tones of Larus's telephone voice, suspicions of blood on a dark jacket.

Varga listened to all of it and insisted that Santry tell it again. Then he circled, squeezed it for more, looked at everything five ways, and finally announced, "We're close! So close I can smell their filth."

He unrolled a large scroll and stretched it out on the table beside a stack of folders.

"While you were in the pines of Lycabettus last night, Nikos hid in a small closet for four hours photographing files." His bear-sized hand pressed flat on the green folders, as if emphasizing their power to bear any weight. "Documentation, Michael. You swear on Bibles; I swear on these: beautiful, hard, irrefutable facts. My oaths and lamentations become suddenly undeniable and exhilarating when backed with these. I think we've got them. I think we've broken through. It's all here: letters, budgets, canceled checks, and secret memoranda. He stabbed at the unfolded organizational chart with a thick, blunt finger and leaned close to Santry, as if summing up his case for an unseen jury. "Korachis is a wild, rampaging octopus. A new species: He doesn't have eight arms, he has hundreds, and more on the way. Look at this. Tentacles everywhere!" Varga's hand moved rapidly across the sheet as he pointed excitedly to clusters of names. "Everything I suspected, and a few surprises. The usual extortion, fund skimming, and international stable of castrated politicians, cops, and judges. Not much heroin moves through Turkey without his tax on it, but he's less active in drugs than I predicted. Then there's high-class theft of exotic valuables like the Fragments for the carriage trade. But his specialty is a network of independent mercenaries and terrorists. In some cases, he sets them up but usually doesn't run them. He gets them started, cuts them loose, and collects enormous servicing fees. He's operating an international certification, employment, supplies, and covers operation. He links killers to qualified buyers who trust his judgment and connections, he sells the guns, munitions, and explosives needed for the assignments, and he covers their asses against detection and arrest. If the Italians had paid him to clear a path for Tocaro through the Roman legions, he'd never have been picked up. Larus and a handful of gunmen are kept on central staff to enforce agreements and take special jobs, but otherwise he doesn't care who gets killed. He'll sell services to anybody.

"Add all that activity up and it's more than an old-fashioned octopus can handle. And that's why Savonon gets early retirement, Ross moves in, and Larus doesn't. Savonon moved up when it was a fairly small direct-action unit. His roots were in the field. He knew how to mobilize a strike force and run drugs through Piraeus, but he doesn't know how to plug in a computer, much less run an international organization. Neither does Larus. He's another Savonon in good health, sexy clothes, and turquoise beads. Ross is what Korachis needs: a professional, hard-charging manager to grab hold of those thrashing tentacles and orchestrate them for the greater good of the usual few."

Santry studied the chart closely while Varga read the international roll call of elite, rich, and powerful public figures prospering from a covert business relationship to Korachis. "What are you going to do with all this?"

"What does a journalist do with an exposé? He shouts it from the rooftops."

Santry walked away from the desk toward the kitchen and coffee. "I don't like what this means for Ross."

Varga slumped in his chair like a deflated balloon, exuberance gone, exasperation lines across his face. "You're his Father, Michael, not his Mother. He's made his bed. The troubling question for me isn't about Ross, it's about you. What happens to Santry? That's what we've got to figure out. The story's grown too big. It can't wait till you die to get published, and I can't control what Korachis or Gabriella or Larus tells the investigators. My story's no problem. I've got the evidence I need without quoting you, and if we get the Fragments to Simonedes in the next week or so, he'll be happy to lock them up and say nothing about either disappearance or return. But the others . . . well, I don't know what they'll do. Trapped people usually want others to feel the same steel teeth."

Santry began talking before Varga had finished. "Stop, Dimitrios, no need to go on like that. You're right. There's no question about running the story. Why else are we tearing around Athens and Lesbos like madmen? It's the only way to stop them." The fingers of one hand flicked over the pile of folders and lists of honored names. "We're down to basics, aren't we? What can anyone do in Babylon? Not much, it seems. No new worlds or anything like that, but maybe you can reduce the slaughter. Maybe not even that. I don't know anymore, but you can't walk away from the possibility when it's in your hands. The story's got to be told. There's no choice on that one. And don't worry about me. I'm not making any public confessions and I'll get those Fragments back to Kallos if I can, but, well, if it comes, it comes. I'm tired of thinking about it. How soon are you going public with all this?"

"Soon, but how soon I don't know. There are problems. Ladrea's one. I can't publish before she's safe because it makes Larus too unpredictable. Right now she's probably all right, because in spite of what Korachis thinks, the man's not crazed. The lure of gold straightens out many emotional kinks. Count on it—he'll deliver the daughter if it's the only way to get the ransom." Varga looked back at the long organizational chart. "The bigger problem is that Korachis has influence and informants in all these rat holes and this story burns them all. He could hear about it a hundred ways before it gets near the presses and pack these files up my rosy ass before dropping me overboard in the middle of the Mediterranean. I've got to come roaring out in a way that steamrolls all objections and gets an aroused public on my side so they can't bury it and me. In any case, nothing comes out till you and I agree on it."

The big man moved toward the projector on the low table and told Santry there were two films he wanted them to look at together, two he hadn't seen out of the twenty that Nikos lifted from Gabriella's office. No, they weren't going to be missed. Seventy-five or a hundred remained on the shelves, and who would be looking for old movies anyway? Savonon was presumably dead, Gabriella and Ross were unconscious, Larus was roaming the plains of Attica like a starved wolf, and Korachis was too busy playing the anxious father to pay any attention to a few deletions from his lover's toy room.

Varga pulled the heavy window shades shut and yelled over his shoulder, "He's also too busy keeping your life in danger. I don't like the smell of your meeting with Ladrea tonight, but I can't think of anything to do about it."

Santry propped pillows at one end of the couch and stretched out. "What's the first one?"

"A surprise," Varga told him as he threw a switch and a beam of light raced to the faded yellow wall with a full-face shot of Santry walking apprehensively up a staircase toward a man with long blond hair, staring in disbelief at an imperious and magnificent Gabriella flanked by two stunning cheetahs, watching a film that anticipated most of his moves, swinging a chair wildly at Larus, and finally lying sprawled on the floor like a rag doll, eyes closed, mouth slightly open, one arm bent awkwardly beneath him. Two unknown, unfamiliar men were walking toward his lifeless body as Gabriella's voice instructed the audience: "The priest's behavior has conformed to the predicted scenario in all essential details, though exhibiting an extreme degree of sexual hysteria. . . ." Her voice stopped abruptly and the film went blank.

Varga switched the lights on and said that a fast meatcleaver editing job had probably been done on the film when Ross returned from the Indies steamed up about the treatment of his friend. He doubted that Gabriella would risk offending the new prince in the palace. Santry didn't know and didn't care anymore, although he suspected the film had not been edited at all but was intended for the victim's eyes in another round of torment. It ended abruptly in order to increase the subject's anxiety about what happened when the two men reached him and the lights went out. He couldn't quite imagine Gabriella trimming her work to satisfy Ross.

"What's the other one?" Santry asked, as Varga slid the second reel onto the projector.

"Haven't seen it, but it's labeled 'L. P. Gerson.' I saved it because you asked about the company. I've seen eighteen of these monsters in the last ten hours and there's a pattern. The content varies, but there's nothing illegal going on and every one of the leading actors has been involved in some way with Korachis's criminal activities. That way Gabriella can do what she pleases and not worry about the police or lawsuits."

The lights went out again and the wall came to life with a black-hooded figure strapped to a chair. Ten minutes into the film, Santry had learned nothing about L. P. Gerson and more than he wanted to know about the extrasensory capacities of the man under the hood, who was guessing the identity of playing cards held in front of his unseeing eyes while being subjected to a range of pleasurable and painful stimulations. Gabriella's voice-over explained the theory being tested—that pain, contrary to received opinion, did not restrict but expanded the mind's reach, and therefore the sightless subject's skill in identifying cards through E.S.P. should increase in direct proportion to the voltage of the current received. Santry, offended by the procedure and bored by the endless cards and unimpressive guesses, would have turned it off, but Varga was entranced and loudly predicting the next card to be turned up. Santry suggested that he volunteer for a film and was thinking about that night's rendezvous with Ladrea when he heard Gabriella's voice say something about removing the mask and allowing the "subject" to see the results of his research.

He glanced back at the wall as the black hood was lifted. A middle-aged man with thinning hair was up there squinting into the camera's lights. Something about the face held Santry's interest and made him watch, then made him get up and walk toward the wall, trying to see the inflated image better, trying to remember where it was that he had seen him. The man was walking off the stage when the spark struck and Santry yelled, "Dimitrios, that's him! That's the man in the red Fiat! Run it again! He's the one who drove Larus to Gabriella!"

Varga flipped the reverse switch and they watched the man walking backward toward his chair, where he sat blinking at the lights until an attendant lowered a hood over his face.

Varga hurriedly checked the files piled high on his desk, while Santry read from the gray, metal film container: "L. P. Gerson: John Phillips."

The priest was staring at the pudgy face seen the night before on a deserted street corner when Varga yelled, "You've got him! According to these, he's been with Korachis for a couple of months. Works in the shipping department and picks up a thousand U.S. dollars a month for feeding information on munitions shipments to them. Larus probably recruited him originally and has taken him into the new organization."

At six o'clock that evening, Korachis's eyes moved over the three faces watching him intently. "The priest must be followed tonight," he announced quietly. "But he must not know—for his sake as well as ours and Ladrea's. He's inexperienced and easily alarmed. One wrong glance, one involuntary start, a single slip of the tongue, and Larus will suspect the trap. Three cars, four men in each, will follow when Santry leaves the hotel. One will keep Santry's car in sight, while the other two trail by radio communication. They'll travel as a relay: exchanging the lead frequently so Santry's driver never sees the same car too long behind him. Apostolos will be in the lead car and will direct all activity. What they do . . ." He paused, then corrected himself: "More accurately, how they strike will be determined by where they are and what they find. But they will strike," he said emphatically. "Apostolos and I agree that given the peculiar game Larus has begun to play, it's doubtful he would end it simply for the gems. We find it too easy to imagine him carrying Ladrea to a distant land and demanding Gabriella herself as ransom in the next note. There are risks, but to wait only increases them."

Ross, bruised along one cheekbone and bandaged across the throat, asked, "What are the risks for Santry?"

Apostolos answered, "If possible, we'll wait till their meeting's over and the priest's gone from the danger zone. If we can, we'll even wait till Larus leaves, trail him with one unit until Ladrea's freed by the other two, then take him out. But I emphasize 'if possible.' We don't know what we'll find."

"I want to be there," Ross said flatly.

"No," Korachis countered firmly. He was courteous but open to no discussion. The matter was decided. "Please, Alexander, you're still reeling from a beating, and I'd say no even if you weren't. Apostolos must have free rein and instant obedience. You know you'd interfere with questions and ideas. These twelve are a highly skilled, carefully trained, and disciplined strike force. They know their job and they must be free to do it. You and I will wait together."

"Where's Santry now?"

Apostolos shrugged. "We don't know. He said he was going to get some sleep and then go walking, but three hours from now he'd better be in front of his hotel waiting for Larus."

Gabriella, whose neck bruises were covered by a glossy purple scarf and who had remained silent and detached through most of the discussion, told Apostolos that he was to bring Ladrea directly to her upon release. "Larus refers to Polaroids in his letter. If they exist, I want you to find them. Be sure nothing's left behind for reporters, police, or the thrill seekers." She stood as if to go, but announced instead that others should leave. "Andreas, you and I must talk, but I need some time with Alexander."

The older man tilted his head slightly to one side as if to say that he understood and suggested to Apostolos that they get something to eat. "I'll return in an hour," he told her. "Ross and I must be together in my office from eight o'clock on. Apostolos, Santry, and Larus must know they can always reach us there." They confirmed their arrangements, gathered their coats, and took off, leaving two dark-jacketed men on duty in the hall. One wore a beret and had a close-cropped beard. The other watched with uncertain eyes and looked away as Korachis passed.

As Gabriella walked toward Ross, he wondered what was coming. It was their first conscious moment alone since Larus had quietly opened the door to her bedroom and found them naked. He had heard nothing. Absorbed in a marijuana high and the undulating dance carrying him deeper and deeper between those lean and golden thighs, Alexander had surrendered to the dark sea roller surging powerfully toward a distant shore he wished they never had to reach. Gabriella had felt first the sudden shift and crash of his body on hers, opened her startled eyes, saw Larus's grimace, his raised fist, and nothing more. When she awoke, Ross was gone and she listened through the frightening roaring in her ears to voices in the other room. Her eyes closed and she drifted unconcerned toward sleep until she heard Korachis and Ross saying something about the night. She had struggled to her feet to stop him from the terrible mistake she knew he'd make if left alone. She reached the doorway and leaned uncertainly against the frame. Too late. Ross had already told the story. She saw that much in Korachis's eyes as both men hurried toward her and helped her to a chair. Andreas asked no questions about the previous night and she offered no explanations.

Her fingers touched the silk scarf on her throat as she faced Ross alone. "What did you tell Andreas?" Her question had a cautious, apprehensive edge.

Ross was cool. "That we were sitting here going over plans for the benefit when Larus came through the door and surprised us with a gun."

She leaned toward him and touched his cheek, then shook her head and turned away. "Why did you tell him that?"

Ross saw the long, thin back beneath the black dress, followed the slight swells at the hips and breasts, remembered skin the color of young deer. He didn't answer.

She faced him, eyes intense and narrowing. "Well?"

"What'd you think I was going to tell him? That we were in the back room balling?"

She called him a fool but called him so quietly and said she knew when she heard their voices in the next room that he'd be lying. "Why do you apologize? Why the hiding? What are you afraid of?"

Ross snapped angrily, "If you have something to say, why don't you just say it, Gabriella!"

"It's pathetic behavior," she told him, more sadly than fiercely. "The frightened adolescent crouching naked in the corner, knees turned inward, hands hiding genitals, eyes anxiously on the lash of some unseen judge."

Ross got cooler. "Okay, it was a mistake," he said casually. "I'm just less committed to the blazing truth than you. It doesn't even interest me that much—but lying's not a principle either. I don't care who knows we're fucking, and God knows Andreas has learned what to expect from you. It's only that, at least in my experience, fucking is always the Great Complicator, and there are a lot more urgent items on our agenda right now. But if it's important to you to tell him, go ahead, fine with me. It was an important night and I'll deal with whatever comes out of it."

"What did you learn last night?"

"C'mon, Gabriella, ease up. The bed's not a classroom. I don't go there for instruction."

"Too bad," she said, looking curiously at him. "I learned something. You're more honest lying down than on your feet. Your body tells the truth. It doesn't apologize. It doesn't hide at all." She hesitated and spoke tentatively, as if walking the edge of a cliff. "I'm the opposite—more honest with my words. It's my body that often hides and doesn't tell the truth. But last night there were no evasions. I refuse to deny that—to Andreas or to you."

He finished the second martini, tapped his empty glass impatiently on the mahogany bar for a third, lit another cigarette, and looked cautiously around the bar. The first glories of gin's velvet glow had reached the suburbs of his mind and tension was fleeing from every pore. Sweet John Phillips, which was what he called himself when talking to no one but himself, had decided that he was in way over his fucking head and had to get out of the rat barrel before they turned the cats loose. He wanted to be dragged across no more beaches, but he wanted even less to be thrown down iron stairs into a crowded cell where men with yellow-stained and broken teeth and black-hole mouths wouldn't beg, pay, or ask politely for his ass. No, no, he told himself, Sweet John couldn't handle that at all!

Going slower now, he sipped the fresh martini and stared clear-eyed at the two facts rattling him: He had to get out, but he was nailed to the floor. It was time to go, but he couldn't move. *Well, it's not quite that I can't move,* he reasoned. *It's that John-John is only half terrified by all the action. The other half of him is really quite pleased. All false modesty aside, he has to admit that there's more to him than meets the eye and if the fair-haired one comes through on promises, this lad will soon depart the cloistered cabinets of L. P. Gerson, burn these frayed clothes, make a fortune, and stride boldly into a sunlit world.*

He paid no attention to the man who slipped onto the stool beside him until he saw the cards. He was playing them out one at a time beside his beer. Jack of diamonds up. Without a care, Phillips laughed and said, "Eight of clubs." He watched an outsized hand flip the next one over lightly: queen of hearts. Phillips laughed and volunteered, "Sometimes I hit 'em, but I'd never make a living at it." Relaxed and friendly and a drink or two beyond giving a shit, he said, "I'm in communications. What's your game?"

"I'm the dues collector."

And there was something about the way the big man said it that kept Phillips's eyes forward and the glass at his lips and his courage just out of reach. "The dues collector?" he finally managed. "Interesting work, I bet. Wouldn't fancy it myself, but now that you tell me, I can see it suits you. Yes, you've got the look of it—that steady-as-she-goes look of the natural sea captain." He felt a spurt of unexpected energy carrying him and giggled nervously. "I can see you before the mast, flogging whip in hand." He looked the stranger up and down. "A bit hefty for flights in grim pursuit on back stairs, I'd guess, and the clothes could use a sprucing, but the face is exactly right. And it's not just the proportions. I don't mean to stare, fellow, but, by God, you do have a trophy-sized head! The moustache and brows alone must make the boys in arrears tremble." More chuckling noises. Then: "If I was in your club and saw those scowling eyes coming after me, I'd pay up, and quick."

He called the bartender and ordered another beer for his "partner."

"Can you imagine this face of mine collecting bills? Or intimidating anyone? Not likely. Maybe if I had turned to it earlier, but not now. No, much too late for me. By the time you're our age, you've got the faceprint that fits your job. Look at this friendly open countenance and take a guess. What do you think I do?"

"You're a clerk at L. P. Gerson," Varga told him.

"Oh, so," Phillips said softly, studying the surface of his rapidly disappearing martini and reaching for his matches. "The dues collector has come to the clerk. You bring a bill?"

Varga said nothing but slid three sheets of paper in front of him. The first was a photocopy of the munitions shipment schedules passed from Phillips to Larus to Savonon and a record of Korachis's cash payments for them. The second was a three-month-old front-page article on the sea heist of L. P. Gerson guns. And the third was a photograph of a woman sprawled on an Athens sidewalk beside a bombed-out car.

Phillips stopped smiling, looked quickly around to see if anyone was watching, and asked, "What do you want?"

Varga ignored the question and whispered roughly, "That's for starters. Last night you met with Savonon on Lycabettus, dropped Larus off on Kalitsis Street, then went to the fat man's apartment and killed him. How much do you think a man should pay for murder?"

Phillips saw lightning flashes ricocheting up and down those iron stairs and heard the terrible thunder of cell doors clanking and slamming. He backpedaled frantically, circled, and came at the stranger with a hard, clear line. "Fuck off, mister. I've got nothing for you. I was right here, right on this stool last night, and dozens of good drinkers will testify when needed." Fear escalating, he began to speed, seized the photocopies from the bar, folded and stuffed them into his coat pocket away from the stranger, and told him, "Those names you said, I don't know any of 'em, but, good buddy, I'm taking these to my lawyer and I'm going to sue your ass." His voice rose toward a shrill tenor as he demanded, "Who the hell do you think you are, coming in here and disturbing me, harassing me, threatening me like this? Time somebody trimmed your sails, Captain. Now, where can I reach you, because there are laws protecting people from this kind of shit. You got a card or something? You must have a card. Just give me your name and address, Skipper, and I'm going to be back in touch with you. You've made a bad mistake, and from now on my lawyer'll do the talking. I've got no more to say, and I'm sure as hell not paying you any dues."

Varga leaned closer and told him, "I didn't say you'd offer to pay. I said I was going to collect. Count on it!"

Phillips slid off the stool and insisted that the man identify himself, realizing he had gotten carried away and had no idea how to reach this shakedown artist whose sticky fingers had reached right into Korachis's goddamned file and come out papered with enough to put all of them away for several lifetimes.

"Tell your lawyer my name's Forticos—Lieutenant Forticos."

Phillips snatched the information like a doper on his last run before a fix and began backing toward the door, his glistening face twitching nervously. "Okay, Captain, you're going to hear from me. And soon! Very soon!" He stumbled backward into a table, apologized repeatedly to the ruffled drinkers, and hurried on to the exit, where he whirled to give the big man a parting shot. He was disappointed to discover he wasn't watching, but fired a finger at the broad back and heavy shoulders anyway. As he ran to the car, he knew he had blown it. How uncool could one get? Thank God Larus hadn't been there to see him falling backward through the crowd. The memory embarrassed him. He had a lot to learn from the blonde. One step at a time. Rome wasn't built in a day. Sweet John Phillips wasn't going to become Jack the Ripper overnight. But he could learn; he had always been quick on the pickup. He was so relieved to reach the red Fiat that he gave the hood a breathless, affectionate pat and sighed mightily when the motor charged to life. As he pulled away and sped toward the yacht harbor, a slight middle-aged Greek in an undistinguished, well-pressed black suit lit a cigarette, released the brakes on his old, dark blue Toyota, and eased into the traffic behind him.

Since the night Varga broke into his room in Detroit and read his incriminating journal, Santry had stopped making regular entries in any book. But the habit of reflecting with pen in hand was rooted in years of practice and was a useful compass. If he could not always find true north, the writing at least helped him see where the needle of his life was pointing at the time. At eight-thirty P.M. on Wednesday night, the priest capped his pen and read over a few of the phrases scattered on the back of an envelope:

> "frightened/impatient/restless; unpredictable wills/ irresistible events rushing toward some final storm; chaos and the illusions of Bellerophon."

He tore the envelope up, dropped the white flakes of paper in the basket beneath the desk in his hotel room, and reached for the phone. It was answered on the first ring.

"Andreas . . . ? Yes, it's Santry. I must go in a few minutes and called to learn of any developments. How are Alexander and Gabriella . . . ? Yes, I'd like to talk to him."

Korachis looked up from the phone by the blue window seat in his office and told Ross to get on the other line. It was Santry. He did not volunteer to get off and let the friends talk privately. There were times when the best of men needed the moral support of interested, powerful observers to help them act and speak correctly. This was such a time. Korachis did not intend to let Ross, a man he valued and trusted more than most, vacillate even momentarily. He kept the phone at his ear and his eyes steadily on Alexander as the younger man lifted the receiver.

"Hello, Michael. I'm very glad you called. . . . Yes, we're all right. A few bruises, no permanent damage. Gabriella's resting in her apartment. The two of us have been sitting here talking about you. Everything all right?"

"Is Andreas on the line?"

Ross glanced across the room. Korachis nodded. "Yes. Why?"

"Because I want to ask you a question and I want him to hear it. This morning, Larus threatened to kill me if there were any surprises tonight. Korachis promised me there'd be no tricks. No one following, no surveillance, no traps. I want you to tell me that's still the way it goes."

If Ross had misgivings about his response, they didn't show in hesitation. "Definitely, Mike. It has to go as planned. Nothing will happen to jeopardize your safety." He paused, then added, "I'm sorry we couldn't talk today. It's important to me that you understand what happened last night."

"Yes, we need to talk," Santry told him, "not about last night particularly, but about everything. One long talk before I go."

Ross was surprised. "How soon's that?"

"After Ladrea's release. Next week, if possible. You should consider leaving with me. I'm serious. Simonedes is still recovering. Forticos and Savonon are dead. Ladrea kidnapped. Larus tried to kill you on Sunday. Last night he settled for strangling and humiliation. I don't know what you believe anymore, but by any reading your life line appears precarious. Remember the night we stood in front of the Pegasus and argued about your excess and my caution? Remember

Bellerophon, the talented rider? He was lucky. His horse tossed him before he got killed. Smart horse. Yours is galloping straight into the flames. You've lost the reins, Alexander, and your feet are caught in the stirrups." Santry stopped abruptly. "I didn't mean to get into all that now, but that's what I want to talk about, and both of you might as well know what's on my mind because even seeing each other again has become a questionable assumption. Who knows what Larus will do when he learns you've killed Savonon?"

Ross shot Korachis a worried glance and asked, "Mike, are you all right? Are you okay for tonight?"

Santry's voice came back with a hard edge. "Am I all right? In a conventional sense, yes, I'm fine, meaning sober, fit, and capable of action. If Larus allows, I'll see Ladrea. If he lets me go, I'll call immediately. You don't have to worry about that. But in any deeper sense, no, I'm not all right, and neither are you—either of you. How could we be? We're caught in a soiled wind."

Korachis wondered, after hanging up, about that emotional intensity. "Does it seem inordinate to you?" he asked Ross. "I can understand fear, but why should Santry feel soiled? Priests don't usually feel soiled by others' foulness, they feel superior to it. What do you think is going on?"

"Savonon," Ross told him. "He followed him, reported what he found, and feels responsible for the death. For Mike, evil's a river with endless tributaries. When it bursts the dam and floods the city, its destructive power is the force of many streams, not one. Santry's torn up because he feels caught in a current he detests and he can't get out. He wanted to get Kallos, Simonedes, you and me behind him. He wanted out. But he's a good man and couldn't turn his back on Ladrea. He has to do what he can to save her, so he stays to help, fingers Savonon, finds me mauled and taped to Gabriella, and still agrees to go alone to Larus, a man who's already beaten him up twice. He ends up feeling trapped in an evil whirlpool. I can understand where he's coming from."

"You're too understanding, Alexander, too ready to make excuses for him. Your friend's caught in the net of bad metaphor. His communal compulsions have turned him against himself. To him, the Church isn't an aggregate of self-interested individuals, each pursuing his paltry ends; it's the mystical body of Christ. Mired in that collective image, he can't see life as it is: an exploding star, splintering irrationally in millions of absurd directions. He insists it's a river surging toward some sea. More tribal subterfuge. The illusion of coherence and solidarity masking the pain and the fact of chaos. Santry needs his guilt and soiled winds. They're evidence of a moral order. Without them, he'd be alone and meaningless—lost." Korachis looked away from a wall tapestry that held his eye while talking and searched Ross's face. "You seem clear of those tendencies. No guilt that I've observed—even little troubled introspection."

Alexander, less recovered from the previous night's assault than he looked, leaning casually against the wall with ankles crossed, agreed. "No, there's not much guilt in my life." His hands went deep in the pockets of his flannel slacks and found a few coins. "Like this afternoon, Gabriella told you the truth about last night. I lied. That gave me a moment's awkwardness but no guilt because no agreement I had made was broken. I assumed she wouldn't tell you, that's the way it usually goes in these affairs, but she wanted you to know. She insisted on it. I'm not sure that's entirely the principled truth-telling matter she claims, but that's not my business. Whatever made her do it, the results gave me a worried moment about your reaction."

Korachis, erect in his chair, caressed the handle of his cane. "And when Santry asked about a trap tonight, how did you feel about lying to him?"

"No feelings at all. I agree with the plan and nothing happens till Santry's clear of danger. Right?"

Korachis tilted his head to one side and watched through slightly narrowed eyes. "What if I said 'wrong'? What then, Alexander? What if I told you that Apostolos has been instructed to save Ladrea at whatever the cost to others? What if the priest were killed tonight? Would you feel only 'awkward' then?"

The footsteps stopped outside his room. He watched the knob turning on the locked door and heard the sharp, repeated taps. He had to get outside, had to be out front by nine o'clock. "Who is it?"

"Santry?"

"Yes."

The voice was muffled. "We're taking you to Larus."

When he opened the door, they pushed him brusquely aside, pulled the shades down, checked bathroom and closet, peered furtively at the street below. One was his size: five-foot-ten, stocky, and with the same corrugated Italian features. The one with the tiny eyes set like coals in a broad Slavic face told him to take off his jacket and wool cap. "Hurry!" he commanded, handing him a heavy, knee-length coat and cap with a beak. "Put these on!"

As soon as Santry changed clothes, they rushed him down rear stairs to a basement exit, a trash-strewn alley behind the hotel, an idling car. The Italian walked out the front door wearing Santry's jacket and cap, moved a few feet from the entry lights, and stayed close to the building. He kept his dark, insolent eyes on approaching cars, stared over headlights, and watched every driver. He waited for the first white-eyeball flash of recognition, the sudden brakes, the opened door, and a half hour of aimless, misleading wandering.

Across the street, five floors higher, a rooftop prowler eased night glasses from his eyes, threw a quiet switch with cold fingers, and spoke softly. "White Porsche at curbside, Santry entering, car proceeding south toward Iannakous Boulevard."

Twelve men listened, keyed up, tensed, and waiting for commands. Apostolos's voice crackled. "Yorgo, follow for thirty minutes and take it out." Immediately, a light gray sedan, ominously full of armed men, pulled from a dark side street and swung downhill.

Moments before, an elderly Greek had finished his ouzo in the hotel lounge off the lobby, talked with the clerk, folded his newspaper carefully under his left arm, walked out front, and shuffled slowly up the street past hidden eyes. "Strato!" Apostolos had radioed. "He's coming out the rear. Get positioned." Minutes later an urgent voice reported, "Two men in alley behind hotel approaching brown Honda Civic, plates numbered four-zero-seven-one-five, heading west in alley, approaching Theodorous Street, and turning north."

Santry pressed himself deep in a corner of the backseat, collar up, cold. No one spoke. Cigarettes glowed from three mouths. He opened his window an inch, stared at white smoke rushing out, glossy bright store windows rushing by, heavy traffic on all sides, and he worried about the mask. There wasn't one. Why? Why did they let him see where they were going? Because they were not taking him to Ladrea at all? Because they were taking him to her, but not to where they kept her? Or because this was a one-way ride? Up front the man who led him to the car muttered something about "O Pappas, the Priest." The driver instantly hissed, "Ochi! No!," and the flat-faced man shut up. Santry caught the angry eyes watching him in the rearview mirror, looked away, and absorbed himself in the long miles of bare-bulb apartment houses, endless strings of colored pennants fluttering over shining cars for sale, waves of heavy traffic piling up at intersections, grim faces over wheels pressing forward in the gloom. He was watching a man in the next lane screaming at the woman beside him when the Honda shot forward, hurtled down a curving highway, pulled right, screeched up a short ramp into a supermarket parking lot, careened through a sharp U-turn into position between two parked cars to face the road and watch for any car racing desperately to catch up with them.

Apostolos saw it all through the rear window of the green van and lifted the hand mike to his mouth. "Strato, pull to the curb at the gas station coming up on your right. He pulled into the supermarket just ahead of you. When he comes out, follow for a mile. Then pass and take the lead. I'll close the box."

In minutes, the Honda edged into traffic and tracked onward. In another thirty, the sea rimmed the road and Santry saw the lights of freighters across the bay, massed outside the docks of Piraeus waiting for a storm to pass. Close, they had to be getting close. The lights were out on a seaside Ferris wheel; dark windows of empty hotels stared at the cold and dismal sky; stacked chairs and tables looked deserted and friendless outside innumerable cafés. And a single, great-domed church threw a long shadow over them as they passed. The man up front leaned forward, the car slowed, a finger pointed. "Go in that restaurant. Two men will be playing cards and drinking cognac. Sit beside them." The Honda scurried up a narrow street, pulled into an alley, stopped. A dry-cleaning van passed. Nothing more. "Go now!"

Santry pushed the door open and crawled out. He stood motionless for a few seconds, watched the Honda speed away, saw a man emerge from a building entrance and come toward him, turned quickly, and walked downhill, intent on the steps behind him.

Apostolos's brisk voice masked his end-of-the-hunt excitement. "Strato, get ready! He's walking toward you."

"Check. We see him on the corner, entering a restaurant named Fassolis. Advise."

"This could be the meeting place. Send a man in to check it out. I'll be across the street at the entrance to the docks. Just beyond those trucks."

"Hold it!" Strato called. "He's coming out. Two men beside him waiting for the light, crossing in front of us. Looks like they're headed for the piers. You should be able to see them about now."

"Got 'em, Strato. Moving down Pier A. Anyone following?"

"No one in sight."

"Where's your man?"

"Still in Fassolis. He'll cover the rear."

"There's a warehouse along the pier a hundred yards from my position. Pull over there and hold. We've got their exits blocked."

"Where's Santry?"

"Approaching the end of the pier, headed for a freighter on the left. If they go aboard, I'm sending two men closer."

Santry followed the men who had been drinking cognac in Fassolis up the narrow iron stairs to the rear deck of the deserted ship, stepped across coiled cables to the rail, and looked down on the black water chopping at the freighter's sides. "Wait here," they told him and disappeared on silent shoes.

The pier below stretched through darkness, clustered sheds, wooden shipping crates, and scattered trucks. A few lights glowed from warehouse walls. Hulls of larger ships lay like beached whales against nearby piers. He shivered in the heavy coat, heard a door slam somewhere within the ship and footsteps approaching on a lower deck.

His eyes fixed on the top of the stairs as someone climbed them, came a few feet toward him, stopped, and demanded from the shadows, "What was our agreement, Santry?"

He waited till Larus stood beside him before saying

with unconcealed impatience, "To come alone, to see her, and to leave. Where is she?"

"You came alone?"

"You know I did." He gestured at the deserted dock below. "We're obviously alone."

Larus leaned against the railing, his face partially obscured by the raised collar of his sheepskin jacket. "You're wrong, Santry, but I believe you anyway. You're too in the zone to know what's going on. And don't get jumpy. You'll see her, but we've got to observe a little street theater first. We don't want to get much closer to the stage, so I'll have to tell you what's going on. It may be even more dramatic that way, because I don't think you'll believe me until you see the exciting climax of act one. Now keep your eyes open and on that clump of trees in the small park at the far end of the pier, the ones you walked through to get here. You ready?"

Santry said nothing as Larus took a flashlight from his pocket and pointed it straight down the dock toward the darkness of warehouses, closed ticket offices, and the empty benches of a city park.

"At this point, the script calls for the sudden appearance of one long, steady flash." Larus flicked on the light, held its powerful beam steadily toward the emptiness of the pier's end for a full minute, cut it off, and told Santry, "Now watch what happens!" In the distance, a flash echoed back. "You know who that was, Father? No, you probably don't. That was the young fellow who followed you into Fassolis. No, you didn't know about that either, did you? That light tells me that two heavy long-haulers have been quietly eased across the access road to the pier and that from here on, no one leaves the theater. Fair enough, eh? If you come to a play, you should at least stay till the first intermission. Others, of course, saw that light, too, but only a few grasped its deeper meanings. A man named Strato is one of them. He's a good man: ambitious, greedy, and malleable at the temperature of congealed gold. He is now telling the two men remaining in his car to sit tight because he's leaving for a few minutes to consult with Apostolos."

In the distance, a car door slammed and a match flared. Larus continued the running commentary in velvet, self-satisfied tones.

"Strato now enters stage left and crosses to the second car. I don't know exactly where that car is, but Strato knows and so will we before long. I'd guess he's close to the door by now. There are only so many places it could be and none of them is remote. So let's say he's now tapping at the window and we should try to imagine Apostolos's surprise to see him there. He didn't tell the dumb son-of-a-bitch to come over. What the hell's going on? But notice how that surprise and mild irritation changes in one rapid-fire series from shock to anger, fear, and finally panic as the men in the backseat lean forward and press the cold muzzles of their guns against his neck. For what happens next there is a historical precedent. One might even say the compulsions of tradition make it normative. You've heard of famous Greek hospitality. Well, there are other dependable behaviors in the Balkans. Did you know that of one hundred nine emperors of Byzantium, sixty-five were assassinated? Believe me, the beat goes on. So listen carefully, because if the play's proceeding as intended by the director, you will soon hear the changing of the guard."

Santry imagined bursts of fire an instant before he heard the guns and Larus's satisfied pronouncement that the "coup's begun." He was surprised by the shots' muted sounds because their power filled his sight with lurid, frightening colors twisting in frenzied, backstabbing treachery. Cannons and rockets would better match his mood. Apostolos dead! He barely knew the man, but they had shared coffee that morning. A few hours ago, young, strong, vivid; now bloodied, breathless, gone. What was he doing here? Korachis promised that no one would follow, no one would interfere in any way. And Alexander! Dear friend and zealous opportunist: *It has to go as planned, Michael. Nothing will happen to jeopardize your safety.* In the instant, a stranger walked across his mind: black beret, beard, blue jacket with a dark, wet stain. There in the doorway staring at Ross and Gabriella, outside in the corridor hearing the entire plan, perhaps now in a dark car bent over Apostolos's seeping body. And he had said nothing about the stain, nothing of his suspicions. Unfortunately, just as well. If he had, Apostolos would be alive, but the blue jacket and how many others would be most certainly dead. On what grounds would he choose between them? There were times when all one could do was walk away and not look back.

Larus's voice, steeped in mockery and self-assurance, cut him. "Your comrades' keen regard for your safety is touching, Santry. They've found a slave who'll run their risks and pay their penalties. It's a good deal for them. They fuck up and leave it to their handy-dandy priest to sacrifice himself for their sins. Gabriella's inclined to sadism. You can't wait to get on the cross. The two of you ought to team up—guaranteed bliss. A great pair: She'll drive the spikes and you'll shriek for joy."

Santry turned his back on the despised mouth and glimpsed the lights of cars coming down the pier as the first blow caught him across the cheek and spun him sideways. Then another and another, back and forth across the face, open-handed cuffing, smashing him from side to side in a blur of stinging slaps that stopped only when the blonde grabbed Santry's jacket and jerked him close, their eyes inches apart, blacks steady and unfrightened on pale blues as Larus demanded, "Where's Savonon!"

Santry's hands reached up and gripped the wrists

jammed against his chest as he said quietly, "Savonon's dead."

"When?" Larus demanded.

"I don't know exactly, but soon after your meeting on Lycabettus."

Larus's hands slipped away. "Second-rate to the end! The asshole was probably overheard in the lavatory bragging about the plot. Well, the tables are well turned now."

"Wrong again," Santry told him, the fingers of one hand feeling his smarting face. "No tables are turned; you've gained no advantage; all you've done is intensify the storm. Now, later, the storm's the only winner."

Larus waved at the men clustered outside two cars on the dock below, called congratulations, and told them he was coming down. Two or three responded with raised fists and shouts of "Bravo, Larus, bravo!"

The blonde looked away from the railing, gave Santry a thin smile, asked if he had heard those cheers, and recited, "The priest sits on the burning deck, offering judgments by the peck. Too lost in God to realize, the Kingdom's just materialized!" He started toward the stairs and summoned Santry with all the contempt of royalty for the swineherd. "Come! And be grateful, little man, because for at least another hour you are useful and alive."

A telephone lay on the table between them. And images of men at carside fawning over their newly crowned sovereign, opening the trunk and proudly displaying the grotesque, blood-spattered trophy, Strato basking in the warmth of Larus's praise, the blonde strutting like a conquistador in tight jeans, riding boots, and Marlboro jacket, firing his disciples with dreams of gold and leading them to Fassolis for red meat and strong drink, while he and Strato took the priest upstairs. Larus was standing, full of success and power, receiver in hand and numbers clicking on the spinning dial.

"I'm calling Korachis," he told Santry. "And you're

going to tell him anything you want. It doesn't matter anymore. Just remember, though, you've fallen into a moral universe and I'm in charge of it. Offenses get punished."

Larus listened intently as the phone rang three times and then heard Korachis's controlled voice say "Hello?"

"Korachis, this is Larus. Put Ross on the extension. If there's anybody else in the room, put them on, too. I'm about to administer an intelligence test."

He winked at Strato in the moment's wait, then greeted Alexander with a sarcastic shot about demon lovers who couldn't get it up without letting their guard down.

"Listen, you two, I hate to be churlish, but you put twelve men on me tonight and it pisses me off. I can't really object to the fracas because it went my way, but neither Santry nor I can stand liars. . . . Of course he's here. Who else can bring us a message from the other world now inhabited by invincible Apostolos . . . ? What others? The other men? No, they're fine and quite eager to see you—if and when I give the word. Right now they're downstairs celebrating liberation day. . . . No, Korachis, just shut up or I'm going to hang up. On international markets, your word now has all the value of wet camel shit. Santry would no doubt say it differently, but he agrees with the general assessment. I'm telling you what to do, and you do it, or you don't do it and take the consequences, but there's no more talk. The deal is this: Santry and Ladrea for the necklace of Hera—and the exchange takes place tonight or not at all. So get those gems ready and wait by the phone for instructions on where to bring them. Santry will have seen Ladrea by the time I call again and can tell you she's fine. But if the necklace isn't in my hands tonight, Ladrea and the priest will be quietly erased. And that is a diamond-vault guarantee. It's up to you. Here's Santry."

The priest reached and took the extended receiver from Larus's hand. He remained seated and ignored Korachis entirely. His voice sounded like that of a man resigned to anything and hopeful about nothing. "Alexander, it's very hard to know what to say to you. . . . What? No, no, none of that. Torture's not his game. I'm physically well. . . . Yes, he's right beside me, as is your faithful servant Strato. Please, you don't have to go through all that. He told you exactly what happened. Apostolos is dead and your elite corp has run up a new flag. From what I've seen, they'll do exactly what he says until Strato or someone else decides it's his turn to lead the killer pack. I must tell you that your unimaginable deceit tonight only increases my hope that you'll get out of all this before you're unrecognizable to those of us who have respected you. That's harsh, but I'm feeling betrayed and angry. I'd prefer to say these things face to face, but that's impossible tonight. Whether it's possible tomorrow, we'll have to see."

Hundreds of tall silver masts, their halyards chinking in a light breeze, stabbed the night sky. Or were they spears, hurled at yachts from a giant's angry hand, each piercing and wounding a sleek, fiberglass side? Varga was more in the mood for wrath and thunderbolts than sunny sailing, and sniffed the damp air for every trace of vengeance's skirts. He didn't know whose throat her bony fingers would soon be choking, but, by God, she was near. Somebody was going to get hoisted, flogged, maimed, or killed. The Hippodrome was overcrowded and every thumb was down. Most yachts he saw tethered to the narrow wooden piers were dark in canvas shrouds, but a few lights gleamed from portholes. The open windows of the parked Toyota in which he and Nikos sat caught every sound: sudden laughter from a shipboard party, a solitary cough along the shore, the slow, plaintive bazouki's song. They heard none of the sounds they feared: footsteps on the gravel approaching from the rear, a man or woman screaming, a well-tuned motor purring within a quiet hull as the yacht they watched pulled away from shore and slipped from sight. None of that happened. All and more than that could happen at any time. The risk was too high. Varga decided, one more time, to get the story by jamming the actors.

Nikos had tracked Phillips to a small yacht harbor, watched him board a forty-four-foot sailing ship, exchange brief words with a man on deck, and disappear below. On the phone, he had told Varga, "You'd better come. The yacht's name is the *Ghost*." By the time Dimitrios got there, Phillips had been on board an hour. They waited another thirty minutes until ten P.M. Santry was to meet Larus at nine. If that meeting happened, neither man was on the yacht, because Nikos had been sitting there since eight-thirty, and only Phillips had moved up and down those piers. So who met Phillips on deck? Varga let his hunches run. It was a guard. Why a guard? What better place to keep Ladrea out of sight and instantly movable? The fact that Phillips waited on board meant Larus was expected. And if Ladrea was on the ship, then Santry would be coming to see her for Korachis. But if they came now, Varga's seat was in the distant bleachers, too far away to help or even see what the hell was going on. It was time to leave the audience and take the stage.

Nikos took the hose and can carried in the trunk for just such emergencies, siphoned off a gallon of gas from the Toyota's tank, and edged slowly toward the *Ghost*. Varga walked beside him, an iron tire-wrench tightly in his hand. The weathered boards of the long pier trembled slightly from their weight, but faces could not be seen from the distant ship and nothing was strange about two men walking. Fifty feet from the lights of the long, low yacht they planned to board, they stopped, watched, climbed quickly to the deck of the nearest ship, soaked its furled mainsail in gasoline, torched it, jumped away from the searing flame, and ran shouting down the pier. By the time they reached the *Ghost*, climbed aboard, and beat on the cabin door, flames from the burning ship were licking the sky red and filling the air with thick, oily smoke.

"Fire! Help! Help! An extinguisher!"

Inside, the noises of quick scrambling, steps on the stairs, the turn of a lock, an angry face peering out and over Nikos's shoulder toward the flames that threatened every ship if uncontrolled, eyes flashing from anger at the intrusion to alarm, strong hands seizing red canisters from wall brackets, and two men rushing out into a night storm of iron blows. The first dropped to the deck like an empty sack. Phillips jumped backward and screamed until Varga blasted the air out of him with a vicious blow to the gut and kicked him backward down the stairs. Nikos dragged the fallen guard into the cabin, slammed and locked the door behind him, listened to the frantic shouts from shore, pulled window curtains back to glimpse dark figures racing toward the fire, quickly bound the bleeding sentry, gagged him, and stuffed him in the john. Phillips lay on the floor beneath a fold-down table gasping for air and writhing like a pinioned snake. Varga said he might be useful and not to crack him, so Nikos tied his hands behind his back, shook him, hissed, "Shut up!," and left him sobbing.

Varga, anxious and breathing heavily, took the guard's gun and carefully searched the ship. He found her in the forward cabin, her black hair tossed and matted, mouth open, wrists and ankles bound, unconscious. Skin pale and cold, lips blue, no apparent wounds or blood, vials of drugs and a syringe by the bed. She had been heavily sedated and probably comatose for days. He cut the tapes from her hands and feet, covered her with a light blanket, and hurried back. Nikos was on deck, taking one more look at the dying fire and the dark knot of men holding dockside hoses and cursing the flames.

Varga dropped to his knees, grabbed Phillips roughly by the shoulders, rolled him on his back, and forced the gun into his whining mouth.

His voice rumbled, "Phillips, listen to me. Your life has taken a sudden turn for the worse. Everybody wants your ass: the Greek nation for terrorism, L. P. Gerson for smuggling, Korachis for kidnapping, and Larus for leading me here."

Phillips mouthed repeated, sucking pleas against the barrel of the gun and rolled his terror-stricken eyes.

Varga edged the .38 an inch deeper in his throat. "You ready to tell me some truth?" When the weeping man nodded desperately enough, Varga removed the gun, leaned grimly toward him, and demanded, "When's Larus coming here?"

Phillips swallowed hard, stared at Varga through red-rimmed eyes, and gasped, "I don't know! But he's coming! Anytime. Please, I didn't know she was here. I never knew anything!"

Varga let him cry. The panic looked genuine and the near-hysteria could be useful. He gestured with his head and led Nikos silently to the forward cabin where Ladrea lay. "I'll help you get her to the car," he told him quietly. "Run her to Dr. Petrides, take those drugs by the bed so he'll know what's in her, and tell him to keep her well and keep her hidden until he hears from me. Then get back here as fast as you can."

She was wearing slacks and a heavy sweater. The addition of a wool cap, jacket, and the guard's shoes made her a believable drunk with arms draped over Nikos's and Varga's shoulders as they carried her past the few people still mingling near the yacht with the burned mainsail. In minutes, she was stretched out on the backseat of the Toyota, doors were locked, and Nikos was on his way. Varga raised one clenched fist and shook it exuberantly after the disappearing car lights. Free! By God, she was safe and free! It was turning into a hell of a night. His heavy shoulders swung toward the yacht, his elation ebbing only slightly as he focused on the troubles coming up.

He found Phillips where he left him—on the floor, hands tied behind his back—and propped him in a chair near the cabin sink. The man had quieted but nursed the look of a cornered small animal. Varga sat at the fold-down table, his back to the wall, his broad, angry face toward the bottom of the stairs Larus had to descend. One gun rested on the table by his hand. Another lay out of sight on the cushioned seat beside him. He knew the blonde had to be kept out of reach because if they ever tangled hand to hand, his writing days were over. Memories of a strangling night in Kallos reverberated along the fibers of his throat and nailed down one resolve: *One wrong move and Larus gets shot. Any hesitation will be fatal. Remember that,* he told himself, and shifted his brooding gaze from the varnished stairs to Phillips. The soft-cheeked man smelled of fear, his eyes avoided Varga, his lips stretched thin and tight in a worried grin, his head bent weakly to one side. Varga had rarely seen such cowering and imagined a tail wagging deferentially between those fallen haunches.

"Jesus Christ, Phillips, ease up! It's not the end of the world. It's just the end of your miserable life."

Phillips stopped smiling. "You've got to turn the lights off and on." The reporter waited, interested and very suspicious. "When he drives up, he blows the horn. If the lights don't go off and on, he knows something's wrong. It's their signal."

"What other signals do they have?"

"The hatch door," Phillips said, too eagerly. "It's supposed to be locked all the time. He lets himself in with his own key."

"Bullshit!" Varga snapped. "You bastard, you're trying to set me up. It's the light going off and on that warns him. I ought to tear your miserable, lying tongue out and throw what's left to the fish." He got up, hot, grabbed Phillips by the shirt, and raised his arm as if to belt him with the gun, thinking even then that as signals went, Phillips made some sense.

The man flinched but stared directly at him for the first time. "No, no, it's the truth. I swear it!"

Varga bent his great, shaggy head close to the desolate, frantic voice and wondered. There was something in the abject cringing, some terror and anguish in the bleary, puffy eyes that made the man ring true. He was sure as hell scared to death. But was he scared enough to tell the truth? "Why are you telling me this?" Varga whispered menacingly. "Why are you helping me?"

Phillips wailed back angrily, his voice rising higher and higher toward some stretched-thin breaking point. "Are you stupid? Are you crazy? Who should I help? Who else has a gun on me? Look, whoever you are, this is John-John talking, a simple man. Why do I help Larus? The dribbling money? Hell, no! No money's worth his weirdness or yours. I help him because he holds the gun or the rope or drags me across a rock beach or just generally beats the shit out of me. I help him because I'm trapped. Can you understand that? Trapped! I've been cut loose from the fucking world! I got nobody but me. And if he kills you, I'll help him again. My only question is: 'Who's got the gun?' I'm just trying to stay alive, man, just trying to get by. I'm not on his side. I'm not on your side. I'm on *my* side! I'm for John-John! And, good buddy, you better believe me, if he doesn't see that signal, he's going back for the heavy-duty whamo, and this two-by-four floating isolation ward is going up in smoke. You and I will be on our way to Timbuktu, because Larus gets off on bombs. So when that horn blows out there, you better flash that goddamned lamp or get ready to circle Athens from about five thousand feet!"

Varga leaned against the wall and applauded. He enjoyed the outburst. The passion roused him, he liked the style, and he was glad Phillips had stopped simpering. "You have a certain dramatic flair, don't you, Phillips?" His great, bristling moustache rose at the corners in an honest, appreciative smile. "Under the clerk's dull robes, a man of authentic speech and telling gestures! That was nicely done. If you're lying, you're a hell of an actor."

Phillips's narrow shoulders relaxed, settled slightly forward, as if a storm had passed. He stared curiously at Varga and asked without defiance, "Who the hell are you? What are you doing in all this?"

Varga judged he had nothing to lose and told the truth. "I'm a reporter on the edge of my biggest story or the last night of my life."

Phillips exploded in nervous laughter at the talk of death, and launched into a rambling discourse on the seductive power of big stories. "I don't mean sex seduction," he explained. "I mean the somebody-else lust. When I was a kid in England, I was big on knights. In my head, I wore white ivory armor. Then I jumped the goddamned ocean and rode my palomino through a haze of purple sage. After that: deep-sea diver, bank robber, and back to pony express. Lately, it's been Jack the Ripper. I swear to God, I'm more real to myself as Jack-the-fucking-Ripper than as Chief Clerk John-John."

Varga asked Phillips how he got tied up with Larus, and the man obliged, speeding again as he remembered the photos Larus flashed in the bar, the casual "you're going water skiing" words on a deserted beach, the mixed terror and excitement when the first munitions shipment schedule left his hand. He careened manically up and down the twisted labyrinth of the last few months and had reached Lycabettus Hill with Larus and Savonon when he stopped abruptly, raised a quivering finger to his lips for silence, and stared at Varga with fear-glazed eyes. Somewhere in the distance, a horn had blown twice, stopped, and blown twice again. Varga sighed deeply, pulled his hand slowly across his mouth, stared quietly at Phillips, heard water lapping against the ship, ran through a fresh calculation of the odds, then reached deliberately and calmly switched the cabin light from on to off, on to off, and let it blaze. He then pulled Phillips by the arm, hurried him through the short, narrow passageway to the forward cabin, ordered him to lie down on the bed, and gagged and bound him.

"I think you're telling the truth, Phillips, but I can't take chances now. If we get through this, I'll do a feature on you: Jack the Giant-Killer. Double agent John-John, who wormed his way into the terrorist camp and brought 'em down. You'll like him more than Jack the Ripper."

Running through the ship, he lurched up narrow stairs and checked the hatch door. Locked! He made sure the guard was still out and his bindings tight, sat, and faced the stairs from the fold-down table, .38 in hand held steadily on the space Larus had to fill when he descended from the deck. He touched the gun on the seat beside him several times, getting the distance right for a sightless lunge, glanced at closed window curtains one more time, listened for Phillips, listened for steps on the wooden pier. He, they, how many were coming now! More than one, walking toward him, steadily forward, unhurried, careful in the dark, taking time to watch for signs, stopping at the burned sail, coming on. *Phillips says he has the troops. Phillips says he's taking over.* Two men walking! Two, no more. Close now. Beside the *Ghost*, right outside, Larus's muffled voice, one man up there on the deck, now the second, a key in the lock, the hatch door swinging open, first legs coming down!

Santry! Grim-faced, suddenly astonished, unbelieving. Varga motioned to one side with the gun. Santry stepped quickly across the room. Polished riding boots behind him coming down the stairs, jeans tight on supple thighs, unbuttoned sheepskin jacket, a glimpse of turquoise about the neck, the long-awaited flash of recognition, and three men still as statues, silent, staring.

Larus studied the gun, a couldn't-miss nine feet away. His eyes rose slowly to the burly man behind it, narrowed slightly as he took in the large owlish head, the hand-combed, rumpled hair, the wild moustache, the angry eyes. "Varga!" He said it quietly, as one surprised but not alarmed, glanced downward at the remaining stairs, and asked, "May I come in, or do you want me to stand here?"

Varga's malice went undisguised. "Step to the floor, turn around, and put your hands high on those stairs."

The blonde took his time, glanced about the room, shrugged carelessly, turned his back, raised his hands, and leaned forward on the steps. "Santry and Varga teamed up!" he exclaimed. "How did I miss it? I knew you were playing a strange game, good Father, but I never thought of this. I salute you, both of you. But what happens now? Is the fox outfoxed, or simply locked in the henhouse? Santry will tell you that Strato is parked at the harbor entrance. He's heavily armed. How are you street fighters going to handle the two of us? I doubt you'll be much of a match when things break loose. A pencil pusher and a priest. I've tangled with Santry. I know how good he is in a fight. My mother'd take him in the second round. And Varga, your pencil may be potent, but you look as dangerous as a pet lamb. I'd advise you to shoot me in the back right now, because I'm not going to leave you breathing this time."

Santry interrupted the threats and asked his question with a word. "Ladrea?"

"Safe," Varga told him.

"Then who's moving in her cabin?" Larus asked.

Varga, too, had heard the shuffling sounds behind him, worried about slipped knots, and reached for the second gun. Phillips had told the truth about the signals, but he was a loose card flipping from deck to deck. The noises stopped.

The priest reported quickly what had happened: the

ride to Piraeus with Korachis's men following, the death trap, Apostolos killed, Andreas and Alexander waiting for Larus's call with instructions on the gems.

"Is that you back there, Phillips?" Larus called, adding a harsh, insulting laugh.

Varga, buying time for Nikos to get back and deal with Strato, encouraged him to talk. "What makes you think he's here?"

"No mystery, Varga. The red Fiat in the lot announced that bumble-boy was on the prowl." The blonde raised his voice and shouted into the stairs, "Phillips, I want to thank you for leading Varga to me! Deeply indebted!" His sarcasm dripped with rage. "It's an action worthy of your keen intelligence. When this little scuffle's ended—and take my word for it, it's not going to last much longer—I'm going to do an autopsy on your anal tract and discover how your brain works."

The smooth-muscled, powerful man on the stairs was getting ready to move. Varga was sure of it, smelled the impending attack, and searched the room for anything overlooked, anything Larus could use against him. He saw nothing but heard the alarming footsteps on the pier. It couldn't be Nikos. He'd never come so well announced.

"Strato!" Larus crowed and waited. He was as tense as a coiled snake, sniffing the air for the slightest shift behind him, eager for the movement that would give him the split-second edge he needed.

"Check the window, Mike."

Larus knew that was it and turned his head slightly to see Santry looking out through parted curtains. His hands worked slowly against the stairs, his legs bent slightly at the knees, every nerve waited for the moment the priest's eyes would leave the pier, go back to Varga, and Varga for one predictable instant shift his eyes from the targeted back, and glance at Santry. And when that happened, Larus chilled them with a horrible scream, hit the light switch with one crashing movement of his arm, hurled himself backward in the collapsing darkness away from the blast of the .38 that roared in the ship's small cabin like heavy cannon in a tunnel, rolled under the fold-down table, and came up hard, driving the wooden top straight into Varga's face. He heard the bones give, the gun hit and skid across the floor, found Varga's moaning throat with his left hand, and had his right palm poised flat as a disc in the black air when Santry caught him with a body block that sent him crashing into the wall. Furiously cool, his right hand reached smoothly inside his jacket, where the knife was sheathed, slipped it out, and listened for the noise that would tell him where to plunge the blade. The games were over. It was time to go to war, sacrifice two lambs, and satisfy the gods. Varga sighed and Larus moved swift and quiet as a leopard toward the pain.

The lights exploded like a bursting star, freezing everyone in place, fixing white ghostly images forever in their minds: Santry low in a tackle's crouch, Varga sprawled on the floor, hands raised against the blow, Larus straddling him, face twisted, knife in hand coming down, and Phillips, stiff arm pointing straight at Larus in harsh and final judgment, snub-nosed gun inches from the long, blond hair, a mask of triumph on his face.

He kept shooting long after the room stopped pounding and the .38 was as empty as the life in Larus. None of the living moved, but stood motionless, entranced, listening to the dead clicks of a firing pin smashing over and over again on empty shells and staring at the body on the floor.

At one in the morning, Santry walked down the glistening, antiseptic corridor of the hospital toward the visitors' lounge and its public phone. The scattered lights and sounds were those of every hospital he had known: labored breathing, the comforting, fluorescent glow of television, low voices murmuring against the fears, a white, starched uniform at bedside, the solitary relative standing watch. A sharp-faced nurse glanced up, gave him an exhausted look, and went back to her charts.

Korachis answered on the first ring. He had been waiting by the phone for hours. "Good news—Ladrea is free and well. I'm calling from Providence Hospital. She's being looked after by Dr. Apollo Petrides, the same man who took care of me after my filming misadventure. Larus kept her immobile with drugs and she's still sleeping, but Petrides says she'll be all right. Wait, wait, let me tell you the rest. Larus is dead. He was killed by one of his own men who shot him and ran off. . . . Where? On the yacht. I don't know the harbor's name."

Korachis and Ross immediately pressed him hard for more details. Santry listened impatiently to the first insistent questions about who killed Larus and where was Strato, easily imagined the torrent yet to come, and stopped them cold.

"Listen to me! I'm very tired and have little more to say. Since Ladrea was kidnapped on Saturday night, I've done what I could to get her back. That's happened and I'm out of it now. Forticos, Savonon, Apostolos, and Larus have been killed in the last three days. You'll no doubt kill Strato and his warriors if they don't get you first. It's not my war. I can't stop it and I refuse to help the slaughter, so I'm not interested in telling you where I've been or who I've seen. Right now, I'm interested only in going to bed. Alexander, call me this afternoon at the hotel, will you? I need to talk to you."

The elevator door opened and Ross saw Korachis's trim figure standing erect outside the visiting room, where patients in green, knee-length hospital gowns and personal robes lounged, smoked, and paged through twice-read magazines. They met toward the end of the waxed, tiled hallway and spoke in near-whispers. "How is she?"

"Fine, apparently. Tired but fully conscious. Gabriella's with her. Odd, though, she remembers nothing at all after seeing your car explode. That fire's her last vivid memory. The rest is vague and patchy, like a disappearing dream. She must have been half delirious when she wrote the note, because she can't recall either seeing Savonon or writing us. We were there when she awoke. It took minutes for the world to come into focus, but when it did, she was immediately frightened and remembered running across a field, hiding like a small child in a castle, and hearing Larus coming for her inside the walls. She's eager to see you—and Santry. He lured Larus upstairs in Mithymna so she could escape."

"There were no Polaroids? She knows nothing about me and Gabriella?"

"Nothing at all. If there were photos, she never saw them. Did you ask Santry?"

Ross nodded. "He saw none on the yacht."

"Would he tell you any more about what happened?"

"Nothing except that he hopes to leave soon. He did agree to help at the benefit Saturday night, though he thought the request was strange. He'd never admit it, but I think he's glad for the chance to do one last good work. It's in his blood." Alexander looked down at his polished shoes, then up into the black glasses watching him. "So what's your assessment? How are you feeling about all this?"

"Quietly exultant," Korachis told him with a smile as confident as it was slight. "All of this has worked together for our best interests. The Dove and I had an extended talk and reached an agreement. He'll deal with Strato and the others, finish a few commitments, and join us next month, bringing his own men with him. A very important moment for us. A gifted man, he's Larus's superior in every way and I've wanted him for years. Our growing empire is now assured an astonishing military wing." He grasped Ross warmly by the shoulders. "It's time to let your ambitions soar. Give them free rein, Alexander. You've finally got an organization worthy of your drive. More power's within your grasp than ancient conquerors dreamed of."

Santry sent flowers and a note on Thursday but didn't see her until Friday. She was well cared for, had more than enough company, and he, Varga, and Nikos had long hours of work to do. "You look wonderful, Ladrea," he told her, surprised to find her standing in a beige robe by the window, pleased to find her arms suddenly around him and her lips against his cheek.

"I lost three days somewhere," she said. "I was far away, out of my own sight, and it was you who brought me back. Everything's more vivid and somehow lonelier. Is it like this in the resurrection?"

Santry, not having come back from the dead, felt less exuberant but far better for seeing her. She relieved his preoccupation with a necessary but joyless task. "Lonelier in the resurrection? I'd be surprised, but I laid such speculations down long years ago. They tell me you don't remember much."

"Only a vast silence."

Santry, reflecting on the noise and confusion of his last three days, suggested, "Perhaps you were in heaven after all. I can't wait."

Her fingers pushed into the thick black hair falling forward on her face and swept it back. "For heaven?" she asked.

"No." He smiled. "For vast silences. Heaven and I have had a falling-out."

She touched the pale yellow jonquils he had sent. "Alexander says you saved my life; he says you risked your life for mine."

Santry made a slight gesture with his hand, as if to

sweep away the praise. "Easy duty," he explained. "The kidnapped woman, a child trapped in fire, the loved one drowning—dramatic crises make heroes of us all. Everyone wins and celebrates. It's harder to fight your friends than to save them. That takes effort—even remorse." He looked away from her slightly canted, green-flecked eyes and stared out the window at the tops of trees. "I'm leaving soon. Not sure where to yet, but far away. I'll write. I'd like to hear from you, but—"

Her hand reached and held his arm, her face filled with questions. "Of course you'll hear. How could you even wonder? I don't understand your mood."

"Look," he said, his voice resigned and quiet, "the next day or two will bring surprises I'd like to talk about but can't. When it's all over, please remember my chief regret was this necessary silence with you."

A shadow crossed her wide-set eyes. "Alexander knows something. He says you're friends but you're going different ways."

Santry had been with Alexander that morning for hours: same arguments, same bitter taste, nothing changed. "Yes, we're friends. And strangers, too. Alexander knows that, but nothing about what's coming. What do you think he means by 'going different ways'?"

"He thinks the men who kept me shouldn't be ignored. He says you do."

Santry shrugged. "I expect Larus and Savonon have had enough attention. The rest? Foot soldiers hired for a job. They take orders, they don't give them." He watched her closely. "They were doing the same or worse for your father. When they killed for him, he praised them. It's hard for me to see why an action's wrong only when it happens to your daughter."

Gabriella's presence in the doorway brought no surprise and little disappointment. He knew she was expected and there was little more he could say to Ladrea. There was no way to make it all come out right. He doubted that she'd ever write. Attacks on strangers were easy to forgive. It was sins against the family that drew the battle lines. He took the newspaper extended toward him by the mother, impressed again by her troubled face and fierce eyes. If anything, she was losing weight and her stretched cheeks shone as if polished from underneath by bone.

"The article's on page three," she told him, then talked to Ladrea while he read the extended account of preparations for the annual War Widows' Benefit. He gave particular attention to these paragraphs:

> Four hundred of the nation's economic, political, and cultural leaders will assemble in the ultramodern Poseidon Theatre on Saturday night. . . .
>
> Gabriella Antissa, the well-known Athenian filmmaker, fashion model, and director of the War Widows' Fund, announced yesterday that the entire proceedings, including the presentation of her new film on the widows of the Peloponnesus, will be televised for the first time to a nationwide audience. . . .
>
> A special feature of this year's benefit will be the appearance of Father Michael Santry, a Roman Catholic priest from the United States. Father Santry is a close friend of Father John Simonedes, abbot of the Monastery of St. David the King on the island of Kallos, who will be one of the honored guests present on Saturday night. . . .

Santry dropped the paper on the bed and interrupted the two women. "You should have talked to me before inviting Simonedes. You know I'm leaving late Saturday night. He'll think it's very strange that I can't visit with him."

No conciliatory trace softened her voice or manner. "I don't ask anyone about the invitation list to my benefit. If you're leaving the hospital, I'll walk with you to the elevator. There are a few final arrangements to make."

Her rudeness barely rippled Santry's surface. He had stopped caring much about Gabriella one way or the other and, because he was not at heart a vengeful man, he took no particular pleasure in her impending fall. "I'll meet you outside in a minute," he told her. "Ladrea and I haven't finished our talk."

Gabriella glanced a question off her daughter and left the room. Santry closed the door and took Ladrea's hands in his. "I've really nothing more to say except . . . you'll be my best memory of Greece."

She freed her hands, slipped a ring from one finger, pressed it in his palm, leaned close, and whispered, "Our circle, Michael. One only the two of us will ever understand. More than memories lie ahead, just as more than silence lies behind. I was less than awake but more than asleep for the last three days." Her eyes brightened close to his. "I don't know who wrote that letter warning my father about Savonon, but I think you do. I wasn't even on the fishing boat in Mitilini. Larus transferred me to the *Ghost* ten miles at sea from Mithymna and sent the *Dolphin* on to confuse the man we saw with a camera on the dock. I heard them talking: Larus, Strato, the man from Gerson's. Terrible things I never knew. And the men who carried me from the *Ghost*, the men working with you, I heard everything they said."

Santry asked, "Did Larus show you photographs?"

She turned away. "Yes, I saw the Polaroids. He left them by the bed. I burned them but they're etched inside my mind, so I took a vow of silence about the past—for my sake more than theirs. I don't tell you this to worry. I tell you only so you trust our friendship. Whatever happens tomorrow, you'll hear from me." She folded his fingers over the ring. "This circle's ours. I won't be the one to break it."

* * *

On the long walk down the waxed and polished corridor, Santry listened impatiently to Gabriella's insistent questions about the details of Larus's death. "He was shot several times," he told her, "and died with a dagger in his hand. As you might expect, its handle was elegant, a single piece of carved ivory. Unfortunately, an appropriate death."

She stopped walking and faced him, her thin arms folded tight across her breasts, as if protecting herself from the cold. "Why do you say 'appropriate'?"

"Because he died the way he lived—carelessly, and with his hands at someone's throat."

"His death was more of God's good work, no doubt."

"No, his death was a waste. So was his life. I can't see much of God in any of this. Though there wasn't much pain or suffering—I suppose mercy's hidden somewhere there."

She switched abruptly. "Santry, do you find merit in the War Widows' Fund?"

The conversation's turn increased his caution. "It seems to be a good project. Why?"

"Because it's finished if someone finds those shots of me and Alexander. I know Larus took them and I know he'd use them, so they're either on him or on that yacht. You've got to help me find them before somebody else does and rushes them into print."

"Stop it, Gabriella. I hear your predictability calculations creaking. 'Ask the priest to get the photos for the sake of distressed widows and he can't refuse.' I have difficulty taking that very seriously. You wouldn't care if every Athens paper ran your copulation scenes in color. There's only one woman you wouldn't want to see them, only one woman whose eyes you watch. Some great love or jealousy there, probably both, and not my business, but something more than Alexander's charm prompts the mother's sudden passion for the daughter's lover. Well, relax. The photos have been destroyed. That's all I'll say."

They walked the rest of the way in silence, but when she pressed the black button for the elevator to go down, she said, "I can't think of any reason for you to lie to me, so I'll believe what you've said."

His slight frown and tilt of the head meant that she could take it or leave it. He took the elevator to the lobby and dialed Varga. "Dimitrios, have you seen the papers? I think you should call Simonedes and get him over here tonight. . . ."

The second call went to Korachis. "As you know, my plane leaves late tomorrow, so I'm free until the benefit and could use a quiet day alone. If your offer still holds, I'd like to go to Mitilini and take a day to wander by the sea. Yes, I do feel the need for solitude. Detroit? Yes, but briefly. I've pretty much decided not to stay. It's one step at a time for a while. . . . Thanks, Andreas, I'm genuinely sorry I can't wish you the same, but you know what I think of your work. . . . No, there's no point in talking more. We're each fixed in our ways and talk would change nothing. Alexander and I talked this morning and we're further apart than ever. He's mesmerized by dreams of glory, convinced that if he doesn't go for the gold, someone else will. . . . What? Well, of course it's true. They'd line up to get his job. There are thousands eager to sell anything and anybody for a buck: drugs, guns, friends—you name it. If you can cash it, they'll deliver it. So what? Larus should kill your daughter because if he didn't somebody else would? Alexander should stick a needle in a teenager's veins because others will if he won't? You should arm some psychopath because—" He broke off. "Forget it, Andreas. Our decisions are made. All the rest is justification."

At close to midnight, Santry looked across his Scotch-and-water, glanced again at the gaggle of young merchants planning great futures at the smoky bar, saw dark eyes prowling behind mascara masks, heard couples steeped in ouzo laughing raucously, and wondered about the solitary woman lounging near the piano player. She had been there for an hour and never left the music. When his hands were on the keyboard, her eyes held intently on an empty space beyond her slender legs, watching the melody unfolding there. Her presence, not her appearance, reminded him of Ladrea. Something remarkably open and intense about them both, some rare capacity for absorption in the present, something, no, someone singular unfolding there. He reached in his pocket and felt the ring Ladrea had given him. He was closing the circle. A year ago, Ross had come to Mitilini to learn about the Fragments and plan their theft. Now Santry had come to take them back. He wanted to hear the circle snap complete. He finished his drink, then walked outside.

Maria, who greeted him warmly upon arrival, would be in bed now and undisturbed by late-night meditations in the library. There was a cold, melancholy sea by the harbor road, a motorcycle droning in the distance, the smell of wood fire and car fumes and, a mile later, the hundred-year-old house beyond the gate with a fire out front to mark his way through oleanders still in bloom. He closed the heavy door behind him, stood hushed in carpeted silence, and saw the note reminding him of food and welcome. Santry entered the library, found the fireplace still glowing, and saw Korachis on the wall, fixed forever in elegant detachment. He stood erect, gloved hands folded on his cane, gaunt, chiseled face unsmiling, arrogant, and stern.

Drapes drawn shut, door locked, materials assembled on the desk, Santry got to work. He crossed the room quickly and stood in front of an undistinguished small frame enclosing what few in the world would suspect was a priceless treasure. The contrast between its unremarkable, drab appearance on the wall and its radiance when gripped by giant olive-wood hands in the center of a vast hall was startling. Santry took it carefully in his hands, placed it on the desk, took a razor, and began his strange work of restoration.

An hour later, the authentic Fragments were in his possession and the copies he had left on Kallos, and which Simonedes had brought to Varga the previous night, were hanging on Korachis's library wall. Santry poured himself a nightcap, sat in a comfortable leather chair in front of the fire, looked up into Korachis's disapproving face, and told him aloud, "The beauty of all this is that no one will ever know. Not you, not Alexander, not the public. As far as Simonedes is concerned, it never happened. He wants no publicity, no investigation, no reporters swarming monastery walls. It's not perfect, Andreas, but as crimes go it's close. Awfully close." He smiled sleepily. "My sins will find me out; my crimes are another matter."

Korachis remained unamused, and Santry, weary of the older man's pretentious glowering, looked away from the painting. Korachis annoyed him. Even in portraiture, he managed to look down his magnificent, beaked nose, as if superior to all he surveyed, despising the herd—except at milking time. Yes, then his patrician distance vanished and he was happy to get in close, grab hold with both hands, and strip them dry. Santry let him go and rested his tired eyes on the fire, inviting its embers to cast their certain spell. Another brandy and the dark room took on the glow of a cabin he loved in northern Michigan. There was a lake there and salmon runs, early walks through stands of birch, and men he trusted. He and a couple of friends, sometimes Alexander, would pile into a car on Friday night and head north. Good times. Maybe the best. He lingered with his drink and thoughts and watched the fire dapple ruby light and shadows on the Persian rug. He thought for a long time before calling but finally picked up the phone and dialed, and heard the sleepy voice from Athens. "Alexander, it's Mike. Sorry to wake you, but—"

"No, it's okay, Mike. What's going on?"

"Not much. I'm sitting here in Mitilini watching a fire and drinking Korachis's Metaxa and thinking about that talk we had this morning. Well, what I said was true and I meant it all. I still do. But it wasn't all the truth. You and I are going different ways and there are things we don't like about each other now, but there are good things we can't let each other forget. We've been friends a long time, a lot longer than we've been strangers. Now we're both friends and strangers and maybe that's more honest. Alexander, we're walking away from each other for a while. I called to tell you I don't want the strangers we've become to forget the friends we've been and make us into enemies."

The television crews backed their heavy trucks up to the rear doors of the Poseidon Theatre at four o'clock Saturday afternoon and began unloading cameras and pulling cables. The caterer arrived at six, earlier than necessary. The champagne, caviar, and fruit would not be served in the candlelit dining hall until ten, but he liked to watch the annual emergence of rich, parasitic butterflies from the black limousine cocoons. The caterer intended no immediate harm. He made his living tickling their palates and kept his mind alive by studying their concerted flights. The War Widows' Benefit provided an unparalleled viewing stand from which to see in one assembly the faces of the powerful shipping magnates, industrialists, and politicians whose names he followed throughout the year.

His helpers were more interested in the women, and especially in Gabriella Antissa, whose well-sheathed body and sultry face prompted some flights of their own. By seven, security guards in business suits had searched the building and taken inconspicuous posts, and the projectionist had checked his equipment and the first minutes of the film. A dozen young women, as beautiful as they were well trained, sparkled under rotating colored lights in the oval-shaped reception lounge and waited to guide the first arrivals to their seats.

The program was scheduled to begin at eight, but expectedly the first limousine didn't pull up out front until close to the hour. But then the stream of black, magic sedans never stopped and for a full hour flashbulbs from a hundred cameras blazed on top of television spotlights' blinding beams, exciting the crowd to push in closer to see the faces, furs, and jewels certain to be reproduced on the late-night news and in the morning papers.

Simonedes had been one of the earliest to arrive and settle in his seat, slightly dazzled by the light storm that cascaded outside the building, but feeling infinitely better than he had the day before, when he arrived in Athens. Santry had met him at the airport and while driving him to Varga's apartment had tried to tell him a strange story. "Michael," he had interrupted, "I've listened to priests' secrets for years and have concluded that some things are best left unsaid. If the Fragments are returned to Kallos, as far as I'm concerned they never left the island. Do this old man a favor and let it rest."

The seats around him were filling rapidly. The eyes around him were on the move, watching every entrance. As far as he could see, he was the only priest there. Upon entering the theater, he had surrendered his coat and hat to a smiling woman but had refused to give up the briefcase now resting on his lap. The fingers of one hand moved gently on its surface, as if to smooth the leather. Santry was nowhere in sight. Their conversation had been brief but good. Simonedes had, with some difficulty, extracted a promise from Santry to come to next year's conference, but the man refused to be a speaker. He said he'd come only if he didn't have to do anything but sit in the rose garden and watch swallows. Simonedes's fingers moved, almost against his will, to the briefcase zipper, opened it slowly, and he peered inside. The Fragments were still there. He sighed quietly, shut the case, leaned back, and stared at the empty stage, where Varga had assured him he'd see an unforgettable performance.

He heard the restless woman in the seat beside him whisper to her husband, "There's Korachis." Simonedes leaned forward to see and watched with hundreds of others as an unbending, unsmiling man with a cane and a slight limp escorted a radiant young woman down the center aisle.

Someone nearby said excitedly, "Ladrea!"

As soon as the two were seated, the lights dimmed and five hundred of the elect turned their intelligent, amiable faces toward the corner of the stage where a woman in a black gown and a necklace of diamonds spoke from within a waterfall of light. There was no podium and, in her hands, no notes. Nor was there any doubt in anyone's mind who stood there in solitary, commanding splendor.

Alexander watched from the rear, leaning comfortably against the back wall just inside the doors. Only two men knew his exact location: Korachis and the Dove. No trouble of any kind was anticipated, but these days trouble was in the air and only a fool would ignore precautions. The Dove had a light force scattered throughout the building and all was quiet. Ross looked over the assembled heads to the stage, where Gabriella was completing her welcoming remarks. It was the first time he had heard her speak in public. She was good: poised and self-sufficient, voice resonant if slightly harsh, and a power-packed body that must drive other women to crash diets. He admired the haughty style. She was taking millions from this crowd and making them feel privileged in the process. His eyes drifted over aisle seats near the front to find Ladrea and Andreas, the one recovering rapidly, the other dying nearly as fast. One of the rare ones, gone in a year at most. More than enough time to learn his way, evaluate personnel, develop plans, and take the lead. His time had come and he was ready. The words "Father Michael Santry" took him back to the stage as the priest walked into Gabriella's circle of light. He was glad Mike had called from Mitilini. Hell, no, they wouldn't be enemies. They didn't even have to be strangers as far as Ross was concerned. Live, let live, and play the game. Play it hard, but play it.

Santry wore his uniform for the occasion: black suit and white, circular collar. He stood the way Ross had seen him dozens of times before: hands comfortably at his sides, shoulders squared to the audience, rugged features quietly composed and waiting for silence. He gave off none of Gabriella's arrogance but communicated distance all the same. He was not one of them. Neither ill at ease among them nor disdainfully disposed, he remained separate. He said nothing until Antissa had gone and the stage was bare, then began quietly. "I would be remiss if I did not thank you and those watching these proceedings on television for the openhearted warmth this stranger has received in Greece. Your hospitality is as famous as it is generous. A special word of appreciation must go to a man sitting somewhere in this audience, Father John Simonedes, the well-known abbot of the Monastery of St. David the King on Kallos. It is not often that one discovers an older brother, and when it happens, one is grateful."

He shifted his stance and looked at the floor as if in thought. When his eyes returned to the hundreds on him, Ross saw a different composure there. It was the look he remembered from Santry's picket lines and encounters with hostile groups: the slight lift of the jaw, the touch of a frown, the ready eyes.

"The War Widows' Benefit is a most worthy project. It is undeniably good to care for those in need, to look after the bereaved, and to speak for the voiceless. It is for this reason that I have taken the liberty to alter the program at this point."

Ross wondered what was going on and saw Korachis look up quickly toward the stage. The schedule had been tightly scripted, and alterations, however benign, would send shock waves through the TV control room and Gabriella's already hot-wired circuitry.

"I read Thucydides's account of the Peloponnesian War when I was a young man," Santry continued. "Twenty years' work in Detroit then convinced me of his astonishing accuracy when recounting the ways of the powerful with the weak. The ancient Athenians had many virtues, honesty and lucidity among them. When triumphantly confronting the Melians with their demands, they put it straight to them: 'We shall not trouble you with specious pretenses either of how we have a right to our empire or are now attacking you because of wrong that you have done to us, for you know as well as we do that right, as the world goes, is in question only between equals in power. The strong do what they will, the weak suffer what they must.' "

Gabriella reappeared suddenly on the edge of the light surrounding Santry, silently prompting him to hurry through his unexpected remarks. Murmurings rose from the audience like vapors, but Santry's unexcited voice continued firmly.

"I've had the good fortune to meet one of your countrymen, one whose name is familiar to many here. He believes the Athenians were right on their facts but concludes that powerful conquerors should not be celebrated. They should be fought. The excesses of the mighty will not be moderated by friendly counsel or pious hopes. Countervailing power is the only language understood. We wish it were not so, but fire is sometimes a necessary scourge."

He raised his hand toward the projection booth high in the rear of the theater, brought it sharply down, and immediately disappeared in darkness as the immense screen that stretched from end to end of the huge stage filled with an enormous Greek face, glistening tar-black eyes, and a slow, rumbling voice that announced through a thick moustache, "I am Dimitrios Varga."

Dark figures scurried on the edges of the stage, a few men rose in their seats, and Gabriella's unamplified voice cut through the growing uncertainty and shouted toward the projector, "Cut it! Cut it off!"

Ross, ready for anything, stood away from the wall and watched Korachis, easily visible in the screen's reflected light. His face was forward, intent on Varga's giant face and the stern voice telling them all, "Please stay in your seats. An action is unfolding over which none of you has control. The projection room is locked and the men inside are armed. Do not interfere with them. A separate copy of this film is being viewed simultaneously at police headquarters and the morning papers will give details. It is in your interest to remain quiet and attentive."

Korachis got to his feet and barked at the audience, "Silence! Hold your tongues!" There was immediate quieting and Korachis commended them, "That's better. Remain composed, and if anyone wants to leave, let him do it quietly. As for me, I want to see this and will then decide the fate of these buffoons."

That was more than enough to settle the eager crowd. No one moved toward exits and Varga had every eye and ear. "Five years ago, I began a search that ends tonight. I was in Africa reporting on a prison break. They were uncommon criminals: European mercenaries, terrorists, thugs—widow-making men. They left a trail of torture, theft, and rape, and stories about a blond 'Ghost.' I learned almost nothing, but I asked reporters in other countries to let me know if they heard that

name. I kept a file. He began turning up in Greece."
The screen swelled with Larus, the camera closed for a minute on the turquoise beads, then pulled back to show him beating an unarmed man to the ground. Varga noted, "He's dead now. Some considered him stylish."

Ross didn't need the script to see the collapse of all his hopes and moved quickly down the far aisle toward the stage, took his steps two at a time, slipped behind the curtain, and eased Gabriella away from the men surrounding her. As soon as they were alone, she demanded, "What's Andreas doing? Why's he letting this go on?"

"He's cool," Ross told her, "but unimportant now." He spoke rapidly and kept his face close to hers. She didn't try to move away. "Listen to me. We've got no more than a couple of minutes to talk the truth you like so much and make some decisions before the main tent comes crashing down on all three rings. Fact number one: Varga's got it together and Andreas is going down. We don't like that, but that's the truth. Fact number two: He'll be dead before he's convicted. Number three: Santry's action probably means Varga doesn't have or won't run the Kallos piece, so I'm shielded. I haven't been around long enough to be responsible for anything else. You're on the edges in any case. Conclusion: It's our show. The whole organization's getting smashed, but not necessarily us. With your capital and my skills, we can build a new and better one while they're tearing the old one apart. And the way I'll do it, there'll be no tonights for us in the future. This kind of nonsense doesn't need to happen. You fund it, I run it, and we split all profits. That's my best offer. Take it now or I'm gone because the heavy shit is about to fall."

She touched his cheek with a soft, black glove. "Starting when?"

He kissed her neck and whispered, "Starting now."

A TV monitor carried the film backstage. Alexander's arm was around her waist while they watched dramatic scenes flashing in rapid succession in front of a captivated audience: a freighter rolling in heavy seas with a cargo of munitions from L. P. Gerson, followed by a filmed interview with a black-hooded man describing how shipments were hijacked and sold for fortunes to any gunmen with the cash. Television clips showed women bleeding to death on Athens sidewalks and Varga's evidence that the bombs had been supplied by an international organization based in Greece. The muffled cries of shocked incredulity and bitter doubt gradually gave way in the face of Varga's meticulous documentation to whispered approvals and occasional shouts of "Bravo!" Correspondence, records of payments, and taped telephone conversations between Korachis and Italian heroin dealers nailed it down. Details of the payoffs by which a multinational organization was kept on the blind side of the law named policemen, bureaucrats, and politicians in seven countries. And Varga explained relentlessly how all tentacles led to a center dominated by a gaunt man in dark glasses who, at the film's conclusion, got promptly to his feet and startled everyone by walking directly to the stage and calling for the lights.

At that moment, an usher rushed to Alexander and whispered that police were stationed at every exit. A few in the crowd began to jeer Korachis. Most, not knowing what to do, sat tight and looked around anxiously. Korachis leaned on his cane and scowled. Someone shouted, "Quiet! Let him talk!" Others repeated the call, the crowd simmered, and Korachis raised his hand and stared them down.

When all grew quiet and waited expectantly, he began slowly, saying, "I've learned that the police are waiting for me outside, so I'll be brief, briefer than they imagine. There is no way to minimize this night's betrayal or avoid its shocking consequences. Nor am I disposed to affirm, deny, or evade what Varga has claimed. I have taken a principled stand throughout my life in favor of excellence and power and I respect those singular virtues wherever they appear. I do not wish him well, but I recognize his strength." His eyes swept the room. "As for the rest of you, we've never been friends. Certainly I've not been yours. Too much of the sheep in most of you. When I walked in tonight, you honored me. An hour later, after hearing in public what you've long whispered in private, you're ready to eat my flesh."

He raised his head toward the projection booth, his dark glasses scattering silver glints from the overheads. "Weakness, mindless conformity, herd behavior—these are the evils. Death, at the right time, is not evil. Death, at the right time, is freedom." He took a deep breath and leaned heavily on his cane. Ross watched from the wings and worried. The man looked faint and unsteady on his feet. With an effort, Korachis pulled himself erect and stared at the hushed crowd. "Varga's revelations can't touch me. The police will have to wait." An unusual smile crossed his lips. "A few moments ago, I took a liberating capsule and will soon be gone." A wave of gasps and cries surged the room. "I leave you with few regrets, no contrition, and considerable scorn. My last words are for those few whose ears will understand: Santry and Varga have declared themselves enemies. They have gone to war and mean to destroy you. Like Noah, I send a Dove upon the waters." His cane tapped the floor for a moment, as if waiting impatiently for an expected call. His head lifted suddenly, the legs buckled, and he collapsed on the stage.

People leaped to their feet, screamed, and shouted for doctors. The theater was in an uproar. Alexander reached him first and helped carry him backstage. Reporters scurried among the powerful with lights and cameras recording astonished faces and shocked reactions. The aisles and exits were jammed with people wanting out pushing against the hundreds more trying to get in who had seen the action on TV and rushed to the Poseidon to catch the final act. And in a small dressing room behind the curtains, a policeman announced an ambulance was on its way, a doctor rose from Korachis's body, and Ross walked to his side.

Alexander led Gabriella and a soft-faced man to an empty space. "Andreas is dead. We'll meet tomorrow morning to deal with the crisis." His eyes went to the tall man. "You are to ignore his instructions regarding Santry and Varga. Their deaths won't help us make a dime."

The Dove looked from Ross to Gabriella and waited.

She answered without hesitation, "In all organizational matters, Alexander Ross now speaks and acts for me."

Simonedes crossed the wooden floor of the restaurant slowly, taking all precautions against a fall in the shadows of the lantern-lit room. As soon as Varga sighted him, he was at his side to help. Santry rose when he reached the table and Simonedes asked if the gesture was in deference to his great age, wisdom, or just his total blindness. "I appreciated what you said tonight, Michael, especially the part about older brothers. I carry a message from a younger one, or, at least, so he claims. As I was leaving, a very handsome American took my arm and asked if I'd be seeing you." Varga and Santry exchanged quick, anxious glances. Simonedes saw them and told them not to worry. He had been very careful and had not been followed. "He asked me to give you this."

Santry held the letter in one hand and hesitated. Then, taking a knife from the bread basket, he sliced it cleanly open, withdrew a single folded sheet, and recognized Alexander's distinct, strong hand. He read it silently:

Dear Mike,

   Relax, the Dove's wings are clipped. Thanks for the shield and *pax vobiscum*.

                              Alexander

He passed the note to the two men at his side, filled their glasses, touched them with his own, and said quietly, "It appears to be over."